Also by Michael Gray:

The Flying Caterpillar

Follow the author at:

www.MichaelFGray.com

Asleep at the Wheel of Time

by

Michael Gray

ABQ Press Trade Paperback Edition

Cover Design by Barbara Goodmiller

ABQ Press
Albuquerque, New Mexico

ISBN: 978-0-9838712-5-5

To my wife, Denise,
my children Matt, Jon, and Eli,
and in memory of Jay Paterson,
who, bed-bound with chronic progressive MS,
encouraged me to read this book to him,
chapter by chapter, never falling "Asleep",
until one day Time caught him napping
and swept him up.

Acknowledgments

The humpback whales of "Star Trek IV" swim through these pages, but I am most indebted to Stanislaw Lem's *His Master's Voice*, which asks the question, "If Earth was contacted by a superior race of beings, would we understand them? Indeed, would we even try to understand them?" I have added a logical corollary: would aliens address themselves to humans, or might they find another terrestrial species more open to what they have to say? I started perusing the slight literature devoted to the study of intelligence in our oceans. John Lilly and his research with dolphins came to the top of that list and I discovered a marvelous book called "Mind in the Waters," lovingly assembled by Joan McIntyre.

In Friends in Time, where I have worked for twenty years with people who have MS and ALS, I found a natural context in which to continue developing these themes. Most affectingly, at a time when he was bed-bound and his speech increasingly difficult, Jay Paterson, a gentle man who has since passed on from his Chronic Progressive MS, would ask me to read a chapter or two of *Asleep* each time I visited--as if my fledgling manuscript belonged in the company of the series of books we had read together over the years. Then Pat Simmons, Rose Rocque and I shared books we were writing: Pat's about her final year caring for a dear friend who had ALS, Rose's about her experience of being homeless, and mine about aliens, humans and cetaceans. In an uncanny way, we recognized a common ground in one another's visions: that when life is falling apart, we can still strive to be our best selves.

For her inventive design and artistic cover creation, I thank Barb Goodmiller. For making the book cover fit just right, thanks go to Amanda Campbell. For creating a book out of a mere string of words, I am grateful to Harlen Campbell. For steering *Asleep at the Wheel of Time* safely into harbor, my appreciation goes to Judith Van Gieson, Captain and Publisher of ABQ Press. For her professional critique and line-edits, thanks go to Lisa Lenard-Cook. And for their encouraging critique of "Chapter Two", which helped me to say, "This book is ready," I thank Carol, Cindy, Lynn, Alice, Waki, Sheila, Phyllis, Tanya and Lisa.

I would especially like to thank two people whose influence continues to sound in me two decades later: Barry Schieber, who in the course of a six month retreat in 1991/92, managed to remind me that I am a writer who should be writing; and Mary Sue Comstock, who read the entire draft of *Asleep* and said, "This seems like a channeled work to me". She herself then—considerably deepening the import of her words—moved to Hawaii to be closer to the dolphins who had invaded her own dreams. I have always cherished what she said. After all, who would not want to be the vehicle for a vision deeper than we ever realize on this brief afternoon sail we call life?

CHAPTER 1

Friday, January 10 (Day -90)

Patrick Murphy skidded to a stop beside the little general store at the edge of the tidal inlet. He could scarcely believe that he had actually made it. He opened the door, leaned back against the seat of his Honda Civic hatchback and savored the sound of surf. After his long drive he could easily have fallen asleep, but he squeezed himself past the steering wheel and stepped onto the icy asphalt. At 270 pounds and a hair under six feet, he was no longer the ten-year old boy who had stood on this very spot—in Anchor Beach, Maine—so many summers ago.

A cold wind blew off the sea, but in the shelter of the storefront the sun was surprisingly warm. He stretched and walked over to where he could see the waves breaking on the beach. He must be crazy—did he really expect to meet a whale in the middle of winter in a boarded-up Maine resort town? Well at least he had taken a first step. This was the beach to which the haunting images of his dreams had driven him.

Standing in his brown work shirt, breathing in the salt-bitter air, he rubbed his broad hands vigorously over naturally insulated ribs and shoulders. Collar-length brown hair, a little darker than his mustache, had thinned on top. His face, at forty-three, still reflected the good looks of his youth, but those extra pounds now slurred the effect, like an ice sculpture melting out of focus.

He heard the squeal of a door hinge behind him, then an elderly woman's voice. "We've got a fresh pot of coffee going. I could make a sandwich."

He turned towards the front of the store, surprised that it was open, and squinted against the brightness of snow and white lapstreak siding. His long drive down from Montreal, broken once by a sugar and caffeine stop five hours earlier, suddenly caught up to him. He felt dizzy as he tried to focus on her face. "That sounds great," he managed to stammer.

He followed her into the store. Without asking, she brought over a cup of coffee and set it on a table in the small luncheonette area near the front. He drank standing up. When she disappeared into the back, he wandered over to a line of windows that looked across the inlet. He closed his eyes and drifted into the muffled crashing of the waves.

Strange how he had been thinking so much about his younger brother, John, lately, especially since crossing the U.S. border that morning. Maybe he should call, assume his role as older brother, but what could he say after so many years? "Hey, John, I've developed this interest in humpback whale songs, so I quit my job and drove down to Anchor Beach, Maine." He knew he wouldn't call. His successful brother, John, would immediately see this most recent instability as further evidence of Patrick's fundamental inability to make a real life for himself.

The woman's voice startled him. "Hope you like turkey and cheese."

Turning around, he saw a twelve-inch submarine sandwich on a large plate, surrounded by pickle slices, potato salad, and black olives.

The aroma of fresh coffee steaming in his cup greeted him as he sat down at the table. He demolished half the sandwich and all the potato salad in a kind of stuporous inhalation. When he finally looked up, he was surprised to see that the woman had been joined by a man who, like her, appeared to be in his early seventies. They introduced themselves as Hank and Emily.

"What brings you to Anchor Beach this time of the year, son?" Hank inquired. Good question.

"My brother and I stayed here a long time ago in one of the cabins down the road," Patrick said, intending to avoid the issue of how he had felt compelled to come back here against all rational considerations. Yet a long buried part of himself had other ideas.

"I needed to get away from everything. Boy, was that long overdue. My brother had the right idea—he abandoned our sinking ship more than twenty years ago, and never looked back once at our screwed up little family. So, this morning, at three a.m., two decades too late, I left Montreal and drove straight here."

Hank was looking at him with a concerned expression on his wrinkled old face and Patrick wished he could take back the bitterness he heard in his own voice. This nice old couple didn't need to know how Patrick's life had taken a wrong turn somewhere. And they definitely didn't need to know that Patrick considered himself a complete failure in life.

The best thing would be to pay for his sandwich now and leave, but Patrick couldn't stop himself from continuing. "John left Montreal with a scholarship to MIT at eighteen. Then he moved to sunny Albuquerque and before anyone knew it had married the prom queen and was a full professor of Astronomy. What did I do? I hung around a few miles from where I was born, looking after a bitter, senile old mother."

In horror, Patrick heard himself picking up steam. His own voice—like some opportunistic puppy bolting for freedom through its owner's legs—now moved on to their mother's death. He told the whole wretched story: how even then, John had not returned; and how he, Patrick—the miserably unprodigal older son—had spent the worst day of his life sitting alone beside their mother's coffin, as relatives and acquaintances reminisced about his brilliant younger brother. "Your Mom was so proud," he heard repeatedly—and everyone knew that it wasn't Patrick's temporary jobs as a computer programmer or his sullen wariness of all fellow humans, that had made their mother's eyes shine.

After fifteen minutes, Patrick ground to a halt. He stared at the untouched half of his submarine sandwich, feeling raw and exposed. An unpleasant whiff of perspiration accosted him from his damp shirt. What had possessed him to dump on these complete strangers? Flustered and angry with himself, he asked how much he owed. To his embarrassment, they declined payment, and when Emily said in a wavering voice, "I just took a lemon meringue pie out of the oven," Patrick suddenly felt overwhelmed by shame. He had given this old couple a guided tour of his emotional and psychological frailty, and couldn't stay a moment longer in their presence.

He hurriedly left the store, climbed into his car, backed up, and had shifted into first gear when he heard the screen door bang. He spotted Hank limping across the icy roadway and reluctantly rolled down the car window. The old gentleman handed in something wrapped in wax paper. "Em thought you might want the rest of your sandwich, Patrick."

He muttered, "thank you," as he took the sandwich and quickly drove away. His first impulse was to drive for a few more hours. Then he suddenly needed to be outside. He swerved left at the first opportunity and headed down a snowy track towards the beach. It ended at a parking lot which in summer would have been crowded with cars from Portland, but which on this early January afternoon, offered a few boarded-up concession stands with deep snow drifts on their north sides.

He pulled his car close to a stand, locked up, put on his gray wool coat, hat and gloves, and headed down to the beach. Loose sand and snow grabbed at his boots, revealing how out of shape he was, and his coat was way too tight, but the brisk sea wind felt wonderful blowing over his face. When he reached the hard packed beach, glistening at low tide, he raised his arms over his head and shouted into the wind. "Freedom at last!" The seam ripped in the back of his coat, and he laughed out loud. That's one way to get freedom. Then he laughed again, relieved to discover that he had not forgotten how.

He headed north, back toward the general store, walking as close to the breaking waves as he could without getting his hiking boots soaked. Strands of kelp cluttered the dark sand —their slippery feel reminding him of wet lasagna. To his left, the sandy beach rose up into low dunes that were white with snow. The sound of waves beating on the hard beach and the acrid smell of salt felt deeply familiar—in spite of the fact that he had only been to the ocean once before.

After walking for ten minutes, Patrick came to an area where sandbars, separated by pools of water, led to a rocky spit a half-mile out. Ten minutes later he was clambering up onto the rock.

From the top he could look in all directions: eastward to open ocean, westward back to shore. And just beneath his feet, facing south, he saw an indentation in the rock—a natural lounge chair, carved in stone. Suddenly he felt very tired. He'd driven non-stop for eight hours on an almost empty stomach, and then sprung that emotional leak in front of strangers.

Moving carefully along the steep rock face he made his way down and lowered himself into the rocky couch. Not half bad. He stretched out his legs and leaned back into a kind of rocky cocoon. A ledge on his left blocked the brisk ocean wind, while allowing the afternoon sun to beat directly onto his chest. He raised his arms so that his gloved hands formed a pillow under his hood. He felt warm and safe, high and dry above the surf crashing against the rocks below.

A small freedom seemed to open up for Patrick. How had he ever allowed his life to become so dominated by obsession? Now it seemed scarcely credible that he had sat in front of a computer screen virtually every night for a whole year. Looking for what? Patterns? An alphabet? A vocabulary that he could somehow relate to human language? Ridiculous. The best scientific minds had no idea how to approach an unknown language.

He had talked to professionals—from linguists to pattern-recognition experts, to whale experts—hoping to find a secret passageway into the language of whales. He had also seen a therapist to see if she could make his obsession go away. But therapy had made it worse—as if something that didn't like being threatened with eviction had taken up residence inside his mind.

Whatever he noticed in his waking moments was the tip of a gigantic iceberg. Beneath the weirdness that invaded his daily life was a vaster landscape he visited in dreams. Sometimes he wrenched out of sleep stammering incomprehensible phrases—his heart pounding with fear. Often he woke up feeling guilty. Was that why he hadn't left his mother for all those years—was he condemned to penance for a crime he couldn't remember?

Usually there were whales and dolphins present, but sometimes he was in a different world entirely. Then when the faces of creatures peered into his eyes, he knew he had gone crazy. Yet he had quit his job to follow the scent of these crazy visions.

He took a few deep breaths of the ocean breeze. Every now and then, after an especially loud crash on the rocks below, traces of sea spray blew over him like fine cologne. Stretching out on the comfortable rock in the warm afternoon sun, he yawned. The exhaustion of his long drive—and perhaps of the way he had lived these last few years—announced itself from deep within his body. It would feel good to rest for a moment out here, on this rocky couch in the middle of the Atlantic Ocean.

The warmth of the sun seeped into his tired body, as another world, repellant but fascinating, lapped at the edges of consciousness. Sometimes it seemed that his mind was breaking apart; yet he did not have the strength to turn away from these visions—which had showed up unannounced one day about a year ago, like distant relatives from another country.

For a moment he tried to hold back. But soon the one who was trying to hold back wasn't there anymore. His body seemed to lengthen in the direction of living time, arms and legs and hands turning homeward. Then he was a dark, glimmering shape, diving into another world.

Far below the ice, his own body vast and sensitive, he watches as two human beings—a father and son—come plunging downwards. They drift down through the beautiful blue light, dragged along by some dark, heavy thing, as life and breath are torn from their lungs. The son is tied to the dark body, but why is the father still holding on? He could let go at any time, yet he keeps chewing the cord that binds his son, with jaws now feeble in the deathly cold.

We rise up into brightness, rising towards the wondrous light. This light, sung about from the old time, is shining inside the father two-legs. How can that be? How can the light be shining forth from one of them? One of them who kills for no reason.

* * *

The sensation of a heavy body slithering across his face tore Patrick from a deep sleep and he couldn't move a muscle to push it away. Something passed over him—alien but strangely familiar—like an embodied remnant of a nightmare. Then he recognized his own arm, numb from having lain pinned back under his head while he slept.

He felt bone cold, shadow covered most of the rock, and the waves crashed directly in front of him. His beard was stiff with frozen spray and sheets of thin ice broke off his clothes when he moved.

He struggled to his feet, almost slipping down the icy surface into the seething water. To the west, a smoldering, red sun had begun its descent beneath the cold rim of the sand dunes.

Stay calm. No need to panic. How high could the tide rise in a couple of hours?

He clambered across the slippery rock until he reached its highest point. Then his mind did its best to reject what it saw. The rock on which he was standing had become an island. He was surrounded by the Atlantic Ocean.

Where was the meandering path of sandbar he had taken out? In its place, open sea raced unimpeded towards the shore. This isn't possible. All he had done was stroll out to the end of a sandy peninsula, and then lie down for a moment.

He looked around. Here and there, waves were breaking, the ruddy glow of the setting sun infusing their sudsy foam with a cold beauty.

A voice started up in his head. No way you're going to die out here. Just calm down and work it out. People don't die because they stroll out to a rock.

Someone would see him and come out in a boat. This wasn't the Arctic Circle. It was a tourist area in Maine. Off-season, admittedly. At worst, he could hold onto this rock during a terrible, freezing night. That prospect felt horrifying, as he tried to rub some sensation back into his numb left leg, but surely this rock would remain above high tide.

Suddenly, with a surge of optimism, Patrick remembered the old couple who ran the general store at the end of the beach road. Maybe they were looking for him and would find his parked car.

A splash of icy water lashed Patrick's cheek and he gasped. With that one terrible sting across his face he suddenly understood that no warm-blooded being could survive a night on this rock. The frigid waters of the north Atlantic were rising and he would die if he didn't get to shore. He couldn't believe it. His visions—and the taste of freedom he felt when he finally followed them—did they mean nothing? Was it all just to get washed up bloated and half-eaten by fish?

Patrick seemed to wake up a second time. He flailed his arms, shouting and shouting until his throat hurt.

Cold recognition gripped his heart. The beach was completely deserted, no one knew he was stranded on this rock, and the sun was setting. He looked down at the base of the rock, where the sudsy water lapped at a dark vestige of sandbar—all that remained of the causeway to shore. I can't. I'd freeze to death before I got anywhere.

But the path he had taken out must still be there, his mind insisted, just below the surface. Someone who knew exactly where to step could make it. Maybe.

He looked at the beach. It was harder and harder to spot any kind of landmark. Where was that piece of driftwood poking through the snow that had stood out from the salt grass so dramatically in the bright afternoon sun? Now he couldn't be sure. Someone could be walking along the beach right now and they wouldn't see each other. Patrick shouted again. But his voice was weak and hoarse. He knew that a person on shore, half a mile away, would hear nothing but the surf crashing.

Patrick could see some of the waves partially breaking before they reached the shore. Probably on the submerged sandbar which he had taken out, he thought. Could this vanished sandbar really be his only hope? If that was where the waves were breaking, then he would be drenched in the bitterly cold sea for as long as it took him to make it to shore. On the other hand, if there were stretches where only his feet were submerged, maybe he could keep hobbling for a while.

He tried to tear his mind loose from these pointless speculations. The decision was a simple one. If there was a chance of being rescued, he should wait. If there wasn't, then every second counted. Every passing moment gave the ocean, and the night, a further, murderous advantage.

But Patrick couldn't make his body move.

Then another dreadful flail lashed him full in the face and Patrick started crawling down the icy rock to the water.

Childhood memories of swimming on this same stretch of beach as a kid did not prepare him for entering the north Atlantic in January. The nerves in his feet and legs experienced a scalding numbness, as if he had stepped into the mouth of a moray eel whose teeth were dipped in Novocain.

Patrick gasped with shock but kept splashing forward. The sandbar was only a few inches under the water and he made good progress toward shore.

A strange kind of clarity came into his mind. He understood that he could die in the next few minutes, and a part of him was ready to experience whatever happened. With ragged, gasping breaths, he heard his own voice. "If this is the end . . . you have a lot of catching up to do . . . You better show a little backbone . . . now . . . if you want another chance."

The water remained shallow as he steadily pulled away from his condemned island. He even began imagining that he could make it, if only his legs didn't collapse under him. Whenever the water became deeper, he turned to either side until he found a direction away from the drop-off. Even after he could no longer feel his legs, he managed to keep on his feet.

Amazing—he really seemed to be doing it!

Perhaps once he got out of this situation, he should visit his brother. It was a shame, really, that there had been so much pain in their family, that he and John had never become friends. Why was that exactly? Brothers should be friends. Especially now that it was only the two of them. Only the two of them.

Then a wave hit, and Patrick fell. It seemed surprisingly comfortable to have his face under the water. He tried to fight off the lethargy and willed his legs to seek the sandy bottom, but all he felt was the bobbing sensation of waves passing overhead. It was as if his body and mind had stopped talking to each other.

His eyes remained open, but it was too dark to see anything other than an undifferentiated murkiness. If there was a sandy bottom below his face, he couldn't see it.

He had enough light, however, to see the eye that appeared within three or four inches of his own.

Then the dark glimmering vanished, and a few seconds later he sensed something pass between his legs and push him into the air. He gasped for breath. Then, as he fell face forward towards the water, a strong presence slipped beneath his chest. He felt ridiculously safe, like a child whose loving parent has lifted him up and hugged away the hurt.

For many years Patrick's only friends had been animals. A whole lineage of stray dogs had unquestioningly come home with him, like old friends falling into step side-by-side. But could this be really happening now? A dolphin?

Patrick could no longer feel his body, or open his eyes, but he willed his arms to embrace this new friend. And then he dreamed his oldest dream.

His father was carrying him in from the car. The wooden crib creaked as he was lain down on the mattress and a knitted blanket pulled over him. The blanket was blue and yellow and white. But the father had no face, just the warmth of an unknown man who loves his baby boy.

CHAPTER 2

John Murphy looked at his wet face in the mirror and wished he were a different person. Someone calm and relaxed would be a good start. How could he feel so stressed after only forty years of life? A tall man with red eyes and a clenched jaw stared back from the mirror—a slur of black stubble broadcasting that he had forgotten to shave again that morning. His well-cut Oxford shirt and beige gabardine slacks revealed an athletic build, but his face looked like someone in line for a heart attack.

He was in the Computing Center bathroom at UNM (University of New Mexico), dashing cold water onto his face, because he had just screamed at a computer operator. The fool had mounted a two-week old disk from the VLA (Very Large Array) and now John's mapping of the surface of Saturn's moon, Titan, was messed up. Again. It had to be the wrong disk. There was no way he could encounter such blatant interference two weeks in a row.

John knew he needed to suppress his anger and go apologize—even though he was still seething over the hours it would take to restore his database.

Leslie, his wife, constantly nagged John about how he never apologized for anything, never took responsibility for a family argument or problem. Well, perhaps he could practice on a computer operator what he couldn't manage with his wife.

John shuddered. He had actually yelled loud enough that two other operators, sorting output in the next room, had stuck their heads through the Halogen seal.

He needed to relax, get more rest. But how could he relax when every night at 3:00 a.m. he awoke in the grips of cold terror?

John dried his face with a paper towel, brushed off most of the slovenly shreds it left in his dark stubble, and returned to the computer room. Bill—wearing a gray sweatshirt, faded black denims and sneakers—was sitting at the console, his back to the plastic-sealed doorway. His sandy colored hair was shorter than most UNM students.

As he pulled a chair over to the console and sat beside Bill, he realized that he didn't know much about this young man.

When Bill didn't look up from the console, John cleared his throat. He hadn't had to do that for a while. The marriage counseling must be getting to him, John thought as he delivered his prepared line to Bill's averted face. "Can we just say that I resembled a horse's ass a moment ago, and leave it behind us?"

Bill glanced up, but remained silent.

Shit! Wasn't that enough? What would Carolyn, their marriage counselor, advise? Probably that he hadn't learned to share during his childhood, with the unspoken insinuation that you can learn now what you missed as a kid. OK, on with the sharing. John took a deep breath. "Look, I had no right to talk to you like that. It was rude and unjustified. I apologize. It's no excuse, but I haven't been sleeping well."

And without intending it, he heard himself add, "I've been having a recurrent nightmare."

That was enough. More than enough. Now he needed to continue processing the previous week's data from the VLA radio telescope, in his search for a stable feature on Titan's surface.

Bill responded, precisely and unsmilingly. "I mounted the disk you gave me today. If a mistake was made it was by someone at the VLA or by you, Professor Murphy."

John felt a pang of misgiving as Bill spun his chair back to the console and pressed some keys on the keyboard. A few seconds later, a page of figures came onto the screen. It was the same summary page that had sent John into a fury ten minutes earlier.

Bill put his finger next to a particular line on the screen. "This signal-intensity range is too large, isn't it? And it looks a lot like the interference you got two weeks ago."

John was stunned. How could a kid who mounted disk packs and magnetic tapes, and burst laser output pick out the crucial discrepancy in a screen full of astronomical measurements? And a Psychology major at that.

Bill pointed at the screen again. "But look at these dates. They cover exactly the period you would expect, one week ending two days ago. If you trust those dates, then this is new data."

John took a sharp intake of breath. Shit. The kid was right. Those were normal date ranges. He had no reason to distrust them. Out loud, he said, "You're right. It looks like we have new data—and more God-damned interference."

Bill continued with rising enthusiasm. "You must have picked up the same thing twice. Could it be something on Titan?"

John heard his own softer tone as he explained, "There is no way this surge in intensity can come from a real object on Titan."

Bill turned 180 degrees on his swivel chair and looked directly at John. "Why not?"

"I'm trying to locate a stable physical feature on Titan's surface, to determine whether Titan is rotating on its own axis." John began, as if he was talking to one of his own Astronomy students. "With Saturn's strong gravitational pull, such a system . . ."

Bill interrupted. "Why can't a strong signal be coming from Titan's surface?"

John leaned back in his chair, in a posture he recognized in himself from innumerable graduate seminars. "In my Titan research, I'm using VLA telescopes to collect the scattered reflection of a signal sent out from the Goldstone transmitter."

Bill continued the line of thought. "So the signal must be pretty weak after 2 billion miles and four atmosphere crossings."

How did Bill know this stuff? It was true that the radio pulse sent out from Goldstone had to travel a billion miles and cross the atmospheres of both Earth and Titan before bouncing off the surface of Titan. Then the reflection had to retrace the same distance and traverse the atmospheres of both Titan and Earth again before registering at the VLA.

"Exactly. The signal is very weak," John said. "All 27 VLA dishes need to integrate that weak signal over several seconds before they can produce a single image of Titan's surface."

"What kinds of things can you discover from these images?"

"You can infer whether the surface is land or water," John answered. "For instance, we've already demonstrated that Titan isn't covered by a global ocean of liquid methane, as was once thought. Titan displays the kind of roughness characteristic of solid surfaces. However I haven't yet found a feature stable enough to allow me to measure rotation." John reined himself in.Enough Astronomy 505 for one day.

"So what substance could reflect the Goldstone signal back as strongly as we're seeing here?"

"Nothing." John responded categorically. "The signal strength of this interference is ludicrously out of range."

Bill's fingers drummed on the table. "Please think about it. What could be on Titan to cause such a strong signal?"

This guy was as stubborn as a good research assistant—too bad John's Titan project had no hard funding. Out loud, John said, "Give it up, Bill. It just doesn't compute. The wave amplitude we're seeing on the screen is about 1000 times larger than can be attributed to a Goldstone signal scattered off any known substance. The only thing that could account for such signal strength would be a transmitter on Titan, more powerful than the one at Goldstone. No. Something is wrong with the data."

Bill seemed not to hear. "So let's have a look. Can you find the spot on Titan where the interference occurred in this week's data?"

John didn't have the energy to point out yet again how this anomaly could not possibly refer to anything occurring on Titan. The pulse was far too strong to be something on frozen Titan or an echo of any terrestrial source.

Bill's eyes were bright. "Wouldn't it be interesting if both incidents of interference occurred at the same spot?"

Bill rolled his chair to one side and John pulled up to the keyboard. He knew it was a waste of time, but it was as if Bill reminded him of something in his own past. Perhaps it was the thrill of the hunt, when everyone around you says you're crazy. But then it turns out that you aren't crazy after all.

John scrolled through screens of summary data from the recent week's new VLA output until he found the spike.

John was aware of Bill staring at the monitor. Those coordinates did look oddly familiar. Without speaking, John got up and retrieved his briefcase from the table. He found his notes about the earlier interference, and started scanning pages. Then he sat stock-still.

Bill's voice intruded into his thoughts, "What is it?"

John looked at the computer screen again and double-checked the coordinates. Then he exhaled loudly. Holy Shit! Both incidents had occurred at exactly the same place on Titan's surface. Just like Bill had predicted.

Suddenly John couldn't fight off exhaustion. He would need to go back to the raw data and look at the jump in signal intensity. He would have to observe those same coordinates from another telescope—maybe Arecibo. But not now.

He turned to Bill. "You were right. Listen, I really appreciate your help, but I don't know what's happening, and I can't think about it now."

John expected Bill to try to pin him down. Instead Bill asked, "Are you having the same nightmare every night?"

John shrugged. "Maybe. Why do you ask?"

Bill leaned forward. "I've studied dreams quite a bit. In fact I'm working on my doctorate in psychology in that area. If you ever want to talk about it, I'm a good listener."

John looked at his watch. He ought to be out the door right now. "If your field is psych, how do you know so much about astronomy?"

"My Dad had a telescope. On clear nights, we'd go out and look at the planets. That is, if I got our 30 cows milked and bedded down in time."

John was caught completely off guard by the wave of emotion that rushed through him. Bill's image was so simple, so mundane—yet the recognition rang deep within him: That's how it feels to have a dad.

Afraid that his lip might start trembling, John launched into professorial mode. "Bill, what if I talk to your boss about you helping me every Friday with my VLA analysis? Interested?"

"Right on!"

"But I have to run now," John added quickly. Then he didn't get up.

Bill leaned forward in a way that reminded John of Carolyn, his marriage counselor, and asked, "How come you're not sleeping well?"

John had to throttle back the impulse to start talking about the dream that woke him up every night at 3:00 am. The dream that wasn't even his own dream.

He knew Bill was still staring at him as he headed towards the Halogen seal, but he didn't look back. He offered no word of explanation for his abrupt leave-taking, and two minutes later he drove out of the parking lot, already arguing with Leslie in his mind about why he was late yet again.

As he turned the corner onto his own quiet street, a memory came back. How once, when the police had brought his brother Patrick home for some teenage vandalism, their mother had accused Patrick of destroying the most important thing in their lives. Now, 27 years later, it was too late to ask their Mom anything; and John's nightmare seemed to push itself through the dim shroud of his family's past—answering questions he had never dared to ask: about his father's death and why their mother seemed to blame Patrick for her loss.

Leslie was paying bills at the kitchen table when John walked in.

"I wish you'd seen a program I watched last night," she said the instant he walked through the kitchen door. "There was a businessman whose teenage son committed suicide. He kept saying how he would trade everything for just a few more nights playing at home with his kid."

"OK, OK. I'll stay home tonight. I won't rush off and make any revolutionary discoveries I may live to regret," John responded, unable to keep an edge out of his voice.

Leslie looked at John before continuing. "I know you're a good dad. But do you remember last month, after you got back from your week in Geneva, how Frankie didn't want you to read him a bedtime story?"

"What, now you want me to give up my work? Anyway, that only lasted a couple of days," he protested.

"And do you remember how you and Frankie used to play on the carpet every night, how you'd lift him up on your feet and you'd both be laughing?"

John was silent.

She laid her hand on his arm. "Nothing we'll do as parents will be perfect, and Frankie is lucky to have you as a dad. I just needed to say something about how important it is to leave lots of room for kids when they're young."

John looked at his wife and remembered the years in which he hadn't even known the names of his oldest son's teachers. Pushing aside the feeling that he had failed Eric as a father, he heard himself say, "Do you mind if I make a few calls?"

Leslie pointed out that most people came home on Friday night to spend the weekend with their families. Then she smiled and John—relieved—put his arm around her shoulder as they walked into the kids' room together.

Two-and-a-half-year-old Frankie was watching "E.T." from one end of the couch and Eric, his long gangly twelve-year-old legs stretched out on the rest of it, was reading a book about dragons. Both boys had dark brown hair and handsome features—Eric's much more angular and sharp than Frankie's round-faced openness. When Leslie asked them how it was going, Eric looked up. "Fine. Did you expect everything to fall apart without you?"

Frankie started chattering. "Boy scared. E.T. scared." He always needed someone there for the scene in the corn breaks, where E.T. and Elliot finally meet. Apparently Eric, reading his book, had allowed Frankie to survive Elliot's high drama yet again.

John whispered to Leslie. "I'll go make those phone calls." Then he slipped out to the kitchen where the message light was flashing on the speaker wall phone.

The message was from Leslie's mother. He quickly saved it, dialed the Arecibo Radio Telescope number, and glanced at his watch. It would be 8:35 p.m. in Puerto Rico, three hours ahead of Albuquerque.

After almost ten rings a man picked up the phone and John explained that he needed to get a couple of minutes of telescope time to observe Titan's surface. No dice. The Arecibo director was out of town for several weeks and they were booked for months ahead.

Next he called the operator and got a few numbers in the Harvard area for people involved in SETI (the Search for Extra-Terrestrial Intelligence). SETI work had always seemed a complete waste of time to John, but their equipment was ideal for investigating his data spike: the Agassiz Radio Telescope scanned the part of the radio spectrum known as the 'water hole,' which included the wavelengths John was using in his VLA observations.

Director Mark Fielding answered, still at his desk at 7:30 p.m., Massachusetts's time. The two men recognized each other's names—not particularly warmly—and John hastily described his problem: two incidents of interference that coincided with a single spot on Titan's surface.

When Dr. Fielding didn't respond, John belatedly remembered how absurd it was to attribute these radio waves to a source on Titan. Why was he setting himself up for ridicule from the SETI people? Then he remembered that he had made a joke at Fielding's expense at a recent symposium.

Laughter erupted from the other end of the phone line.

"I'm really very interested," Fielding said. "We have an adjustment scheduled for early tomorrow morning. Give me the coordinates you were observing, and I can get you something by Monday."

Fielding chuckled again, then remarked, "For 15 years, I've searched the farthest reaches of time and space across the entire 'water hole' spectrum and have never found any sign of alien intelligence. Just imagine if intelligent life was discovered in VLA photographs of a backyard moon, using the frequency broadcast by Goldstone. And a final irony: you're the one who finds it!"

"I appreciate your willingness to work with my problem, Dr. Fielding." John interjected, ready to provide the co-ordinates and end the call.

Fielding seemed in no hurry to hang up. "By the way, did you hear about the comet that passed behind the Sun this morning? Cloudcroft Observatory picked it up during a routine solar flare watch, and then tracked it for about 20 minutes. Judging from how long it took to cross the penumbra, it will stay behind the Sun for a few weeks now."

John had trouble concentrating. Leslie came into the kitchen with Frankie and he heard her say, "Go tell Daddy that it's time for supper and he needs to stop working."

John barely managed to catch Frankie before he crashed into the leg of the kitchen table. Unaware of his close call, Frankie carried out his mission.

"Daddy no work. Supper."

Meanwhile Dr. Fielding was still going strong. "They may have got enough of a track for someone to find it on an old sky chart. That could give us some idea of where it's headed—if it doesn't crash into the back side of the Sun, of course."

John managed to give Fielding the information he needed and hung up. As Leslie popped a container of leftover rice and chicken into the microwave, punched in four minutes, then emptied a can of green beans into a saucepan and turned the flame to medium, he told her how he had got a better reception from the lunatic fringe than from the establishment.

“Supper will be ready in three minutes. Go wash Frankie's hands and tell Eric to set the table," Leslie interrupted.

John called out from where he sat, "Eric, come and set the table!"

Leslie, already washing lettuce leaves in the sink, gave him a dirty look, and John headed toward the bathroom with

Frankie. So much for Carolyn's advice to share his day with his wife.

He looked into Eric's room on the way down the hall. Eric was lying on the top bunk with earphones, continuing to read his fantasy novel. John waved through the door until Eric nodded—while Frankie continued down the corridor, repeating, "Wash hands. Wash hands."

Once they were all seated around the kitchen table and everyone had been served from the casserole dish, Leslie turned to John. "I'd like to talk to Carolyn about your dream next week."

That was one conversation he wasn't ready to have. He hadn't even shared with Leslie the weirdest thing about his nightmare. There was no way he could be remembering anything that had ever happened to him personally. How could he (who had been in his mother's womb at the time of his father's death) possibly have a dream about it?

Abruptly Frankie chimed in, "Uncle Patrick coming. Uncle Patrick coming."

John stared at his youngest son, certain that he had not once, in Frankie's two-and-a-half years of life, referred to his brother as "Uncle Patrick." He glanced at Leslie, but she simply repeated her question, "Can we talk to Carolyn about it?"

Forcing himself to remain calm, John managed to answer. "I guess we should." Then, scrambling to change the subject, he started talking about the two jumps in signal strength he had found in his Titan data. To John's surprise, Eric laid aside his novel and asked, "So how would aliens on Titan talk to us? Would they send pictures, or talk English?"

Pleased that Eric was showing some interest in his research, John turned to him and said, "Unfortunately there can't be any aliens on Titan, Eric. It's too far away from the Sun to support any kind of life, let alone intelligent life. Voyager II measured the surface of Titan at about minus 200 degrees Celsius. Basically Titan is too cold, too dark, and if it has any oceans then they're ammonia, not water."

Eric's eyes started to glaze over and he returned to his reading. John refrained from telling him to put his book away at the supper table. He felt a pang of recognition at how easy it had been to become a remote father figure with his older son and he wondered, yet again, whether growing up with a single and traumatized mother had left him emotionally unprepared to be a good parent. His dream's image of his mother, holding her pregnant belly and wailing, seatted on the artic ice-flow, threatened to overwhelm John, and he tore his mind back to the family kitchen. Whatever had damaged his relationship with his only brother, Patrick, he hoped he had not passed that wound on to his own two sons. He stole a glance at Leslie and—as if she could read his repentant thoughts—she smiled back. Reassured, John let his mind return to how he would pursue his investigations into the Titan anomaly.

He needed to confirm the two VLA observations on another telescope. His call to Fielding had been a start, but he also needed to contact other observatories. As for analyzing his current VLA data, that was not his area of expertise. So whom could he ask? His UNM colleagues didn't need to know about it, if John, in his sleep-deprived condition, had made some completely amateurish error.

The Santa Fe Institute! He would dash off some e-mail as soon as his family was in bed. But what could he say might have caused this data spike? A military experiment? A glitch in his software, which somehow misfired at just those coordinates? Alien life? No explanation made the slightest sense.

But John knew he wasn't a fit judge of anything these days. He still felt completely unable to explain—to colleagues or to himself—why he had abandoned, about a year ago, his very successful research into galaxy formation. Why had he started this project to map the surface of Titan? That still made absolutely no sense.

Leslie had to repeat herself. "Eric suggested that we walk to the Pot O' Toffee for some dessert." John pulled himself back quickly and looked around the table. Then, forcing himself to summon some enthusiasm, he said, "Hey, it's Friday night."

John put Frankie into his backpack. With Leslie's help, he slung his arms into the straps and the four of them set off on the two-mile trip to the local coffee/dessert hangout.

On the way, Eric outlined a theory of how aliens were running the VLA installation and giving his dad a series of puzzles to solve. If he succeeded, then the whole Murphy family would have an opportunity to travel to another galaxy.

Leslie rolled her eyes, in mock exasperation, and Eric pitched his voice closer to Frankie's and started chanting, "Please, Mom! Can we go? Can we go? Please!" As Eric doubtlessly intended, Frankie joined in.

John knew he was missing an opportunity to engage Eric's playful interest in the VLA mystery, but he couldn't bear to think about aliens controlling his mind. It struck too close to what was happening to him every night. Muttering something about needing to exercise, he strode ahead.He and Frankie reached the 'Pot O' Toffee' first, and waited outside until Leslie and Eric caught up.

As usual it was crowded. Standing in line, John glanced at Leslie and saw that she was upset. He put a tentative arm around her shoulder. Finally, in a barely audible voice, she said, "One day I hope you'll decide that you want to be with us."

He felt a stab in his heart. This was the crux of why they were in therapy, and now he had flunked yet again. He mumbled an apology. When she leaned against him, he squeezed her hard—for once not resisting the feeling of sadness that swept over him.

Surrounded with unwelcome glimpses of how he had been a rotten brother and an inadequate dad, and how now the professional life for which he had sacrificed far too much, seemed threatened, John knew that without Leslie he would have long ago been completely lost.

His face must have registered something of these feelings, because after looking at him, she laid her head on his shoulder and with her arm encircling his waist, she held onto him with a fierce intensity.

CHAPTER 3

They should have closed up hours ago. Hank wondered yet again why they bothered opening the place in winter. They should be in Florida like all the other aging owners of marginal general stores, not freezing in the middle of miserable north Atlantic storms when there weren't any customers anyway.

He knew why they did it. Emily was waiting for their son to return from the sea, hang his oilskins on the wooden peg in the kitchen porch and announce, "I'm, famished. What's for supper, Mom?"

He sometimes heard Dan's footstep himself, even though the memory of their son's swollen body rolling in the surf never left his dreams. Ever since Dan had died, three years ago, Em hadn't been much for traveling. She preferred to pass the cold winter months in their snug apartment and open the store for any strangers who found themselves dead-ending at the edge of their inlet. Usually the car would U-turn and race back to the main intersection several miles back. But now and then he and Em would hear a rap on the window, and then she would bustle up front, ready to put on coffee and make heaping sandwiches. Never mind that the travelers could get something at the FINA a half-mile back up the road. They were all waifs in the storms of life.

A good example was that heavy-set man—Patrick—who came by around noon today. He seemed to need to talk, but his eyes kept darting around, as if they weren't comfortable in his own head. He said he and his brother had come to

Anchor with a neighbor's family 30 years ago, and he mentioned at least three times how much fun he and his brother had together that week. It gave you the impression that fun had not been his long suit in life.

Something about Patrick had reminded them of their son, Danny, and it wasn't just their Irish names. Why else was Em out in the store with the lights still burning at 7:00 p.m. on a Friday night in January, when not a single customer had been by for more than three hours?

Hank had spent most of the evening grumbling to himself in their warmer living quarters behind the store. Their apartment was snug but comfortable, with two bedrooms and a bathroom facing north, overlooking the inlet, and a large combined living room and kitchen on the east wall, with views directly out to the open Atlantic. Every 30 minutes or so, he went up front with a cup of steaming hot tea for Em. And there would be the old cup, sitting where he had left it, cold and untouched. She was so tense that he felt afraid to touch her, as if she would shatter into a thousand pieces. The truth was that Hank himself hadn't got through more than a few pages of his book in the past three hours. He'd read the same paragraph in his thriller, then next thing he knew he'd be staring out to sea.

And now his eyes were acting up. For some time, he had been imagining that something was flashing out on the water, as if an oar, dripping in the wind, had caught the parking lot floodlights. But that had to be his mind playing tricks. Danny had washed up at dusk, after rowing his dingy into an early morning storm.

Whatever was cooking on the stove was making Hank ravenous. Hunger helped him force his stiff body out of the rocking chair and he made his way once again into the front of the store. Em must have heard him, but she kept staring towards the windows that faced out over the inlet. He could see that her eyes were red.

Finally she sighed. "Well, dear, you've humored me enough for one night. I guess we better close up."

He walked behind the cash register, flicked off the switches for the outside floodlights and bolted the front door.

Then once Emily had reached the apartment, he turned off the store overheads and followed her back into the kitchen.

She already had the lid off the pot of lamb stew which had been simmering on the stove all afternoon. The delicious aroma traveled with the rising steam like a dinner bell. Some warm food would do them both good.

Emily's voice sounded distant and frail as she spoke. "Be a dear and get us some of those hard rolls from the store."

Then the ladle clattered to the floor.

Hank bent down, grasping the counter to support his arthritic knees, picked up the ladle, rinsed it and laid it on the counter next to the stove. Then he rested his hand gently on his wife's shoulder. Her body felt like glass. When she didn't turn around to let him give her a hug, he patted her back lightly. "Sure thing, Em. I think some crusty rolls will go just fine with your stew."

He left the door to their flat open to give himself a bit of light and made his way through the familiar aisles until he reached the far wall where they kept the bakery goods.

The line of windows above the shelves looked out over the inlet, where light from a full moon glanced across the black water. From inside the darkened store, the water seemed alive.

He supported himself on the upper shelf and felt around underneath in the small collection of bakery goods they carried at this time of year. Sure enough, he felt a bag of crusty rolls.

As he straightened up with the plastic bag in his grasp, he experienced that sense of something flashing again. Something steadier than the restless face of the sea.

"Damn," he muttered under his breath, "either I'm getting dotty or there's something wrong with my eyes."

Being in no hurry to acknowledge either of these ailments, he leaned toward the window and cupped his right hand around his face. At first he saw only the water and the wavering band of moonlight riding on the swell.

Then he saw the dolphin. In all their years living out here, Hank had never seen a dolphin in the winter months. And even in the summer, he had never seen one this close to land leaping clear of the water. It was as if she knew Hank was there. With each leap her glistening tail reflected moonlight straight into his eyes.

For a moment, Hank stood there, completely stunned, as it gradually sunk in that this dolphin had been out there trying to get his attention all evening. How long ago had it been since he looked up from his book and felt something flashing in his eyes? Ten minutes ago? Fifteen?

He immediately put aside the urge to call Em so she could share in this magnificent sight. Something told him that time was of the essence.

He ran to the front door, unbolted the lock and threw the outside floods back on. On the way out he shouted to Emily to call the FINA station. Then, not even taking the time to close the door behind him, he ran across the icy asphalt in his shirtsleeves, ignoring the pain shooting through his old legs.

Gasping with his unaccustomed exertion in the freezing, salt-bitter air, he struggled through 40 yards of loose sand to the hard-packed beach. The night was full of booming surf and the clacking of pebbles as each wave slipped back into the sea. It was as if something was breaking into the shadows of his mind, something that he had been ignoring for a long time. Long suppressed emotions dashed against his chest like a hurricane tide.

He was still 25 yards from the water when he saw the huge clump of kelp, bobbing in the surf. After each wave, this immense cocoon would lie stranded on the glistening sand. Then, with the next wave, it would start to float back towards the sea. As Hank watched, the dolphin rode in on a large breaker and gave the tangled mass of seaweed a shoreward nudge. Then he gasped, choking on the freezing air.

A pale human face gazed sightlessly straight into his eyes.

This can't be happening. He didn't have to look too closely to know who it was. It was the man who had visited their store that afternoon.

Its effort to keep the man's head above the reach of the surf was obviously costing the dolphin. As Hank watched, it lay there stranded on the sand. Then with a painful rasping sound, it managed to use the next wave to get back into deeper water.

Hank knelt down beside the body and looked at the man's face. His skin was pale blue and completely cold to the touch. Pressing his fingers on the man's neck, he could feel no pulse.

Good Jesus, what should he do now? Should he risk getting the car stuck in the loose sand? He knew that even with Em's help they would never be able to lift this man themselves. He wondered if Em had already called the FINA station. Did he dare to leave for a few moments to get some blankets? In his uncertainty, he turned to look back up towards the store.

There was Em, hurrying towards them with her arms full. When she reached the water's edge, she pulled a hot water bottle out from the midst of the blankets and thrust it beneath the man's grey coat. Then she took charge. "Quick, take Patrick's other shoulder! We need to get him higher up the beach. This poor, dear creature is going to die if we don't."

Together they managed to pull Patrick's head above the breakers, using the slithery kelp to slide him over the rough sand. Then they covered his cold, silent body with blankets.

While holding Patrick's hand in both of hers, Emily turned to face the dolphin who was now about 50 feet out from shore. Hank could scarcely hear her voice above the bitter wind. "I'm so sorry I didn't understand sooner. I didn't know it was you. I thought it was just my own mind, drowning again with my boy. It kept telling me, 'It's too late, it's too late. He's gone.'"

Behind them, a Blazer shot straight over the three-foot embankment, hit the sand skidding, and then did a slalom turn twenty feet from the surf.

Burt, the man from the local Fina station, jumped out of the 4-by-4, ran to Patrick's side and immediately started CPR. A sickening amount of water gushed out of the blue mouth, but no pulse came back.

Burt said it was over. But Emily wanted to bring him to the hospital in Portland. As they were laying Patrick across the back seat of the Blazer, she removed the hot water bottle from inside his coat.

Burt found a slight indentation in the sand bluff further along the beach and used it to reach the road. Pausing just long enough to shift the Blazer into two-wheel drive and slap a flashing light onto the hood, he turned onto the dark coastal road and they headed into town.

Emily pulled the blankets off Patrick and rolled her window down part way. Hank had no idea why, but he figured it didn't really matter any more. Patrick was dead. He pulled a damp blanket over his own shoulders against the biting air coming into the vehicle.

"Patrick will be OK. I just know it. But we have to keep his body cold." Hank wished that she would just let it go, maybe cry a little. In his mind he tried to tell his wife to let go of this horror from their past, not to reach out to this blue corpse. Out loud, hidden in the darkness, he muttered something reassuring, willing to pretend for her sake that there was still a chance.

The only witness to their departure was the dolphin who had brought Patrick to land.

Strange how she had been called to come here. It had taken five hours of strenuous swimming to reach the rock where she had found the two-legs almost dead in the water. Now she was exhausted and weakened by abrasions on her belly from a piece of metal that had torn at her from the sand. She wondered if she would be able to make it back to her pod.

She felt a small glimmer of hope. The unconscious two-legs, and the two who had pulled him up the beach, all seemed to have the capacity to hear the voice. The 'old ones' had been right—some two-legs could learn language. If enough of them learned, perhaps there was still a chance for the world.

But there was almost no time left for any of them.

CHAPTER 4

Monday, January 13 (Day -87)

John's head was full of screaming. For a while that was all there was, that and a sense of cold, terrible loss. Then he awoke to his body, lying in bed, damp and stiff and trembling, and to his mind, stunned with grief and horror.

John knew from experience that he would not be able to get back to sleep. The clock radio indicated 3:04 am. He felt exhausted. It had been almost midnight on Sunday when he had finally fallen into a fitful sleep. Damn! He had forgotten to set his alarm for 2:45 a.m. Throughout the weekend he had kept intending to do that, but he never remembered it when he was in the bedroom.

He glanced at Leslie and saw that she was still asleep. Amazing. John experienced the screams which filled his mind as if they were torn from a living moment. The sense of succumbing to intolerable pressure and cold was so vivid that he could not believe he had just kept lying quietly beside his wife. But apparently the physical terror remained locked inside the world of his dream.

John grabbed his bathrobe and a pair of heavy socks from the chair at the foot of the bed and made his way through the darkness of the hall into the study. He switched on the desk lamp, pulled on his socks and tightened his robe against the cold air, then sat down in the oak chair. The swivel mechanism creaked. He opened his journal to the next blank page, but before picking up the pen he closed his eyes and let himself remember.

It seemed that each night he could remember more. Whether he was retrieving larger passages each time from a dream that was always the same, or whether the dream itself was growing as he paid more attention to it, he did not know.

Their marriage counselor, Carolyn, had been quite fascinated with John's dream when Leslie had made him tell her about it, as if she thought it was some repressed memory—which she, of course, felt obligated to help him excavate. Towards that end, she had told John to get a journal and to write down everything he could remember immediately upon awakening.

It was ridiculous to imagine that the dream could refer to an actual experience. John had never seen a whale in his life. He had been on ice, but only on rivers and lakes in Canada, where he had grown up. He had even fallen through the ice once as a child, but this dream went way beyond the fear of drowning which he had experienced at the age of ten, when he had broken through the ice of Lac Saint Louis, 50 feet from shore, and would likely have drowned if the water had been deeper.

Then, of course, there was the story of his father's drowning. But John had seen the legal documents. His father's death certificate was dated more than three months prior to the date on his own birth certificate. He'd heard of early repressed memories, but prenatal memories—that was absurd. It was strange, though. Now that he thought of it, the woman in the dream, as she sat there wailing in anguish—wasn't she holding her belly?

Why was this dream so vivid? Why did it come back night after night to rob him of his rest and peace of mind? Well, time to do his homework. John picked up his pen and began writing.

The dream always started with a child of about three standing on an ice floe. There were always two adults present who seemed to be the boy's parents. But John had never been able to convince himself that they really were his parents. In a dream full of vivid images, the faces of these two adults seemed to be always averted, caught in the act of turning toward another dimension.

John picked up the pen and started writing.

They are on an ice floe with a research vessel moored alongside. The man is pushing a metal sled with some kind of heavy machinery on top. A twenty-foot-long chain, with one end welded onto the sled, drags behind across the crusty surface. Sunlight reflects off the snow blindingly.

A padlock—its open hoop hooked into one of the chain's links—bounces across the hard snow. The three-year-old picks up the lock. It takes some effort, because the heavy links of the chain come with it. The hoop of the open lock fits nicely into a rawhide thong on the zipper of his snow suit. He keeps playing with the lock, the chain dangling like a heavy necklace. The two adults must be busy with other things during this time.

The child succeeds in closing the lock with an audible click, and the man looks up, shouting. He pulls a set of keys out of his pocket and takes a step toward the child.

Suddenly there is a loud crack. The ice, which seemed so thick and solid, is rent by a gash that passes directly under the sled. The man grabs the chain and starts to pull the sled towards him. It is hard to get it moving, but he succeeds. What had seemed a recipe for disaster shifts into a manageable emergency merely requiring prompt and decisive action. The man keeps pulling the heavy sled—with his tethered son walking beside him—and it slowly moves across the gap. The gap itself has meanwhile stabilized into an eight-inch opening on the surface of the ice.

A shudder passes under their feet and the gap opens further, holds for a moment, then with a roar a third of the entire ice floe breaks away. The calved section of ice must have been thinner—its underside carved out more deeply than the remainder of the floe—because its surface immediately sinks down by about five feet.

The heavy sled totters at the broken edge. The man is kicking his boot heels fiercely into the hard, crusty surface, desperately trying to keep the sled from slipping into the water that has opened in front of them. He is shouting something at the woman, who seems immobilized with horror. Is he telling her to get a knife out of his pocket and cut the rawhide? Is he telling her to pick up the keys which have fallen on the ice?

Should she join him and help pull on the chain or push down on the front of the sled, which is bobbing up and down? Perhaps she already feels the hell that is opening up for her and her children, and is frozen with fear at its approach.

She chooses to join her husband at the end of the 20-foot chain, but her foot hits his foot and he slips forward a little. In the instant which it takes him to recover, the sled lifts clear off the ice and slips into the black water. Then she is standing there utterly alone.

The point of view shifts to hundreds of yards beneath the surface. Something or someone is looking up at the ice floe and watches as the sled and the two humans are plucked away from the ice, with the father, still conscious, holding onto the chain. He is trying to chew through the rawhide loop binding the child to the chain, and he is still holding on when his heart stops beating.

Even in recollection, writing in his journal with his hands illuminated under the yellow warmth of the desk-lamp, John experiences this part of the dream like a hammer striking his heart. He is both the father who is dying, trying to save his only child, and the father of two boys asleep in the next room, sons whom he has been too busy to really get to know.

John has to force himself to keep writing, as a sudden urge to check on his own sleeping children pulls at him like chains wrapped around his heart.

Grasping his pen tightly, John feels like he is in two places at once. He is sitting in his house in Albuquerque, New Mexico, and he is also rising up towards the light in frigid Artic waters, catching a sled and the bodies of the two humans on his broad head. Sitting in his den, John knows that it is the father's sacrifice that has prompted this huge, compassionate creature to lift them to the surface and butt his head against the edge of the ice floe with enough force that the sled and the two humans slide onto the ice.

The whale knows that the father is dead but that the child can be revived. He swims around under the ice, unable to communicate to the wailing mother that her son still lives.

Then the dream images begin to break apart, but now John knows that, in the process of clutching at both cold bodies, the mother starts the boy's lungs breathing again. Then he is completely back in his warm Albuquerque home, shaking with the silent scream that is now the constant companion of his days.

John stood up from his desk and walked down the hallway to Eric's and Frankie's room. From the light spilling in from the hallway, he watched his two boys and listened to their slow deep breaths. And in that moment he realized that during all those years that he devoted to his scientific theories and calculations, he had been counting trees, unaware of the forest in which he was walking.

CHAPTER 5

John turned on his computer, fired up his communication software and logged onto his University account. It was still only 3:30 a.m., Monday morning, far too early to try and call anyone, but maybe he would have some e-mail from Fielding or the VLA scheduler. He wondered whether the SETI people had really scheduled a Titan observation for the weekend.

There were three new messages, all from Mark Fielding. He put the most recent, which he noticed had arrived only 15 minutes ago, on the screen. His throat tightened as his eyes rapidly scanned the text. He could scarcely believe the address list to which Fielding had copied this e-mail. In addition to johnmurphy@unm.edu, Mark had sent it to administrators in NASA, the White House, the Planetary Society, and the Pentagon. The letter announced that an intelligent communication had been picked up from Titan. Mark Fielding stated categorically that—based on the tracking path of the Agassiz radio dish over a 30 minute period—the source was a fixed location on Titan. It could not be some occluding satellite. He also affirmed that the signal strength was three orders of magnitude too high to be a scattered signal from Earth.

Then came the real shocker, and obviously the reason Fielding had copied this note to the Pentagon. Fielding stated that he had accidentally intercepted a confidential military transmission, and requested official sanction before taking the next step. He didn't elaborate, and his letter ended.

John felt dizzy. Could Fielding have already decoded something which had scared him? And now he was claiming that he knew nothing about its content?

The next message was from a Near Earth Asteroid Watch group (NEAW), forwarded by Fielding: more about the comet sighting Fielding had mentioned on the phone. An amateur astronomer had found something on an old sky chart that might be an earlier sighting of the same object. If this could be confirmed, then he was predicting that it would cross Earth's orbit in three months, alarmingly close to where Earth herself would be at that time. John deleted this e-mail in a fit of irritation and moved on to the earliest of the three messages from Fielding. This letter, written exclusively to John, provided a password for www@seti.com/fielding/titan/jm. Fielding's file was more than 5 gigabytes, too big to download over his Comcast connection in a reasonable time-frame, so he would need to use the University high-speed link.

He grabbed a handful of flash drives, quickly dressed, left a note for Leslie on his pillow, and slipped out of the house. Then he drove through the deserted streets to the Physics Department.

John couldn't get a handle on what was happening. And now Mark Fielding was actually calling it an intelligent transmission! What did he think it was? A classified mission to Titan's surface? A high power transmitter in space somewhere, bouncing a signal off Titan's surface? None of these speculations rang true.

He was relieved to find the building parking lot deserted. He grabbed his shoulder bag and entered the darkened building.

Working quickly, with a sense of urgency, John fired up one of the SUN computers, established an FTP link to Fielding's computer, and then initiated the file transfer. Sure enough, he needed to supply the password. The transfer began and for about 30 seconds appeared to be proceeding normally. Then a message flashed on the screen announcing abnormal termination.

He quickly restarted the FTP transfer protocol. This time he received the message, "File Not Found."

He checked his spelling and retyped the command. Same thing. He tried to list the contents of Fielding's directory, which he had successfully done just a few moments ago.

"Permission Denied," flashed on the screen.

He checked to see if he had received anything from the aborted transfer and found a 1 gigabyte file in his home directory. It was only 20% of the original, but at least it was something. He quickly copied it onto his high-capacity flash drive and deleted the original.

He was about to log off when a notice of new e-mail flashed on the screen and he re-entered his mail program.

The letter, which had originated from a General Fischer at the Pentagon, stated that the data picked up on Fielding's telescope was vital to national security and that no one without top clearance was permitted to see it. He ordered John not to tell anyone about this incident nor communicate the coordinates from which the radio waves had originated. The letter concluded with the promise of an official visit in the near future.

John's mind raced. He knew that an experienced system programmer would be able to tell from the systems logs everything that John had done this morning. From Fielding's end they would know that a partial file had made it across the internet to a UNM computer. From the New Mexico end, they would easily discover that John had copied the partial file onto a thumb drive. They would want it.

He needed to download this file, somewhere no one would look. He couldn't do it at home. That was the first place they would look.

Suddenly he remembered Bill. Maybe he would be working a graveyard shift at Computing Center Operations. If not, maybe they could give him a home number. He picked up the phone then slammed it back down. They could also look at the phone records for any calls made from the physics department around 4:00 a.m.

He grabbed his thumb drive, shut down the computer and turned off all the lights. Then he left the Physics building, drove to a Seven-Eleven and dialed the Computer Center from a pay phone.

When Bill answered, John spat it out in one breath, "I need to make a back-up of a file that could get anyone who helps me in serious trouble."

Bill's response was unhesitating. "Lead the way, Professor."

John laughed and said, "Meet me outside in five minutes."

John drove to the Computing Center and parked at the edge of the lot, turned off the car lights and waited. After a few moments, Bill came out of a side door.

He spotted John, sprinted over, and slipped into the passenger seat.

Without preamble Bill said, "I've got the perfect place to stash your file. Our network guru is down in Hawaii for a few weeks, setting up a new super-computing node."

Bill held up a key. "I managed to get this from my boss's drawer without anyone noticing. But he's due back from break in five minutes."

John handed over the thumb drive. "The file's called LGM."

Bill sprinted back to the building and disappeared inside. John felt his legs trembling, like when he woke up at 3:00 a.m., and he knew why. His nightmare had just stepped into his waking life.

The side door opened and closed so quickly that John would have missed it, if he hadn't been looking in that direction. Keeping the lights off, he drove over, retrieved an envelope leaning against the stucco wall, and sped out of the parking lot.

John arrived home a few minutes before 6:00 am. Before entering the house, he switched on the Honda's overhead and opened the envelope. Bill had written his home phone number and a short note. "If I can help in any way—and I mean ANY way—call me. Great file name. Little Green Men: exactly my sentiments".

John entered the house. Except for the light under the door into his office, the house remained quiet, still wrapped in January darkness. He hid the thumb drive under a stack of three year old computer listings. 'The best hiding place is in the midst of everyday clutter' came into his mind, as if it were a familiar saying from childhood.

Feeling calmer than he had since awakening almost four hours earlier, he went into the kitchen and made a pot of coffee.

Well into the first cup he found himself smiling at his recent behavior. What had all that been about? Why the cloak-and-dagger trip to the Computing Center? What did he think he was saving, and from whom? Once he had the information on his thumb drive he could have made that transfer later. No one was going to notice that he had transferred a file from Mark Fielding's directory. And if they did, he could just tell them that it hadn't worked.

However, by the time Leslie came into the kitchen for a cup of coffee, about 30 minutes later, his mind was racing again. That e-mail from the Pentagon had ordered him to stay away from the data. It had informed him that government agents would be visiting.

But there couldn't be anything transmitting on Titan. That was completely impossible.

Sipping her coffee, Leslie held up the note he had written hours earlier. "You've already been to campus this morning?"

John was probably more amazed than Leslie at how he responded. "If our government isn't doing something illegal on Titan, then something inconceivable has happened."

Neither of them said anything. They just looked at one another, and their silence had the effect of making John's statement stand out and appear momentous.

He knew Leslie wanted him to say something more. But what could he say?

"Christ, John! All you've done is look at some data that the VLA sent you. What in the world are you feeling so nervous about?"

John made the decision not to tell Leslie about the file he had transferred across the internet earlier that morning. It didn't feel like a lack of trust in his wife. No, he was protecting her, wasn't he? After all, if John looked nervous, it would be better if Leslie didn't look nervous too.

He was madly trying to work out how to explain his silence to Leslie, when she said, "Don't look now, but a black Oldsmobile just pulled up in front of our house. And two men in dark grey suits are getting out of it."

CHAPTER 6

Patrick was looking for his body. It struck him that this was a strange thing to be doing. There must have been countless times in his life when he had been asleep without the slightest awareness of being inside a body, and with even less concern about that fact. But this was different than being asleep. He was trying to breathe, trying to open his eyes to see light and color—and absolutely nothing was responding to these efforts.

He was very much in touch with his mind—it just had no body connected to it that he could find.

Could this be what happened in death? One thing was certain; there was no point worrying about his body if he couldn't find it.

Then a burning strangulation stripped away all comfortable indifference. His skin was being torn off by millions of vicious little mouths. Terror of dying enveloped him: terror of physical pain, of the threat of personal annihilation, and terror of losing his mistaken life, just at the very moment when he could almost remember why he had been given this life.

He caught a glimpse of meaning—something to do with reaching out to other beings, under inhospitable circumstances, like a flower breaking through asphalt into sunlight.

For a brief instant, almost matter of fact in its calm detachment, he could see himself lying in the back of a vehicle, his head in the lap of a grey-haired woman, with two men sitting in front. His own body appeared to be stone dead.

Then he was being cradled in his father's arms, while on all sides whales and dolphins swam past. Their sad, attentive faces looked on as the man held his lifeless child and tried to speak. Air bubbles came out of his father's mouth as they slowly sank into the darkness of ocean depths.

Then his brother was calling him. What was he saying? It sounded like, "There's only us two". John, his brother, was a young boy again and they were at Anchor Beach.

But surely he could not remember these things if he had no living body? He tried to hold onto that thought, as if it gave convincing proof of his existence.

Perhaps he should take some kind of inventory. When was he last aware of being in his body? There had been an experience of pain and strangulation, but maybe that was how consciousness tore away from the body, like a Band-Aid being ripped away from tender skin. His body had certainly looked dead in the car.

A more plausible candidate for embodiment was just after he had sunk beneath the water and had looked into that eye. But that had seemed too completely weird. That must have been a dream, a bridge between the experience of freezing in the water and the familiar dream which had followed, where his father was carrying him in from the car.

Perhaps what he was doing right now was dreaming up a world in an attempt to stave off annihilation—now, during a brief respite, before the Lord of Death spotted him and ran him to earth for good.

Even if he got a body back, what would it matter? He would still be stuck as he had always been stuck in this unending stream of wretched half-truths, in these muddled fantasies that only made him feel disappointed in everything real in his life.

As if to emphasize his continuing inability to be grounded anywhere, every familiar landmark vanished. He felt as if he had been locked in a dungeon. Time seemed to go by, a lot of time maybe, but without any personal landmarks he had no way of knowing.

Abruptly, he found himself inside some kind of body that had no arms or legs. He was deep down under miles of water. The pressure was intense, even to the body that had evolved in this alien sea. He tried to see where he was, to reach out to companions who would protect him. Images kept flashing and disappearing as if he was experiencing something above, on a distant surface, while his body suffered in dull blindness. Visions of a vast landscape appeared and disappeared: lightning flashing jade and ruby brilliance over ice cliffs, jagged glaciers towering at impossible angles, and fierce jets of hail and sleet ravaging everything.

Then he was rising higher, above the ocean, above the cliffs, until he could see the whole surface—frozen, cruel, inhospitable to life. Yet there was life. It was in the ocean.

Intermittent sheets of lightning lit up the thick cloud cover. Now and then a jagged flash discharged into the water below, and for a moment a mysterious world could be glimpsed under the surface—submerged, floating islands, with tunnels and ramparts, sailed past, as if housing, or imprisoning, some inconceivable civilization.

Then rising up even higher there was only cloud and smog, thick as dirty milk. Miles and miles of it. Then out into space. But it wasn't just space. Overhead, a huge body—round as the belly of a whale—filled half the sky.

Looking down, he lost his balance and everything disappeared. Then another flash came and he found himself back in the cold, deep ocean, locked inside a squirming body—more like a serpent than a whale.

Then, abruptly, another shift. In vain, his mind called out for something to grasp. But he had no body, no breath, not even a familiar mind, to touch down upon.

Floating across the surface of the water, transfused with light, an immense sculpture appears whose interior is filled with exquisite lattices of ice. Sparkling as in a vast and intricate jewel, light reflects among its countless surfaces. In its scale and grandeur, it resembles an immense, radiant cathedral. In the delicacy and fineness of its construction it exceeds the perfection of a spider's web. Translucent mists of jade and ruby swirl around a radiant central core. And it is all growing out of the surface of the ocean, like a breath freezing in winter air.

Then the mists turn into heavy rain. The fine lattice details melt as gathering torrents wash over them.

The entire sculpture, which had extended hundreds of feet into the air, dissolves back into the sea within a few seconds.

A small bright light is all that remains. This small shining object continues to hover above the ocean waves. As he looks more closely, the object grows larger. He sees that it is a crystal sphere with billions of perfect facets sparkling and glittering. Then he can see inside this sphere. In fact, he is falling faster and faster straight through its radiant circumference.

Before any impact can occur, the ball opens up into the great open space of the solar system. The crystal sphere explodes into orbiting shards of ice as he plummets though it, each frozen comet glinting in the pale light of the distant Sun. As he continues to plunge toward the center, faster and faster, the Sun grows larger and larger, and one by one the familiar planets pop out of the vastness of space. The strangest thing is the way that he can recognize and keep track of the entire solar system, as if he can continue to see each planet and its moons, and each of the billions of icy comets at the very edge of the system, while at the same time flying towards the Sun like a pebble flung into a pond.

Then all of that disappears, and there is only the ocean, cold, raging and dark.

He is in the presence of something profoundly alien. An alien intelligence living on a world marked by inconceivable transience. There is something living there, in a world of water, in a world where the illusion of permanence is not allowed.

In a world so marked by transience, there are no cathedrals paroling the centuries, no family plots joining generations of beings to particular fields or mountain vistas. Against the inroads of time, there is only the mind's deep penetration of the balances and rhythms of nature.

From long practice at hiding his feeling, Patrick wants to retire into a private place of his own. Then it suddenly dawns on him that a dead man doesn't have to protect himself from grief.

With feelings of immense sadness, Patrick returned to more familiar memories. He had felt so isolated all his life, never really sharing anything with anyone else. He remembered how he had felt when, at three years old, he realized that his father had vanished from his life forever. He remembered how the heart of a young boy had closed down at that time, and how for the rest of his life he had always skirted intimacy like a hungry ghost.

It was as if the melting of the beautiful cathedral of ice, scarcely come into being, had unleashed deep pain for all the losses of his life. And out of this unfamiliar openness, he found himself thinking of the family who ran that little store at the end of the beach road. He found himself saying a little prayer for their happiness. May they not lose whatever they have found in this world of beauty and love.

It felt like he was learning a foreign language, and that by sending kind thoughts to these strangers he was communicating with an intelligence alive in his dreams. It was a strange intuitive move for someone who had lived his life in the shadows, allowing no voice to his intuition.

If he could have his life back, he would try to do something. But how could he be alive? Everyone knows that a human being can't survive for more than a few minutes in freezing water.

Suddenly he was back inside the solar system. He could see everything in orbit around the Sun, down to the smallest flecks of matter streaming through the emptiness of space. But this time something had changed. There was something he was supposed to see.

Then he saw it. Something far more massive that a fleck of matter riding on the solar wind. Something approaching one of the planets on a collision course.

Then he was in a hospital room, floating near the ceiling, looking down on his own body. His body was connected to a lot of tubes and pumps. Shafts of white light were streaming down into his body from a radiant pool, and a shaft of blue light was streaming upwards from his throat into this pool of radiance. Why were there tubes and monitors? Did that mean that he wasn't dead?

For a moment he tottered in this wide perspective, overlooking everything with equanimity and detachment, and then he was poured back into the enveloping, devastating realm of sensation, painful but suffused with warmth.

His last image, before sinking completely into the mute darkness of embodiment, was of the woman, Emily, rising to her feet and crying out.

"He moved! Patrick moved!"

CHAPTER 7

It was too early for the Jehovah's Witnesses to be calling. And something about the way the two men stood told John the bulges under their jackets weren't copies of the Watchtower.

John opened the door and the taller of the men spoke. "Are you Professor John Murphy of the University of New Mexico Physics and Astronomy department?"

When John indicated that he was, this tall, lean-faced man took out an ID case and displayed it through the screen door. "I'm Agent Miller and this is Agent Sullo. We would just like a few moments of your time."

John opened the screen door and the two agents came into the front hallway. John introduced Leslie and then said, "You're out early this morning. Would you like some coffee?"

Agent Miller responded. "We won't take any more of your time than we need to, so we'll decline your offer for coffee. Professor Murphy, is there somewhere we can talk privately?"

Feeling a pang of anxiety, he realized that he had been counting on Leslie's presence to keep everything low-key and friendly.

Just then a bedroom door opened and Eric walked out in his terry-cloth bathrobe. He was in a hurry as he was every weekday morning, to shower, grab breakfast and his lunch, and make it to the bus stop by 7:10 am. But he found the time to glance down the hall at the two men standing with his parents and remark, "My parents read the Bible every day," before going into the bathroom.

Agent Sullo, the shorter, more visibly muscled of the two men, failed to suppress a smile, and the distraction gave John the few moments he needed to compose himself. "My office is right here, Agent Miller and Agent Sullo. Please come in. We can talk privately here."

Meanwhile Frankie had started crying in his room and Leslie hurried off to see what the matter was.

John closed the door, pointed to the couch, and sat down in his computer chair. "How may I help you, gentlemen?"

Agent Miller leaned his long body forward as he spoke. "Let me say straight off that this is a completely routine visit, Professor Murphy. There is absolutely nothing for you to be concerned about. I know that being visited about national security issues can make the most honest person in the world feel a bit nervous so let me put any concerns you might have to rest. But we do request your cooperation on a certain matter which has come up. You accidentally stumbled on something unusual in your research at the VLA, and I understand that you then contacted your colleague, Dr. Mark Fielding, to try to learn more about it."

Both agents were looking at John, and Agent Miller was obviously giving him an opportunity to say something about this unusual material. John wondered if they knew anything about his attempt to download Mark Fielding's file. Well, if they didn't know yet, they soon would. "That is correct." John said.

When he didn't elaborate, Agent Miller spoke again. "Why did you need to switch to another radio telescope?"

"Because I hoped to find out more about the interference. All I see now is a bright spot in the middle of the picture."

Agent Miller continued. "Ah, so you just hoped to eliminate an anomaly?"

John hesitated and finally decided to tell as much of the truth as possible. "I encountered this same interference twice in one month. At first, I assumed it was interference, and simply excised it out of my observational database. But then I got the same thing two weeks later. When I noticed that both incidents had occurred at exactly the same spot on Titan's surface, I felt I needed to investigate further."

"What conclusions have you come to?" Agent Miller pressed.

"I haven't come to any conclusions. Every hypothesis that comes to mind leads to an absurdity. Terrestrial interference doesn't work, because it wouldn't be dependent on what part of Titan I was observing at the time. On the other hand, what could there be on Titan to account for such a strong signal? A top-secret space probe, landed there by our government or the Russians? That doesn't make any sense. How would it have got there? Some natural source of radio waves? I can't think of what that could be. Aliens? I think we can let that hypothesis go, don't you? So, no. I haven't come to any conclusions. It simply makes no sense, any way you look at it." Then he added, "I have no idea what's going on here. Can either of you gentlemen enlighten me?"

Neither agent so much as blinked, as John went on. "I mean, your presence here is very disappointing. It suggests that what I've stumbled on may be yet another boring military experiment."

This time Agent Miller immediately responded. "Why would you be disappointed, Professor Murphy?"

John felt his heart racing. He shouldn't have said that. Calm down, for Christ sake. Just remember that you're completely entitled to pursue your scientific research. And don't sit there tense and silent. That's the single worst thing to do.

He took a deep breath and started speaking, in what he hoped was a casual, professional manner. "Well, maybe 'disappointed' is too strong a word. But, you know, even an astronomer like myself can get excited at the idea that one day something extraordinary could happen. One day an observation will revolutionize our view of the solar system."

The shorter, more muscular man, Agent Sullo, now spoke. "Have you been in communication with Dr. Fielding since you gave him the Titan coordinates for further observation?"

Then it hit John that the stocky Agent Sullo was the boss of this two-man team, and he realized that this was a question he wasn't ready to answer.

Both agents were looking at John. Their eyes seemed to sense every nuance of hesitation. He realized that he had to make a choice. Should he gamble that this really was just a routine visit? Or should he make some kind of confession to these agents? Perhaps it would be better to tell them now, voluntarily, whatever they could discover later from university system logs. They would be less likely to investigate further if they left his house this morning with what seemed like a complete explanation for his behavior.

Recognizing that his explanation now had to also explain his inability to immediately answer Agent Sullo's question, he started talking. "Well, for starters, you may wonder why I have so much trouble saying whether I have communicated with Dr. Fielding."

A glance at the two intelligence operatives confirmed that they were indeed wondering about it. They looked like two vultures, one short and one tall, ready to step closer if the individual before them didn't get back on all fours pretty soon.

With little idea of how he was going to satisfy them, while also hiding his determination to look at the fragment he had snatched off the Internet, he continued. "The thing is, I haven't talked with Dr. Fielding, but this morning I logged on and found an e-mail message from him. He included the password to a file of new Titan observations, so I went into my department to download it."

"Don't you have an internet connection on your home machine?" Agent Sullo asked.

John told him that the file would have taken too long to port across at home.

"And did you retrieve that file?" Agent Sullo continued.

The moment of truth. Should he let everything ride on the hope that Bill had successfully transferred the file fragment and that no one would find it? Was Leslie right, when she claimed that he would be a completely open book to professional investigators such as these? If so, he needed to tell them about everything—everything except his trip to the computing center—if he was to have any chance of satisfying them.

He made his choice. "Yes, I tried to download the file. Unfortunately, I was locked out in the middle of the transmission."

He looked at the shorter of the two men and tried to gauge if he was on the right track. Met with Agent Sullo's unwavering gaze, he had no choice but to plunge on in the dark. "I think I got about 20% of the original and I made a back-up of it. Of course, it may not be readable in this fragmentary form."

Agent Sullo didn't miss a beat. "Did you read the e-mail which told you that you should not concern yourself with this confidential information?"

"Yes, I read it. But only after I had attempted the download."

Agent Sullo pressed on. "Did you read it before you made the back-up? And where is this back-up, Professor Murphy?"

John had already decided to give up his thumb drive gracefully. He still had the original disk with the VLA data, which he planned to send to the Santa Fe Institute for analysis. He knew people at the VLA and he should be able to get some more observational time to view Titan again. And, most importantly, Bill had made a copy of the same Fielding file fragment, which Agent Sullo was now requesting.

He stood up and retrieved the thumb drive from under the pile of papers. The squeal of his swivel chair stood out in the silence as he sat back down.

Agent Sullo appeared uninterested in the thumb drive, as he continued. "So you left your house early just to transfer a file. Then you copied it after being warned not to. Exactly what time did you go in, Professor Murphy?"

"I think it was probably around 4:00 am."

Agent Sullo's eyebrows lifted. "Let me see if I understand this correctly, Professor Murphy. You get some e-mail telling you about a file and it causes you to leave home four hours earlier than usual. When you try to download this file, you find that you've been locked out. You check your e-mail again and find a message telling you that this information has been confiscated. So what do you do? You copy this confiscated material onto your private media."

Agent Sullo paused for a moment before continuing. "That sounds like someone who is very motivated to see this data, wouldn't you agree? Why?"

Why indeed? What could he possibly say to these two bureaucrats from the sinister world of big government? Out of a sense of utter blankness, he found himself looking directly at Agent Sullo and asking, "Wouldn't you be interested?"

Agent Sullo didn't answer for a moment. "I wouldn't try to steal state secrets. I wouldn't be that suicidal."

John felt something shifting in him. Sullo's hesitation made the agent seem more human and John felt anger begin to stir. He leaned forward in his chair. "How did you guys get onto this so fast? What does Titan have to do with the intelligence community? This all just blows my mind."

Then, before either agent had an opportunity to make the slightest gesture of response to this question, John's voice rose into an impassioned harangue. "Let's get real here, gentleman. I don't have the slightest idea what any of this means. And now I wonder whether you do. We aren't talking about some run-of-the-mill top-secret military experiment, are we? I mean, how in the hell could someone secretly land a transmitter on a moon one billion miles from here? And why would anyone want to keep such an amazing accomplishment secret?"

Agent Sullo didn't respond for a moment or two. "I can't tell you that, Dr. Murphy. Our government has national security activities which you don't need to know about. Especially as a Canadian, let me add."

"Why can't you tell me what's going on?" John persisted. "Because it's a state secret, or because you don't know? Is the military trying to hush this up because they're scared shitless? Are we talking about something so completely inexplicable that people in high places are daring to breath the A-word?"

Both agents looked genuinely at a loss. Finally Agent Miller asked, "Which A-word is that, Professor Murphy?"

He heard his own voice continue. "I could never look my kids in the face if it turned out that I was the one who intercepted an alien transmission, and then just shrugged and let it go."

Agent Miller glanced at his boss with an expression of unmistakable consternation. His boss didn't return his look, but his face was grim.

Then John fell into a familiar fear of authority and desperately tried to back-pedal. "Hey, lighten up. I'm joking. I wanted to look at the data because it's part of my research. But now that you've asked me to hand it over, I'm doing so voluntarily."

He reached out with the cigarette-lighter-sized drive, but Agent Sullo kept his hands on his knees. After a moment, the younger agent leaned forward and took the flash drive.

John had the impression that the two agents felt angry with themselves. After a few moments, Agent Sullo seemed to pull himself together. "Professor Murphy, I need to inform you of a few other actions we have taken. All your data from the VLA has been confiscated. I've been assured by several of your colleagues at the VLA that your Titan database only records summarized integrations of the raw data, so we have left your own Titan material intact. Everything else that you worked with last Friday has been deleted off the Computing Center machines."

Agent Sullo continued. "A few other things you may also wish to know. I don't believe that you will succeed in getting additional time on the VLA radio telescope. The staff in charge understands the importance of leaving Titan well enough alone, until the U.S. government has answered a few questions. And one other thing, I would rather you don't pursue your e-mail to the Santa Fe Institute at this time."

As John sat speechless, Agent Sullo turned to his younger cohort. "I need to make a few phone calls. Give Professor Murphy our standard paperwork to sign, and make sure he reads the juicy parts about national security offenses. I'll be in the car."

Then he turned to John. "You don't have another copy of that file hidden away somewhere, do you?"

John felt the dryness of his mouth as he shook his head. Agent Sullo looked intently at John for a moment or two and then said, "I can let myself out. Thank you for your time, Professor."

After Agent Sullo had gone, John signed everything that Agent Miller gave him without asking a single question. Then he watched as Agent Miller expertly perused the recent systems log on his home computer.

Protest seemed futile. Part of him wished that he had never heard of Titan. Then he wouldn't be doing this insane thing. There was something transmitting from Titan? Fine. Let someone else go to jail over it.

Finally John walked with Agent Miller out to his front yard. Talk about looking guilty. Why on earth was he following the man out of the house?

When Agent Miller offered his hand, John took it willingly, almost eagerly. But after he had watched the dark Oldsmobile pull away from the curb and turn out of sight around the corner, John knew that something had remained behind. Something unknown had come to roost in the midst of his comfortable, ordinary life. And, for better or worse, he would never be the same again.

CHAPTER 8

Tuesday, Jan 14 (Day -86)

George Ball, armaments honcho extraordinaire, did not enjoy being called into the White House, especially to see that sleazy, asshole President. But best to keep an open mind–this might be the chance he had been waiting for. He better be careful though, say as little as possible. That was always a good rule of thumb these days—ever since a year ago, when his epileptic fits had started. It would never do to have a fit in the President's office. That would nix any chance of getting his technological brainchild launched into space, as that weenie, Phil Black, the President's Chief of Staff, had hinted could happen. No one needed to know that Georgie Boy got his brainstorms during epileptic fits. It didn't make the brilliance of his discoveries any less brilliant.

George followed the Secret Service agent, an athletic-looking, blonde man, about 6'2', down the White House corridor. George knew he could break the jerk's neck before he had a chance to lift a finger. That was a strange development too. George had always been a tough kid, but ever since the fits started he had been able to move with inconceivable speed and power. A few weeks ago, a damn pit bull had picked the wrong guy to growl at. Before either of them knew what was happening, he had tossed it onto a second story balcony where, instead of snarling and baring its teeth, it was whining for its mommy.

The agent knocked on a door, and a moment later it was opened from inside by Richard Todd, director of the FBI. That pet monkey, Todd, might be some use to him yet. Good thing he had him over a barrel.

When George entered the room, the President himself stood up and walked forward with hand extended. Probably a good time to smile. "George, come on in. I'm delighted to finally meet you. Director Todd and Phil have just been filling me in on your incredible missile tracking system." George forced himself to shake the President's hand—throttled back the impulse to go wash in the ivory washstand at the edge of the room—and sat down in the chair the President indicated. He nodded to the President's Chief of Staff—another asshole, if there ever was one—and made like he was giving his undivided attention to the Commander in Chief.

The President continued. "I believe Phil has already filled you in a bit. We have a problem, and some of the Generals at the Pentagon think you may be the one who can solve it. Let me just summarize briefly."

Summarize?!! All the President knew how to do was wave his hands and spout bullshit. Out loud, George forced himself to say, "That would be useful, Sir."

The President leaned forward and continued in a lower voice. "George, I realize that we may have a bit of a problem with the legality of your technology. I understand it's missile defense umbrella stuff that was never approved by Congress. But, under the circumstances, we can let that go. I want you to know that you can talk candidly."

The President looked at George, like they were both men-of-the-world who understood what was needed and would roll up their sleeves to get the job done. Hopefully he didn't need George to respond to him in this vein. Better keep your mouth shut, Georgie Boy. Umbrella technology? Shit no! No one on Earth had ever seen anything remotely like what he had put together. The earlier Strategic Defense Initiative project (nicknamed Star Wars) was kindergarten compared to what he had developed. He hadn't used shit from the earlier Star Wars technology. And it bloody well showed in performance trials.

The President apparently wasn't waiting for George to respond, because he was talking again. So what else was new?

Presumably this was the President's idea of "candid talk," although it seemed more like expedient bullshit to anyone who had a brain in his head. And Georgie Boy had a brain or two or three in his head.

"It's too early to know if we have a real threat here, George, but it's possible. We'll know more when it swings around from behind the Sun, probably in a week or two. But based on two early sightings, before the comet disappeared behind the Sun a few days ago, it looks like we may have a problem."

Phil Black intervened—about time; the President didn't know his asshole from his belly button. "We have a comet sighting, here, George—like I told you on the phone this morning—and people at NASA are concerned."

As the President continued, Phil handed George a graphic that showed the probability cone of possible Earth-orbit crossings. "I talked with Henry from NASA this afternoon, and he told me we're only talking one chance in a couple of thousand of an actual collision. But he also told me that this is the first time—in 65 million years—that there has been this kind of intersection between Earth's orbit and the projected trajectory of a sizable object."

The President paused for a moment before continuing. "So, tell us, George. If we need to launch a missile to blow this sucker up, do we have the technology to do it?"

This time, the President did wait for a response. And George was more than happy to give it. "Let me put it this way, Sir. If Canaveral has the rocket to get the bomb there in time, my tracking system will pulverize the sucker. My tracking system can pulverize more than 100 objects a second. It can track a bowling ball 100 million miles away moving at 100 miles a second, and it will get it. All I need is the rocket."

George throttled back the urge to say more. He had been about to start boasting about the hundreds of hummingbirds he had vaporized in his test barrel with a series of precise laser bursts. Not everyone liked to hear that. But what the hell? What better way was there to test his system's ability to hit a moving target?

He looked up with a start. The President was standing and looking down at George. Shit. What was happening here? He really had to be more careful—must have wandered off for a few moments. But maybe it had only been for a second, because the President was smiling. George stood up and tried to tune into what the President was saying. "We can't say for sure what we have here, Mr. Ball, but we're going to need all hands on deck for this one. Phil will put you in touch with Henry and the NASA team. Then we'll do what needs to be done. Right?"

That was probably one he should answer. "You're absolutely, right, Sir. We'll do what needs to be done. Yes, Sir!" Hey, not bad. Maybe he was getting the hang of it.

And as if to confirm that George had in fact succeeded in appearing quite normal, the President reached his hand across the table while George—like a regular person—quickly offered his own hand and performed what he considered a good, American-know-how, handshake with the Commander in Chief of his country.

The President left the room with Director Todd, and Phil suggested he and George get to work right away. That was OK with George. He'd talk with the pet monkey, Todd, later.

As they walked along the corridor together, George listened to Phil Black only as much as he needed to. Just enough to be certain that the President definitely wanted to use his intruder-defense system mounted on a space-borne, nuclear-armed missile. Could BallMaker Electronics put this together in a week? Are you kidding? Does the Pope shit in the woods? Ride 'em cowboy! NASA here we come. Better watch out for Georgie Boy. You'll be able to spot him real easy. He's the one with the grown-up toys that shoot real bullets.

CHAPTER 9

For some time now Patrick had been sensing his own breath. Blurred voices—like a radio station not quite coming in—threaded in and out of consciousness. He heard voices talking about someone not expected to recover. But one woman's voice sounded different. She made Patrick feel that all he had to do was decide to open his eyes.

Images of his surroundings slipped in and out of focus. It seemed he was in a hospital, or maybe a nursing home. Inside his head he tried opening his eyes, moving his arms, screaming—but the voices outside just kept droning on, as if he wasn't there. It all felt like a horrible, bad joke. Back in Montreal, instead of jumping off a tall building in despair, he had taken a trip, followed a dream. Bad idea, apparently. Really bad idea. For a few moments it had looked like he was on his way to somewhere new, finally open to new possibilities—but now it was pretty clear that he had thrown away his sorry life. The only difference he could see was that now he had more than his own life to lose—now he was being sucked into the void with a very important message locked inside.

His recurrent dreams had continued. Now they felt like the old Lone Ranger serials that they used to show in the Boy Cub shack when he was growing up, where the new episode would start further back from the way the previous episode had ended. And, instead of the Lone Ranger being hurled out of the saddle off the edge of the cliff, there he was hanging from a vine and Silver had somehow shaken the reins within reach. Similarly in the visions of the solar system that ran through his mind, over-and-over, he would see a catastrophe: a missile hitting a comet and a while later a cloud of fragments would utterly destroy Earth. But then the serial would rewind, and the comet would sail out from behind the Sun, past Mercury and Venus, and somewhere in the neighborhood of Earth and her Moon a smaller explosion of light would ignite on the comet's surface and, like an elegant courtier in a waltz, the comet would continue, unperturbed, back out beyond the outer planets.

The message was clear: A comet was heading straight for Earth and it would be a fatal mistake to shatter it with a bomb.

Maybe if he really concentrated he could open his eyes. He tried and then tried again. Then, when he had given up trying, he found himself looking directly into the eyes of a woman. She was looking straight back at him. How strange. She didn't seem at all surprised that Patrick was looking at her.

The woman seemed vaguely familiar: around 70 with a slight build, hair more silver than white, and eyes that were an astonishingly bright green. Her mouth was firm, even intense, but her eyes seemed to swim in waters devoid of any harbor. Now he recognized her as the woman who had served him a sandwich at the Anchor Beach general store, just hours before his fateful trip out onto the sandbar. And he also recognized her from his childhood.

She still didn't seem surprised that he was looking at her. Could it be that his eyes had been open all along and only his mind had been living somewhere else?

Maybe if he could see, he could also talk. He struggled to open his mouth and speak. He managed some kind of noise but even to himself it sounded like someone gargling. Then, coughing and hacking, in a voice phlegmy with disuse, he managed an almost audible, "I remember you."

The woman rose from her chair, and clasped her hands together. "Patrick, you're awake! You've been in a coma for three days."

Three days? Then—his voice improving with every attempt to speak—he said, "I've taken a long trip. Yes, I remember you from three days ago. You're Emily. But I also remember you from a long time ago." Coughing and swallowing, he continued. "You did something wonderful."

Emily interrupted. "I knew it! I knew you were in there. When we brought you in, they couldn't find a pulse or respiration. I think they thought you had been gone too long."

An image of lying on the back seat of a vehicle, with Emily and Hank and another man shivering with cold, came back, along with a sense of Emily's unshakable certainty that he was still alive.

He felt a wave of gratitude, but he didn't want to lose his thread of memory in the sea of impressions that swamped his mind. Still coughing after every word, he managed to get his sentence out. "You were very kind when John and I came to Maine years ago."

Emily gave him her full attention as Patrick coughed and continued more strongly. "I was looking at some cupcakes with pink marshmallow topping on them and my little brother told me to go ahead and eat them, that I would always be fat and useless anyway. Then you knelt down beside John and told him that I was your older brother and he should treat me with respect".

More coughing. "What you said really affected him."

A nurse burst into the room, pushed the emergency call button, and shouted through the door for a doctor. She took Patrick's wrist and felt for his pulse.

Within moments, the room was full of people in white coats. One doctor peered into Patrick's eyes with a flashlight, another read the EKG monitor and a third questioned Emily about whether Patrick had moved any part of his body.

Emily kept her poise. "Why don't you ask Patrick?"

Some of the faces turned away from instruments and looked at Patrick.

Patrick cleared his voice and said, "I haven't tried to sit up yet but my mouth seems to be working just fine."

The room froze. One of the men in white coats recovered enough to ask Patrick his age and his parents' names.

Patrick responded. "I'm 43 and my parents are both dead. Their names were Claire and Frank. What happened to me, Dr. Singh?"

Dr. Singh went rigid. Then, following Patrick's gaze, he saw the nametag he was still wearing from Grand Rounds earlier that morning. "Your eyesight is amazing," he observed.

When Patrick continued to stare at him, Dr. Singh shook his head and finally responded. "What happened to you? Well, you have been in a level 4 coma for three days. When you arrived in the Emergency Room you weren't breathing and we couldn't find a pulse. But your heart was beating down in there; otherwise we couldn't have revived you after all that time. You had been in complete respiratory arrest for at least 30 minutes, because you were in a car for about 20 minutes, and before that you were in the water for some unknown amount of time."

Patrick interrupted. "I was at least half a mile away from the shore when I lost consciousness in the surf."

He turned his head to listen as Emily interjected. "I know the dolphin was out there for at least another 20 minutes before Hank and I found you. I think you must have been like that for more than an hour, Patrick."

Patrick looked back to Dr. Singh and asked, "Essentially dead for at least an hour? How is that possible? I don't seem to have suffered brain damage."

Dr. Singh glanced at some of his colleagues, who continued to crowd in through the doorway of the Intensive Care Unit. He seemed reluctant to speak but after a moment he did. "You were not quite dead. But even so, I am amazed. I think your weight must have helped you. To put it bluntly, you have a lot of blubber around all your vital organs—not so unlike the adaptations we see in Arctic mammals. But the main thing that must have saved you, since you had stopped breathing for an hour or more, is something called 'the diving reflex'. It's the same reflex that allows a Sperm Whale to dive deep below the surface for an hour, on a single breath of air. Basically the heart slows way down and a reduced flow of blood is redirected away from extremities to the vital organs. In human beings, this reflex is triggered by cold water impacting the lungs."

The area around Patrick's ICU bed became increasingly crowded with people in white gowns peering over one another's shoulders. Abruptly Dr. Singh, who appeared to be Patrick's primary physician, cleared the room of everyone who did not have a prescribed medical procedure to perform.

Then he pressed his palms together, nodded, and left the room.

As soon as they were alone, Emily leaned closer to the bed and said, "Hank has been coming by every night to see you. We both want you to stay with us once you're well enough to leave here."

Patrick felt exhausted but managed to answer, "That's wonderful." Then he slipped back into the dream world that had been his only resting place during three days of coma. But this time he went as a traveler, one who knew the road back home.

CHAPTER 10

Saturday, Jan 18 (Day -82)

Even though it was mid-morning on a Saturday, John glanced nervously at the street before inviting Bill into the house, then quickly led them into his office, closed the door, and gestured toward the couch.

After a frustrating week, at work and at home, John had been ready to collapse into a mindless weekend of entertainment. Then Bill had called to say, "Your photographs are ready."

Bill leaned the skateboard (did graduate students actually ride those things?) against the edge of the couch, pulled five CD's from the pockets of his jacket and handed them to John.

Neither man spoke as John created a new directory, loaded the first CD and started transferring data onto his C-drive.

It really had been an unsatisfactory week. Agent Sullo's threats had come true: John's research on Titan had ground to a halt as door after door closed. At home, they had all been operating under some strain. In fact, listening to the news, the whole world seemed to be experiencing stress. It seemed every day someone had shot somebody—himself, a neighbor, or a complete stranger who just happened to get in his way. Kidnapping, accidents, and bizarre behavior were on the rise and, more and more, driving to the mall or into work, they would see people with placards announcing the end of the world.

Each evening, Leslie and John watched the news. People were gathering around the globe, chanting, waving placards, or facing off with armed police. Commentators were already predicting that these demonstrations could evolve into riots and massacres.

John was still getting e-mail from Fielding and other colleagues about the possibility that an unusually big comet would emerge from behind the Sun in a few weeks. Based on two observations, there was some chance it was on an Earth-crossing orbit.

As John loaded the second CD, he asked Bill, "Did you run into any problems getting these?"

As if he'd been waiting for a sign, Bill immediately launched into his story. Late, yesterday afternoon, a small window of opportunity had finally arrived at the end of graveyard shift. Bill, working a double shift, had seen Sam, senior networking analyst back from Hawaii, mounting a disk pack on the mainframe computer and had rushed downstairs with his CD's. Yes, Sam had left his door open. Jumping at every noise in the hallway outside, Bill had copied the data onto his CD's, deleted it from the hard drive (where he had stored it from John's thumb drive on Monday), and left the office—just as Sam's heavy footsteps were pounding down the stairs.

John, continuing to load those very CD's onto his home computer C-Drive, said, “I think I know how you felt. When I was making my copy of this file at the Physics building, I jumped every time my chair squealed.”

"Why are you waking up every night?"

As if Bill's question followed naturally from their conversation, John found himself telling Bill everything. They became so involved in this discussion—Bill taking over the job of replacing CD's each time the previous one finished copying, that they were surprised when there were none left to load.

John fired up the program that he used to graph radio waves. As they were waiting for something to appear on the screen, he turned to Bill. "I haven't even told my family about this file. I figure if they don't know anything, they can't look guilty. As far as my wife and eldest son know, I'm mildly pissed off because the FBI confiscated my data."

Bill nodded. "It's between you and me."

The first panel appeared and John was stunned into silence. This was not his usual mapping data. John avidly continued to press the ENTER key, as a succession of screens—each incredibly different from the previous one—flashed by.

"What's going on?" Bill's voice sounded far away, as if from another plane of reality.

Whatever this stuff was, it had nothing to do with the scattered echoes of the Goldstone signal that he mapped. Any frequency graph was going to show variations, but his Titan observations had never before shown such a strong and rhythmic coherence. And these graphs reminded him of something.

John continued paging through the clusters of oscillating lines and leisurely, graceful swoops. When John finally turned away from the screen and rubbed his eyes, Bill asked again, "Do you have any idea what it is?"

John slowly shook his head. Then he terminated the program and turned off the computer. Passing the CD's over to Bill, he said, "You keep these. The FBI guys are probably wondering why I gave up my only copy of this file so easily."

Bill put them back into the two side pockets of his jacket. He was forcing the zippers closed when there was a knock on the door of John's study.

The door opened and Leslie stuck her head in. Shit. He hated being insincere with his own wife, but it was safer for them all if she didn't know what he was doing. He stood up and introduced Bill to Leslie.

He heard himself say, "Bill is getting a doctorate in dream therapy. So you can imagine what we've been talking about."

Leslie didn't seem interested. Even when Bill asked her what she thought about John's recurrent nightmare, she just shrugged. "We all have dreams. They just mean we aren't happy about something—maybe because we aren't communicating with the people in our life."

Bill, seeming to sense that Leslie wasn't inviting a conversation about dreams, said, "I need to get going."

John walked him out and watched as he mounted the skateboard, then rolled down their walk and flew off the curb.

After John had closed the front door, he turned towards Leslie, feeling anxiety jab at his gut.

"Why are you lying to me?" Leslie began without preamble. "You know there's nothing I hate worse than being lied to."

John racked his brain for some clue. Had she overheard his conversation with Bill? Was she sensing a lack of sincerity in his manner? Did he just have to tell her everything now, to preserve any kind of harmony in their marriage?

"What's the use of having a family if you don't share things with them? You have no trouble sharing things with this guy who meant absolutely nothing to you last week, but you can't tell your own wife anything about what's happening? Carolyn is right. You've never learned to share anything important. You can tell all your adoring graduate students how the universe was born, but you can't tell me the first thing about how you feel."

John held up his hands in dismay, and tried to stem the tide of Leslie's outrage. "Hey! Slow down. Slow down, please. I'll talk. I'll tell you anything you want to know."

But Leslie stormed on. "What chance does our marriage have if you treat me like someone you can't trust with anything important? You obviously aren't aware of it—you always just completely deny having any kind of feelings at all—but ever since those men in dark suits were here yesterday morning you've looked like a criminal."

Not knowing what else to say, John managed to get out, "Really?"

Leslie continued, "Yes! You look like you've robbed a bank. And now you're wandering around looking at the ceiling and whistling. When I try to talk to you, all I get is superficial garbage."

John had to laugh. That seemed to help Leslie lighten up. Enough that John was able to get a few words in. "Seriously, Leslie. I'll tell you whatever you want to know. I guess it didn't make sense to try to keep it from you."

"I want to know what the hell is happening. I want to know whether our kids are going to lose their father because he's decided to be an amateur spy and get shot."

John gave up. They put Frankie in front of a video and poured cups of coffee. Then John told her everything. He began with the file he and Bill had hidden from the FBI. When he was finished, he offered to show it to her.

But now that John was being open with her, it seemed Leslie was in no hurry to see the actual slide show. He marveled at how she always wanted to feel connected with him, but then the content of this connection seemed almost immaterial to her. Oh well, maybe one day he would understand.

So instead of him showing off his discovery, they simply sipped their coffee quietly, enjoying the moments of peace and quiet before Eric emerged from his room for a late, Saturday breakfast and Frankie's video ended.

Suddenly Leslie looked up. “I forgot to tell you,” she said. "There was something interesting in the paper this morning."

The newspaper was still on the kitchen table and she quickly found the article. "Listen to this. It says that thousands of people have congregated in Bodh Gaya, India, and that it's a completely unscheduled event. People have just gathered there. Let me read you what an American says about why he came."

Leslie found the page and began reading. "I was having a recurrent dream—about a fiery dragon that wants to devour Earth. This dream always included images of me being here at Bodh Gaya. Well, after a month I figured the dreams weren't going to stop until I came here, and you know what the most amazing thing is? Everyone here has a story like mine."

Leslie turned to the continuation page and then looked up from the newspaper. "The interviewer asked him if his dreams have ever been prophetic. Here's his answer. “Not particularly. But I absolutely believe this one. Something unprecedented is about to happen. This gathering means something important.'"

Leslie put the paper down and after awhile, John said, "That guy's dream isn't like mine. But it kind of is, in some way. Something's going to happen—night after night—and you feel you should go somewhere and do something about it."

Leslie looked frightened. "It's really happening, isn't it? Something is heading our way."

Then Frankie tottered into the kitchen and Leslie lifted him onto her lap and held him tight. After a moment, Frankie said, "See Uncle Patrick."

John glanced at Leslie, wondering if she had any clue, but she seemed surprised too.

"Want see Patrick," Frankie persisted.

Leslie hugged him and whispered, "Maybe we can give Uncle Patrick a call sometime."

Frankie clapped his hands together. "Go to park, Daddy. Go to park now."

John laughed and said, "Let's go for it, Frankie," then turning to Leslie he added, "That will give you a chance to look at the frequency graphs on my computer." When Leslie agreed, he went and started the program and showed her how to move through the images by pressing the ENTER key.

Then he and Frankie got dressed for the park and stepped out into the warm afternoon with its bright light and clear blue sky. Walking down the sidewalk, with Frankie perched on his shoulders, John felt relieved that he had told Leslie everything. It crossed his mind that in some ways he was like a miniature model of government itself—secret, treating people like children who are unable to handle knowledge, and operating inside a graveyard of accumulated habits and unquestioned assumptions.

Well, it was time for him to change. And maybe he was misjudging the government too. Surely he would be able to get some information from his colleagues at NASA. The new NASA was doing wonderful research on a shoestring budget. It was stupid for him to feel that they would ever be part of some conspiracy of silence. It wasn't the Cold War anymore.

Out loud, John said to his youngest son, "Time for a change, Frankie. Don't you agree?"

"Come soon. Come soon, Daddy."

John lifted Frankie off his shoulders and held him in the crook of an arm, so that he could see his son's face. Then he asked him, "What's coming soon, Frankie?"

Frankie looked different to him all of a sudden. Was Leslie right? Had he been at work so much that he had missed some crucial growth spurt in their son? Some new level of thoughtfulness and articulation? Or was it something else?

John kept looking at his son, not sure whether he was still waiting for a response from Frankie or whether he was just taking this opportunity to look at his boy with fresh eyes. As he looked, he remembered the many times that Frankie had struck him and Leslie as a different kind of child: cheerful, open, and immediately empathetic at the slightest indication of distress in anyone else. Recently an old woman in Smith's Supermarket had taken one look at Frankie and exclaimed, "What an old soul you are, you dear boy!"

John brought his attention back to the present. Surely Frankie wasn't still thinking about John's question. Yet he seemed so focused, almost contemplative, as he continued to rest in his Dad's arms and as the two of them just stood there under the softly soughing winter branches.

Finally Frankie spoke. "Live in ocean. Come here now."

John just stared at his son. After a moment he had to put him down on the sidewalk because a feeling of dizziness started to permeate his entire body. He sat down on the curb, with his feet in the street.

Frankie started climbing up on his back and John instinctively leaned forward and put an arm behind to support Frankie's assent. He allowed Frankie to pull his hair as he scrambled all the way up onto John's shoulders.

They sat like that for a few minutes without speaking. John had a hundred questions he would have liked to ask, but each time it seemed too ridiculous to ask them of a two-year old boy. After awhile John got up and they continued on to the park.

They played on the swings and slide together for a while. When John sat down on a park bench to rest, Frankie continued to play nearby, eventually sitting down a few feet away on the edge of the concrete walkway that encircled the park. After five minutes, John started wondering what was keeping Frankie so engrossed and he walked over to see.

Frankie was playing with a thick piece of sidewalk chalk he must have found somewhere. To John's surprise, he was slowly drawing lines that looked like writing. After awhile John recognized three letters: "P", "A", and "I".

He sat down on the sidewalk and looked closely at his son's face while Frankie added something to the third letter.

With complete concentration Frankie drew a line straight across the top of the "I". Now it was "T". Then he laid the chalk down, looked at John and said, "Where Uncle Patrick?"

John couldn't answer. Frankie had never written anything before. And why was he suddenly so concerned about his uncle? Someone must have been talking to Frankie about Patrick.

Frankie's voice became urgent. "Daddy answer. Where Uncle Patrick?"

John felt compelled to answer. "Uncle Patrick is probably still in Montreal. I haven't spoken with him since before you were born. Frankie, who has been talking to you about Uncle Patrick?"

Frankie, increasingly agitated, kept repeating phrases and adding new words. "Uncle Patrick live in ocean. Phone Patrick."

John started questioning Frankie. "Who lives in the ocean? Uncle Patrick doesn't live in the ocean. He doesn't even live near the ocean. I can't understand what you're talking about, Frankie. Are you saying that Uncle Patrick telephoned our house when I wasn't there?"

Frankie started to cry.

What the hell was the matter with him? His own child takes his breath away and moments later John is shouting with anger.

John felt like crying himself as he spoke. "Oh, Frankie, I'm so sorry. I'm just so confused. I wish I could understand. Did Patrick telephone?"

Frankie rubbed his eyes and then shook his head.

"Do you think I should telephone Uncle Patrick? Is that what you're saying?"

Frankie smiled and nodded his head.

John eagerly followed up. "Does Patrick live near the ocean now?"

Frankie nodded.

John hesitated, wondering if there was any possibility of really understanding Frankie's statements. Finally he said, "When you said, 'Live in ocean.' Were you talking about Patrick?"

Frankie immediately shook his head. Then after a moment he added, "Your Daddy gone."

This time John had no refuge in his mind to which he could retreat. He just had to bear the full impact, like a body blow to his psyche, of the stunning recognition that these tatters of phrases being uttered by his two-year old son could not possibly be explained in any ordinary way.

Frankie knew about John's dream.

Was it possible that Frankie also knew things about Patrick, things unknown to John? Fearing the likely affect on both of them if he tried to pry out further clarification from his son, John gave himself over to the feelings that were coursing through him.

He felt totally unprepared when two streams of memory suddenly joined. Frankie was almost the same age Patrick had been when their father had died. Looking at Frankie, feeling how unbearable it was to think of him ever being left alone in the world—and realizing that the terrible loss depicted in his nightmare had literally happened to his brother—it was as if his immense love for his own son spilled out onto the parched desert of his feelings for his brother. Almost immediately, this desert swallowed up the meager rainfall, but for a moment, John felt a terrible sadness sweep over him.

Reaching for Frankie and hugging him fiercely, John felt young and innocent and hopeful, as if all hurts could one day be drenched in a soft rainfall of forgiveness.

CHAPTER 11

Friday, Jan 24 (Day -76)

It had been a week since Patrick had come home with Hank and Emily, and every day he grew stronger. Now he could walk for an hour on the beach by himself, but the apartment was a small space for three people who didn't really know each other that well. So when Hank offered him the use of a summer rental cabin they owned further down the beach, Patrick leapt at the opportunity.

Emily put together a box of provisions and Hank drove him down to see the cabin. "I think you'll like it, son. It's within spitting distance of the ocean and we've fixed it pretty good for winter use."

"No one lives in it during the winter anymore?"

Hank didn't respond for a moment. "It's available now, son. The man we fixed it up for drowned a few years back."

Hank pulled off the main road and drove past several cabins with salt-dark cedar shake sidings and boarded up screen porches. The dirt road, which still had traces of snow from the last storm, ended on a low sand dune where a single cabin stood by itself, surrounded with last year's salt grass rattling in the wind. They got out of the car, and while Hank unlocked the porch door, Patrick looked out at the ocean.

In spite of the drifts of snow and his breath clouding in the air, he was reminded of the cabin that he and John had stayed in 33 summers before, when their neighbors in Montreal had invited them down for a week. The view of the open ocean, and the feeling of the wind as it rose up the beach and swept across his face, were intensely familiar.

Hank left Patrick to his thoughts for a few moments then said, "This is one of the finest views on the point and this cabin has two bedrooms. That's why we fixed it up to be year-round."

Hank led the way up three steps, opened the door and walked in. When Patrick followed, he was greeted by a whiff of cottonseed oil in the cold air. Hank showed him through the rustic housekeeping cabin, pointing out the rough-hewn rock fireplace, the thermostat that controlled electric floorboard heaters, the pots and pans, and the bedding. All the rooms—porch, kitchen, living room and two bedrooms—were finished in oiled pine.

"Now son, the only condition on you living here is that you have supper with Em and me at least three times a week."

"I knew there had to be a catch." Patrick said, pretending to debate the terms. "Chicken dumplings. Fresh cod chowder. I think I can manage it."

After Hank had left, it didn't take him long to put the milk, eggs and bacon in the fridge, and the cereals and canned goods in the cupboards. Delighted that Emily had put tea and coffee in her box, he found a kettle, rinsed it out and put it on to boil, before putting away his personal belongings.

He had just started putting clean sheets on the double bed when the kettle started to whistle. He found an old thermos under the sink, washed it, put in three tea bags and filled it with boiling water.

By the time he had finished making the bed, put out clean towels in the bathroom and opened the shutters on the porch windows, the tea was ready. He found a small, unused table in the extra bedroom and put it in front of the porch swing. The January wind off the Atlantic chilled the uninsulated porch, but Patrick decided that he wanted to have his tea out there. He remembered seeing some extra blankets in the linen closet outside the bathroom and he went to get one.

As he was pulling a heavy green blanket off the top shelf, a glass-fronted portrait almost crashed to the floor. He managed to catch it as it came sliding off. Even viewed upside-down, he could see that it was a photograph of a couple holding a baby. Before putting it back on the shelf, he turned the picture around so he could see it more clearly, curious about who had lived here before—a man who had apparently since died.

The couple looked vaguely familiar, but then all old photographs, with their brownish tint and dated garments, tended to look familiar. He took the picture out to the porch with him and leaned it against the outside wall while he poured himself a large mug of tea and added milk. Steam billowed into the cool air.

Ah, wonderful! He sipped his tea, while swinging gently on the porch swing which hung from the rafters by steel chains. Warmth from the hot tea began to accumulate under the thick blanket he'd wrapped around him. Then time began unfurling like a scroll—a scroll covered with symbols that seemed oddly familiar. He could hear the rhythmic tumbling of the breakers through the single-pane porch windows. Threads of his life came tantalizingly into focus, gossamer threads floating in and out of a column of sunlight. Memories intersected in strange patterns. Some connections were obvious enough. Sitting now in this cabin was bound to remind him of his week at Anchor Beach when he was ten. But now other things were besieging his mind, as if they also claimed to be vitally connected with his own past. One was the image of a whale trying to save a man and his son from drowning. He supposed it was one of the countless images that had beset him while he lay unconscious in the hospital—and which he was now doing his best to forget—but this one affected him more than the others.

He kept looking at the framed photograph propped against the outer wall of the porch, six feet from where he sat, but was too comfortable to disturb the blanket wrapped around his legs. When he eventually retrieved the picture and laid it across his knees he saw that the couple seemed in their mid-twenties—the man holding a baby while the woman rested her hand on the swaddling blanket.

Patrick pried back the pins which held the cardboard-backed photograph into the frame, slipped the photograph out and looked to see if anything was written on the back. Penned in a neat script, he read, "Daniel Henry Seaver, aged 3 weeks, and his loving parents Emily and Hank."

In a flood of recognition, he realized that this cabin had been fixed up for their son. Suddenly he understood something that had happened in the hospital room in Portland after he'd awoken. Emily had called him by the wrong name. That hadn't seemed like any big deal. But it had stuck in Patrick's memory that her eyes had welled up with tears and she had excused herself to walk out in the hall for a few moments. The name she had called him was, "Danny."

Now they were letting Patrick stay in the house they had made for their son, a son who had apparently died. Having grown up with a single parent who basically didn't seem to like him very much, Patrick could scarcely conceive that anyone would ever want him around.

He carefully put the photograph back in its frame and hung it on an empty nail within view of where he was sitting on the swing. Then he finished his tea, put on his new winter parka, turned down the thermostat and went outside.

He struggled through loose sand and snow until he reached the hard-packed beach. The roar of the breakers filled him with energy and he spontaneously broke into a run, as if he might lift into the air—a gull skimming across sun-burnished wave-tops.

He soon slowed to a walk, his legs trembling and his lungs burning in the crisp winter air. But he couldn't have done even that a week ago.

First he headed south, exploring an inlet until it intersected with the beach road. Then he walked back north, past his cabin, until he reached the sandbar which he had taken out to the treacherous rock. It was a little after four in the afternoon, just about the time that he had decided to plunge into the frigid water two weeks earlier. Apparently, he had made the right decision that day. And he hadn't made many of those in his life.

The sandbar now formed an unbroken bridge out to the island. Two hours till supper. If he didn't lie down and go to sleep, what could be the problem with walking out again? He would just have to keep his attention on the sun and make sure to leave a good half hour of light for the return trip.

But his feet refused to move. The memory of how he had almost died and then returned to life filled him like the afterglow of a strong drink, and he couldn't stop his legs from trembling.

He forced himself to step forward onto the sandbar. Walking quickly, to give himself more time, his senses became increasingly alert and his mind clear. Then, whenever the sandbar seemed to thin out, or dip down close to the level of the water, he stopped to make sure that the sand was broad and high on both sides. That way, even if he had to hop across a small patch of water here and there, the path would still be visible at either end.

With his heart pounding, he reached the barren island and clambered up on top. From there he could look in all directions. Behind him, there was an unbroken causeway back to land. Looking out to sea, he could see waves breaking on a distant sandbar, and it occurred to him that these breakers were taking the power out of the Atlantic swell before it reached shore.

Facing into the cold sea wind, he pulled the cord on his hood tighter and combed the bright surface of the ocean—gentle undulations flashing in the late afternoon sun. A great expanse of sky and water, with lines of surf breaking a half-mile further out. No black body breaking through the shining carpet of the sea.

After a while he noticed that there were no sandbars visible further out, and that the waves were not breaking out there anymore either. Now the Atlantic swell was riding in towards shore and towards where Patrick stood.

Then it hit him. It wasn't just a gradually rising tide he had to fear. At this very moment, open sea was sweeping inland. And like flood waters breaking over sand bags around a swollen river, the waves could inundate in minutes the sandbars he had taken out.

He clambered down the rough rock and reached the sandbar on the run. Running as fast as his winter boots allowed, he tried to recall the sandy path ahead of him. At first the waves were small and choppy. Then larger waves rode past, crashing onto the beach in front of him.

The waves became increasingly impressive with every passing moment. As he ran—the tender lining of his lungs burning and his legs threatening to crumble under him—he slowly relaxed. He could now see that he was not going to get trapped this time. But why did he keep flirting with his own extinction?

A voice answered in his head, loud and clear. You need to tell humans about the intelligence in the waters. Patrick wasn't in the mood for any more assignments from disembodied voices, and out loud he shouted, "No, I don't."

By the time he reached shore and looked back at the island, it was hard to fathom his folly. White plumes riding across the dark water were breaking over the sandbar he had just crossed.

He struggled up to the dry sand and sat down. Then, feeling dizzy, he lay back and looked up at the sky. Dark blue with traces of dusky red in the clouds. He had to roll over to cough a few times, but eventually his lungs didn't burn and his legs had recovered. What had that voice said he should do? It probably didn't matter. Dr. Singh had told him to take it easy, and not pay attention to weird images and voices. "They'll go away after awhile," he had said. Well, those were doctor's orders that he was more than willing to follow.

Patrick looked at his watch—it was 5:10 p.m. Just enough time to hurry home and change into dry pants, socks and shoes for dinner at Hank and Emily's. Home. He liked that sound.

It was a few minutes after six when he pulled into the parking lot in front of the general store and hurried around to the back. As he stepped onto the porch, delicious aromas greeted him. Hank opened the door, helped him off with his coat, and pressed a glass of wine into his hand. After toasting one another, Patrick downed most of his drink in two quick swallows.

"Supper's almost ready," Emily announced, continuing to stir a pot on the stove. Then, looking over her shoulder at Patrick, she asked, "Did you get your message?"

The depth of his surprise was a measure of how completely removed he felt from his ordinary life. Setting his empty wine glass down, he said, "What message? No-one knows I'm here."

"I need to get the food on the table while everything's hot." Emily responded hurriedly, ladling chicken and dumplings into a white china platter.

He couldn't read Hank's expression either, so he stood and watched Emily bring the platter to the table and set it down on a wooden rack. She glanced at Patrick briefly, but then went back to the stove and turned off the heat under the potatoes.

A message? Surely she couldn't mean the voice that had spoken in his head as he raced back to shore? He watched Emily's back, as she poured the potatoes through a colander in the sink.

Hank returned Patrick's gaze with eyes that were kind and considerate, but said nothing. Without Emily's question, he might have forgotten that voice.

Maybe he had received a message.

The three of them sat down at the table. The potatoes were now stacked in a platter which matched the larger platter in which chicken, dumplings, carrots and onions swam in their broth. Both sent up signals of steam, announcing their excellence.

At a glance from Emily, Hank closed his eyes. "We give thanks for this wonderful food and for the ability to taste it and appreciate it. Thank you also for the companionship with which we sit down now to enjoy these bounties."

Hank didn't speak for a moment but when Patrick looked he saw that his eyes were still closed. Patrick closed his own eyes again. "And we thank you for guiding us when we need it. Give us the ears to hear your guidance, and the humility to accept your help. Wisdom can come from anywhere, because You are everywhere. Amen."

Then, as if he had said nothing in the least reverent, Hank announced, "You've outdone yourself again, Em! Let's dig in!"

Emily insisted that Patrick take generous portions of everything, while Hank refilled Patrick's glass with claret.

He hadn't really had lunch and had covered a lot of miles that afternoon. The wine gave wings to his appetite and he ate with gusto until, gradually, the silence around the table drew his mind back to Emily's question.

He looked up from his food and saw that Emily and Hank, while enjoying their supper, seemed to be waiting for him to speak. He laid down his fork and swallowed the food still in his mouth.

Patrick didn't know what to say. What he wanted to say—that he couldn't remember feeling this comfortable with fellow human beings ever before in his life—could so easily ruin everything. "Intelligence in the waters." The phrase suddenly came back to him with a force that he could no longer deny.

"I don't understand how you know about my message," he began. Then he told them how he had suddenly recognized that the surf was on its way in. He shared how, while running for his life and wondering why he kept flirting with his own destruction, a voice had spoken in his mind. "It was the kind of guidance you just talked about, Hank. I suddenly knew that I have to wake up to how completely my life has changed. I can't go on as if nothing has happened. I have all these new connections . . . with the ocean . . . with you two. . ."

Emily immediately asked, "How do you feel connected with us?"

Patrick was afraid to answer. For a moment, he felt dizzy, unable to look at them. When he did, risking a glance in both their directions, he found two immensely kind faces turned toward him.

He told them about the photograph he had found of them with their baby boy, and how it had become connected in his mind with a dream he had had for as long as he could remember—a dream that seemed to be about his own father.

He told them how his mind was inundated with images of life in the ocean and how he experienced things from the perspective of creatures who lived in the sea—sometimes a dolphin or a whale, but sometimes an alien being, not of Earth.

When Hank and Emily continued to give him their full attention, he took a deep breath and said, "Dr. Singh said I am bound to feel confused with all the hallucinations I experienced, but that over time they should go away. Except some of them haven't gone away. There's one that keeps getting more and more intrusive. It's about a comet. This comet is heading straight for Earth and I'm supposed to warn people about it. But how can I do that? Who would believe me? Even I don't know if it's true."

"A comet is heading toward Earth?" Hank interrupted. "What do you know about it?"

Patrick told them about his vision of the ice sculpture which had turned into a model of the solar system. While struggling to convey how deeply it had affected him, and how it had been far more vivid and convincing that any mental image he had ever previously had, or felt capable of constructing himself, he was gripped by an anguished feeling that maybe he really had been called to an important task— which he had not taken a single step towards fulfilling.

He stopped talking and took a sip of wine. When he looked up he saw that Emily was holding both hands in small fists in front of her mouth. He wished he could get up and give her a hug, but she was probably remembering her son, and for Patrick to approach would just make it worse.

After a moment, her voice shaky, Emily said. "Dr. Singh doesn't really know much about you, Patrick. He doesn't understand how the sea gave you back." Then, struggling to get the words out, she said, "You are like a son to us."

Like a hungry dog at the edge of a campfire, Patrick didn't know what path to take out of his familiar shadow world. He was relieved when Hank took over. "I don't have Emily's intuition, but I've never seen a dolphin behave like the one who brought you to shore. If you think that someone is talking to you inside your head, I'd pay attention if I were you. How else could a dolphin talk with you, except inside your head? He can't call you on the phone, like the man who telephoned here this afternoon, wondering if we'd seen you."

Patrick's stomach did a somersault. "Someone telephoned me this afternoon? How could they possibly know I am here? It wasn't your friend, Burt, from the FINA, was it?"

"What you were saying seemed important and I didn't want to interrupt you," Emily said. "That's why I didn't just blurt out, 'Oh, your brother called here this afternoon, wondering if we'd seen you.'"

Patrick thought his insides were going to either dissolve or explode. He had to force himself to listen as Emily continued. "We had a very nice chat. He told me that he'd called your apartment and that your answering machine message had said something about being in hot pursuit of a happy week of childhood. Apparently he immediately thought of here. He was quite amazed when I reminded him about the marshmallow cupcakes.

"He's very keen on getting together with you as soon as possible. He wanted to know whether he should come here, or whether you'd rather go to Albuquerque and see your two nephews."

This time, Patrick found words. "Two? They have another son? I only knew about Eric."

Emily smiled. "Yes, their Frankie is two years old. John told me that 'Frank' was the name of your Dad. Patrick, he sounded very nice to me, and he really wants to see you. He told me that you two have been estranged for years and that he feels to blame for that."

Patrick couldn't keep the harsh quality out of his voice. "Why does he need to see me all of a sudden? Why now, after so many years, does he need to see his worthless brother?"

Emily made no comment on Patrick's changed manner, and her voice remained warm and concerned. "He said that he's going crazy with a nightmare. He's been having it for more than a month and he finally figured out that it's not his experience that he's dreaming about. It's yours."

Patrick couldn't disguise his interest. "So he wants me to help him get rid of a nightmare. I figured it had to be some practical problem he needed to fix."

Emily continued. "He said his nightmare is making him have strange thoughts about everything, including some message about a moon somewhere. Patrick, whatever pain there is in your past, there's one thing I know. Your brother needs you."

Patrick's insides had finally decided that they were more ready to dissolve than to explode, as Hank leaned across the table. "I took the liberty of calling the airlines. If you want him to come here, there's a flight leaving Albuquerque tomorrow morning at 7:30 am. If he caught that, you could pick him up at the Portland airport at 2:30 tomorrow afternoon. I know Em and I would both love to meet him."

Before Patrick could sputter out an objection, Hank took a piece of paper out of his shirt pocket and laid it down on the table. It had John's phone number on top, and underneath he had written flight information, including an 800 number for reservations.

Emily pressed. "It's getting close to 8:00 p.m. in New Mexico. John said you could call anytime, but I imagine your new nephew may be asleep by now. And if I remember, once a two-year old is asleep, the rest of the family doesn't always have much energy left to do all the things they didn't get done all day."

Patrick probably looked like he needed one last nudge, because Emily added, "We have a phone in our bedroom. Take all the time you want."

All the time he wanted? How about half a century, gone forever? As for a telephone call with John, a few minutes should be more than enough, he thought bitterly. That would blow their old record out of the water.

Patrick stood up on legs that were trembling slightly, took Hank's piece of paper, tried to smile, and then headed into their bedroom before he lost his nerve completely.

CHAPTER 12

Ted Sullo knew he didn't have a fix on that astronomer, John Murphy. How do you figure a guy like that? Here you have a man who seems to have everything—a beautiful wife, two bright, attractive children, and a full professorship at 40. Why would a guy like that hide a file when he'd been warned that it was top secret and that he shouldn't mess with it?

And how do you figure Murphy's abrupt shifts in attitude? One moment he seemed to think the VLA had picked up a U.S. military transmission, and that therefore the content was completely immaterial to him. Then the next moment, there he was telling you that he had left the house in the pitch dark just to take a back-up of this so-called immaterial data.

Ted had plenty of experience with people who were trying to hide something and he knew that's what Professor Murphy was doing. Murphy appeared to have handed over his only back up of Fielding's file, but he must have copied it somewhere. Where was it? Ted had checked all the computers to which Murphy would normally have had access at the Computing Center and at the Physics department and had found no trace of the Agassiz file anywhere.

And what was this file anyway? Why was everyone so interested in it?

The truth was that no one was telling Ted anything. If he didn't know what Professor Murphy had on his mind, he sure didn't know what Richard Todd, his boss at the FBI, had on his. All he knew was that he'd been given the job of coordinating round-the-clock surveillance on Professor Murphy, bugging his home, office and car, plus doing a complete background on his family, friends and colleagues. Todd was really on him to find out every last detail about Murphy's habits and contacts.

Why the hell was a strong signal coming from Titan? No one would tell Ted what it was, or why his agency had immediately taken it so seriously. Now their telephone taps had picked up John Murphy tracking down his brother in a little general store on the coast of Maine, and then booking a flight to Portland for tomorrow morning. There was another story for you. What do you make of his older brother, Patrick, jumping in his car one night, driving 400 miles, and then a few hours later getting admitted to a Portland hospital, seemingly as dead as a door stop? Then, after three days in a deep coma, he wakes up and checks out—apparently in better shape than ever—and goes to live with an old couple who don't seem to have ever laid eyes on the guy before.

Ted felt torn. Should he keep hanging around Albuquerque in the hopes that he could get inside Professor Murphy's house and computer, and really have a close look at what he had there? Or should he follow Murphy to Portland? What was the name of that dead-end coastal road? Oh, yeah—Anchor Beach.

One thing was sure, if he hung around Albuquerque much longer, he was going to have to check out of this sleazy motel. Considering this assignment was supposed to be such hot shit, why didn't they give him a decent expense account? Enough to let him stay at the Hilton would be just fine with him.

Ted picked up the phone and called American Airlines. Then he placed a call to his home office in Washington.

Twenty minutes later he had not only booked a flight to Portland for that night, but his request for a full surveillance team to join him at Anchor Beach had been granted. Pleased at this sign that his boss still valued his work, Ted decided that he was being kept in the dark because sensitive issues of national security were at stake.

The hard part would be to escape attention in a little tourist community like that, which would be basically shut up for the winter. The important thing would be for Ted himself to stay completely in the background, since his would be the one face recognizable to Professor Murphy. For the rest, even a boarded-up beach town had some winter residents who needed telephone service when their telephones went on the blink. Which they were about to do.

An hour later, Ted checked out of his fourth-rate motel on Central Avenue and drove to the Albuquerque International Airport. International? What a name for a desert stop-off from which, to his knowledge, not a single direct international flight originated. Now, now, Agent Sullo, you shouldn't let your bitterness show like that. It means that you don't like something about this case. But when Ted tried to bring to mind what he didn't like about this case, it wasn't the face of Professor Murphy that arose before him. It was the face of his boss, Richard Todd—closed, evasive, refusing to shed the smallest glimmer of light on the fundamental questions Ted had asked him. Why the hell was the government so interested in this small blip in the stream of radiation from the universe? The very thought that this data could refer to something real was unthinkable. But such thoughts had begun to come to Agent Ted Sullo at night with far more disruptive effect than the slamming doors and growling low-riders had produced during his stay at the sleazy motel on Central Avenue.

And then there was that image which Ted couldn't shake out of his mind, of Professor Murphy saying how he couldn't face his kids if he was the one who picked up first alien contact, and then turned his back. The guy might really have been joking, like he later claimed. But ever since, Ted hadn't been able to still an insistent voice inside him. Who the hell had sent this message? And why wouldn't anyone tell him a single word about it?

CHAPTER 13

Saturday, Jan 25 (Day -75)

Patrick decided to make a day of it. John's plane wasn't due to arrive until 2:32 p.m. that afternoon. It was 8:05 a.m., and with a stack of buckwheat pancakes under his belt Patrick was enjoying his second cup of coffee. He knew he needed to take it easy. Dr. Singh had said there was still some infection in his lungs from all that saltwater, and yesterday's jaunt out to the island hadn't helped.

Patrick poured himself a third cup of coffee, tilted his chair back against the kitchen wall, and laid the newspaper on his lap. He had picked up a Portland morning paper at the Fina minimart during his pre-dawn walk two hours ago.

He scanned the headlines and started turning pages. In between sips of coffee he reached the classified ads. He wasn't really reading, but a box under "Opportunities," leapt out at him:

EARTH—MOON—VISITOR
Last stop for the future
A morning talk by Hal Nagen

The talk was to be held at 10:00 a.m. at a Unitarian church in Portland, and Patrick knew he was supposed to be there.

He quickly rinsed his dishes, grabbed some warm clothing and closed up the cabin. His Honda fired up on the first try and he headed down the muddy track to the paved road, turned left and headed south. He drove along slowly with the window cracked open a few inches, appreciating the fact that, this time, he was doing the driving himself, inside his own breathing, sensate body.

He found the church without too much trouble and was seated in a pew near the front by 9:50 a.m. He had the pew to himself until almost 10:00 a.m., when an athletic man of about forty-five, with blond hair, came and sat beside him. This felt a bit strange, because there were only six other people sitting in the church. The man didn't say anything. He just sat looking toward the front where a chair had been placed next to a table on which a candle was burning.

At 10:05 a.m. a couple got up and left. Patrick heard them whispering on the way down the aisle. "This is not what I expected." Then a middle-aged woman, who had been kneeling, stood up, bowed toward the stained glass scene up front and left. By 10:15 a.m. the church was empty, except for Patrick and the blond man beside him.

Patrick looked at the candle burning at the front of the church, and decided to stay a little longer. John's plane wasn't due for another three hours.

He stole a glance at the man beside him. Why had he sat there? He could probably just ask. But how? Patrick sighed, turned toward his neighbor and said, "I hope someone comes. I really felt certain that I was supposed to come to this."

"This talk is definitely for you." The man had a foreign accent—Scandinavian, maybe—and his deep baritone voice resonated like a baroque organ in the now empty church.

That was as good a conversation-stopper as any. But Patrick heard himself responding. "Isn't it for you, too?"

"I showed up ready to give a talk. But the interest wasn't here. You saw how few people came, and how ready they were to get out of here."

Patrick let himself digest that, before speaking again. "So, what is the visitor?"

"You of all people don't have to ask me that, Patrick."

Patrick spun his head so fast that he felt a jab of pain in his neck. Fighting off panic, he said, "Hal Nagen, I presume."

No smile, no response of any kind. Just a steady gaze that felt like it was penetrating more deeply into Patrick's inner thoughts than he cared to be penetrated.

"Yes, of course, I am Hal Nagen. But I doubt very much that is why you look white as a ghost right now. Why don't you ask me about something that concerns you? You will probably not have a chance to see me again for several weeks.

What did Patrick have to lose? "How do you know my name?"

Hal shrugged. "A friend of mine swam hundreds of miles to save you. She survived, you will be happy to know. Another friend of mine talks to both you and your brother in your dreams. You listen a lot better than John does, by the way."

Maybe he did have something to lose, after all. Like his last shred of sanity. In self-defense, Patrick turned around and stared at the candle at the front of the church. It would probably be best if he didn't ask any more questions right now. Dr. Singh had spoken quite firmly to him about the danger of cultivating hallucinations that had taken root during a disembodied state of consciousness. "Always go with whatever you can touch and feel right now," Dr. Singh had said. Maybe Nagen was a hallucination. Maybe Patrick was still asleep in his bed in the cozy cabin.

Hal interrupted his thought. "I understand your concern, Patrick. And the doctor who brought you back to life is a good man. In fact I visited him yesterday and I think he can be of help to me personally. But consider this. Your visions did not commence with your near-drowning experience. Did they?"

Patrick didn't want to get drawn in, but he couldn't prevent himself from asking, "What do you know about my visions? Is it a real place I'm seeing?"

Hal's voice was gentle, as if he were calming a skittish animal. "You are having visions of Saturn's moon, Titan. I think you know that, but let's start by talking about things I know you know. All Titan species are ocean dwellers. Life formed in magma-heated lakes, on an otherwise frozen, barren world. Later they learned to harness Titan's rotation to produce heat and light on a planetary scale."

Like a Catholic reciting Hail Mary's to ward of danger or temptation, Patrick tried to hold onto Dr. Singh's advice, "Stay with what you can touch and feel." Intelligent life on Titan? He could almost hear Dr. Singh's contempt at the mere notion.

Patrick decided to stick to a potentially verifiable assertion. "Voyager II didn't find any rotation. And if our own moon is tidally-locked, with just Earth's gravity pulling at it, then Titan really has to be locked with massive Saturn grabbing at it."

"One would think so." Hal allowed. They both knew that Patrick had witnessed Titan's rotation for himself. Hal continued. "It takes 6000 Earth years for Titan to complete a single pirouette on its own axis, relative to Saturn. Saturn is so close that tidal effects on Titan are 400 times greater than lunar tides on Earth."

Patrick's mind was full of clear visual images of tiny Titan crossing in front of massive Saturn's glowing face, but he struggled to break free of them. This was just what Dr. Singh had warned him about: he must not allow any voice or vision to talk to him about things for which there was absolutely no outside corroboration.

But Hal's voice wouldn't stop. And Patrick couldn't shut it out. "Saturn spins very rapidly, once every 10 hours, and its magnetic field turns Titan like a bicycle tire turns a dynamo. Titan is the dynamo wheel, running on the surface of Saturn's magnetic field." That was a new metaphor for Patrick, and he had to admit it helped explain some things he had seen.

Hal stopped talking until Patrick looked at him again, at which point he asked gently, "Do you want me to continue, Patrick?"

Patrick meant to sound indifferent, but it didn't come across that way, even to his own ears. "Sure."

Hal now insisted that Patrick look at him, refusing to talk until Patrick had locked into his gaze. And once Patrick had done that, he lost all sense of being grounded in a church in Portland, Maine. Hal's voice seemed to surround Patrick's consciousness.

"Let's look at it together," Hal said.

Then the church disappeared and Patrick was looking at Saturn and its much smaller Moon, Titan. But instead of a tiny orange dot crossing the face of Saturn, with its spectacular band of rings, Patrick could see how Saturn's magnetic field flowed over and around Titan. He could see how some force on Titan was causing electrically conductive material to concentrate and become magnetized on the hemisphere facing Saturn, and how this in turn caused Titan to spin very slightly.

Patrick tried vainly to remember Dr. Singh's advice—to dismiss from his mind anything that he knew would sound absurd to another sane person—yet now it wasn't his own mind that was talking. It was this stranger, narrating the images that had taken over his mind.

"Titan's ocean faces away from Saturn," the compelling voice continued, "like a huge eye looking out over the cosmos." And Patrick could see directly how as Titan spun its ocean kept moving away from Saturn, creating tidal movements able to climb almost vertical walls. The extreme cold of Titan's surface (about -200 Celsius) immediately froze any liquid left behind by the migrating ocean, and as the mountains grew bigger, there was less and less water left in the ocean. "So, why is there still an ocean on Titan?" he heard Hal intone.

Patrick knew the answer, but he couldn't speak as Hal's hypnotic voice continued. "Volcanic forces undermine the foundations of these mountains causing gigantic glaciers to plunge into its sea." And now Patrick could see how Titan's ocean migrated continuously towards the East, in a cataclysmic process that subjected the Titanians to constant danger, even miles below the surface.

Gradually Patrick could make sense of the images that swamped his mind: of Titan's thick atmosphere, hundreds of miles thick, organized into conductive filaments and pockets of neon-type gasses, shining for the ocean-dwellers beneath.

He continued to watch his own mind as if Hal was providing a voice-over for the images that flowed through it.

Hal's deep baritone continued. "So Titan's rotation around its own axis creates fantastically high tides and an ocean that migrates in its deep basin of ice. More importantly, it feeds the planet's internal, volcanic furnace, whose lava is used to produce an ocean temperate enough to nurture the warm-blooded Titanians. Yes, that's right, warm-blooded."

Patrick couldn't take much more of this invading presence in his mind. And as if Hal had recognized Patrick's breaking point, his voice now sounded quiet and soft in the nearby pew. "Do you ever wonder if the Titanians are talking to you directly?"

As the church came back into focus, Patrick answered, "Yes, of course."

"It's a good question, isn't it? Are Titanians present on Earth? And if so, whom are they talking to? Well, I only know of two humans who can talk directly with Titanians. One is your nephew and the other is my brother. As for how Titanians—one billion miles away—can communicate clairvoyantly with humans—I don't really know. What I do know is that you and I aren't talking directly with them. We are talking with the whales and dolphins of our own Earth. But you already knew that too, didn't you?"

Patrick didn't know what he knew. But, given a choice he'd rather be talking with a fellow mammal on Earth than with inconceivable creatures on an alien world. So he nodded.

"I understand that you are afraid of losing your grip on reality, Patrick." Hal continued. "It's an important issue for you. But please try to be open to the possibility that I could tell you things that would help you to feel sane. It's not all that surprising that you feel a little over the edge sometimes. People who are chosen for special roles often feel that they are going crazy."

With a great deal of effort, Patrick wrenched himself away from Hal's gaze. He watched the candle for a while and squeezed the edge of the pew until his hands hurt. When Hal remained silent, Patrick turned his head back and looked at him again.

Hal continued talking, in the kind of tone a concerned parent might use with a child who has shared a secret difficulty. "This may not make a lot of sense to you right now, Patrick, but there is a good reason that certain humans are having visions of this ancient race of alien beings. These beings have been in contact with Earth for a very long time, for hundreds of thousands of years, but never before with humans."

Amid the deluge of visions and images, any one of which would have had the power to shake Patrick's sense of what was real, this last fact penetrated directly to the core of what he had always believed about life on Earth. That alien beings had been communicating with the whales of Earth for a thousand centuries most definitely did not belong within his scheme of reality. So why did he believe it?

"Can you see the problem?" Hal asked.

Oh, what the hell. Of what use was a little sanity, anyway? "Sure, I can see the problem," Patrick said. "These aliens talk just fine to whales and dolphins, but humans don't talk to anyone but themselves. So if you need something from humans—like using a bomb on a comet without creating a thousand fragments—how are you going to get their attention?"

Hal broke in with a sharp sense of urgency in his voice. "Exactly! That's excellent, Patrick! I'm impressed. So now, tell me this: what do you and I have in common? Why are we both in contact with cetaceans?"

Patrick quickly went from the warm glow elicited by Hal's compliment to a conviction that he had not the slightest idea what Hal was talking about.

Hal continued. "OK. You don't know anything about me, or my brother. So just answer for yourself. Why have you been chosen to represent the human race? Here is a hint. It has something to do with what happened to you at a very young age, and something to do with the condition you have ended up in as an adult. Think family. And then ask yourself: how are you like the human race as a whole? If you can answer that for yourself, then you will also know why I have been chosen. And why our brothers have been chosen."

"Oh, of course." Patrick couldn't keep the sarcasm out of his voice. "We'll walk two-by-two into the ark. I don't know how you know my name—and a few other things—but I came to hear a talk. I didn't plan on being converted to some 'you are God's chosen' cult. I need to meet my brother at the airport."

"That's what I'm talking about! You're meeting John. You're way ahead of me there. I don't even know who my brother is. That's what Dr. Singh is going to help me with. He took some DNA samples from me, and he's going to run some data base searches. It's a long shot, but my lost brother may show up somewhere."

"Why go to all that trouble?" Patrick snapped, throttling back the awe he had felt moments before. "Why don't you just ask your cetacean friends?"

"I have. They don't know him." Hal responded, seemingly unaffected by Patrick's tirade. "But they have a very bad feeling about him?"

"Excuse me? They don't know your long-lost brother, but they have a bad feeling about him? I think you're slipping a little bit there, Mr. Nagen. Not quite up to your strong beginning, I'm afraid." And when Hal made no response, Patrick added, "I mean, if you don't know your brother, and the cetaceans don't know your brother, then who has a bad feeling about him?"

Hal stood up. When Patrick didn't follow suit, Hal leaned over until his face was a few inches from Patrick's face. Then in a low whisper, he said, "I believe the Titanians know my brother. The whales think they are using him for something, and that this has destroyed his sanity."

Knowing a thing or two about having his sanity threatened, Patrick felt his tantrum subside. He had a thousand unanswered questions slithering through his mind, and this was the first time in his entire life that he had every met someone who appeared able to answer some of them. Not that he welcomed either the questions or the answers that he was receiving, and above all, not the way they invaded his mind as if it were a brothel available to anyone who cared to drop in. But in Hal he sensed the presence of someone who knew his way in these alien waters.

"It was hard for me to come here today," Hal said, still standing a few feet away. "And now I must leave. We'll talk again soon. Stay focused, Patrick. Trust yourself to know what is true, as bizarre as it may seem. You have a good heart, and your basic sanity moves me deeply."

Without another word, Hal turned around, strode to the front of the church, blew out the candle, and disappeared through a side door into the late morning sunshine.

Patrick found himself sitting all alone in an empty church—a tiny whiff of smoke rising from the extinguished candle—while the thousand unanswered questions rolled over him like breakers flashing on a sunlit sea.

CHAPTER 14

Patrick and John sat in matching wicker chairs with steaming mugs of tea and watched the well-seasoned logs catch flame. Patrick had picked his brother up at the Portland airport three hours earlier but they hadn't talked about anything consequential since. It felt too risky. The man sitting in front of him, he realized, was the person before whom he was most afraid of exposing any kind of weakness.

Meanwhile Patrick's mind kept returning to that unsettling meeting with Hal Nagen. The few certainties he had counted on now seemed as insubstantial as fog rolling in off the sea. Adding in his fear of John, Patrick didn't know how to make a sane-sounding statement about any of it.

But it was important to try. To his surprise, he felt himself laying claim to his status as an older brother. It was an unfamiliar feeling, because John was the breadwinner for a family, an eminent scientist and university professor, taller, stronger and more confident than Patrick had ever been. Yet, for the first time in many years, Patrick felt called upon to lead the way.

"Do you remember this cabin?" he asked finally, laying down his mug of tea. As he spoke, a memory, which he had first glimpsed when Hank showed him this place, fell decisively into place. This had to be the cabin he and John had stayed in as children. This must be the room in which they had discussed the future, during a game of Monopoly, more than 30 years ago.

"I'm afraid I don't remember much," John said. Then he shook his head and added, "Judging from what your friend Emily told me, I probably wasn't very good company to have around."

"Actually, you were great company," Patrick shot back before he had a chance to think about it. "You told me that you were going to be a cosmologist and I told you that I was going to be a vet. Neither of us mocked the other's dream. But I guess you knew how to realize yours and I didn't."

John looked as if he wanted to say something but Patrick couldn't stop himself from adding, "Whatever you have on your mind must be pretty important—maybe as important as lecturing in Switzerland the week your mother dies."

John looked pained. After a moment he said in a subdued voice, "I need your help, Patrick. I don't know what's happening to me. I'm waking up at 3:00 every morning in the middle of a terrifying dream. I swear I'm seeing our father drown night after night and then a whale saves you. That would be bad enough, but then my VLA mapping of Titan's surface revealed that something is transmitting from there. And I'm now a subject of interest to the FBI because I tried to investigate it."

Patrick couldn't prevent himself from being drawn in as John described how he'd managed to capture a small but amazing fragment of what the Agassiz Radio Telescope had recorded from the Titan transmission. Then, in the middle of a vivid account of his and Bill's recent cloak-and-dagger derring-do, John stopped abruptly and said, "Can we talk about my dream now?"

Patrick sat in silence, unable to respond. He was stunned by the discovery that they were both having a similar dream, even though Hal had told him as much. Averting his eyes, he poured more tea into their cups.

Patrick would gladly have avoided this question entirely, but his conversation with Hank and Emily the night before prevented him from retreating into his usual defenses and excuses. Hal's guided tour of Titan had, belatedly broken through: Earth was in danger and he needed to share what he knew. What he now knew that he knew. And here was another human being actually asking for him to share this knowledge. Unfortunately it was the one person in the world whose mockery he feared in every cell of his body.

He forced himself to hold John's gaze and began to speak. "I know more about these things than you do, but I have a problem. You'll find what I have to say completely unbelievable, and I've already had an overdose of your disdain. Understand?"

John nodded. "Try me. I may not believe everything, but I realize I'm way out of my depth. To tell the truth, I don't feel very good at most things these days." Then John's voice raised an octave. "Am I dreaming your dream?"

Patrick looked levelly at this brother for a moment. "Yes, I'm the boy with the padlock," he finally admitted, then added, "but it's not my dream."

John sounded more like a frightened kid pleading for help than a professor with all the right answers as he asked, "How can it be about you, but not be your dream?"

Patrick answered, "How could it be my dream? I don't live inside your head"

Then Patrick forced himself to respond more gently. "It isn't your dream. But it isn't mine either."

John stared at Patrick with his mouth open. After a moment he asked in almost a whisper, "Is it a memory of something that really happened?"

Patrick suddenly felt unable to get enough air in his lungs. He swallowed some tea and forced himself to answer. "Yes, I believe we're both dreaming about an event that really happened."

John kept coming after him. "Where does this dream come from? Why does it grab me every single night? I've tried to stay awake so I won't have to have it, but after waking up in terror every night for more than a month, I can't remember to reset my alarm clock whenever I walk near it."

Empowered by John's vulnerability, Patrick started talking. "You're dreaming night after night about a scene in which there are several living beings present. You find this dream so convincing that you don't believe yourself capable of having composed it in your own unconscious mind. You feel a strong impulse to find some living mind to which you can attribute a memory on which this dream could be based. Well, then, ask yourself: Whose mind could it be coming from? Let's eliminate the witnesses, such as Dad and Mom, who are now dead. Let's eliminate the unborn child, you. Who does that leave?"

John answered right away. "You and me."

Struggling with old resentments that welled up in him, Patrick said. "No! Don't be so Goddamned intellectually lazy, John! Who else was there? A full grown adult with a heart larger than you or I will ever have! Who the hell do you think is talking to us? Pick up the phone, man. This call's for you."

"That's not possible." John said in a whisper. "How could that be possible? You can't mean that."

Patrick turned the screw. "Who do you think I mean? Spit it out. If you don't just say it now, out loud, then you're never going to get a handle on this. Say it, John, now!"

John obeyed, in a low hesitant voice. "A whale. You're telling me that a whale saved your life, and that now he's trying to talk with us." Then, like a child who can't back off from his own preoccupation, he asked imploringly, "You have the same dream? You really have the same dream?"

Patrick felt an unwanted catching in his throat. Was it his dream? Of course it was. This dream was a living memory of how their father had died, and it proved that he was responsible for their father's death.

He tried to tell himself that a three-year old boy couldn't be to blame. But he did blame himself. He had always blamed himself.

As painful as these realizations were to Patrick, at least he had had a lifetime of guilt to prepare himself. When you've never made it in your own eyes, when your personality is like a harbor of broken ice, it isn't as threatening to recognize the superior intelligence of a different mind. In fact, if this mind is outside the order that has made you feel worthless, you welcome it. But how could John possibly make sense of all this?

It was time to tell John what he knew. But where could he start? Should he mention his meeting with Hal Nagen that morning, and Hal's corroboration of what he and John were experiencing? Maybe later. Just remembering their meeting in the church, Patrick felt his chest constrict. Should he just start blathering about all his dreams and visions—in comparison to which John's single dream seemed like a Readers Digest excerpt—or did he need to pick and choose very carefully things to which John might be open? One unthinkable but undeniable fact loomed over everything else—they had both been contacted by a non-human mind, and neither of them understood how or why this was happening.

"Let's take a walk," Patrick said, standing up and heading toward the pegs at the front door, from which hung winter jackets and the two identical red woolen toques that he and his brother had chosen to bring with them.

CHAPTER 15

John lagged behind, vaguely aware that his older brother was striding up the beach at a fast pace. No problem. He could catch up whenever he wanted.

He needed to sort out a few things. Everything was happening too fast—especially this new possibility that he and Patrick could be friends. The wasted opportunities of a lifetime would have to be acknowledged. But maybe to really be there for his own two children, he was going to have to face up to what had happened in his own childhood. Carolyn, their therapist, would be proud that he was even thinking about such possibilities.

So his nightmare was about real events. But how could a whale talk to them? That was ridiculous, and he hadn't gotten where he was in life by being ridiculous.

The truth was that he felt split in two—the scientist in him watching helplessly as irrational feelings increasingly determined how he acted.

John looked up and saw that Patrick had moved at least 100 yards ahead of him, so he broke into a jog and caught up. As soon as Patrick turned, John leaned closer and shouted, "Do you know anything about a transmission from Titan?"

Patrick shouted back. "I know it's very important."

"Why?" John asked.

Patrick made no response, and they continued to walk side by side next to the crashing breakers. The waves were larger than John remembered—maybe a storm was on its way. Fine, don't answer. What could you know about Titan anyway?

John felt Patrick's hand grabbing him by the elbow. He turned and saw that Patrick was talking but he could only catch a few words. " . . . Titans talking with us . . . heading straight for Earth . . . "

John suddenly felt exhausted. It wasn't just the wind drowning out his brother's voice. He could have loosened his hood and leaned forward to catch every word. It was simply too much to swallow. How could he have gotten so caught up in these ridiculous fictions? He was probably suffering more seriously from sleep-deprivation than he realized.

When Patrick kept talking, John clamped his gloves around either side of his hood. Apparently Patrick got the message, because he turned abruptly and walked toward the dry sand above the high tide mark.

John forced himself to follow and they clambered through the loose sand until they reached the other side of a knoll. There, sheltered from the booming surf and gusting wind, Patrick sat with his back against a piece of driftwood and John sat cross-legged facing him.

Seeing how upset Patrick looked, John forced himself to speak. "I'm sorry, but my nightmare feels a lot more real to me than visions of aliens and doomsday warnings. I realize there's a lot going on that I don't understand, but when you start talking as if my entire understanding of the solar system is nonsense, I close down. I need to keep my basic sense of reality. Titan is a frozen moon and no native of Titan can be sending a message from there."

That was all John had intended to say but he continued. "Face it, Patrick. There aren't any aliens around in this solar system. And you'd be smart to question your own motivation in claiming to be so central to everything."

As anger flared on Patrick's face, John immediately regretted his last remark. Why had he never learned to be friendly to people? And especially now, to Patrick, when Patrick might know some things that John also needed to know?

"Let me reply to what you just said." Patrick began, his voice surprisingly even. "You're entitled to keep your opinion of me and we both know that it's not all of a sudden going to be a very high one. Fine, let's both be honest. You want some reprieve from your nightmare and then you'll be on your way back home—back to your family, your work and your normal life. You really don't want much else out of this trip."

John felt he should deny that he had a low opinion of Patrick, but somehow he let the moment pass. Instead he did his best to pay attention as Patrick continued. "A comet is heading straight for Earth and we need to tell the world about it. You especially. The military establishment will let this comet destroy everything, before they voluntarily share anything they label as a state secret."

John agreed with his brother's diagnosis of the military/industrial complex, but heard himself saying, "How do you know what the military will do? Last I heard you weren't all that up on current events."

"My information doesn't come from some new interest in world affairs," Patrick responded. "It comes from dreams like yours. You're dreaming night after night about a boy and a whale? Well, I'm dreaming night after night about a bomb hitting a comet and breaking it into thousands of pieces—each one capable of sending Earth into a new ice age."

John knew from personal experience how miserable that felt: a dream that never goes away, until you listen to what it is trying to tell you.

"Unless they're pushed," Patrick was saying, "they simply won't get around to it in time. That's our job. You don't need to believe everything I tell you. But you need to acknowledge that you've paid up your ante and that you're in the game."

Patrick grinned and raised a gloved hand in the direction of the ocean. They struggled to their feet in the loose sand, then retraced their steps back to the beach. Back in the midst of howling wind and crashing breakers, Patrick pointed to a rock, about a half-mile off shore, which appeared to be joined to the beach by a causeway of sand.

When Patrick started to run in the direction of the sandbar, John quickly fell in at his side. Even though three decades had passed and they were ridiculously encumbered with heavy winter coats and boots, John suddenly remembered doing this before. Running for the sheer pleasure and freedom of it as the surf crashed and drained away through glistening sand. As if the primal waters of their planet could wash away all the confusions of a human life. At least this was real. And John knew in his heart it was why he had come.

CHAPTER 16

By the time they reached the general store after their visit to the rock, darkness had fallen across the wind-lashed ocean and a fierce wind scourged their faces with pellets of snow. John had grown up with Canadian winters, but after decades in New Mexico, it was a relief when Patrick closed the porch door and they were standing in the warmth of Emily's kitchen.

Hank took John's ski jacket and hung it up on a wooden peg. Hot rum toddies were passed around and Hank proposed a toast. "To reunions and safe harbors in the storms of life."

John inhaled the aroma of honey and lemon-laced rum and was about to take a drink when he noticed that the old couple was still looking at one another.

He felt strangely affected by the way the two old people looked so deeply into one another's eyes. It flashed through his mind that he never looked at Leslie like that. He was always too busy working on some agenda or other.

Eventually Hank raised his glass to Patrick and to John and took a drink. John didn't waste any time talking a large swallow himself, closing his eyes with pleasure as the hot liquid flowed down his throat and into his belly.

He soon drained his glass and was wondering if he would be offered a refill when Hank turned to him and said, "John, our phone was dead for awhile this afternoon but two minutes after the service man got it working, a call came in from your wife. Apparently she had been trying to get through for hours. She said a young man on a skateboard found something missing on your computer at home."

John had to set his glass down on the table. After a few moments he managed to ask, "Did she say whether all copies of the file are lost?"

"All I know is that something is gone." Hank responded quickly, seemingly uncomfortable with the subject of computers.

John's mind raced. The agents must have broken into their house. They would have had no trouble finding the Titan file on his hard disk. But did they know about Bill and his back-up CD's?

John phoned home. When there was no answer, he tried Leslie's parents. Her mother picked up when she heard John's voice on the answering machine, but she hadn't seen Leslie.

Enraged at how the authorities felt entitled to hide knowledge from ordinary people, and afraid of what they might be willing to do to protect that compulsive secrecy, John tried to calmly think about this new situation.

Should he call Bill? But was any telephone line secure now? Maybe they even knew he was here at Anchor Beach and could tap calls made from Hank and Emily's phone. For that matter, had Hank and Emily had a real telephone problem this afternoon, or were the FBI on to him here?

This is not the time to get completely paranoid. He tried to tell himself.

Patrick's voice intruded on his thoughts. "I don't know exactly what you lost, John. But you're still involved—now, more than ever. You need to tell people what you and I are being shown." John felt his fists clenching as Patrick continued, "And whatever else happens, no one can take away your knowledge."

"With knowledge and a buck you can buy a cup of coffee," John responded. "And the military establishment dosen't need me to tell them about the comet. They know a lot more about it than I do."

"The comet?" Patrick interrupted. "They've seen the comet?"

John couldn't believe that his brother was being so dense. How could Patrick ever imagine that the military wouldn't know about the comet sightings?

Patrick was still talking, with mounting excitement. "Do they know it's a threat to Earth? Once they do, they'll want to contact anyone who knows more about it than they do. We've got to keep them interested in you."

John could scarcely suppress the rage he felt. He managed to keep his voice under control as he responded. "First, the authorities know more about this comet than I do. Secondly, they're not going to ask my advice just because I've stumbled onto something on Titan. And thirdly, it is ludicrous to think I would want the government to be interested in me and my family. It takes my breath away that you could imagine I would deliberately create the impression that I know more than I do. You're talking about people who would be ready to have me murdered if it suited them." John's voice, which had sounded harsher than he had intended, softened as he concluded. "Really, Patrick. I came here to ask for your help and you've come through with flying colors. But I don't need your advice on how to play games with the FBI."

Even as he spoke John recognized that his feelings about the Titan transmission went much deeper than he was acknowledging.

Then it hit him out of left field. Patrick hadn't known about this comet sighting. He'd only known about the comet itself. His surprise that a comet had been observed was unfeigned: he really only knew about it from his dreams.

John started to listen more closely to what Patrick was saying. "Your reaction is perfectly understandable, John. You have to protect your family. And I certainly don't expect you to pretend to know things that you don't really know. But tomorrow morning you will have new knowledge."

Patrick abruptly turned to Emily. "I'm afraid we're holding up supper. It smells absolutely wonderful, Emily."

Emily announced that a meal of prime rib, roast potatoes, Yorkshire pudding and brown gravy, was ready to serve.

Hank carried the platter onto the table. With one accord everyone, except John, was suddenly moving. Patrick washed his hands at the sink, Hank started carving the roast and Emily took a salad from the fridge and poured thick gravy into a green china boat that matched the main platter.

At Hank's request, Patrick opened a bottle of Merlot and poured it into four glasses. Within a few moments everyone was seated, Grace had been said and the food passed around.

John ate ravenously and accepted thirds of everything. The others finished eating first, and then started talking in a way that seemed almost surreal to John. Hank and Emily treated Patrick as if he were their favorite son. But how could that have happened in just a few weeks?

Then a question from Hank yanked him back into the moment. "Have you shared your visions of Titan with John?"

Patrick kept his eyes on John, as he responded to Hank's question. "No. John isn't open to that."

Hank persisted. "Did you tell him that you were rescued and brought to Emily and me by a dolphin? And that after three days in a coma you awoke with clairvoyant powers?"

John and Patrick continued to look steadily at one another as Patrick shook his head. "A little bit. You have to realize John is here because of his nightmares. He's not ready for visions of Titan dancing in his head."

While the two brothers continued to look unwaveringly at one another, Patrick continued. "John is not interested in my visions of Titan. Even though his two year old son, Frankie, has also talked to him about the Titanians."

John's fork slipped from his hand and clattered onto his plate. Patrick had absolutely no way of knowing what Frankie had said. John had not breathed a word to anyone. Not even to Leslie.

Patrick gave John no chance to speak. "I see two ways of getting John involved. One is to slip in a little bombshell, like I did just now. The other is his dreams. And, by the way, John, I doubt you'll be dreaming about Dad's drowning much now. That's served its purpose, which was to bring you here."

John didn't really want to continue this conversation, but he seemed unable to prevent himself from asking, "What will my dreams be about now?"

He had intended a world-weary skepticism to come across in this question, but instead an unintended tone of urgency came out.

Something like a vast hunger arose in him, as Patrick responded. "It's a dialogue. A living being is talking with us. The more we pay attention, the more we can receive. I'm pretty sure you'll wake up tomorrow morning feeling very differently about the Titan transmission." And then, seeming to sense something new himself, Patrick added, "These images from Titan are hard for me too, but I bet after tomorrow you won't ever again think they're coming from an American probe."

Maybe it was the respectful attention with which the old couple listened to Patrick. Or maybe John's nightmare had shaken him more profoundly than he realized. Patrick looked different—not just that the years had changed him, but during the past few days Patrick had radiated a new confidence and certainty.

For a few moments no one at the table spoke. The sound of the storm outside gave the kitchen a feeling of sheltered warmth and security. An image from childhood came into his mind. He was jumping over deep drifts of snow in downtown Montreal with a 50 mile-an-hour wind pushing at his back. All the houses and trees were plastered and the roadway was so completely buried in drifts that it was lost beneath a white vastness. To move down the street, on which not another soul could be seen, he jumped straight up. Then the wind drove his body forward as if he were a sail in the flow of time.

John turned back to Patrick and said, "This may be a good occasion to mention that I might still have a copy of that Titan file. I'll let you know as soon as I get back to Albuquerque." Then, before Patrick could say anything, John continued, "Now let's get me ready for my next conversation with the whale."

As if something had shifted, they both laughed. And something had shifted. They were on the same side.

CHAPTER 17

Eric didn't see why they had to stay at a hotel, but he certainly wasn't complaining. He had just spent the past three hours swimming in this neat pool where part was inside the building and part was outside—and outside, in the January air, steam puffed out when you breathed. Now he and Frankie were watching an HBO movie that they would normally not be allowed to watch— because their Dad was in Maine somewhere and their Mom was asleep on the other bed.

Eric looked over towards Frankie and saw that his baby brother was asleep too. He turned down the sound on the TV and dimmed the lights. Before sitting back down on the bed, he went to the sliding door that led outside. He unlatched it and stepped out onto a small balcony. Their hotel room was on the seventh floor and had a great view across the city all the way to the west mesa. There was enough city glow to see the volcanoes and enough light from a quarter moon to see the snow on Mount Taylor, 50 miles further west, if you knew where to look.

Sometimes he had the strangest feeling these days. And he was feeling it more and more lately. This afternoon it had hit him more than ever before. Seeing how freaked out his mom had been this afternoon had pushed him into a very strange place. It had something to do with his dad and uncle, but he had no idea what. And what was his dad actually doing? Other people's dads didn't have the FBI breaking into their houses.

They might not have ever found out either, except that their neighbor across the street had happened to notice the panel truck parked out front. She had started wondering why there was a Jones Intercable logo on its side panel—seeing that his dad had been quite disapproving of cable at a recent neighborhood association party. "Why settle for five channels of crap when you can have 100 channels of crap?" he had asked the neighbors, more than a little sarcastically. This neighbor, who apparently had cable herself, seemed quite pleased that the Murphy's had finally succumbed.

But they hadn't succumbed.

Between his mom remembering a file his dad had shown her more than a week ago, and Eric having a knack for computers, they had been able to determine that something was missing. That was when his mom had freaked, tried to call his dad, then thrown some clothes in a couple of bags, pushed them all into the van, and driven to this hotel.

And now, standing in an uncomfortably cold breeze seven stories above the city streets below, Eric felt again how his mind was not exactly the same as he remembered it. Why was that?

Take right now, for instance. The movie playing in the hotel room behind him was very boring compared to the stuff happening in his own head. But was any of it real? Was Frankie really dreaming about some long room with a stone floor and paintings of weird demons on the walls where men in red and orange robes were all looking at him? Was his mom really having some nightmare about losing Frankie in a shopping mall? And were his dad and uncle really starting to talk with each other after all those years? More specifically, were they at this very moment sitting around some funky kitchen table, drinking coffee with some old geysers and talking about some whale they both knew?

And that wasn't the weirdest part of what was happening in his head. The really weird part was that a voice kept telling him to remember everything, because he was going to be the one to send some important message somewhere or other. This voice even had a face behind it: out of focus, unfamiliar, but intense, a blond guy who seemed to be in charge of dealing with some global catastrophe.

Well one thing he knew. It could be a good thing if his dad felt a little friendlier towards Uncle Patrick. It was really weird to have an uncle and never see him. And it kind of seemed sometimes that if his dad could get over whatever problem he had with Uncle Patrick, then maybe he wouldn't be such a stiff at home. Like, it would be nice if at least once you could throw a ball with your own dad. Or sit in the same room together and feel he would listen if you told him something. But for as long as Eric could remember, his dad hadn't really been there. He would make some kind of response if you actually spoke to him, but it wasn't real. In some ways, his dad might be able to understand some things better than his mom. If only he was listening.

Cold and shivering, Eric opened the sliding door and went back into the room. Without stirring where he lay on the bed, Frankie opened his eyes and said, "Daddy have new dream now. Like Uncle Patrick."

Eric had hoped for as long as he could remember that his dad would wake up and pay more attention to the rest of his family. Now that it seemed to be happening, it was not at all what he had expected. Too much else was changing at the same time. Now there didn't seem to be anything he could count on to stay the same.

CHAPTER 18

Sunday, Jan 26 (Day -74)

John sat up in bed, completely awake, and looked around the room. In splashes of moonlight shining through loose-woven curtains he recognized Patrick's cabin. It seemed familiar in an uncanny way, which the single night he had slept there could not explain. Maybe his dream had dislodged an old memory that was now hovering in the shadows.

He made his way through the darkness of the cabin, checking to see that the door to Patrick's bedroom was closed before he turned on the kitchen light. He put on the kettle and then went back for his journal and a pen.

He was living another life: glistening bodies breaching in sunlight, constantly on the move, feeding incessantly; clicks and pings sketching out a landscape of knowledge and feeling in a mind vast beyond individual consciousness. These sensations so completely inundated John's mind that by the time he heard the kettle's furious whistling, the wall behind the stove was wet with steam.

With a force of clarity he could not doubt, he saw a giant comet on the far side of the Sun—a dark marauder about to descend toward unsuspecting flocks. Its volatile ices were buried deep beneath a rocky mantle, itself bubbling in the searing heat.

The concepts at his disposal seemed completely inadequate to explain the images that crowded his mind. To help himself see more clearly he took his time making coffee.

He had dreamed about whales and dolphins. He had dreamed about a comet. And he had dreamed about something else—a distant world so completely alien to his understanding of life that he didn't know how to begin to describe it. But this is what he most desperately wanted to document, before his ordinary, waking consciousness washed it away.

He brought his mug to the table, took a few sips, opened his journal to a blank page, and started writing. "There isn't a single center. When we have only one place to live, it is dark and annihilating. The gesture of reaching out creates a window into other places. Perhaps even other times. Like being the whole sea instead of a small boat getting smothered by the waves. It's more than imagination; the whole sea knows the boat and supports it. Life has to have a foothold in the water, but then it can have eyes in the sky, even above the clouds, even in other worlds. It's not possible to leave the water. Too cold. Would die. But can fly too. Like light dancing on the waves. Like ice branches growing in the mists. Like an eagle foraging above the nest, never forgetting the nest, but seeing every detail for miles around."

John recognized that he was increasingly imposing his own translations onto images which didn't themselves include eagles or nests. He stopped writing and poured himself a second cup of coffee. Then he asked himself if he could remember anything fundamental about the vision. It would be more useful to remember even a single bizarre fragment of the original experience—just as it had appeared to him—than to write a long, lyrical appreciation of the feelings it had stimulated.

He sat back down at the kitchen table and, holding his cup in both hands, closed his eyes and let himself drift. At one point he felt he was in the landscape of the dreaming again. He must have sat like that for quite a long time. The metronome of the Atlantic surf continued to measure out the darkness and quiet of a sleeping world. His coffee was still warm, but no longer hot. He remembered that he had closed his eyes in order to try to retrieve at least one fragment from the dream. Now he had much more than the original dream images to express. There had been a kind of dialogue.

He picked up his pen and began writing again, this time with a sense that he didn't have to hurry. The images in his mind would not vanish if he tried to understand them. "There are other beings in our solar system. There isn't much sunlight reaching the frozen surface of their world. Parts are warmed by a flow of lava. There is no solid ground on which to build things. More like dolphins than humans. Their environment doesn't satisfy their need for wider perspectives. In order for intelligence to evolve and journeys to be taken, it was necessary for something to develop in the direction of greater openness. On Earth, human evolution has been dominated by firm ground. Therefore hands are able to grasp and legs are adapted to push against solid surfaces. Dolphins and eagles live in water and air, and have limbs like oars and sails, accordingly. Observing dolphins can give some feel for how an advanced intelligence could exploit other faculties than those required to manipulate objects. If you ask how the descendants of whales could ever imaginatively leave their planet, you have something interesting to think about."

John wrote many more pages. At some point he stood up and stretched. He glimpsed sand dunes beginning to emerge from the blackness of night and walked out to the porch to get a better look. He was heading towards the swing when a movement in the shadows made him freeze.

"That coffee sure smells good."

Patrick, well wrapped in blankets, spoke from the darkness of the porch swing. "I've been dying for some coffee for the past three hours."

They went into the kitchen and John stood, mute, as Patrick made more coffee and prepared two plates of toast and jam. Then he could no longer restrain himself. "You've been up for hours?" Did you have the same dream? Is that what happens—we get a conference call with both of us on the line? Then how come I had my questions answered in that call, but I didn't hear you asking anything?"

Eventually John ground to a halt and demolished his two pieces of toast. When he eventually looked at Patrick again, he felt a stab of terrible loss. It was one thing to have never had a father, but this brother should have been his best friend during all those cold years in Montreal.

"It's not too late, John." Patrick's voice broke into his thoughts. "We have eleven weeks of life left. For some of us, maybe more. We have time to remember the meaning of our lives. Perhaps we both now understand that you and I will never be completely apart again."

John didn't recognize what was so strange about his brother's voice, until with a shock he realized that Patrick had not spoken out loud. The scientist in him started to ponder what might make that possible. Then, almost effortlessly, he accepted the inconceivable: it wasn't just a whale talking to them. Patrick was opening a door of whose existence John had not even dreamed.

He could feel years of unwept tears gathering inside, like raindrops joining on a windowpane. Decades of feeling, corralled within the confines of a tiny spectrum of intelligence, were now kicking down the fences. A lifetime of losses paraded through him like an army in defeat. But that was not the most amazing part. The most amazing part was that John finally understood that nothing had ever been completely lost.

CHAPTER 19

Ted's legman, posing as a telephone repairman, had installed bugs in the old couple's kitchen; and Ted himself had risked entering the brothers' cabin while they were out for a walk. Now the microphone he had placed on the stone fireplace was transmitting constantly because the sound of the waves kept it on. So he wasn't getting much sleep.

Some of the conversations he had recorded were beyond belief. More than once he had shuddered at the thought that excerpts of this material would probably go as high as the President.

The Secret Service guys would love the part where Patrick said they needed to get close to the President. Not a good idea, John and Patrick. And not for the first time, Ted wished he could edit some of this material before it fell into the hands of his "superiors".

These recordings told the story of a respected scientist moving by degrees—more like precipitous leaps—toward a position in which his scientific detachment had become completely corrupted. In its place had arisen the fervor of a visionary. With every breath, Professor John Murphy sounded more and more like his fruitcake brother.

Now there was a specimen for you. Admitted to a mental health facility, Patrick would be medicated within the hour.

In writing his summary of the contents of these recordings, Ted had identified three main themes. First, Professor Murphy now believed that intelligent life, native to Saturn's moon, Titan, was trying to warn humans about a comet on a collision course with Earth. Second, Patrick believed that he and John were both in communication with a whale that had supposedly saved Patrick 40 years previously, in an incident during which their father had died. And the third main theme—which would doubtlessly appear the most important to his superiors—was that, after having been made aware of a problem with his home computer, John Murphy had made unequivocal reference to his continued ability to access a copy of the Titan file. Ted didn't know what worried him the most. Was it the failure in his own surveillance assignment (he had already initiated an exhaustive search of every computer storage media Professor Murphy had come close to in previous weeks), or was he afraid for the safety of the two brothers and the unknown kid on the skateboard?

Ted's anxiety went deeper. These two brothers were both dreaming about the same things. One of them had picked up an intelligent radio signal from a moon one billion miles away, while the other had survived three days in deep coma after being brought to shore, seemingly dead, by a dolphin.

Whoa. Time for a reality check, Ted.

He couldn't shake these coincidences out of his mind. They turned everything around inside him, making him doubt his own role as government enforcer. It was one thing to try to keep Professor Murphy quiet, while the Administration tried to figure out where the hell that message had come from. It was quite another to collaborate in the suppression of knowledge that might be vital to the whole world.

The Murphy brothers were talking about a comet. Ted watched the news most evenings and had heard nothing about a comet, but they were describing its exact dimensions, which was off the charts,as well as the exact moment when it would pass a few miles from the Moon, headed directly towards Earth.

They weren't just talking vaguely about unexplained radio waves, either: now there was an urgent message being sent by intelligent inhabitants of Titan, whom both brothers described as if they were gossiping about their friends and neighbors.

Ted Sullo had met a lot of mad people in his time, inside and outside of government, but this was the first time he had found himself unable to stop thinking about what the loonies were saying. He had even started wondering if there might have been a comet sighting which hadn't yet made it to the evening news.

Worst of all, Agent Ted Sullo couldn't free his mind of haunting images of an ocean planet. He couldn't free his mind of a vision of a beautiful blue light transfusing ice caves at incredible depths in some alien sea.

Ted took out a CD. After several fast-forwards he found the cut he wanted.

Patrick was speaking. John had just asked him to describe his vision of Titan. Patrick's voice had a quality which reminded Ted of the Catholic Masses of his childhood —an association that made him feel more than a little uncomfortable. "There is a beautiful blue light descending like rain. The impression of rain falling comes from oxygen bubbles rising to the surface. The bitterly cold water, in which warm currents cycle here and there, is infused with light down to a depth of several miles. The ice walls themselves are glowing, far beneath the levels to which surface illumination could ever penetrate."

Despite his suspicion that Titan was a barren, dark world, completely inhospitable to oxygen-based life, Ted was drawn into these images, as if something intensely familiar were being invoked for him.

"We are swimming in the depths of a beautiful, radiant ocean. This is our embodiment. At the same time, another part of our intelligence can look down on the surface of our world from above. From a perspective miles above the surface, we see that a glowing light is concentrated in the ocean. Elsewhere, vast regions of ice are ravaged by savage cold and dark."

Patrick's voice ceased. Ted remembered how, on the original tape, the silence had lasted for more than five minutes.

Patrick's voice, now undeniably ecstatic, resumed. "If you become really quiet you can hear the song of the magnetosphere gently caressing Titan, as Saturn rocks her smaller partner in the embrace of her gravity. You can sense the extraordinarily intimate bond that exists between these two entities, like that between a strong body and a nimble mind. You feel numb with a dawning recognition of the vast grounds of consciousness at work in the Saturn system."

With a sudden start, Ted realized that the RECORD light had come on for the bug in the old couple's kitchen. He stopped the tape and switched his headphones over to what was coming in: water running, bang of metal against metal, swoosh of a gas jet.

Those microphones were impressive. He could almost see a kettle heating on the stove.

Then he heard Emily's voice. "Well, everything's ready except the tea. Any sign of them, yet? John has to leave in less than two hours to catch his plane."

Hank announced that they had arrived. The microphone picked up the sound of feet stamping in the back porch and four voices suddenly talking all at once.

Ted had to stretch the cord on his earphones full length to reach the coffee maker. Listening intently, he poured himself a cup of coffee and then sat down with his yellow pad of paper in front of him. He wrote the date and time on top and the names of the four people present in the kitchen. Then he stared off into space.

Deep space.

CHAPTER 20

Sunday morning was warm and clear. John and Patrick had taken a long walk in the fresh-fallen snow—thanks to Leslie's insistence that John bring a pair of galoshes. The receding tide had left a swath of wet sand where walking was easy, but on the dunes the winters of his childhood reigned.

They drove over to Hank and Emily's around 11:00 a.m. Everywhere snow was melting off rooftops and branches. Here and there asphalt peeked through the plowed roads.

Lunch was on the table when they entered Emily's kitchen. With John's flight back to Albuquerque leaving at 2:10 pm, they only had an hour in which to eat. They immediately sat down and—after Hank had said Grace—dug into a curry and rice invention that featured Emily's leftover roast beef.

After they'd finished, Patrick turned to John and asked, "What does the scientific community know about Titan?"

John had been turning this over in his mind, trying to find a starting point from which to talk with his fellow scientists, if he ever got the chance. So now he felt ready to talk as if his only knowledge of Titan derived from scientifically legitimate sources.

But before John could launch into a lecture, Patrick asked, "Does anyone think it could support life?"

"No." John responded. "Titan has a lot of nitrogen in its atmosphere—the only known planetary body in our solar system, other than Earth, that does. So it's possible that it has the kind of organic molecules that were present when life started here."

"Then why couldn't Titan support life?" Patrick interjected.

"Because its surface doesn't receive enough sunlight." John continued. "The Voyager fly-bys measured temperatures of about minus 200 Celsius on the surface. Saturn is about ten times further from the Sun than Earth. That far out, even a planet without Titan's smoggy atmosphere would be dark on its surface—something like dusk just before people turn on their headlights. So the composition of Titan might be Earth-like but it's too cold to have evolved life comparable to what we find on our planet."

Patrick interrupted, "But surely life elsewhere could be based on a different model."

John forced aside an image of massive, gliding bodies—which seemed to be listening to him as he spoke—and continued his outline of orthodox theories about Titan. "Someone once described Titan as 'Earth in a deep freeze.' If our Sun flared up into a hotter phase, then Earth would get sizzled and Titan would warm up—then perhaps its rich soup of organic molecules could kick in and life could evolve there."

Patrick summarized. "But meanwhile, no one thinks Titan could have intelligent life on it now because it's too cold and dark."

John nodded, "But the scientists who monitored the Voyager space craft readings haven't seen what you and I have seen."

Hank interjected. "John, please tell us something about what you and Patrick have seen."

Emily added, "I sometimes see pictures—things that the dolphin who saved Patrick shows me. But I know I've never seen this other place—this Titan that you and Patrick talk about. Please tell us what it looks like."

John realized that he had a chance to say something to a completely sympathetic audience, and this new sensation was quite thrilling. At first he hesitated (because his brother knew so much more than he did) then, looking alternately at Hank and Emily as he spoke, he dove in. "I've seen a planet whose surface is mainly ice, some of it slashed by gigantic faults which would dwarf the Grand Canyon. Most of the surface is frozen and dark, but there's one area of open ocean where a spectrum of bright light fills the water and the clouds above it."

Hank interrupted. "I've read a bit about the Voyager expedition to Saturn. Didn't they think that Titan's oceans were made of ammonia and methane?"

"That's correct." John responded. "But we never completely mapped Titan's surface, so we could easily have missed an isolated body of volcanically-heated water."

John glanced quickly at Patrick before continuing. "In any case, I feel certain that these beings were showing me their home. They live under the water. They can survive either near the surface, or miles below at the bottom of the ocean. They manipulate volcanic flows of lava in order to carve out habitable areas from the great mountains of ice.

"The source of energy in the sky is a later development, analogous to our power plants and combustion engines, but I don't believe it is the major source of heat. In any case, the lava under the sea is the energy source which permitted life to evolve on this moon in the first place. Life on Titan originally evolved in surface ponds created by naturally produced volcanic vents."

John grew more animated as he continued. "The Titanians live in the ocean but are able to see the surface of their world and beyond to other worlds. This is a mystery. How can they fly if they evolved at the bottom of an ocean? Maybe they're not flying but somehow they can view Titan's surface from above."

Hank interrupted. "How do they communicate with Earth?"

John thought for a moment. "I think they have ways of doing things that don't involve a lot of technology. It involves mastery of the material universe but not the kind of manipulations which we humans associate with intelligence. I think they have a way of spanning space, and of adopting perspectives within space while their bodies remain within the specific ecosphere that spawned them. They seem able to extend their mental presence outside their physical bodies. I don't know how they do it, and I don't really know how much of them gets projected in this way. It almost seems like their senses can be based outside their physical bodies. Maybe even more than their senses."

At this point Patrick interrupted. "I think it's important to always remember that the Titanians have never talked directly with us. Whatever the nature of the contact between our two planets, it's the whales and dolphins who answer the long distance call on the Earth end. What we get is a local call from an individual whale. The content of that call includes information from which we can speculate about the Titanians' bodies and minds—but I don't believe we are in direct contact with either."

This was definitely news to John and he wasn't sure whether he believed it. He voiced his skepticism. "How can you have images of another being's world and feelings of what it is like to live there without being in direct communication with that being?"

Patrick answered. "The whale who is talking with us is a good story-teller. He is able to communicate an experiential sense along with the images that he has received."

John felt like arguing. "I'm not sure I believe that either you or I can be so completely confident in our interpretations. Especially about something as subjective as how a species is managing to communicate with us."

Patrick didn't miss a beat. "It's not at all subjective. I asked the whale and the whale told me. He told me that sperm whales receive the Titanian transmission at this end. A sperm whale can generate a very fine mesh of brain waves which extends throughout its spermaceti field."

John interrupted. "I think I read something about that, about how brain waves can propagate through the colloidal mass located in a sperm whale's head."

"Exactly," Patrick answered, so quickly that John had no opportunity to follow up. "This colloidal mass hosts a neural mesh. Then this mesh of brain waves is modified by the Titan radio waves. In effect, the whale acts as a kind of radio telescope. And since the receiving instrument is itself a living mind, it is able to selectively tune in at an inconceivably fine level. And with sperm whales distributed over the world's oceans, they form the equivalent of a radio telescope as large as our planet."

While another part of him could see the sense in what Patrick was saying, John could feel his mind closing as Patrick continued. "The humpbacks help to distribute this knowledge to other whales. This is achieved partly through their songs. However, far more information is distributed telepathically. The songs serve to underscore the reality of this knowledge, which is especially important when teaching the youngest whales. Also the songs of the humpback directly stimulate certain centers in the whale's bodies—similar to the use of mantra and chanting in many human religions."

John felt tired. He tried to remind himself how convincingly Patrick had predicted the change in his dream, but there was a limit to what he could absorb all at one time.

And it was hard to give up yet another scientific given. All his working life he had 'known' that organic matter could not receive radio waves and make sense of them. He managed a weak smile as he turned to Patrick and said, "Oh, well, maybe I'll come around on that one later. For now, we better think about getting me to the airport."

John stood up and shook hands with Hank. Emily insisted that he give her a hug.

As Patrick drove out of the lot, John turned in the passenger seat and saw Hank and Emily standing in front of their store waving. He waved back, thinking that both he and Patrick could have used an uncle and aunt like them, growing up in Montreal. Patrick's voice broke in on his reflections. "Things will heat up for you pretty soon, John. In a few days, some powerful people—maybe the President—will want to talk with you. Don't try to do it on your own. If you get a chance to speak directly with the President, you need to remember that, while you are an important bridge, the traffic that flows across it doesn't come from you."

John looked at his brother. He realized that he still couldn't take Patrick as seriously as he wanted to. He tried, with limited success, to accept Patrick's right to give him this kind of advice. Finally he said, "I'll try to remember. Modesty is not my forte, but I'll try, Patrick."

He was about to turn away, when Patrick reached under his sweater and pulled something out of his shirt pocket. It was a thumb drive. He handed it over to John. For a moment

John had no idea what his brother had given him. Then he remembered that in one of their conversations over the past two days Patrick had mentioned a digitized file of humpback whale songs. Feeling less than enthusiastic, he said, "Thanks. I'll have a look when I get back, and call you."

"Supper time is the best time to try and catch me at the store."

The two brothers looked at one another for a moment, then John excused himself, leaned back in the Honda's passenger seat and closed his eyes—leaving Patrick to navigate the winding beach road into Portland.

CHAPTER 21

Tuesday, Jan 28 (Day -72)

Ted Sullo was as nervous as he had ever been in his life. His boss, FBI Director Richard Todd—lean and mean in his checked suit and thin mustache—had just informed him, as they were rushing down the hallway towards the Oval Office briefing room, that they were about to meet with the President of the United States. Ted had been called back from Maine to attend this hastily scheduled meeting. The President had expressly requested that Agent Ted Sullo be present. Why? Because Ted's pals, the Murphy brothers, knew things which no civilian should ever know.

They entered a small conference room where several people were already seated. Ted recognized one of them as the President's Chief of Staff, Phil Black, a short, slightly chubby man with thick black hair and a mustache waxed at the ends. Another man, who was not familiar, glared at Ted without a hint of welcome. Ted had to force himself not to stare at the man's thin grey lips and greenish skin. As soon as he saw him though, an inner alarm went off. Physical danger.

Ted's boss pushed him toward a vacant seat. Then, almost immediately, they were all rising as the President entered the room, two Secret Service men a step behind.

The President's sandy colored hair was graying slightly at the temples—not bad for a sixty four year old white male, Ted thought. At 6" 2" and 200 lbs., he seemed larger than he appeared on TV, and a good half-foot taller than Ted. He welcomed Ted by name—leaning across the table to offer a firm handshake—then nodded to the others, sat down and said "I have just come from a meeting at the Pentagon, where career military brass are shitting their pants. This audio recording," —he brandished a CD above his head— "outlines highly classified material, for which the individual speaking most definitely has no clearance."

The President handed the CD to Ted's boss and said, "Play it for us, Richard."

Ted's boss, looking like a ferret with his pencil-thin mustache, inserted the CD into a slot on the Sony system and pressed PLAY. For the next five minutes they listened to Patrick Murphy describe how several waves of space-faring, nuclear warheads could be launched from American and Russian missile pads. The earliest launches could target the comet with nuclear armament, utilizing laser echo timing to trigger detonation while the probe was several miles away from the comet. Subsequent waves of missiles could provide a safety umbrella, in the event that the huge comet shattered.

On the recording, astronomer John Murphy's voice objected that this technology did not exist—at least not in a form that could be launched on a few weeks' notice.

Ted noticed that the other four men became even tenser as Patrick Murphy's voice responded to his brother's objection. "Even the President doesn't know how sophisticated this technology is, let alone Congress—who doesn't know about it all—but it definitely does exist. There's a firm called 'BallMaker Electronics', run by a man named 'George Ball', which has developed some amazing technology for the Pentagon. At this very moment, the capability exists to launch deep space missiles that behave like cruise missiles do over terrestrial terrain, locking onto a target and automatically working out the path needed to get to it. These missiles can carry either nuclear armament or laser cannons and can hit something whizzing past at 60 miles a second."

At a nod from the President, Director Todd punched the STOP button and ejected the CD. The room remained silent.

Ted looked at the President, wondering if the Commander in Chief might be hearing this material for the first time. He was still wondering when Phil Black broke the silence. "It so happens that this drivel is true."

The President, looking even grimmer, turned abruptly to Ted. "So, Agent Sullo, please tell us what the hell is happening? At first we thought we had an astronomer who just happened to pick up something unusual during his Titan research. Now we discover he has a brother who knows more about our nation's armament-preparedness than my own Administration does. Who are these guys? How can Patrick Murphy know this kind of thing?"

Ted suddenly knew that he should have been paying a lot more attention to the other brother. The bugs were still operating in Patrick's cabin and in the old couple's store, but he hadn't listened to them since leaving Anchor Beach two days ago.

Ted started talking—he couldn't just sit there with his mouth hanging open when the President of his country had asked him a direct question. "All I really know about Patrick Murphy, Sir, is that he lived in Montreal working as a computer programmer. He had a brief, unsuccessful marriage, and then for years he looked after a mother who apparently had a nervous breakdown—later diagnosed as Alzheimer's. She died three years ago. Apparently his obsession with whales started about one year ago."

A woman with red hair, whom he didn't recognize, interrupted. "What do whales have to do with anything?"

The President's attention didn't waiver for an instant, so Ted continued. "A couple of weeks ago he quit his job, jumped in his car and drove to a boarded-up summer resort area on the Maine coast. He had only been there a few hours when he was pulled out of the ocean and taken to the Portland General Hospital, seemingly as dead as a post. Three days later, he suddenly opened his eyes, and, a few days after that, checked out on his own two feet and went to live with the same old couple who brought him in. Apart from that, I don't know much more than what I've heard on the recordings, such as the one which Director Todd just played."

The President continued to give Ted his full attention. When no one else spoke, Ted continued. "I spoke with some of the staff at the hospital where Murphy was taken after his drowning accident. A Pakistani doctor, named Singh, told me that they would probably not have tried to revive him if they'd known how long he had been without oxygen—about two hours they now think. He also told me Murphy had experienced a lot of clairvoyant-type visions."

The man whom Ted did not recognize produced a contemptuous hiss. Ted spun toward him, and their eyes met. What was it that he found so repellant about this man? With effort Ted returned his attention to the President and was surprised to see that the head of his country had not appeared to react to the hiss. He was waiting for Ted to continue. Feeling out of his depth, Ted went on. "I mean I certainly didn't discuss clairvoyance with this doctor. But he told me that many of Murphy's dreams had taken that kind of form—as if he was being shown visions about Earth's future."

Ted's boss cleared his throat, apparently ready to intervene, but the President held up his hand, and kept his eyes on Ted.

Sensing that every time he opened his mouth, he just dug himself in deeper, Ted was relieved when Phil Black spoke. "If I understand you correctly, Agent, you are suggesting that we should treat this fruitcake as someone with special powers."

From various appearances at FBI functions, as well as numerous unofficial stories that circulated about him, Ted knew Phil Black as shrewd, arrogant and dangerous. Turning directly to the President and scrupulously ignoring Phil Black, Ted continued. "Mr. President, my assignment has been to investigate astronomer John Murphy and his interest in Titan. The revelation that Murphy's estranged brother, Patrick, has access to top-secret military information—I have to say I find that completely stunning, Sir. It makes me wonder if there isn't something extraordinary actually occurring on Titan."

Phil Black interjected, apparently with the President's permission. "Are we talking little green men here, Agent Sullo? Little green men with hearts of gold who are looking for some pet humans to adopt?"

Ted winced. Part of him did in fact hope that a higher wisdom would intervene in the apparently hopeless plight of human affairs on Earth. However, he reminded himself, apart from his unfortunate reference to alleged clairvoyant powers in Patrick Murphy—a subject whom he was supposed to be investigating—he had not in fact said anything out loud explicitly to that effect. Still giving all his attention to the President, he continued. "I do not believe I have said anything about how this unusual situation could have arisen. If Mr. Black wants to believe there are little green men behind it, well that's him talking, not me."

The President smiled and said, "Tell me, Ted, how do you think that Patrick Murphy came to be in possession of factual information of an extremely confidential nature?"

Ted glanced around the room, before responding. "Sir, I believe I would provoke an unproductive argument if I started talking about things I don't understand."

"Please go ahead and talk off the top of your head, Agent Sullo," the President insisted. Then, glancing at his Chief of Staff, he added, "We're all used to differences of opinion here."

Not knowing what else to do, Ted started talking. "This is how I see the situation, Sir. I think we need to take the contents of these recordings seriously. If Patrick Murphy knows about top-secret Pentagon contracts with BallMaker Electronics, then we should take seriously the other things he says. For instance, he claims that a comet will hit Earth less than three months from now—unless all resources are immediately committed to diverting it."

Ted had not intended to be a mouthpiece for Patrick Murphy's message, but he seemed unable to stop himself. "I realize that Murphy's warning by itself will not persuade you to launch a full scale mobilization, Sir, but maybe it can help us to be better prepared. Once we confirm the presence of this comet, no one will care too much how Murphy breached Pentagon security."

Ted was ready to leave it there, but the President pressed him to continue. "I appreciate your analysis, Ted. Now please give me your personal hunch about who in the world—or not in this world—might be capable of penetrating Pentagon security."

Ted glanced at the other people in the room hoping for some revelation, and when no such guidance was forthcoming he said, "I'm not sure my opinion matters very much, but I wonder if we have been addressed by an alien race of beings."

Ted looked around the room again. No one had fallen off a chair. Even Phil Black sat there quietly doodling on his pad of paper, perhaps scowling a bit more than usual but apparently not about to explode in indignation. Finally, as if the subject wearied him, Phil Black leaned toward Ted and said, "Agent Sullo, you yourself must have heard from these recordings that a comet has in fact been sighted. More to the point, we know that John Murphy was perfectly aware of this sighting so he didn't need any aliens to tell him about it."

Holy Christ! A comet really has been sighted, and everyone here is scared shitless about it. But no one told Patrick Murphy about this comet—at least not in any ordinary way.

Ted felt an icy sensation in his spine. He glanced at the unpleasant man and found himself looking into the eyes of a coiled serpent waiting to strike. The fear he felt was of something completely immune to fellow human feeling. Why did no one else in the room seem to notice anything strange about this man?

Ted's attention was yanked back as the President addressed him directly. "Agent Sullo, do you believe that we have been addressed by aliens who are indigenous to Titan?"

Ted felt a kind of soft, slow motion explosion go off inside. The President's question, and the fact that it was the President who was asking it, turned a key in his mind.

He looked around the room, trying to gauge from the four faces trained on him what he should say. It was not a spirit of open-minded inquiry that greeted him. He felt as if he could be ripped to shreds if he made a sudden move.

Because the face of the President seemed most sympathetic, he spoke directly to him.

"That's a very hard question, Sir. The scientific community has dismissed the idea that there could be life on Titan. So it would be ludicrous for anyone to propose that there is not only life there, but that we have been contacted by this life. It's only in this very moment, in response to your question, Sir, that I have to say, 'Yes. I believe that we have been contacted by intelligent life indigenous to Titan.'"

The room was silent.

Phil Black leaned toward the President and whispered something. A moment later the President announced that he had another appointment and thanked everyone for sharing their thoughts. Then the President, Phil Black, and the two security men who had been standing at the edge of the room, quickly left.

That left Ted, his boss, and the snake. Ted remained seated, waiting for his boss to say he could leave, but his boss seemed completely unaware of Ted. He seemed to be waiting for some sign from the snake. After a moment the snake did speak. "Tell me, Richard, when you assign someone to a sensitive case involving national security, do you run a recruitment ad in the Personals or do you assign one of your regular agents? Mr. Sullo here seems to have a good relationship with his feminine side."

His boss responded. "George, in retrospect I might have looked a bit more closely at Agent Sullo's record before assigning him to the Murphy case. At the time, however, it seemed we needed a computer expert with experience in the field. Agent Sullo came to the top of the list."

George nodded, as if considering the wisdom of having selected a top systems man for this assignment. Then he turned to Ted, and flashed a chilling smile. "Correct me if I'm wrong, Agent, but I believe your reasoning goes something like this. Someone makes an ass out of the American intelligence community. They let us know they have access to information about our nuclear deterrent capability . . ." Ted felt a deep revulsion growing inside him as George Ball continued to speak. An image of this man beating someone to death in the back of a warehouse, while talking sweetly to the victim, flashed into his mind. Meanwhile George was still talking. "These guys are so smart they can't be from Earth. They must be a race of superior beings who have come to save us from our folly. They must be higher beings. Why? Because they've broken our security and dumped their fantasy doo-doo on the floor!"

Ted was speechless. What was going on? His boss, who had played virtually no role in the meeting with the President, now breathed not a word in Ted's defense. Was there some complicity between these two men, which they had been careful to hide from the President? George seemed to be tied into some fantasy of his own. Then with a sense of shock, it dawned on Ted that George had not denied the presence of aliens—he was expressing his abhorrence of them.

Before Ted could process this insight, George abruptly nodded to the FBI Director, stood up, and left the room—a solitary reptile in a three-piece suit.

Alone in the conference room with his boss, who sat staring down at his hands, Ted remembered that they had never liked each other. After a moment, Director Todd looked up and said, "I want you to take a few weeks off. Keep your mouth shut. If Murphy contacts you, refer him directly to me. Just go spend some time at a beach somewhere and don't talk with anyone about any of this."

Ted made no response. Apparently none was required because his boss stood up and left without another word. When his escort arrived a few moments later, Ted got up and allowed himself to be shown out of the building.

A beach somewhere. Not a bad idea.

CHAPTER 22

Friday, Jan 31 (Day -69)

John had been back in Albuquerque for most of a week. At work he had limited himself to lectures and finishing up some research projects that didn't require too much concentration. He'd missed two faculty meetings and had three unanswered calls from his department chairman—but he couldn't worry about that now. Any sense of what his life was all about had dissolved in the face of his experiences in Anchor Beach. As for his dreams, which earlier had hit like hammer blows at the same time every morning, now they arrived whenever they choose. He had even canceled a lecture this week, because—while walking along the corridor between his office and the classroom—he became convinced that Titan did indeed have a small rotation: caused by a dynamo running off Saturn's magnetosphere! Better not to talk with his graduate students if that kind of hallucinatory fluff might pop out of his mouth.

John had not talked directly to Bill since returning from Maine. For one thing, the VLA had canceled his Titan observations, so he no longer had any data which justified time on the Computing Center mainframe. He also was wary of drawing attention to Bill.

However, on a late Friday afternoon, he found himself at the Computing Center. The dispatch area, where users picked up their output, was deserted. He glimpsed Bill through the cubicles, separating print jobs as they came off the large laser printer.

John quickly slipped an envelope out of his briefcase, randomly grabbed some discarded printout sheets from a recycle receptacle, and called through the cubicle where his own output was normally filed. "Hey, Bill. Someone else's job was attached to mine."

Bill turned around and slowly came over. Another operator, whom John didn't recognize, came into the room and seemed to be making a show of looking for new output on the laser, even though Bill had already taken it all and the laser was not printing anything new.

Bill, glancing over his shoulder at the other operator, said in a loud voice, "Sorry about that, Professor." Then he grabbed the papers, quickly stuffed them in another cubicle and disappeared into the mainframe room.

Shit. Now his letter was sitting in a bogus clump of papers which didn't even have a header page. If this new "operator" looked, he would find John's incriminating letter in which he warned Bill that the FBI were probably looking for him. Great. John had just laid his Judas hand on Bill's shoulder.

He struggled against the impulse to grab the papers back and instead sat down at a terminal to run a small print job.

A few moments later, Bill came to John's cubicle with the new printout. The vigilant "operator" was suddenly in the room again. John tried to grab the printout from Bill's hands but Bill held it for a moment before pushing it deeper into John's grasp. Feeling something thin and hard inside the papers, John hurriedly wished Bill a good weekend, turned and walked out of the building.

He drove home, not daring to look inside the printout until he had parked in his driveway. His hands trembling, he discovered that the hard object was a thumb drive with the letters, L-G-M, penciled on the label.

He went directly into his den and turned on the computer. While it was booting up, he laid the thumb drive down on his desk and made a quick trip to the washroom.

When he returned, Frankie was in his room, holding the thumb drive. John had to struggle not to holler. He quickly knelt down and took the flash drive away from Frankie. Strangely, Frankie did not object.

John slipped the drive into his computer and copied its contents onto the hard drive. Then he fired up his program, pointed it to the new input file and waited for patterns to appear. He felt tremendous relief when an image finally flashed onto the screen.

Seeing the familiar images, he laughed out loud. There was something absurd about the connection he felt to these jagged lines which in any ordinary sense were completely meaningless. The only meaning that these frequency modulation mappings carried for him was his certainty that they did not belong to any naturally produced radio waves. And, not for the first time, he wondered why these modulations seemed familiar.

Gradually, as he continued to scroll through the contents of Bill's drive, John started to sense that the patterns were in fact not precisely as he remembered them. It was as if they had been spread out and slowed down, like an old 78 record turning at 33 rpm.

But how could that have happened? Had Sullo's gang messed with his program and reset a timing parameter? Was it possible that Bill had rewritten the data in a different format? While going through various possibilities in his mind, he muttered out loud, "This is really strange."

"Uncle Patrick give you." John spun around in his chair and stared at Frankie who was standing beside the desk, smiling. His eyes darted to the corner of his desk: the “LGM” drive that Bill had given him was still lying exactly where he had laid it!

There was a dizzy pounding in his ears as he verified that the flashdrive he had been viewing was the humpback recording that Patrick had given him. And gradually the revelation sank in: humpback whale songs are beaming to Earth from Titan!

"Call Uncle Patrick." John scarcely paused to wonder that he was following the advice of his two-year old son. His fingers felt clumsy on the phone's small keypad as he dialed Hank and Emily's number. It was 4:30 pm in Albuquerque—suppertime in Maine.

"Hello, this is Hank and Emily's residence." It was Patrick's voice.

John threw all caution to the wind. He didn't care if all their phones were bugged. His voice was trembling as the words spilled out. "The Titans and the humpbacks speak the same language! They are talking to each other across a billion miles of space!"

After he finished telling Patrick how the contents of the two drives looked almost identical, all he could hear on the line was his own and his brother's breathing. It was enough. It told him that Patrick was as stunned by this revelation as he had been.

Finally Patrick spoke, "You know what's really strange? We can't speak either language, so knowing that they are the same won't help us decode either one. Two and a half months isn't enough time for us to scratch the surface of what either is saying to the other. It took us decades to read the Dead Sea scrolls, and that was trivial compared to this communication between two non-human species."

John interrupted. "Are you saying that we can't use this information? That we might as well not have found any of this out?"

"No. I'm not saying that. I'm saying I don't think we'll be able to understand this language through any kind of analysis. Believe me, I've banged my head against that wall for a year. We'll continue to be dependent on the whales talking to us in our own language—or whatever it is they do to show us images."

John considered what his brother was saying. As radically contrary as it was to a lifetime confidence in analysis and research, he had to acknowledge the truth of what Patrick was saying. Then, in an equally unfamiliar reversal of his usual indifference to what his brother thought, he heard himself asking, "So what should I do now?" Such a simple question, but even as he asked it he realized that he had not invited anyone's input like that in thirty years. When Patrick started chuckling on the other end of the line, John looked at Frankie and they both smiled.

"The first thing is to tell the authorities that the Titans talk humpback whale language," Patrick told him. "This phone call has already accomplished that. The other thing is to tell everyone about the comet—its exact trajectory, its size, its

ETA. Do you have a program that can plot movements of objects in space?"

This time John laughed. "Funny you should mention that. I've been working all week on that. I already have a pretty decent slide show. It shows how the comet spawned, how it has orbited around the Sun three times in the past 500,000 years, and how in less that three months it will rendezvous with Earth."

Patrick whistled through the phone. "The authorities will want that. Why don't you make an extra back-up while you're waiting for them?"

John continued to listen as Patrick became increasingly enthusiastic about how John's discovery would change everything: ordinary people would be amazed, the scientific community would become passionately involved, and the authorities would finally wake up and do something.

While Patrick was talking, John took out a box of blank CD's and started making back-ups for the FBI. Now and then he interrupted Patrick to ask some practical question or other. Then, as he was completing the backup of his "history and projected impact of a comet with Earth," a question entered his mind that punctured his enthusiasm. "What about the cetaceans?" he blurted out, interrupting Patrick in mid-sentence. "Don't we have to collaborate with them?"

Patrick made no response. He didn't have to. In the silence that followed, John contemplated the bleak prospects for a transformation in human consciousness. If Patrick was right—that a carelessly delivered bomb would shatter the comet into a lethal Armageddon—then human beings needed to learn to accept the guidance of whales.

Patrick and John were still staring into this unthinkable future—now less than ten weeks away—when Leslie stuck her head into John's office and said, "There's an Agent Miller at the door. He says he would appreciate a moment of your time".

CHAPTER 23

Saturday, Feb 1 (Day -68)

The pale light of a quarter moon made the cold night visible, without adding the slightest breath of warmth to the stiff pre-dawn wind at his back. Patrick was glad for the thermos of hot coffee and blanket in his knapsack, and the hooded parka on his back.

As he made his way out to the rock, splashing through a few puddles in his padded mukluks, he felt a quiet exhilaration. Strange. In some ways he was out on the periphery of events—one of billions of people living comfortably beneath the unperturbed heavens. His brother John was much closer to the center of the cataclysm that was about to break out. And that was as it should be—the authorities would obviously much rather deal with a respected scientist than a raving psychic with zero credentials. So let them get everything from John—dealing with John would be unsettling enough for them.

Sometimes Patrick wished he had brought his computer from Montreal. It would be simple for John to send a portion of the Titan file over the Internet as an e-mail attachment. Then he could see with his own eyes the conversation going on between the Titanians and the whales of Earth. But he didn't really need to see it. John's discovery had stunned him on one level, but he had known for a year that the Titanians and the whales were talking to one another. What was amazing was that between John and himself they could now prove it.

Patrick reached the rock and found the crevice where he had fallen asleep—three weeks ago today—then opened his knapsack and took out the blanket and the thermos. He made himself a comfortable nest and poured a cup of hot, milky coffee into the plastic lid of the thermos. Steam rose, luminous in the early dawn light, and a rich smell of coffee mingled with the smells of the sea. He sipped the hot liquid and watched the sun come up over the ocean.

What should he do next? He felt strong, now that he had shed fifty pounds, and he felt more confident than ever before. He must be one of the best-informed people alive, at least about what was going to happen on planet Earth. Surely he had a role to play. Should he go to Florida or San Diego or Hawaii, and make a determined effort to contact a dolphin?

Nothing.

What about Hal Nagen? Was he already playing some central role in all this? Patrick now felt ready to renew his contact with this man, who—if anyone could—seemed most capable of providing some guidance. But where was he?

Patrick's questions did not elicit any inner response. That probably meant he should stay put, and leave things to people with the connections able to impact world affairs. For instance, his brother John had put together a computer-simulation of the comet's trajectory, which he could explain in a vocabulary familiar to other scientists. And perhaps John could convince people to implement the new vision that had been in Patrick's mind when he woke up that morning: how to nudge the comet closer to the Moon so that gravity-assist could slingshot it away from Earth.

Patrick poured himself another cup of coffee and welcomed the morning sun on his shoulders. Sea gulls were whirling far above the water. Every once in a while one would dive and come up with a fish.

He felt relaxed and warm, but there was also a sense of gathering cataclysm, as if enemy bombers were about to cross the peaceful horizon.

Suddenly Patrick knew what he most wanted to do before the world came to an end. He wanted to see his two nephews. It was time for Uncle Patrick to come in from the cold.

Of course, John had not invited him to visit. Well, he could ask. Patrick pushed himself up to standing. It never occurred to him the idea hadn't been his own.

CHAPTER 24

For the past week—ever since John had returned from seeing his brother—Leslie had been on edge. It was no longer just that John was working with a confiscated file—the FBI man had appeared satisfied with whatever John had given him—but their whole family now seemed to be operating in some kind of intuitive quagmire. Sometimes they would all know something and then suddenly realize that none of them had ever said anything out loud.

Leslie popped a tray of chicken nuggets into the oven and turned the heat to 350 degrees. She would much rather have gone out to eat tonight, but with everyone feeling so uncommunicative she knew it would be a mistake. Actually, it was mainly John who was acting remote. So much for her hope that seeing his brother would somehow reconcile John to his own childhood and thereby stimulate him to espouse his role as the father of his own two boys. If anything he and Eric had interacted even less since his return.

She felt tired as she started rummaging through the freezer for a package of green beans.

Eric's voice startled her. "Hey, Mom, what are you doing? It's Saturday night." She looked up to see her son standing in the doorway behind her. To her further surprise, John appeared behind Eric with Frankie's backpack carrier in his hands.

It took her less than a minute to turn off the oven and store the start of supper back in the fridge. Then they headed out on the two-mile walk to Los Ninos, their favorite local family-run Mexican restaurant.

John, who had become a bit obsessive about exercise since being told that his cholesterol readings were too high, stormed ahead with Frankie on his back, arms swinging to shoulder height with each step—while Leslie and Eric continued behind at a slower pace. She listened with mixed feelings as Eric began jabbering about some TV program he had seen the night before. She wasn't interested in the sitcom he was describing, but it was a relief to discover that he would still talk to her at all.

Abruptly Eric stopped in mid-sentence, as if he had become bored, and they walked along in silence for a couple of blocks. Something about Eric's manner made her anxious, but she pushed aside the impulse to ask him what was wrong. Direct questions didn't work with Eric, especially about feelings.

"Montgomery Mid School really sucks," Eric eventually muttered, in a low voice she could barely hear.

Leslie moved closer and said, "Teachers can be blockheads, can't they?"

"They're not as mean as kids can be." Eric shot back. Then he walked in silence for another block. When Eric didn't elaborate, Leslie risked another probe. "Are some of your classmates giving you a hard time? I know that used to happen to me sometimes."

"Melvin Mandler," Eric stated flatly, then added, "If you ask him his name, he says it real fast. 'Melvin Mandler.' Then if you ask him again, he says it even faster."

Leslie had to wait Eric out for another block, but this time he resumed talking on his own. "There were about ten kids standing around Melvin. One jerk said, 'I'm sorry, I don't think I've met you before, what's your name?' So Melvin said his name. Then another jerk said, 'I'm sorry. I didn't catch that. What did you say your name was?' Melvin said it again. More and more kids gathered around. Melvin looked like a mouse cornered by cats."

When Eric didn't talk for another block, Leslie couldn't stop herself from trying to guess what was bothering him. "I bet you would have liked to do something to get everyone off Melvin's back."

Eric shot back, "All he had to say was, 'Screw you! I've already told you my name. Do you need to borrow a Q-tip to clean your ears?' But he just kept answering them, and the other kids just kept getting meaner and meaner. It made me sick."

Eric stopped walking and faced Leslie. "I wasn't laughing or anything, but I was in this crowd—like when two kids are fighting and you just get drawn in. Melvin was really pale, and his face was wet. I felt like I was going to throw up. When I looked at Melvin, he was staring at me. He didn't open his mouth but I heard him as clear as anything, 'Please help me, Eric. I'm going to faint.'"

John and Frankie must have reached a major intersection several blocks further on, because Leslie saw them striding back in their direction, with John's arms still swinging stolidly back and forth.

Eric and Leslie had now stopped walking entirely. Watching John and Frankie bearing down on them from the distance, Leslie suddenly remembered something that had happened years ago. Without thinking, she started telling Eric about it. "A woman with a baby once asked me for some money outside a thrift store. I was in a hurry, so I pretended I didn't hear her. Then later I couldn't get her out of my mind. I even went back to look for her, but she wasn't there."

Eric might not have heard his mother's confession, as he continued with his story. "I tried to tell him some one-liners he could throw back at them. Things like I already told you. But Melvin fell on the ground kicking and squirming. The kids who had been acting the meanest split really fast. But I couldn't move."

John and Frankie reached where they were standing. "Aren't you guys hungry?"

Leslie knew Eric would talk more freely with just her there, so she said, "Go ahead and get us a table. We'll meet you there."

John seemed relieved and strode off in the direction of the restaurant again, his arms bobbing up and down like oilrig pistons. Leslie immediately returned to the scene in the schoolyard. "I sure wouldn't know what to do with a kid having a fit."

Leslie was amazed to hear that Eric had experienced a telepathic communication with another kid at school. As the only one in the family who didn't have these kind of experiences, she was dying to learn more about it, but she was even more concerned about how Eric had handled this situation on an ordinary human level, and how he was feeling about himself as a result. She tried to bring the conversation back to this perspective. "Did a teacher come and help out?"

Eric put his hand against the roof of a car, as if he needed the support, before continuing. "I couldn't see anything or hear anything. It was like I was trapped inside his mind while he was weirding out. I couldn't have got through it on my own."

Leslie couldn't prevent herself from interrupting, "You weren't alone? I mean, it doesn't sound like Melvin would have been much of a support to you at that moment."

Eric looked almost embarrassed as he answered. "It was really strange, but I could feel someone else there. It made me less afraid. Anyway, I'm starved. What are you going to order?"

And before Leslie could find out anything more, Eric was expressing impatience that they weren't closer to the restaurant. She would love to have learned more about what had happened, but Eric's uncharacteristic openness had passed, and she had to hurry to keep up with him.

CHAPTER 25

Los Ninos, John's favorite restaurant, was always crowded at meal times. Tonight there were about ten people ahead of them waiting to be seated, but the line moved quickly and Frankie, perched high in the back pack, was in a talkative mood. With the exception of one man sitting alone at a window table next to the front entrance, Frankie was charming everyone. The strange thing is that Frankie kept trying to talk with this solitary man, calling him 'Billy', even though his efforts elicited an icy stare.

Leslie and Eric arrived and their party of four was led to a table in the inner of the restaurant's two dining rooms. Within minutes the waitress brought water glasses, silverware and—John's favorite—made-on-the-premises salsa and tortilla chips. She immediately pulled her order pad out and John ordered chicken enchiladas with green chili, Leslie the combination plate, Eric a bean tostada with no onions or chili, and for Frankie a chicken taco with no salsa. Since it was Saturday night, John and Leslie ordered beers.

The drinks arrived quickly but they only had time for a few sips before the waitress was back with the food, which she laid out with the refrain, used in all authentic New Mexican restaurants, "Careful, the plates are very hot."

Everyone except Leslie dug in. She poured Frankie's milk into a sipper cup, which she produced from her purse, then took another drink from her Corona bottle. John, already well through his plate, swallowed a mouthful of food, and said, "Aren't you hungry?"

"I'm thinking of what Eric talked about on the way here."

John laid down his fork with a sigh and glanced at Eric. Eric was plowing through his tostada, seemingly oblivious to everything else. Why is everything always tottering on some sort of emotional brink? Why can't we just go out and enjoy our food? Out loud, he said, "What did Eric have to say?"

Leslie filled him in on the incident with Melvin Mandler and John quickly forgot about his half-eaten food. Listening to his wife, he felt as if he himself had been transported to the schoolyard; and by the time Leslie finished talking, he felt completely stunned. When John glanced at his oldest son, he saw that Eric had finished his tostada and was staring off into space.

John cleared his throat—but that apparently only worked with graduate students. He knew he should say something—that Leslie expected it—so he turned to Eric and said, "Your Mom says you had an unusual experience at school."

Eric muttered something without looking away from the window and a sudden flood of emotion rose up in John. Unable to control himself, he heard his own agitated voice saying, "If you have the ability to hear someone else's thoughts then that isn't some video game you're playing. You need to take it seriously, Eric. Don't you understand what's going on?"

"No, he doesn't." Leslie snapped. "How could he understand what's going on? You haven't told him anything. Why don't you tell Eric something about what happened with Patrick? Why don't you tell me, for that matter?"

John didn't know how to respond. What Leslie said was completely true. He was the one who wasn't following through. He was the one who was failing to change how he acted. Drawing deep within himself, he managed to mutter an apology, and to his amazement Eric turned away from the window and said, "It's OK, Dad. I guess none of us really know what's going down here." Feeling moved, John wanted to say something but didn't know how. He managed to nod to Eric and offer a sheepish smile.

For some time Frankie had been restless but now he actually climbed down from his booster chair and headed for the front door. Welcoming the call to action, John looked at Eric and said, "Duty calls" then took off after Frankie. Frankie had already reached the outer dining room by the time John caught up with him. John noticed that the restaurant had already started to thin out. The owner had hung up the CLOSED sign and there was a key in the inside of the locked front door. He also noticed that the sour-faced man was just getting up from his table next to the front entrance. Actually, it was Frankie who noticed—trying yet again to get a smile out of the guy.

John corralled his son, then went back to their table, handed a squirming Frankie over to Leslie, glanced at the check and pulled out his wallet. He was about to pick up the check and head for the front cash register, when he realized that the restaurant seemed unnaturally quiet. Glancing over his shoulder, John saw the sour-faced man standing on the other side of the wide archway that separated the two dining rooms. He was turning in circles, as if he thought he was being attacked from all sides. As he turned, the gun in his left hand whipped across the restaurant.

As his frantic gaze swept across their table, John felt the man's mental state—like food that has gone rancid. Still turning in all directions, the man started shouting. "Everyone stay real quiet. Then no one needs to get hurt. If anyone makes a sudden move I'm going to have to put a bullet in his head. Now you all enjoy your meal. I really don't like to see people waste food."

The restaurant remained quiet, but now you could actually hear the clink of forks as customers pretended to lift mouthfuls of food off their plates. The look on Leslie's face impressed John more deeply than the man with the gun.

For a few more moments they could hear pots banging and water running. Then abruptly all kitchen sounds stopped.

Suddenly the man with the gun dashed into the other room, towards the counter where the cash register was kept. They heard him shouting. "Keep your hands on the counter or I'll blow your brains all over the fucking wall." Then they heard the owner's much quieter voice. "Please. Please. Take whatever you want."

John glanced at Leslie. She was deathly pale.

Suddenly Frankie started talking. "Birthday. Happy birthday." In the silent room, it really stood out. Leslie, John and Eric all hissed at the same time, but Frankie started bouncing up and down on the padded chair, chanting, "Happy birthday! Happy birthday!"

To their horror, the gunman appeared in the opening between the restaurant's two dining rooms. The gun, gripped fiercely in his left hand, remained aimed back towards the cash register, while he and Frankie looked intently at one another.

With a low wail, Leslie stood up and tried to lift Frankie off the chair on which he was now standing. But Frankie clung tenaciously to the edge of the table. Sounding like a hawk caught in a trap, the gunman screamed. "Get back in your seat, lady! Now!"

"Leslie," John whispered, "Leave Frankie where he is. We have to let this guy get whatever he wants." Leslie let her hands slip off Frankie and sat back in her chair. The gunman acknowledged the wisdom of that move, almost as if he felt friendly towards her. "Thank you very much, lady. You have a lovely son and I earnestly hope he will be alive when I leave here. I once had a son, but that fucking bitch stole him."

Suddenly he whirled back towards the cash register and raised his pistol up and sighted along the barrel. "You make another move you mother-fucker and, and . . ."

"Happy birthday. Happy birthday. Happy birthday to you."

The gunman whirled back to Frankie. He took a few steps into their room—as far as he could while still keeping the cash register in his range of sight. "What did you say, kid?"

Frankie immediately responded. "Your birthday."

"How the hell do you know that?" The gunman shot back. But Frankie wouldn't be stopped. "Happy birthday, Billy. Happy birthday, Billy." The gunman's left hand, still holding the gun, came down to his side—and Frankie wouldn't let it go. "Mommy, Daddy, Eric—sing."

John started to experience whatever it was that Frankie was picking up. He struggled against having his mind invaded —knowing the importance of remaining alert to the great physical danger they were all in. But, as if he couldn't help himself, he let himself go into Frankie's mental space and, in a voice that was at first weak and off key, he began to sing. "Happy Birthday to you. Happy Birthday to you."

No one else joined in. Not surprising, really. John felt a moment of panic as he caught a glimpse in Leslie's eyes of the insanity of his behavior. He looked at the gunman, expecting to see a deranged beast who had only been momentarily distracted. To John's amazement, he saw instead a man who seemed to have tears in his eyes, his gun hand dangling limply against his leg.

John whispered to Leslie and Eric. "Sing!" Leslie's mouth looked like it was glued shut, but Eric, his voice sounding like a squeaky wheelbarrow, joined in. "Happy birthday, dear Billy."

The gunman—Billy, apparently—looked like he might drop the pistol onto the floor. He had completely turned his back on the other room and on the entrance to the restaurant. If there had been anyone trained in how to disarm a man with a gun, they could surely have had him on the floor by now. But no one moved.

John continued to sing as he stood and moved away from their table. Waving his hands in time with the song, he looked pointedly at the faces which stared back at him from the other tables. A few brave souls dutifully responded. There was one elderly woman, sitting at a table where everyone else looked terrified, who actually started clapping her arthritic hands in a semblance of rhythm. Behind him, he heard Frankie's voice continuing undaunted, "Birthday, Billy birthday," not particularly in time with anyone else.

John was now standing close enough to Billy that it would have been simple to reach out and take the gun that dangled limply at his side. He made no move to do so, whether out of fear that the situation could change in a flash, or because he was being drawn into the man's private hell, he couldn't have said.

The singing ground to a halt, there not being a huge amount of irrepressible joviality behind it. Silence filled the room and John—a reluctant actor—had forgotten his lines, on which he realized the whole drama turned. Then suddenly they came back to him, and he was talking to the room in a loud voice. "Today is Bill's birthday. Let's all contribute a dollar so he can have a birthday present from us."

No one responded.

John took out his wallet, extracted a dollar bill, and held it up. A few men tilted sideways on their chairs as they dug in their back pockets. Gradually everyone in the room was digging out dollar bills from purses and billfolds. Some of them just grabbed the first bill their fingers touched, unheeding of whether it might be a $1 or a $50, as John went around the room gathering together the handfuls of money. When he had something from most of the tables, he asked the owner to unlock the front door. The owner stammered that the keys were already in the door and didn't budge from behind the cash register.

John moved a step closer to Bill and held out the wad of money. The room was completely silent. His arm started to feel like lead, as Bill made no move to accept the cash. Finally Bill did move: he slowly raised the revolver until it was aiming at John's chest. John forced himself to hold the man's eyes.

Then, in the silence of John's mind, someone started talking to Bill. They spoke with confidence and conviction, while John stood there mute and trembling. "Bill, your birthday would be a good day to lay aside that gun. You can live the next 31 years of your life in a new way."

As if in confirmation of his willingness to trust the words that were arising, John started understanding what was going on for Bill. He saw the abusive home life that had deposited Bill on the streets at the age of 14. Then a decade of growth, a wife and son, a job selling appliances. He had got himself off drugs and had achieved some freedom from the angry voices in his head. Then his marriage had turned bad and he had lost his son.

Birthdays were not good for Bill. After a party held on his seventh birthday, Bill had angered his father by boasting about how many presents he had received. His father's response had been to make Bill lay them all on the table. Then his father had slowly destroyed every one of them, making his son stand at attention while he did so.

With a fierceness that a year of therapy had been unable to achieve, John wanted all those years of Eric's childhood back.

Still looking into Bill's eyes, John willed himself to think, "You see, you can hear me and I can hear you. Let's try to cut your losses. Do you want to do that?"

"No."

The message behind that single word, spoken out loud, was beyond debate: Bill didn't have a single positive thing going for him in life.

Refusing to give up, John told Bill about the comet, the whales and dolphins, and the aliens. He explained that it was somehow through the Titanians that he and Bill were able to communicate now, and it was through them that Frankie had known it was Bill's birthday. That seemed to catch Bill's interest. John urged him to lay down his gun. They'd walk out of the restaurant together—no harm done. For a moment it seemed that Bill might actually do it. John could feel the man's mind softening.

But then the police came in through the kitchen with their guns drawn. "Freeze! Both of you! You, drop the gun! You, drop the money!" With numbing shock, John knew that there weren't any bullets, and never had been any bullets in the revolver that Bill had bought that afternoon at a local gun shop. Bill turned slowly towards the two policemen and started to draw a bead on the one who had spoken. Four shots rang out, two from each officer's gun.

Male voices seemed to be coming from the other side of a thick pane of glass. "Drop the money, now." John didn't struggle against the loss of consciousness. As Bill's mind turned dark, John let his own body crumple to the floor. Perhaps the Lord of Death had come for both of them.

When consciousness returned, John found himself lying on his back. He was surrounded by people, their legs towering above him. He could hear the owner, now quite composed, explaining everything to the police officers.

One of the policemen, very young, knelt down beside John — "Hey, man, no problem. Take it easy. You did good." He got up quickly and disappeared from John's vision. From their brief contact, John knew that this young officer had never before killed a man. The discovery that the dead man's gun was empty had thrown him into a deep pain he was having trouble facing.

John got to his feet. The body, lying on the carpet in the midst of a large stain, seemed to call out to him to follow into the shadows. He wrenched his eyes away with a shudder of fear.

Customers were being led out of the restaurant. A few snatched a glance at the corpse, but most could not quickly enough escape into the night.

Then he felt Leslie collapse into his arms. As they stood there, plastered together like two wet leaves, John realized that she had gone through much of what he had gone through. He heard her silent, agonized protest. "He had no bullets!"

Without the need for any kind of utterance—neither verbal nor mental—they quietly understood that something was shifting into a higher gear—both for their family and for the world.

CHAPTER 26

Monday, February 3 (Day -66)

Well, Georgie Boy, I believe we have a wrap. George Ball switched off his computer, stood up, stretched, and then did a back flip. Not many guys could do that after sitting at a computer for two hours. He felt good. Really good. His dream was about to be realized. A year of incredibly dedicated work, with at most a few hours sleep a night, was about to culminate in an unprecedented test-in-action. No wimpy half measures for Georgie Boy's brainchild. Bring on the real live comet, gentleman. Scheduled launch time, weather permitting, was this Friday!

It was way past midnight when George left the BallMaker building. He felt so good that he smiled at the security guards as he walked through the metal detector. "Good night, Sir." They responded in unison. A pair of pet ducks, if ever there was.

George drove quickly through the deserted streets until he reached his apartment building near Dupont Circle in downtown Washington. As he was walking through security, the guard said, "Your brother left you a message, Mr. Ball."

What a jerk. He gets your name right, and then starts blathering about some non-existent brother. George collected his mail on his way to the stairwell. He lived on the 18th floor but no one would ever catch him inside one of those mousetraps on a string. He took four stairs at a time, in an easy stride that allowed him to open his mail as he ran. Bills, junk mail, a couple of dividend checks, and one envelop addressed by hand to a George Nagen.

George stopped running and glanced at the sheath of handwritten pages. On the first page, he read, "I believe you are my brother."

He swore under his breath, ran up the three remaining flights at a sprint, ran down the hall, unlocked all three deadbolts, opened the door and slipped inside. Closing and locking the door behind him, he punched in his alarm code, then allowed his breath to return to near-silence before walking stealthily into the dark kitchen. As usual, his senses prickled, on the alert for any unusual sound or smell.

He set his mail down on the kitchen counter—everything but the handwritten letter. The city glow seeping under the balcony door curtains was more than enough light to read by. For a fleeting instant he felt an impulse to look at this letter again. The name, "Nagen," was well known to him. Instead he ripped the pages into pieces and stuffed them into his kitchen trashcan. Then he continued through the kitchen into the dining room alcove.

"I have a copy." A man's voice, like a chain saw ripping into the silence.

George whirled to his left. In the dim light he saw him—sitting in an armchair in the corner. George left the light off—his night vision was legendary—and in three quick strides he moved to the center of his living room. Facing the intruder from ten feet away, he went into a crouch and waited.

One thing was clear: this must be the author of that letter. How had this asshole got past his alarm? A curious man might let him live a few more minutes, in order to find out who he was. But maybe he would just change the alarm code and not worry about who he was. Except then he would probably always wonder how he had got in. Better find out a few things, before breaking his neck. And since he needed to talk with this guy anyway, maybe he could solve a few other puzzles while he was at it.

"How did you get in here?"

The stranger—he looked as relaxed as a cat in that chair, even though he was built more like a rugby player—responded. "I took a guess on the code. I used Dad's birthday."

George had to fight off the impulse to snap that lying asshole's neck then and there. His hands seized into such tight knots that he had to back away toward the far side of the room. He took his eyes away from the stranger for only the instant needed to step around a hassock in front of the couch. But when he looked back at the armchair in the corner of the room, it was empty.

George froze. His eyes picked up no flicker of movement, as he spun around and scanned the rest of the room. Running up 18 flights had scarcely raised his heartbeat, but now his pulse was pounding in his ears. He felt an impulse to fall onto his belly and begin searching in corners. But instead he kicked off his shoes and ran silently through the rooms—like a heat-seeking missile whose target has no escape. Yet the stranger was not anywhere. George raced back into the living room and there he was again, sitting in the same relaxed posture.

"You're a hard guy to talk to, George. I came here hoping that we could talk about a few things. But now I'd settle for anything. Its obvious you aren't open to any real conversation."

This time George wasn't going to take his eyes off him for a second. Like his "Intruder Interception" system. Closer. Yes. Smooth as silk. Weight centered, both feet ready to launch in any direction. That's good. Close enough. Now!

George struck. His fingers tore through the skin of his prey and tore out guts. But it was cotton stuffing from the back of the chair that he squeezed in his steely grip.

"Forget about being brothers, then, since it upsets you so much to think about it. We still need to talk, George. I need to know what you think you're doing with this tracking system of yours. You do realize that it's not your private toy, don't you?"

George tried to spin in the direction of the voice—which seemed to come from very close to the back of his head—but he couldn't move. When he forced himself to turn a few inches, an agonizing stab tore through his right arm all the way from his fingers to his shoulder.

The voice continued. "I'm sorry that this is the only way we can talk. But having you try to kill me definitely puts limits on the kind of conversation we can have. Let me ask you once more: if I let you go, will you let me say a few things to your face? I'm willing to answer any question you ask me. Anything. I'll hold nothing back."

George put all his force into the spin, willing to tear every ligament and muscle in the right side of his body, in order to get his left hand on the guy's jugular. Amazingly he spun without any resistance and stood face-to-face with the stranger. He almost lost his balance but recovered immediately and stood on the balls of his feet, the offending face within striking distance.

Something made him hesitate. Was it doubt that the face would still be there when he struck? Was it astonishment that another human being had actually beaten him? Or was there a tiny vestige of curiosity about what this man could tell him? In any case, George felt his body slowly back away.

"Thank you." The stranger didn't move as he spoke. "I appreciate this. I know that you don't want me to stay here for more than a few minutes, so let me offer you three alternatives. I can tell you a bit about our personal past. I can tell you something about the process through which you receive the ideas for your "Intruder Interception" tracking system. Or, I can tell you about the evolution going on in our solar system right now—in which you and I have an important role to play."

George knew he probably had to let the guy say something before he would leave. What would be the least dangerous choice? Maybe if he kept the conversation on Georgie Boy's agenda, he could actually find out something useful. Whoever this guy was, he seemed to know his ass from his elbow. Maybe almost good enough to be a brother. But he wasn't about to talk about all that. No thanks. Georgie Boy had no parents, no brothers. His mother had died in childbirth and he had grown up in a series of orphanages and foster homes. End of story. Even if some asshole claimed to have had the same father, of what fucking use was that to him? Just because Georgie Boy had found out his birth father's name (Nagen) and birthday (used in his six digit alarm code)—acting on an obsessive urge he didn't understand—that didn't give anyone the right to claim kinship. Georgie Boy had no kin. It was the central fact of his existence.

"I'll ask you a question," George began. "You just be sure you don't slip in any bullshit in your answer. OK, my discoveries come in big bursts. But don't you try to tell me that they come from someone else. All brilliant scientists have visions, OK?"

The stranger nodded, then returned to stillness.

"So, I get these visions and then I make them real. Do you have a problem with that?"

What the fuck was he doing? He didn't have any questions for this asshole. That was the total story. This guy needed to get the hell out of here—now!

"What you have succeeded in making real is truly phenomenal," the stranger said, without moving from where he stood. "If anyone says you didn't do it yourself, then they don't know you. But there's one little problem, isn't there?"

The rage that had become George's constant companion couldn't turn away—as if some undisclosed hunger lurked at the edges of consciousness. The stranger continued. "The problem is that you get more than visions about scientific breakthroughs. You also get visions of writhing serpents that want to make you do things. They tell you how you need to use your discoveries, don't they? These days they are telling you that you must not hit this comet directly with a bomb."

George couldn't stop himself from shouting back. "No one tells me how to use my system. My system will deliver the President's fucking bomb. And the whole world is going to know about it!"

The stranger was talking again. "The whole world is depending on your system. I know your system can deliver a bomb. But it must deliver it in the right way at the right time. You won't ever have a moment of peace if you don't listen to me now. When you experience your vision of serpents, that's when the Titanians are talking to you. If you listen to what they are telling you, then your nightmares will go away."

"Stop!" George heard his own voice screaming. "You're my fucking nightmare. And I know how to make you go away."

He'd read it somewhere. A story about how confronting a hallucination with some internal inconsistency made it disappear. George walked into his bedroom and withdrew a loaded Lugar from a drawer in his nightstand. Then he turned around and saw that the stranger had followed him. Good. He raised the revolver to his own temple.

"I know I can't hit you. Because you don't really exist. But since you claim I have an important destiny, let's see if you really believe it. If you don't leave my apartment right now, I'm going to blow my brains out."

Might not be a bad idea actually. It would be a shame to miss the fireworks next month, but a man has to draw the line somewhere. Writhing serpents were one thing—because George knew they weren't real—but a ghost claiming to be his brother, that definitely didn't fit in with his life plan.

George pulled back the firing pin and began to slowly put pressure on the trigger.

"No! I'm going!" The ghost moved to the front door—too fast to be real. Then it took the time to unlock the dead bolts, before slipping out into the hallway. Now that was a class act. Just maybe, George might let this ghost in again sometime. A ghost claiming to be a long lost brother might actually be better than a pit of vipers, who threatened to never leave if Georgie didn't do their bidding. At least this Mr. Nagen Jr. could take a hint. At least he knew enough to leave when he wasn't wanted.

But ghost or no, no one was going to turn Georgie's bomb off. Once it was off the ground on Friday, no one would be able to turn it off. It had been a good idea to pull out that cable. Wouldn't want some tricky ghost fooling Georgie Boy into sending the wrong code up, now would we? And if it wasn't a ghost, then he had to worry about that wimpy President—who always leaned whatever way he thought would make him most popular with the most people. Yes, yes. Sometimes old Georgie Boy knew what he was doing. This time he had beat the hallucinations at their own game.

George felt so good that, a few minutes later, when he walked through the kitchen and felt the impulse to look for the letter in the trashcan, he walked on by—really not giving a damn. Nothing could destroy his hold on reality. He knew who he was. Let the images rain down, George Ball knew how to stay dry inside.

CHAPTER 27

Wednesday, Feb 5 (Day -64)

Ted never made it to the beach. First thing Monday morning a call from his boss's secretary had ordered him to remain in the Washington area, and now—early on a Wednesday morning—a phone call he had been tempted not to answer announced that a limo would pick him up at 8:00 a.m. He hung up the phone and glanced at his watch: 7:40 a.m.

He showered, shaved and dressed in record time and was waiting at the front door of his condo when the agency driver rang.

Director Todd himself, seated in the back of the car, motioned for Ted to take a seat across from him. "You really managed to piss everyone off," his boss growled, without so much as a good morning. "They're saying the Murphy's have contaminated your judgment." Then he leaned forward, looked directly at Ted and said, "Do you have any idea what this morning's meeting is about?"

Ted shook his head.

"Think Galileo."

Galileo. Wasn't that the name of a probe orbiting Jupiter? Then, in a flash it fit together in Ted's mind. They had spotted the comet—using the Galileo probe—and now they were suddenly less picky about whom they invited to their meetings.

Unable to repress his excitement, Ted exclaimed, "So they turned Galileo around and found the comet!" Then, sensing that he had just stolen his boss's thunder, he quickly added, "How did Galileo know where to look?"

Director Todd frowned. "That's an interesting story. Let's just say that your pal, Professor Murphy, drew them a picture. You'll hear a lot more about it this morning."

Director Todd stared out the window at the passing traffic for a while, before turning back to Ted. "Your astronomer friend has been acting pretty strangely. One of our agents followed the Murphy family into a restaurant this past weekend. An hour later, some weirdo is dead and our agent's report sounds like an X-files episode. Care to guess what happened?"

Ted shrugged, but Director Todd wasn't looking for a response. "Our agent says their two year-old kid read the weirdo's mind and then the professor got everybody singing. To make a long story mercifully short, the police came in through the kitchen, shot the guy, and our seasoned agent is now on professional leave. Permanently. According to the shrink, he thinks someone is talking inside his head."

Ted was dying to ask questions, but was afraid to expose too strong an interest. Both men remained silent as the limo made its way through increasingly narrow streets.

They pulled into an underground garage in a nondescript building and Director Todd quickly led them to a small conference room on the second floor. Entering the room, Ted saw four people seated around an oval table, their chairs all pointing towards a modern-looking viewing system with a 60" screen. Ted recognized Phil Black and his sidekick, the snake. Also present were a man who was unfamiliar and a woman whom he definitely recognized.

The Chief of Staff invited Ted and his boss to take vacant seats and the lights immediately dimmed.

In the darkness, Phil Black's voice rang out sharply. "Some of you have already seen this, and some of you haven't. Keep in mind that no one knows where this stuff really comes from, and it may just be a lot of bullshit designed to confuse us. But the President of the United States is taking it seriously and so we need to study this material very carefully. I've asked Henry to give us a blow-by-blow. Sorry we don't have any popcorn."

The large projection screen briefly came to life with a snowy image, then it turned black again. Or almost black. As Ted sat in the silent, darkened room, staring at the silent, dark screen, he gradually became aware that there were little white dots here and there. As he continued to watch, the dots turned into small, moving balls of light. They reminded him of molecules of gas bouncing around in a container, except that these little balls just sailed out of the picture, replaced by other little balls sailing in.

The screen had a rectangle in the upper right-hand corner with a number in it: 5,000,000. Outside the rectangle there were two letters: BC. After awhile he noticed that this number was decreasing: 4,990,000, 4,980,000, 4,970,000—10,000 shaved off every few seconds.

A man's voice—presumably Henry's—started up in the darkness. "That little rectangle is a date counter. You can see that it started with the year 5,000,000 BC. The dots represent comets flying around in the Oort Cloud. For those of you who don't know what that is—an astronomer named Oort developed the hypothesis that a spherical cloud of comets, left over from the earliest days of the solar system, encircles our Sun about a third of a light year out. The Oort Cloud is too far away to see directly with earth-based telescopes. That's why we call it an hypothesis."

With this recognition—that he was looking at the undulations of comets in the Oort Cloud—Ted felt himself being drawn in. He imagined himself floating in the midst of drifting hunks of ice—each so distant from one another that any sort of contact was rare and fleeting. Now and then he glanced at the date counter. Every 100,000 years or so, one comet would slowly catch up to another comet, like two hikers meeting in the Himalayas. Some kind of mutual attraction would develop in the midst of all that vast emptiness. They would become a twosome, strolling along shoulder to shoulder through time and space.

At first, Ted noticed the inadequacies of the software that had created these thousands of programmed comet-dots, but gradually his mind became increasingly able to fill in missing details. He increasingly felt as if he himself was floating in the vastness of deep space.

Henry's voice continued. "Now we're coming up to 3,000,000 years ago. See how the picture is zooming in on two larger objects? Now watch. Look how those two clusters come together. There! See how the whole conglomeration suddenly rounds out into a single spherical shape? It has to be at least several hundred miles across to do that."

Ted looked on with mounting excitement. As the perspective widened again to include thousands of dots of light, he managed to keep track of the large spherical object.

Not much changed for the next 1,000,000 years, and Henry let the images speak for themselves. Then the perspective gradually widened, until it was possible to see both the Sun and a neighboring star.

Henry picked up his narrative. "What we're seeing here is that about two million years ago a neighboring star approached our own solar system. In a moment, the image will focus in again and you'll be able to see the effect this has on the Oort Cloud."

Sure enough, when the perspective narrowed down to the field of comets, it was obvious that waves were running through the Oort cloud like heavy sea crossing broken ice. The comets rose and fell and collided—some of them fragmenting and some of them climbing on top of their companions and staying there.

The large comet—which had now become the star of this film—started to fall. It fell right out of the Oort Cloud and didn't turn back. And surprisingly, a second, even larger comet, perhaps a mere hundred million miles or so away, fell out of the nest at about the same time.

Over the next 500,000 years, these two comets slowly drew closer and closer to one another, and eventually started to orbit around one another. At that point Henry resumed his narrative. "These two objects are both far more massive than any comet observed in historical times. They are both hundreds of kilometers in diameter. Compare that to the ten-kilometer diameter of the asteroid thought to have killed the dinosaurs. As for the difference between comets and asteroids, you'll soon see that they can look the same."

The two monster comets were about halfway to the outer planets when they started their slow waltz. Because one of them was more massive, it looked as if the smaller comet was very slowly getting sucked into a drain, of which its larger companion was the center.

The calendar in the upper right hand corner of the screen now showed about 500,000 BC. It took another 200,000 years for this pair of comets to reach the outermost planets. As they approached Jupiter, gas jets started to erupt from both comets. Henry picked up the thread. "The first material to volatilize is methane. Once they're inside the orbit of Venus, water vapor will join in. Inside Mercury's orbit, even rocks start melting."

As the comet pair swung around the Sun, accelerating constantly all the way, Ted's hand reached up and unbuttoned the top collar of his shirt, as if he was himself baking in the fierce heat of the Sun. Then they started their flight out through the planets once more. With the inner solar system to provide a measure, it seemed that the larger of these two comets was comparable in size to a small moon.

On the way back out, the pair passed within a few million miles of Uranus. It was clear that this slowed them down. This time they only made it about a quarter of the way back to the Oort Cloud before falling in towards the Sun once more.

On their second pass through the planets, the venting of gases was at first much more restrained. Henry explained. "Most of the methane close to the surface has already been vaporized, so you can see that it's only now, as they pass inside the orbit of Venus, that they really start spewing again."

Sure enough, the comets turned into Catherine wheels, reeling through space with their gigantic, high-pressure fire hoses open full nozzle.

Passes three through six were much the same.

Then came the seventh pass through the inner solar system. When the pair of cometary bodies rounded the Sun for the seventh time, the calendar had reached 7,000 BC. The film slowed down now, as if out of respect for the human beings who must have been looking out from planet Earth, awestruck by the cometary blades slashing across their heaven.

Henry commented on the familiarity of the twin forms that now emblazoned the screen. "We don't know where Murphy got any of this, but these two swastikas are possible profiles for comets with multiple jets. Four equatorial, evenly distributed jets spewing off a rapidly spinning comet would probably look like this."

Henry stopped talking as the two comets continued to slash through the blackness. After a minute or two he added in a quiet voice, "Watch what happens next."

Ted gasped. The smaller comet was suddenly flying away from the Sun, alone. The larger comet had plunged straight into the belly of Venus. Massive internal hemorrhaging erupted as thousands of volcanic vents opened on the second planet from the Sun.

The film followed the remaining comet as it swept out to the third planet, her beautiful blue face unperturbed by the horror rending the body of her sister. The date continued to blink in the upper left-hand corner. It was 6976 BC.

Surely the peoples of Earth would have recorded these events. Deeply affected, Ted kept asking himself—could that really have happened to Venus at a time when humans were already writing and drawing? Could Venus have been turned into an inferno within historical times, just 9,000 years ago?

The film continued tracking the bereaved comet, changing perspective as needed to provide a context for its elliptical path away from the Sun. The surviving comet continued to vent small quantities of gas all the way to Jupiter. Henry commented that probably traces of methane were still being brought to the surface by traumatic venting of water vapor closer to the Sun, and that this methane then vaporized on the trip back out.

The solitary comet continued out past all the planets, slowing down more and more as it entered the cold, dark outer reaches of the solar system, billions of miles away from the Sun. But this time—probably because of its close encounter with Venus—the remaining cometary body was far closer to Uranus than the Oort cloud when it came to a stop and then slowly began its plunge back into the region of the Sun.

There were four more passes around the Sun during the next seven thousand years. When the counter reached zero, Henry pointed out that the letters "BC" had changed to "AD" and that the number was now counting up towards the present.

Another uneventful pass followed. By now there was not much venting, certainly no whirling swastikas.

Ted felt a painful tension in his neck and shoulders as the comet fell among the outer planets once more. By the time the comet was approaching Saturn again, Ted had already been born. All surface gases (Methane and water) must have been consumed in previous passes, because there wasn't any cometary train discernible as the comet fell toward the Sun, crossing the orbits of Mars, Earth, Venus and Mercury.

Ted wondered if anyone observing it for the first time would call it a comet. He visualized a giant baseball, hundreds of kilometers across—its rocky core still surrounded by volatile ices—but now wrapped in a mantle of the dust and dirt left behind after the expulsion of surface gases during previous passes.

Just before the comet slung around the Sun, the counter moved through the present and into the future. The comet was about to become visible from Earth, after several weeks eclipsed by the Sun.

A new planet had been born with no planet's orbit of its own—a barbarian outsider with nothing to lose. The counter remained frozen on the present year, but now another rectangle appeared. Inside was written: Feb 5. This date started advancing—Feb 6, Feb 7, Feb 8. As time moved into the future, the rogue planet swept past the orbits of Mercury and Venus. During a viewing period of about 10 minutes the date counter moved into April.

Abruptly, another insert appeared on the screen. It showed a close-up of Earth with the Moon orbiting around her.

The next five minutes seemed to take forever. The wider of the two perspectives unfolded with a horrifying kind of clarity. It was like watching an expert billiard shot in slow motion where, long before impact, the mind senses that two particular balls are heading straight for each other.

Inside the insert, the Earth and its Moon waited, a mother sheep and its lamb tethered in the yard of an abattoir.

Then suddenly the predator was inside the pen. At first, with the higher resolution of the insert image, it was possible to imagine that the comet would miss Earth after all. But then the Moon's gravity reached out. The comet was tugged inward by a degree or two and free fell for 200,000 miles in this altered direction. By the time it approached Earth, it was several thousand miles closer than it would have been. More than close. The comet plunged straight into the belly of Earth.

Ted couldn't be sure later whether he had heard a scream at the moment of impact. And he couldn't have said whether it was his or another's voice that he might have heard.

The image of molten material, exploding outward in a horrendous spume, disappeared. Ted felt a mixture of horror and relief as he sat in the darkness.

But the film didn't end there. After a few moments, an image returned to the screen. They were back in the great openness of space. The comet was still on the far side of the Sun, approaching as before.

A groan of protest rose. No one wanted to watch the last 30 minutes over again. But it wasn't a democracy, and Phil Black growled, "It's a different movie this time. Henry, tell us how it's different."

Henry got up and went and stood to the right of the viewing screen. He pulled a retractable pointer from his coat jacket and extended it. As soon as the insert popped up on the screen—this time at an earlier point in time—Henry pointed to a tiny ball in the lower right portion. "This is Earth. See this little spot of orange leaving the surface? That's meant to be a rocket." Then the tip of his pointer shifted to the larger, inclusive image. "You can see that the comet is still close to the Sun. What will happen in a few moments is that the insert will take over the entire screen. At that point, the picture will have a diagonal of only 60 million miles. You'll see the rocket travel from Earth—which is situated in the lower right corner—towards the upper left corner. Shortly before the rocket reaches the edge, the comet will enter the screen just in front of it."

Henry stood silently until the rocket and the comet could be seen approaching one another in the upper left corner of the picture. He remained silent until comet and rocket had arced toward one another, met, and an explosion had occurred.

"Now watch carefully." Henry continued. "What just happened is that the comet was nudged very slightly. Just enough so that it passes on the other side of the Moon. Since the comet is still 60 million miles away from the Moon at this point, it didn't take much of a nudge to aim it 2000 miles more to the left. Actually, a lot of us at NASA think this is a pretty good idea—provided that the comet really is on the path depicted here."

It didn't take long to recognize that the comet's path had been affected. As Henry had predicted, this time the comet passed behind the Moon (in the wake of its orbit), instead of in front of it. The difference was crucial. Now the Moon acted to pull the comet away from its path into Earth, and the deadly sphere swept past—like a torpedo passing across the bow of an ocean liner.

The film ended abruptly, bright lights came on, and Phil Black barked out, "Washrooms are down the hall. I want everyone sitting around this table in 10 minutes, ready to stay here for the next three hours."

Then he strode out of the room, without the slightest acknowledgement of the experience they had all just endured.

CHAPTER 28

Ted availed himself of the restroom, then returned to the viewing room and poured himself a cup of coffee. He'd been shaken by the film they had just watched and wondered how much of it could be confirmed. One thing was certain: Dr. John Murphy knew his craft. His video had recounted a cosmic story that had required a broad range of talents, from astronomy to computer graphics.

Phil didn't waste any time. "Everyone in their seats, now! Let me catch you up to speed, Sullo. Twenty-four days ago, a comet was spotted as it disappeared behind the Sun. Astronomers have been looking for it on old sky charts ever since, but the only other confirmed sighting is in an earlier solar observation from CloudCroft, about three weeks earlier. The problem is that distortions from the solar glare make both sightings too imprecise to draw a bead on where the comet should be now.

"That's where matters stood until Agent Miller picked this film up from Professor Murphy last weekend. Using Murphy's data, we turned the Galileo probe around and had it take a look. Well, guess what. The damn thing is exactly where Murphy says it is!"

Phil's voice went up a register as he continued. "So how the hell did he know where it was? According to other astronomers, Murphy hasn't even been looking for it. And this sucker is big—try 200 miles across!"

Ted's gasp was the only sound in the room. He looked at the others and wondered if they realized how incredible it was that John Murphy had known where to look. And not for the first time he wondered when these government big shots would understand that their familiar world had disappeared forever. And who were these people? Ted recognized Chief of Staff Phil Black, George the snake, and Richard Todd, his own boss—but who was Henry, the guy who had narrated John Murphy's video? And who was that good-looking woman sitting beside him?

As if he had read Ted's mind, Phil Black continued. "I'm not going to ask you all to go around the table and tell us why you're here. This is not a support group. Suffice it to say that Henry and Jane over there are from NASA. We are all here because we work for the United States government and our boss has given us a job to do. Jet Propulsion Labs will determine whether the comet has a chance of hitting us. Our job is to figure out what the hell we do if it does. We don't have much time. Within 24 hours all this stuff will be out on the internet, everyone's grandmother will know about this comet, and the evening news will be crowded with astronomers shooting their mouths off."

Phil abruptly turned to the short, balding man with wire-rim spectacles who had narrated the film. "Henry, tell us what Professor Murphy says we should do and what you NASA people think about it."

Henry cleared his throat and began speaking. "John Murphy says that we need to avoid hitting the comet directly with nuclear weapons. He says that's the worst thing we can do because it would shatter the comet. In that case, we couldn't even be sure that its massive core would significantly deflect from its current course."

Phil Black interrupted. "Explain."

Henry responded. "Imagine punching a giant feather pillow which has a rock in the middle. If the feathers are loosely packed, and the outside covering tissue-paper thin, then the force of the punch could get completely absorbed in moving individual feathers around. The rock in the middle might not be subjected to any of the force exerted by the punch on the outside. And you might also then have a lot of feathers flying around. In other words, a nuclear bomb might produce a lot of new comet fragments, and still not nudge its central core off course."

Henry looked around the room, pushed his glasses further back on his nose and added, "Murphy's hypothesis is plausible, if the comet's surface is honeycombed. If this comet is more like an egg, with a strong shell around a condensed interior, then a nuclear explosion could plausibly nudge the whole thing clear."

The woman sitting beside Henry—whose striking red hair exerted a gravitational pull of its own on Ted—interjected at this point. "But if Murphy actually knows that the surface is honeycombed, as he claims, then we need to warn the President to hold off on all bomb launches. It's very important that we tell the President what Murphy is saying. Let me add that some of us at NASA are taking his warnings very seriously. As for stopping the feathers from flying around—to borrow Henry's metaphor—Murphy made some diagrams which address that issue."

When she didn't elaborate, Phil shot back, "Spit it out, Jane. What else does Murphy have to say?"

Jane didn't appear to be troubled by Phil Black's abrasive tone. "Well, of course, if you gave us the opportunity to talk directly with Professor Murphy—instead of having to cull clues out of excerpts from bugged conversations—I could tell you what he says. He hasn't said anything directly to anybody in this room—except briefly to Agent Ted Sullo. However, he did include a diagram in the material he gave Agent Miller, which looks like some kind of shield has been interposed between the explosion and the surface of the comet. Using Henry's analogy, if you coated a giant pillow with something stiff, then the whole thing might move a bit when you punched it."

At this point, George cleared his throat loudly and at a nod from Phil spoke. "Where are the engineering diagrams for the construction of this barrier? We can nail this sucker without Murphy, and we sure don't need his hoax keeping us from doing it."

Phil looked surprised. "We have a confirmed comet heading in our direction, and Murphy told us how to find it. We have an artificial signal transmitting from Titan that no one can explain. I don't think 'hoax' is the word I would choose, George."

Phil looked as if he was about to acknowledge someone else's raised hand when George pounded his fist on the table and exploded. "So what if someone knew about a comet before we did? And so what if they have something on Titan? Those two things are the same. We spotted the comet from Galileo. They spotted it from something they have on Titan. Big deal. Only an idiot would believe all this garbage!"

Ted was amazed at George's rough tone, especially considering that the President himself was included among the idiots he was condemning. Ted was even more amazed when the President's Chief of Staff stepped back and leaned against the white board, visibly giving George space to continue. "If we buy into all this garbage about using the Moon to slingshot the comet, we'll miss our chance to just blow the sucker to smithereens while we have the chance. I hate this crap. Someone will burn in Hell for it. Probably the Russians."

Phil interrupted. "Thanks for your take on this, George. You think that the Russians have a probe on Titan and now they're playing games with us. As you are aware, that's one of the scenarios we are working with. Namely that a political enemy (the Russians, the Chinese, whoever) wants us to mobilize, in order to get confirmation of their intelligence data about our nuclear arsenal. But, meanwhile we still have this comet—and already JPL has confirmed that it will pass close to if not straight through our neighborhood—so let's stick to the President's agenda. How do we respond to this potential threat?"

Phil gave Jane the nod and she immediately turned and looked straight at George as she spoke. "George has a vested interest in not listening to Murphy's cautions. George doesn't want anything to stand in the way of his own agenda, which is to immediately launch a huge bomb and see what happens. That is where the real danger lies here."

George leaned back in his chair, his knuckles white, and kept quiet. Meanwhile Ted's mind was racing. Have these people really confirmed that a gigantic comet is heading straight for Earth? Why haven't they made an announcement? But he pushed his questions aside as Jane continued. "Let's review. Murphy has given us a lot of accurate information about a large comet hurtling in our direction—about its position, dimensions and trajectory. It is vitally important that we talk to this man and find out what else he knows."

Jane rapped her pencil on her note pad and continued. "What else does Murphy's communication say? Well, as George has just implied, there is a suggestion that—through a relatively minor shift in the comet's path—we can harness the Moon's gravity to slingshot it away from Earth. Let's not get confused about what we have here. Murphy may not be what he pretends to be, as some of us here today believe, but if this confirmed comet is really heading straight for Earth, then it doesn't matter very much how Murphy knew about it before we did."

Phil interrupted. "Do you have anything else?"

Jane raised her index finger and looked steadily at Phil as she spoke. "Three things. First, there is our capacity to launch missiles. I agree with George that we should leave all options open, including blasting the sucker to smithereens. Where I disagree is in his allegation that the senders of this message would have somehow done us a disservice by allowing us to locate the comet while it's still behind the Sun."

As Jane counted off her second item, she looked directly at George and raised her second finger in what looked suspiciously like a vulgar gesture. "Secondly, we have communications from the Murphy brothers from which we are already drawing information. And if we ever develop enough huevos, we will take the radical next step of talking directly with these gentlemen. The fact that these communications don't appear to convey the kind of engineering data we would need to actually carry out their suggestions doesn't mean that there isn't valuable information to be gained from them."

Ted felt his pulse go up as Jane looked piercingly into his own eyes. "Thirdly, we may receive another communication that does provide engineering data. The authors may be holding back practical instructions—which would require a lot of effort on our part to carry out—until they know that we're listening."

Jane looked away and Ted raised his hand, suddenly ready to say something. However George, with a cursory, unacknowledged wave of his hand, took the floor. "Bullshit heaped on bullshit! Now we not only have to eat the crap that's already been dumped on us. She wants us to put on our bibs and beg for more!"

Ted noticed that Phil allowed himself a faint smile in response to George's unequivocal disdain for Jane's remarks, but he interrupted the tirade. "Let's keep this meeting in order, Gentlemen . . . and ma'am. Wait until I give you the nod."

Hands were raised again, including Ted's, but it was Phil himself who spoke. "Let me fill the rest of you in on what Jane means. She thinks that we should treat what the Murphy brothers say very seriously because they are the messengers for superior, alien beings who want to help us."

Now Ted really wanted to say something. Phil smiled winningly at Jane and continued, "And Jane is here today because our President specifically requested that she participate in this meeting. Now who else has something to say? Agent Sullo, I think I saw your hand waving in the air a few moments ago."

Keeping his eyes on Ted, Phil continued. "I'm sure Director Todd has told you about the recent antics of your friend, Dr. Murphy. After this meeting, he'll play you a very interesting debriefing tape."

Phil glanced at George briefly before continuing. "There are some influential people, led by the First Lady, who are trying to convince the President that he needs to include Murphy on his emergency planning team. And there are some equally powerful people who will do everything in their power to keep Murphy away from here."

Phil looked grimmer than Ted had previously seen him as he continued. "Agent Sullo, we're in a very difficult situation with Dr. Murphy. On the one hand, if he knows where this information is coming from, then we need to get that out of him. On the other hand, his wild fantasies about life on Titan make him seem like the kind of loose cannon we can't trust for a second. So how do we go about finding out what he really knows and if it's information we need?"

Phil averted his eyes for a moment, before continuing. "To make a very long story short, Agent Sullo, the President has asked that you try to get to know Dr. Murphy better. The President believes, based on the audiotape of your initial interview with him, that Murphy trusts you. So we want you to try to cultivate that trust. Personally see that he gets his VLA tapes back. Become his friend and ally. See if you can find out why he has suddenly bought into these radically unconventional ideas about Titan. We need to know who he talks to. We need to know how a prodigy of the Astronomy world can overnight turn into such an Astrology kind of guy. And we need to know why the hell his prophecies have a way of coming true."

Ted had wondered why he was rubbing shoulders with these high-echelon administrators again. Now he had his answer. As he looked around the room, the faces that looked back at him seemed to be waiting for him to make a response. Ted glanced at Phil Black and Director Todd, but he held Jane's eyes as he spoke. "It will be an honor to do whatever the President asks me to do. But I need to know more about Murphy's diagrams. Otherwise I won't be able to recognize the points on which Murphy seems to have an inside track."

George interrupted. "You don't need to know shit, Mister! You just start Murphy talking and get it on tape. We don't need you feeding information to that psycho."

Ted shifted his chair back from the table. His martial arts training was telling him that George's body was primed to launch across the table on an instant's notice. This guy was definitely not your typical career bureaucrat.

Ted forced himself to shift his gaze to Phil Black as he continued. "Tell me more about the Titan message to the whales. Can you make any sense of the content?"

There was complete silence for most of a minute. During that time Ted could see a sign language of raised eyebrows, averted glances and grimaces passing among Phil, Henry, George, and Ted's boss. But his own eyes looked deeply into Jane's eyes. He had to force himself to look away. When he did, he saw that George had crossed the room and was now speaking in a whisper to Phil Black. Reading the snake's dark lips, Ted decoded his words. "You told me this jerk didn't have clearance on the new Murphy tapes."

Looking at them whispering together, the thought flashed into Ted's mind that George held some kind of power among these people. Then with a sick feeling, he realized this was George Ball, the man whom Patrick Murphy had talked about on the tape the President had played a week ago. George was said to run both the Defense Intelligence Agency, reporting directly to the Pentagon, and BallMaker Electronics, the world's largest armament conglomerate. In particular, BallMaker Electronics was said to have continued working on Star Wars defense initiatives, even after Ronald Reagan left office.

Ted stood up. He focused on Jane as he began to speak. "For those of you who may not have noticed, George is experiencing doubts about my reliability. That is why he is now whispering to the President's Chief of Staff. What has occasioned this doubt is that I somehow know that the electromagnetic energy reaching Earth from Titan is for the whales, not for us. That, by the way, is why no one has made any sense out of it—because it is a conversation between two intelligent species, neither of whom happens to be human."

Ted stopped talking and glared at Phil Black. Phil Black glared back. "How do you know this, Agent Sullo?"

Ted answered. "How do you know it, Mr. Black?"

George lashed out. "Answer the question, asshole!"

Ted looked at George and forced himself to hold his gaze. It was like looking at a venomous snake, while trying to gauge its striking distance. "We've all heard the tape where Patrick Murphy speaks about communication between the Titans and the whales. No one needs to be amazed that I believe him. I believe a lot of what the Murphy brothers say. And yes, Mr. Ball, that means I believe we have been addressed by aliens who are telling us to wake the hell up."

Ted turned his attention to Phil. "What surprises me is that the rest of you are acting like this communication has been demonstrated. What happened since I was yanked off the case? Did the Murphy bothers tell you something about the Titan transmission? This is not the time to be coy, Mr. Black. Because one thing is sure as shit—if people who know something don't start talking to each other, then we're already dead."

Ted looked around the room. "We have nine weeks of life left. Every single living being on this planet has nine weeks of life left. And that asshole, George, thinks he can scare me. What a miserable little shit-head you are, man!"

Ted sat back down and Phil Black took charge of the meeting again. It was as if Ted's tirade had cleared the air, while reassuring those present that he didn't really know anything about whatever they were trying to hide. George's expression made it clear that Ted had made an enemy; however, no one proposed to take him off the case.

The meeting adjourned thirty minutes later. As soon as the others had left, his boss immediately launched into the obligatory reprimand. "Where the hell do you think you are, Sullo? What makes you think you can talk like that to your superiors? I've never seen such unprofessional conduct in an agent. Why the President asked for you specifically, I'll never know."

Without another word, his boss pulled a DVD out of his briefcase and put it into the player. While Ted was waiting for the footage to start, he tried to sort out what he had learned. The most stunning item was that a comet had been sighted and that it might actually hit Earth. But his mind was even more drawn to the unexpected reaction his question about Titan-Cetacean communications had caused. Surely the Anchor Beach tapes didn't account for the look of panic he had seen in Phil's eyes. Was it really possible that whales were talking with an alien race of beings—and that the authorities now accepted this as a given?

And what about George Ball? Images of George kept breaking into his thoughts, interfering with his capacity to think rationally. But he needed to think rationally, especially about George. One thing was certain. George's presence at all these meetings seemed to affirm the existence of the revolutionary, deep space tracking system that Patrick Murphy had predicted. Now that Ted had been reassigned to the case, it was time he listened to all the recent tapes of what Patrick and John Murphy were saying. He would have to be careful in his investigations from now on—he was at best a marginal participant and he had just created a powerful enemy, in Mr.

George Ball. Another thing was obvious: Phil Black and George Ball were both running scared.

Once the debriefing file came on, Director Todd left Ted to watch it by himself. It was not the sort of item that the FBI would have wanted to misplace. The agent being debriefed had tailed John Murphy's family into a restaurant, and whatever had happened had left him hearing voices.

Director Todd returned just as the interview ended. He laid his briefcase on the table, snapped it open, then turned his back to Ted as he retrieved the DVD. Ted found himself fingering a miniature surveillance bug in his pocket, while looking at his director's open briefcase. A strange, hypothetical question came unbidden to his mind. Where would he place a bug if he had been assigned Director Todd as a surveillance target?

A memory came back to him, of his boss brushing shoulders with George at the end of their meeting that morning. Ted could have sworn that Director Todd had cringed as George whispered something.

His boss was still facing the player, as he slipped the DVD into its jacket. Slowly Ted stood up and leaned across the table. His hands rummaged in the FBI Director's briefcase for a fleeting moment, then he straightened up and pushed his chair away from the table. By the time Director Todd turned around, Ted was already walking toward the door.

His boss placed the DVD inside his briefcase, snapped his case closed, and followed Ted out into the corridor. Whether he had his mind on other things or was giving Ted the cold shoulder, Director Todd didn't give Ted a glance, as a Secret Service agent escorted them out of the building. The two men left the White House grounds separately.

As Ted rode back to his office in a taxi, his thoughts were drawn back to the material he had seen on the debriefing tape. One phrase kept repeating itself in his mind: "They're like giant eels and they're bigger than any whale." Ted shuddered for a moment. Then a blue, effervescent illumination filled his mind.

Nine weeks. In a way it made everything so clear. So many anxieties vanished in the light of this inexorable deadline, like dust washing away in a cool shower.

CHAPTER 29

Saturday, Feb 8 (Day -61)

Patrick's plane landed mid-morning in Albuquerque and as soon as he exited the enclosed ramp he spotted John. Beside his brother stood a tall attractive woman with strong features and long blonde hair tied back. It wasn't until she smiled warmly that Patrick recognized Leslie. Could that tall kid really be Eric? He was already as tall as his Mom, his hair dark like his dad's, and an angular look that promised more sprouting to come. And the toddler sitting astride John's shoulders was obviously Frankie, with a round face and eyes that seemed ready to laugh. He returned Patrick's gaze with a steady attentiveness that seemed unusual—not at all Patrick's idea of how a child looked. But then what did he know about kids?

It felt easiest to interact with Leslie. She closed the gap, held her arms wide for a hug, and Patrick felt a surge of feeling as he embraced her and thanked her profusely for inviting him. Then he turned to Eric and said, "I know distant uncles always say this—but Eric, how you've changed!"

Eric feigned amazement. "I know. It's pretty radical. Who are you by the way?" Still feeling out of place in this long-postponed meeting with John's family, Patrick was relieved when Eric smiled and added, "It's great to see you, Uncle Patrick." They shook hands vigorously until Eric grabbed his wrist and said, "Mom, do we still have our health insurance?"

Then John and Patrick shook hands. They looked directly at one another and held their arms out strongly—perhaps to ward off the possibility of an embrace. Coming closer to his brother also entailed moving closer to Frankie, who continued to sit on his dad's shoulders. On an impulse, Patrick said, "I'll trade you my back pack for Frankie."

When John didn't respond, Leslie stepped in. "Frankie, do you want to ride on Uncle Patrick's shoulders?"

Frankie stretched his arms out and said, "Ride on Dolphie." Patrick stood frozen to the spot, scarcely able to breath, while Leslie lifted Frankie off John's shoulders and told her husband to take Patrick's backpack.

He felt Frankie's weight, small hands pressed against his forehead, as the incredible, unmistakable words came out again. "Now swim, Dolphie." A memory of lying draped over the back of a dolphin infused his body. Centered in his chest and heart area, warmth and light began to pulsate upwards through the back of his neck, where his young nephew was pressing against him. In a kind of radiant glow, they walked through the airport.

Patrick's senses had never been this brilliant. He recognized people who had shared his flight out of Chicago, and now he knew why they were traveling—business, family, two funerals. He noticed two men who repeatedly came in and out of his field of vision. They seemed to alternate. One had a cellular phone that he used repeatedly. The other seemed to be taking every opportunity to delve into a paperback novel—except, whenever he looked up, his eyes were very focused on his surroundings.

The one with the phone appeared to be waiting for luggage three roundabouts over, but ten minutes later Patrick saw him walking through the parking lot without any bags.

The drive from the airport was delightful. The Sandia Mountains, overlooking Albuquerque from the east, boasted fresh snow against a deep blue sky.

His brother's house had a peaked roof, like the house they had grown up in, but there the comparison ended. The adobe-colored bungalow and the empty winter branches of a huge cottonwood tree in the front yard made Patrick feel like he was in a foreign country. Standing in their driveway, he drank in the sound of the wind blowing through a towering Ponderosa pine across the street.

Inside the house was friendly and somewhat cluttered with toys. He was pleased to see that the TV room, where a pullout sofa was to be his bed for the next few days, had a sliding door with curtains. Family life would be more appealing with the possibility of some privacy.

Patrick stowed his bags in the TV room and accepted a cup of coffee. Then they sat down in the living room around a coffee table, with Leslie and the two boys on the couch and John and Patrick in two stuffed chairs. Feeling awkward, Patrick took two sips of his coffee in rapid succession. It was painfully obvious that he had never played any role in John's family, and he felt like a distant cousin interrupting their lives.

"Are you smart like Dad?" Eric's voice broke into Patrick's ruminations.

"Why do you ask?" Patrick responded without thinking.

"Well, I just figure Dad's brother would be smart, like he is."

Patrick felt a familiar sense of shame ready to flood into his mind—the shame of never measuring up to his talented brother. But he forced himself to push aside this old reaction and said, "I think I see why something would seem strange, Eric. Your Dad's a famous scientist and I've spent the past ten years working at low-level programming jobs."

"And I'm a stay-at-home mom," Leslie said.

Patrick appreciated her effort, but looked at John. After a moment John averted his eyes, and Patrick suddenly couldn't remember why he had come. How could he have imagined that John's contempt would not have rubbed off on his children? He was unsuccessfully reminding himself that he and John had an important job to do—whether or not they liked each other—when Eric spoke again. "It seems like you and Dad didn't get along very well. But ever since he visited you in Maine, Dad has been talking about you differently. Like you hold the keys to the castle, or something."

Like a drooping plant revived by a spring shower, Patrick felt his confidence return. So I'm that fragile, he thought, as he smiled sheepishly. "I really don't know what's going on with me, Eric. Part of me feels like a complete washout, but another part feels that my life is finally important. And if I can only hang on and learn to cope with ordinary life, then I can develop this new possibility. Does that make any sense?"

Eric answered with enthusiasm. "I hear you, man. How do you survive the crap long enough to get a real life?"

Patrick started laughing. Everything seemed strangely familiar. Then Frankie joined in the merriment, and the sense of familiarity exploded.

At that precise moment the phone rang and Frankie's face became completely attentive, as John got up and went into the kitchen. Then they all sat in silence listening to John's end of the conversation. "Ah, Agent Sullo. It's been awhile. When am I going to get my VLA data back? Oh, really. Well . . . I guess so . . . OK. Sure. Come on over. I'll be here."

John came into the living room and sat back down in his chair. The room remained silent as they all waited for John to say more about the call.

"Well that's interesting." John began. "That FBI guy, Sullo, is going to drop by with my VLA tapes in a few minutes." John glanced at Patrick and added, "He's the one who tried to confiscate everything about Titan. Did I ever tell you I got a funny feeling from him—almost as if he believed I knew something?" Patrick shook his head but felt his pulse quicken.

Agent Sullo must have been outside because a few minutes later the doorbell rang. When John opened the door, Patrick saw a short, stocky man standing outside, a box under one arm. Sullo passed the box over to John and accepted an invitation for coffee. Standing at the edge of the living room, the agent looked closely at each person as John made quick introductions. Patrick's legs were actually trembling as certainty dawned: This man is John's doorway into the White House.

After the introductions, Ted turned to Leslie and said he was sorry if he and his partner had been heavy-handed on the previous occasion. Leslie averted her eyes, then said, "Everyone has a job to do and I'm glad I don't have yours. Please have a seat, Agent Sullo."

The agent sat down and rested his hands on his knees. Then abruptly he turned to John and said, "I don't know how else to say this, Dr. Murphy. But do you really think we've received a message from beings on Titan?"

"Who's asking?" John shot back.

"I am. I really want to know what you think."

John shrugged. "It's a bit like believing in God, isn't it? Sometimes you're certain there's no other explanation for what you're experiencing. Other times you can't help but notice how subjective your interpretations are. Right now, I wouldn't be completely amazed to discover that someone has been slipping LSD into our water supply and that I'm hallucinating."

Ted Sullo pressed on, "Last time we spoke, you speculated that the administration might be running scared—because they had no explanation for this message from Titan. I think that was more dead-on than either of us realized at the time. If you're hallucinating, you've done a remarkable job of substantiating it. Your hallucination now includes an actual comet, which you told them how to find."

John glanced at Patrick but made no response to Sullo's remarks.

Suddenly Frankie started laughing. His face was playful, like a two-year-old child's face, but he looked unwaveringly at Ted Sullo.

Ted glanced reflexively towards his left shoulder, and Frankie laughed even harder. Suddenly Patrick couldn't stop himself from joining in. He was back in a time of innocence, laughing helplessly at some shared absurdity.

It was out of that space of strange familiarity that Patrick started talking. " Frankie is giving you his seal of approval, Agent Sullo. Even though you're recording this conversation he thinks you're a man who can be trusted. What do you want to know?"

Ted looked at Patrick, then at John as if he wanted clarification of the situation. But John didn't respond.

"I was hoping that Professor Murphy could tell me something about how he came to know certain things," Ted said.

Patrick interrupted. "Mr. Sullo, let's be frank with one another. You've been given the job of monitoring my brother because he is considered a security threat, but one who may have important information. Obviously you don't feel entitled to tell us that. Your bosses would consider it a major blunder —and they're listening to this conversation at this very moment. Meanwhile, you personally have powers that our world needs right now. Please don't pretend you don't have them. When I say that Frankie gives you his seal of approval, I'm not kidding. Frankie is pivotal here. Not your President, not Dr. John Murphy, not me. For God's sake, look at him."

Ted's eyes were very wide as Patrick repeated his exhortation. "Don't look at me. Look at Frankie!"

Ted complied. While Ted and Frankie were looking intently at one another, Patrick pressed on relentlessly. "Are you willing to be a bridge? It's no accident that you are here right now. Why did you come immediately after I arrived? I don't mean that those two clowns who were tailing us at the airport told you that John had returned home. I mean why are you and I meeting right now, ten minutes after my first encounter with Frankie? How many of your thoughts are clearly your own these days?" Then Patrick said, "Now look at me, Ted."

Ted, his face ashen, looked at Patrick.

Patrick experienced his body as something spacious and electric, his voice a skein of threads from many spools. "You are close to the President, whose decision is needed to implement the Titanian's plan for harnessing the Moon's gravity."

Ted visibly winced, as Patrick plowed on. "But you are far from the beings whose participation is crucial if we are to save our planet. Of all of us, Frankie is closest to them."

Hal Nagen had told Patrick two weeks ago about Frankie, but Patrick hadn't really believed it until now. Now there was simply no denying it: Frankie was directly in touch with some incredible cosmic force. And just sitting next to him, Patrick's mind was flooded with conviction and clarity.

Patrick's gaze did not waver from Ted's eyes. He could sense the profound stillness that had gripped the room. "The dolphins and whales are closer still. In fact, without them, we humans have no chance of overcoming our dark history of indifference to other species. Our only chance, and the only chance for all living creatures inhabiting this beautiful planet, is to ally ourselves with the happier future of whales and dolphins—a future they have earned."

Patrick continued. " I need you to tell us who else you know who is open to all this. Preferably someone closer to the President than you are. Who would you trust to come with us to Hawaii, so that we can communicate with whales and dolphins there?"

Ted turned pale. He leaned forward and then he slid onto his knees and laid his forehead on the floor. When Leslie started to rise, Patrick gestured for her to remain seated.

After a few moments, in which the only sound was Ted's labored breathing echoing off the oak floorboards, the agent slowly raised his head and pulled himself back into the armchair.

The room remained silent as Ted stared at the fireplace. Finally he spoke. "Her name is Jane and she works for NASA. I don't know her last name. She's been studying Dr. Murphy's charts. She's the only person I've met in Washington who seems convinced there are beings living on Titan."

Patrick knew he was functioning within the compass of some mind other than his own, and he felt driven by a sense of urgency as he spoke. "Find an opportunity to talk with her. Tell her that we know a missile has been launched and that Earth may be destroyed as a result. Tell her that our only chance to avert the horror of a shattered comet pulverizing our world is to communicate with the cetaceans next Friday, February 14th, six days from now."

John's voice broke in with a bitter edge. "Next Friday sounds like as good a time as any to meet the Cetacean Civitans. But do you mind telling us why we have to wait until then? Are they busy the other nights? They don't play bingo, do they? No, I don't suppose so—having no hands could be a problem there."

Patrick was too angry to speak. He tried to center himself, tried to remind himself how jealous John might feel, witnessing the uncanny connection Patrick had made with this youngest son. But images of rage broke over Patrick like a violent sea. He could hear Leslie and John arguing. John was protesting that a little clairvoyance didn't entitle anyone to elect themselves chairman of the board.

Then Eric's voice broke into the argument. "Wow, what a concept! Humans have to talk with the whales to save the planet. Is that really true, Dad?"

Patrick's rage subsided as he looked at Eric, then at John. John's face softened, as if he had recovered a part of himself, and after a moment, in a voice that sounded almost apologetic, he said, "I'm way out of my depth here, Eric. I guess I've never been that great at sharing with people, let alone another species. Maybe this is a good time to let someone else lead the way. To tell the truth, right now I'd rather be able to talk to my own family than to aliens."

The way Eric and John looked at one another told Patrick that this kind of openness had not been the hallmark of John's life as a father. Glancing at Leslie, whose eyes were glistening, it was clear she was witnessing the fulfillment of an ancient prayer. The room remained silent for several moments and it was still silent when Frankie started chanting, "Friday. Friday. Friday."

Everyone stared at the little boy, and at first Patrick felt as perplexed as the others. Then a deluge of images rushed over him, like high tide breaking over a sea wall. Reminiscent of the visions he had experienced in the Portland hospital, Patrick found himself witnessing a vast field of space and time. Now it was clear that Frankie was revealing things to Patrick which he was supposed to tell the others.

When Patrick became present to his surroundings again, he saw that everyone in the room was staring at him. He wiped a line of saliva off his chin, unsure of how much time had passed, and had to clear phlegm from his throat before he could talk.

He noticed that this time John was also listening with complete attention. "Frankie has just shown me things I have never really understood before. He told me why we have to wait until next Friday. The Titanians can only communicate with Earth while their ocean is facing in our direction—and that only happens for half of Titan's 15-day rotation around Saturn. The Titanians will be on the far side of their world for the next six days, and during that time the sperm whales cannot receive messages from them."

Patrick looked around the room before continuing. "If I make claims to personal authority on the basis of information I receive clairvoyantly, then I apologize. Meeting Frankie has helped remind me that I'm only a link in a network which has its center elsewhere. Where I occasionally get bursts of insight, Frankie is in continuous contact with other beings. Among all of us, Frankie has by far the strongest connection. I don't know why, but he does."

Patrick looked first at John, then Ted. "I don't think that the President of the United States is going to base either his career or the fate of terrestrial life on what a two-year-old says. You need to talk to Jane, Ted. It's vitally important. There's an abandoned dolphin research station in Hawaii. We need to pump salt water into its holding pools before Friday."

Patrick knew a huge gamble had just been taken. Agent Sullo was wearing a microphone under his left collar and everything said today would be heard by the President of the United States. Had he just compromised Jane, the person best positioned within the administration to become their ally? Or would her position be all the stronger for the President knowing that the Murphy family had accepted her?

He didn't know.

Well, the cards had been dealt. The ante was in. Now the hand would be played out, one way or another.

CHAPTER 30

Monday, Feb 10 (Day -59)

Ted was standing in his spacious suite at the Albuquerque Marriot (the fruit of his Presidential assignment), still dripping from a shower, when the phone rang. The clock radio showed 6:32 a.m. as he picked up the phone and heard his boss's voice on the other end. "Monday, 800 hours, a jet is leaving Kirtland Air Force Base for Washington. You'll be picked up in 30 minutes. Be ready." Click—without so much as a Good Morning.

As he toweled himself off, Ted wondered if his boss thought Directors were supposed to talk like that. Then, as he threw his things into the suitcase and called the front desk for a take-out breakfast, he tried to imagine what new turn of events was calling him back to the hub.

Four hours later, the jet lurched slightly as it touched down at Andrews AFB. A government car was waiting with its engine running and they drove straight to the White House.

Ted felt a sour sensation in his gut as he spotted Director Todd at the White House entryway. He knew he was going to be crucified for the way the conversation had turned at the Murphy's, but as they hurried through the building, it dawned on Ted that his boss was not talking about the Murphy's. He was talking about something horrifying: three days ago the President had approved an historic launch of a nuclear warhead into space.

Ted felt his legs grow heavy as a vivid memory of Patrick Murphy talking about a nuclear launch—two days ago in John Murphy's living room—flooded his mind. He had to force himself to keep up with his boss's quick march down the corridor.

They entered a sitting room that overlooked White House lawns and gardens. Jane, George and Henry were already seated. Ted felt a rush of pleasure as Jane returned his glance and smiled.

They had scarcely sat down when the President walked in. Everyone rose and remained standing until the President had taken his place at one end of the low coffee table. Without preamble, he turned to Ted. "Thank you for joining us on such short notice, Agent Sullo. The recording you wired us yesterday has caused quite a stir here, I can tell you." Then turning to the others, he continued. "Let me state straight off: JPL has determined that the comet now has a 10% chance of hitting Earth. The question for this meeting is what are we doing about it. I'll start."

The President straightened slightly in his chair before continuing. "We launched a missile from Canaveral last Friday. It's carrying a high megaton hydrogen bomb and some impressive new technology. JPL is already calling it a perfect shot."

Even though he had heard Patrick refer to a missile launch —and his boss had confirmed it moments before—Ted couldn't suppress an audible intake of breath at the President's words. He knew enough about NASA's budget woes to know that the proposed asteroid defense program had received zero funding. So what kind of deep space missile had they scrounged off the shelf to launch on such short notice? Had the administration actually slapped together and deployed—without consulting Congress or world opinion—some rudderless, untested missile carrying a huge nuclear payload?

The President continued. "This launch is only a first step. We launched something immediately because the farther the comet is from Earth, the smaller the nudge needed to push it away from its current course. Meanwhile we are assembling a top notch team from the Voyager and Galileo missions to put together a more versatile platform for subsequent deployment."

The President glanced at George before continuing. "I am happy to say that even this first launch carries some breakthrough advances in target-tracking, continuous-course-correction, and nano-second-reaction delivery systems."

The President sounded like he was practicing for his Address to the Nation, as he continued. "We need to remind ourselves that there is still a month remaining until this missile intercepts the comet, at which time our knowledge of the situation will be far more extensive than it is now." The President looked directly at George as he continued. "The exact configuration of our weaponry is highly classified. So I won't elaborate. George, is there anything you would like to add about the missile launch?"

Ted noticed that George looked more at ease than he had at their last meeting—probably because his "blast the sucker to smithereens" philosophy had prevailed. When George shook his head, the President picked up the coffee thermos nearest him and offered some to Ted. Ted heard himself accepting, while inside he struggled to quell his horror. He glanced at Jane. She was staring at her coffee cup and looked like she could explode at any moment.

The President poured coffee into his own cup, took a sip, and continued. "Now I would like to hear from the rest of you. Henry, the radio waves from Titan went off-line four days ago. But just before then, the patterns changed. Please fill us in."

Henry responded immediately. "Yes, that's correct. The transmitter now appears to be on the far side of Titan, and—if we can believe Patrick Murphy—it won't reappear for another four days. Friday to be exact. Just before disappearing, the wave configuration did change, as you have pointed out, Sir. We still know nothing about possible content, but our pattern recognition programs and grammar-checking analyzers indicate that we are now picking up a totally different message."

The President took over. "So, we have no idea what they're saying, but now we think they're saying something different."

Ted stole a glance at George, wondering how he would react to the President's last remark. A half smile played on George's face, as if a private joke had come to mind. Then he noticed Ted looking at him, and his smile vanished.

The President was addressing Jane. "As you know, Patrick Murphy wants to meet with you, Jane. Hold off for now, but as the First Lady passed on to you this morning, I want you to investigate everything he says. Go ahead and find out if whales and dolphins are congregating down there. Isn't there some kind of Sea World in Hawaii?"

Jane responded. "Yes, Sir. I've been in touch with them. Actually, it's an abandoned dolphin research station, Sir. You wife and I are working together to get it functional."

The President continued. "I understand you've also been talking with JPL about John Murphy's proposal for nudging the comet into the Moon's gravitational field. Please fill us in."

Jane seemed hesitant as she responded. "Permit me to say, Sir, that many JPL scientists share the Murphy brothers' concern about the nuclear launch that has already been made. They have a bad feeling about it."

The President responded brusquely. "As I will tell the nation on Wednesday evening, nothing irrevocable has been initiated, Jane. Our strategy has been to launch a first line of defense as soon as possible—for the reasons that I have just enumerated. However, if it appears that detonation is too dangerous, we will simply shut this first missile down."

Jane's red hair was lustrous against her grey flannel jacket. She apparently felt that she had not yet used up her allotted time, because as the President was turning towards Director Todd, she abruptly resumed her report. Ted found himself growing excited as he watched the freckles turn darker on her throat. "Sir, as I know you are aware, many of us at NASA are afraid of this missile. We are encountering problems in some of the control systems. It's acting like a rogue that doesn't respond to ground control. If we can't get control of this thing, then I recommend that we explode it immediately."

The President glanced at his watch, told Jane that JPL was reporting all problems to him directly and would continue to keep him informed, then he turned to Director Todd.

"Richard, what did you and Helen, I mean the First Lady, come up with?"

Ted stared in amazement at his boss. What was happening here? The FBI was collaborating with the First Lady?

Ted's boss linked his fingers together and seemed to be having difficulty finding words. "Sir, as I'm sure the First Lady has already told you, we have been monitoring a number of situations in which unusual phenomena are occurring. The First Lady likes to call them shifts in consciousness. In ordinary times, I think we would say that a lot of people are hallucinating."

Without taking his eyes off Director Todd, Ted became aware of how intently both Jane and George were listening. As Director Todd continued, Ted wondered if George was hearing something new. "An audio recording came in this morning of a talk given by a woman in Canada. As you requested, Sir, I've shared it with the First Lady." The FBI Director appeared increasingly uncomfortable as he struggled through his report. "The woman on the tape claims to be a channel for some dead guy. I think they call it being 'on the other side', Sir. She was talking to more than 1000 people in an auditorium at the University of British Columbia."

The President interrupted. "Give us a thumbnail sketch."

"She's from New Zealand but is presently traveling around Canada, Sir, talking about the comet. That's why we sent our agent up there. On the CD you hear this woman talking like an ordinary person about the comet and how the Titanians are trying to help us."

Director Todd seemed increasingly uncomfortable. When he fell silent for a few moments, the President cleared his throat impatiently and the FBI Director quickly continued. "No one says anything for a couple of minutes, then a man's voice takes over. Our agent said it was still the woman talking, but from the CD you would never know it. Anyway, this man's voice starts talking about Titan. How heat and light are produced to support life. How Titan and Saturn form a coherent, living system. She kept comparing it to mind and body. I can add that the First Lady is very interested in this Titan material, Sir."

The President nodded. "I'd like it made available to anyone here who wants to listen to it. Now, let's move on. Richard, fill us in on what's happening with the Murphy family. I understand we have a very interesting recording of a conversation at which Agent Sullo was present. I haven't had the opportunity of hearing it myself, but my wife told me a bit about it this morning."

Director Todd responded. "Yes, Sir. I have forewarned Agent Sullo that you would be interested. Agent?"

Ted felt all eyes upon him. What to say? He knew his loyalty to his department had become fundamentally compromised, but it was more important than ever to build a bridge. He took the plunge. "As you mentioned, Sir, they want to meet Jane."

When Ted didn't say anything else for a few moments, several people stirred. Looking directly at the President, Ted forced himself to continue. "It's the whole family, Sir, especially the youngest boy, Frankie. The astronomer's brother, Patrick, seems to be some kind of channel for—I don't know what. When you see John and Patrick together, John sounds like your regular, skeptical, college professor and Patrick sounds like a charismatic preacher. What he preaches about is Titan, the comet, and the cetaceans."

The President interrupted. "My wife has started talking a lot about whales. I think she may accompany Jane down to Hawaii to meet some in person. What does Patrick Murphy have to say about them?"

Ted felt his own excitement mount as he responded to the President. "That would be wonderful, Sir. Apparently the whales and dolphins are absolutely central to all of this. I might as well just say it. Apparently . . . that is, Patrick Murphy claims . . . the Titans have been communicating with whales for hundreds of thousands of years. The only reason that they are now trying to establish contact with us is because of this comet; and because whales and dolphins don't have the technology to avert the threat which this comet poses."

His boss interrupted. "Agent, why does Patrick Murphy want to meet Jane?"

Ted wondered why his boss was hitting on this point, when the President had already agreed in principle and even seemed willing to have his own wife participate. He nodded to Director Todd but looked at the President as he spoke. "Patrick Murphy explicitly asked me if there was anyone in regular contact with you, Sir, open to the view that we have been contacted by alien beings. I mentioned Jane to them because, on the one previous occasion that I have met her, she did in fact indicate that she was open to this hypothesis."

Ted ran out of words. He hoped that he hadn't already destroyed Jane's credibility.

Then George was talking. "Please tell us, Agent Sullo, does your training make you at all concerned that this clearly unstable individual wants to get closer to the President of our country?"

Ted shivered. How could he straddle these two worlds? How could he preserve something of his own marginal credibility with the Administration, while at the same time trying to build a bridge with the Murphy's? Maybe the President's wife would be the key.

Still in the dark, Ted responded. "Yes. Patrick Murphy asked me to contact Jane. And I have gone through the appropriate channels in communicating this request."

The President asked, "What is Jane supposed to do?"

Deciding to trust the President's apparently genuine interest, Ted responded. "I think Patrick Murphy hopes that Jane can persuade you to be open to this radical thesis about the whales, Sir, and to the new knowledge that contact with another species would bring into the human world. I think Patrick Murphy is trying to build a bridge."

The President immediately followed up. "A bridge usually joins two shores. What is at the two ends of the bridge that Patrick Murphy wants to build?"

Ted looked closely at the President. Was he more sympathetic to the Murphy's than Ted had realized? Was the First Lady already playing the role for which Jane had been a candidate? Ted didn't know, but he did need to respond to the President's question. "I think that ultimately the bridge would be between you and the authors of the Titan message. I think Patrick Murphy is interested in me because I'm closer to the administration than anyone he has previously met. Now he hopes to get closer still. I think the concept is that Patrick

Murphy thinks of himself as a link and he is trying to find adjacent links that would lead him to you. I suppose he must feel he already has adjacent links in the other direction, in the direction of the cetaceans and the Titanians. I feel out of my depth here, Sir."

The President said, "We all are, Agent. We all are." Then the President spread his hands wide and addressed the gathering as a whole. "I'm afraid I have to leave now. Richard, play that Canadian CD for Jane and Ted. You should be able to find a quiet place somewhere in the basement." Then he stood up and walked out of the room through a side door, closing it behind him.

Henry and George (who made no attempt to disguise his contempt for the conversation that had just occurred) both hurried from the room and into the corridor.

Director Todd said nothing. He got up and gestured for Jane and Ted to follow him. He walked quickly through the building, as if trying to dissociate himself from the two people rushing to keep up with him.

Jane and Ted didn't look at one other, but Ted suspected that her pulse must be pounding in her ears—like surf beating against the shore—perhaps even as loudly as the waves crashing inside his own head.

CHAPTER 31

Director Todd put the CD into the built-in audio system. Then he left the screening room and the door automatically locked after him.

As soon as they were alone, Jane pushed the play button and a moment later they heard a woman's voice. "May this reach you who have ears to hear it." Then there was a subtle shift in the quality of the background ambient sound. As a veteran mixer and dubber, Ted knew that an introductory phrase had been added especially to their copy of the recording but that now they were listening to a large space full of people. Gradually the room quieted and then the woman spoke for five minutes about the Age of Transformation that had arrived on Earth. The vehicle that was about to open the curtain on this new age was a giant comet, even now rushing towards them from the far side of the Sun.

Then she said, "I think Isaac can say it better. Are you ready for him to come?"

A low murmuring came through the quadraphonic sound system. The small basement room in the White House became an auditorium, packed to the rafters. The agitation gradually subsided. Then a new voice started talking. As Director Todd had said, you just couldn't find the slightest resemblance between the voice of the woman who had spoken a moment before and this new, masculine baritone.

"All Titan species are ocean dwellers," the voice intoned. "A thick crust of ice surrounds 90% of the barren surface of their world. After the Pioneer and Voyager expeditions to

Saturn, no one thought about the affect of tidal forces—because no one thought Titan had any rotation relative to Saturn. It was assumed that the tidal pull exerted by Saturn on Titan would have dampened any rotation that Titan may once have had—as has happened with Earth's tidally-locked Moon."

Ted glanced at Jane. Her eyes were closed and her face seemed as smooth as a child's.

"But Titan does rotate. . ."

Ted heard someone breathing deeply. With a start he realized that he was hearing himself. It was like the sound of someone falling asleep, yet he felt alert, his mind full of clear visual images of tiny Titan crossing in front of Saturn's glowing face.

A tinkling sound filled Ted's mind, like millions of bells, or ice crystals, resonating with a deep, throbbing tone. He thought of opening his eyes to verify that he was still in the screening room, but it didn't seem quite worth the effort.

"The magnetic effect of Saturn's magnetosphere would ordinarily not penetrate very far within Titan's thick atmosphere, which is hundreds of miles thick. However, Titan's atmosphere is organized in such a way that there are filaments, call them neural pathways if you wish (made of material far more conductive to electricity than copper. Electrical current flows through these networks of conductive material (which are insulated by nonconductive gases) until it reaches the lower levels of the atmosphere on the far side of Titan, the ocean side. This current eventually fires into pockets of neon-type gasses, providing light for the ocean-dwellers of Titan."

This was followed by a few moments of silence. Then the deep voice continued. "On Earth we have two main rhythms, corresponding to our year and our day."

A dynamic model of the solar system came into Ted's mind, in which both Earth and Titan could be seen, as the masculine voice continued. "On Titan, geography and life have been molded by three astronomical rhythms.

"First, there is the dim light from the Sun, circumnavigating Titan every 15 Earth days—the time it takes Titan to orbit Saturn.

"Second, there is the cycle of the seasons, lasting 30 Earth years—the time it takes Saturn to circumnavigate the Sun.

"And thirdly, the ocean circumnavigates Titan once every 6000 Earth years—the time it takes Titan to orbit once on its own axis, relative to Saturn."

A long silence followed. Ted opened his eyes and saw Jane looking at him. But she closed her eyes as soon as the voice resumed. "I know some of you have had the feeling that another mind is present. Is that not so?"

There was a soft but decisive murmuring of affirmation. "You may wonder if the Titanians are talking to you. You may wonder whether there are Titan representatives present on your planet.

"No, the Titanians themselves are not present on Earth. But we can have access to them. Clairvoyant humans alive at this time are crucial in this communication. Looking at the human species as a whole: you, in whom these clairvoyant powers have come alive, are as important as ears and eyes are important for an individual human being. But whom are you actually listening to, during this age of unprecedented clairvoyant communication?

"You are listening to our brothers and sisters of the sea. You are listening to the whales and dolphins of our own Earth."

Suddenly the sound changed radically and Ted glanced at the tape player. The tape was still rolling forward. But now the room was suddenly full of the haunting songs of humpback whales.

It was as if a soft mallet struck against Ted's chest. Then he was tumbling through space. The long strands of the whales' singing provided the only reality that he could grasp—like a forest of kelp with a million intricate branchings, orbiting around him in deepest, darkest space. There was nothing else to touch. Yet to grasp this vast skein of song required him to first shatter in what felt like the foundations of his life. As he started to shatter, something flowed into him like a surging tide.

Ted only realized that he was sitting there, with his eyes closed, when he felt his shoulder being shaken and Director Todd's voice saying, "Fall in, Agent. Now!"

On their way out of the building, Ted was vaguely aware that Director Todd was lecturing him on not going native. He forced himself to nod his head in agreement a few times.

Then Ted was standing at the edge of the parking lot. Thinking he was alone, Jane's voice startled him. "I have a car. Can I drop you off anywhere?"

"I haven't eaten anything since breakfast," Ted responded. "And a bottle of red wine would go down pretty good about now."

Jane smiled and pointed at a blue Toyota Prius a few yards away. They drove in comfortable silence through streets unfamiliar to Ted, eventually parking in front of a small restaurant with a French-sounding name.

Over their first glass of Bordeaux, they started talking, and Ted felt himself entering a world that still resonated with the experience they had just shared in a basement room of the White House. He wondered if that deeper world would include the woman sitting across the table from him, and he also wondered if there would be any time to explore that possibility.

CHAPTER 32

Wednesday, Feb 12 (Day -57)

John put all his effort into his bike ride home, determined to be in front of the TV in time for the President's Address to the Nation which was scheduled for 6:00 p.m. Mountain Time. He put his bike in the garage and headed into the house, peeling off bike gear as he went.

The shit was about to hit the fan. Word was out on the Internet that a large comet (still behind the Sun for Earth-based telescopes) had been confirmed by the Galileo probe in orbit around Jupiter: the very comet that would soon emerge from the solar umbra for the inhabitants of Planet Earth. The information available now on the web was very different from what had made a mild splash on the net several weeks ago—namely that something had been glimpsed disappearing behind the Sun and that astronomers were waiting for it to reappear on the other side. Now there was real news spreading like a rogue wave across the World Wide Web.

Apparently someone at NASA was leaking classified information about the comet. John had spent more than an hour reading it that afternoon. A lot of accurate, soon-to-be-verified facts were now common knowledge.

Most striking was a graphic—based on bootlegged JPL pictures—that showed a probability ellipse with a dot in the middle. This ellipse showed the range of possible points at which the comet might cross terrestrial orbit, based on current observations. The dot in the middle of the ellipse was the single most probable point of intersection.

Well, Earth itself wasn't on the dot. It wasn't even at the center of the ellipse—but it was inside. Earth was about 100,000 kilometers from the dot—a hair's breadth in astronomical terms.

Not for the first time, John felt like two people. One part of him looked at this graphic and found himself praying that the comet would stay far away from Earth. But another part of him simply wondered when the graphic would get it right.

John entered the TV room just as the TV anchor announced that the President would be speaking in two minutes. As they waited, Leslie quickly filled John in on what the commentators had said. "The President held a special closed session with Congress this afternoon. He told them about the comet. Of course, both parties were outraged. Why hadn't they been informed sooner? How could the President authorize the deployment of a nuclear weapon against a planetary body without consulting anyone outside his own staff? And so on."

Leslie fell silent as the picture abruptly switched to the President sitting at his large desk with an American flag visible behind him. After a brief moment the camera moved in closer to his face and the President began his address. "Many of you will have already heard something about the subject of my Address to the Nation this evening, and you will have also heard that I spoke this afternoon to the United States Congress about several important issues. I want you all to know that a few days ago we acted decisively to counter an emergency which may threaten our planet. And today, we have acted just as quickly to inform Congress, the American people and the world community, about every aspect of this situation. That is why I have requested this opportunity to speak directly with you about issues which vitally concern all of us."

The President gave his trademark grandfatherly grin and John felt a sour feeling in his stomach. That reassuring smile would probably inoculate millions against personal anxiety over the looming threat to everything they knew and loved.

John held his unopened can of soda tightly as the President continued. "So, now I'll get to the heart of what I have to say to you tonight. A comet has been located which may pass quite close to Earth eight weeks from now."

Even though John had his own inside track on anything the President could possibly say these words caught him off guard. It was as if the executioner could be heard sharpening his axe in the next room.

The President allowed a brief silence before continuing. "This comet is presently on the far side of the Sun. For the moment, it cannot be viewed from Earth-based telescopes. We saw it for the first time two days ago, using cameras on board Galileo, a NASA mission to the Jupiter system. As early as tomorrow evening, weather permitting, you may be able to glimpse a new speck on the Western horizon, but only for a few moments immediately after sunset."

The President paused and deliberately gazed into the camera, as if to let the nation know that, in hard times, he was there for them. "You will, of course, want to know whether this comet poses a threat to Earth, and if so what we are doing about it. First of all, let me tell you plainly: in all likelihood this comet will sail clear past Earth; however we need to mobilize all resources just in case it heads in our direction. That is why, as your Commander in Chief, I ordered the launch of a nuclear missile yesterday morning."

John had to struggle against being physically ill, right there on the carpet. "The launch went flawlessly—a tribute to the expertise of American scientists and to American military preparedness. With this launch, we deployed our first line of defense. However, you can rest assured that we will not detonate any nuclear device until the situation is understood better than it is at present. This first element of our strategic preparedness will rendezvous with the comet on March 18th, 33 days from now. The comet will, at that point, still be about 60 million miles from Earth. At that distance, it will take only a small nudge to deflect the comet onto a different path."

The President paused and took a sip of water before continuing. "I want you to know that we have not committed the American people irrevocably to any course of action which might appear unwise a few weeks from now. Basically the situation is this. We have launched a missile, and now we have more than a month in which to decide if the detonation of a

Hydrogen bomb, near the surface of the comet, is the right thing to do. It was judged important to launch a missile without delay, because the sooner we encounter the comet, the farther it will be from Earth; and the farther it is from Earth the greater effect there will be from any alteration induced in the comet's path."

John sat there stunned. He scarcely knew which was more appalling. The revelation that there really was a comet after all, and that it wasn't just some hallucination he and his family had invented. Or that the administration, a.k.a. the Pentagon, had already acted unilaterally to do something about it.

When Leslie remarked that the President was at least doing a good job of explaining the situation, John almost lashed out at the imbecility of anyone who wasn't terrified of this elected idiot.

The Commander-in-Chief continued. "Now we have a job to do. And we have two months to do it. The missile launched yesterday will rendezvous with the comet in one month. But we have a full two months before the comet will approach the neighborhood of Earth. Fortunately, we have a wealth of technology and knowledge at our disposal. We have already set in motion our first response to this comet and it may be all we need. It may be the case that it will be necessary to detonate this bomb near the surface of the comet in order to nudge it clear of the vicinity of Earth. We did what was necessary to initiate this option, so that we would have it available—should we decide that it is the correct action to take. However, what is at stake here is too momentous for the Office of the United States Presidency to take unilateral action. That is why we are sharing this information tonight. We consider it essential that everyone who is living on this planet have an opportunity to provide input into the ultimate response that is made to this comet. We need all our best minds thinking about it, analyzing it, coming up with ideas. We have a lot of options, and now we have time to develop them."

John turned to Leslie. "Boy, he must really have been tarred and feathered by Congress. Just listen to him. All he's doing is trying to cover his butt. All he's telling us, over and over, is that, whatever happens, he sure meant well. When the hell is he going to tell us about the Titanians?"

The President talked for another 15 minutes. John didn't hear a single word about why the Galileo probe had just happened to spot this comet. He certainly didn't hear anything about any communication from Titan.

Finally the President concluded his prepared remarks. "I would like to invite you all to approach this historic time in a spirit of hopefulness and exploration. As never before, we have an opportunity to show the greatness that resides in the human spirit."

John spent the next 20 minutes switching around among the networks. They all had one panel of experts or another discussing what the President had and had not divulged. Eventually Leslie protested. "Can't we just leave it on one channel? How about PBS? That man from the Washington Post sounded interesting."

John muttered an apology and handed the remote to Leslie. Together they listened to Mark Shields, looking paler than usual, raise some penetrating issues about the Near-Earth Asteroid Tracking System (NEAT), and the difference between an asteroid and a comet. Then John sat riveted to the couch as he recognized the next guest. It was an Administrator at the VLA—the same man who had told him that he wasn't likely to get the telescope back onto Titan for several weeks. John listened avidly to this discussion for about five minutes.

Eventually it sunk in. This man wasn't breathing a word about John's confiscated VLA tapes. All he was talking about was how the VLA, along with the rest of the world's radio and visual telescopes, would be aimed at a particular spot at the edge of the solar umbra tomorrow evening in the moments just after sunset.

Silently, John got up from the couch, fetched his telephone index and a city phone book from his office and then went and sat in the kitchen, within reach of the speakerphone on the wall.

First he called the Agassiz telescope station. Fielding answered the phone. As soon as he recognized John's voice he said, "Did you find the President less than completely candid about certain things?"

Leslie came into the room as he leaned toward the phone and said, "I'm contacting the local TV stations. I've been fooling myself that the authorities would do whatever was necessary. Now I see that was bullshit. What about you, Dr Fielding? You have more of the transmission than I do."

"Not any more, I don't"

John glanced at Leslie and said, "What happened?"

John and Leslie listened in silence as Mark Fielding described how his computer was no longer working and how all record of the Titan transmission had been destroyed. He ended by saying that he felt like a criminal conspirator, because he hadn't treated the transmission from Titan as a real message—and now he had no record of it. Who was going to believe an old SETI researcher who claimed to have heard aliens but had nothing to show? The alien who got away.

John felt a terrible sense of urgency. He told Fielding about his own partial copy of the confiscated file, then quickly hung up.

As he was dialing the number for the local NBC affiliate, Leslie tried to dissuade him from doing anything rash. She reminded him that they were all going to fly to Hawaii on a military jet tomorrow morning. She urged him not to spoil his chance to work with the authorities—now that it seemed possible to do so.

But something had shifted in John. When someone picked up the phone at KOB, he introduced himself and then plowed on with his agenda—as if Leslie had not said anything. "This is Dr. John Murphy. I need to talk to someone who can make a news programming decision for a national broadcast."

Maybe his name actually carried some clout. He was quickly given the newsroom editor, the same man who had interviewed John when he had been awarded The Newton Lacy Pierce Prize in Astronomy two years ago.

The editor was interested. He immediately accepted John's offer to show him the humpback look-alike transmission captured from Titan on the Agassiz radio telescope. They arranged to meet in an hour at the Murphy's home—in order to view the radio transmission on John's computer.

At KOAT, John had to leave a message for the senior newsroom editor to call him back. After hitting the local news affiliates, he intended to get on his computer and blog everything he knew.

He had his hand on the phone, ready to dial KRQE, when it rang at his end. John pushed the external speaker button, and a familiar voice came on the line. "John and Leslie, get out of there! Fast! There's no time to pack. Take your kids and get the hell out of there. Right now! You have about three minutes!"

Leslie reacted more quickly than John. "I'll get Frankie and Eric. You go start the van!"

Leslie was halfway down the hall, screaming out Eric's name as she went. John had not yet stirred from the kitchen table when he heard Ted Sullo speak again through the open phone line. "Two minutes, 48 seconds."

Suddenly John came to life. He almost collided with Eric coming down the hall, looking like he'd just woken up. John shouted. "Don't bother looking for your shoes. Out to the van. Now!"

John ran to the garage and grabbed the bag of CD's out of the stack of firewood.

They all piled into the van about the same time. For the first time in Frankie's life, Leslie just held him on her lap in the front seat, clutching him fiercely with one arm, as she slammed the passenger door shut with her free hand. "Go!" She shouted.

The tires squealed as John backed out blindly into the street. Fortunately no one was driving by. He drove to the corner, took a side street east over to Carlisle and headed north toward Interstate 40. They were held up by the light at Indian School and Carlisle. No sound of an explosion yet. Maybe Ted was imagining things.

Suddenly Eric leaned between the front seats and pointed through the windshield. "Check out the Dracula limos."

Two identical black sedans with black-tinted windows were pulling up to the intersection on the north side. They didn't wait for the light to change. One turned west on Indian School. The other crossed the intersection through a tiny gap, causing on-coming traffic to slam their breaks. John watched in the rear-view mirror as the second car speed down Carlisle, then turned west on the same residential street from which the Murphy's van had emerged moments before.

Leslie had to point out that the light had changed. John's hands were trembling as he pulled through the intersection. Where the hell did they go now? Should he pull onto I40? Leslie's decisiveness filled a void. "We shouldn't be driving this van around. Pull in behind Blake's. I need to put Frankie in his car seat before we do anything else."

They parked in the lot behind the burger stand, hidden from traffic passing on both Carlisle and on the I40 on-ramp. He felt stunned. Why had he called the news stations? What a stupid thing to do. There must be hundreds of people who knew about the Titan message. Fielding at Agassiz, astronomers at the VLA, not to mention the FBI. Surely there would be someone who would share this information with the public. A man with a wife and kids had no business putting them all in danger.

Leslie's voice dragged him back. "We can't stay with this van. They're probably already looking for it. And we can't risk the airport. Maybe we could ditch the van near a city bus stop. Then go to the Greyhound station and travel to some other city."

John felt critical and angry. "Get real, Leslie. Pictures of us are being faxed to every transportation terminal within 500 miles of here. How long would we last?"

Leslie lashed back. "I don't hear you coming up with anything better. And I'm not the one who called the TV stations, against his wife's advice."

Frankie said something that sounded like "seaward."

Eric joined the discussion. "What about that guy who gave you the CD's?"

John turned around and looked at Eric. "Bill! What a great idea. I think I even remember his home number." Leslie pointed out that there was a pay phone at the front of the restaurant, which would be better than having a cell-phone call traced.

Grabbing a handful of change from the dash, he went and made the call. Bill answered on the third ring and—as soon as John had given the location—said, "Stay there. I'll pick you up in 15 minutes." Before John could add anything, the phone hung up on the other end.

John returned to the car and told Leslie that Bill was coming. She might not have heard him. Keeping her focus on Frankie, she said, "Tell Daddy what you said."

John forced himself to pay attention. It sounded like Frankie said, "Seaward. Talk with Patrick."

Feeling obliged to respond, John said, "We can't go see Uncle Patrick now, Frankie."

Leslie interrupted. "Listen to what he's saying, John! Sea World."

When Frankie spoke again, he was able to understand. "Sea World. Talk with Dolphie."

Things fell together in John's mind. Their phone was bugged, and Ted had been carrying a wire when Patrick had talked about Hawaii. If they were in danger in Albuquerque, then they would be in Hawaii also. That meant they needed a new place to meet the whales and dolphins.

Frankie had just told them the new place. Sea World.

John's task had become clear. They needed to be in San Diego by Friday, two days from then. That was when the Titan Ocean would swing around into view, and eight more days of communication with the Titanians would begin. For humans, and for whales and dolphins. Except that most humans wouldn't be listening, unless someone like John told them to.

He now understood that he really did need to go viral with his little slide show. He muttered an apology to Frankie. But how do you treat a two-year-old who now and then calls the shots, and the rest of the time makes a mess, is only partially potty-trained, and would run out into the middle of traffic if you didn't watch him every second?

And they still had some very serious, adult problems to solve. Like getting to San Diego without being shot by whoever was so dead set on keeping the world in ignorance.

He glanced at Leslie and felt immensely relieved when she smiled. Perhaps together they would work everything out.

Bill pulled up beside the van in a beat-up blue Datsun hatchback. He didn't waste any time. He was standing beside the van before John had finished rolling down the window. "I've cleaned the Datsun out so now you have four seats. It's gassed up. Here's my Chevron gas card and my Visa. I've written down my social security number and my birth date, in case anyone asks. You don't want to use your own cards or write any checks after you leave Albuquerque. And don't tell me where you're going. I'd suggest you draw out all your charge card limits now and then don't touch any plastic on the road."

Leslie was already out of the car. She threw open the sliding door and asked Eric to help her with Frankie's car seat. Then she prodded them all into the Datsun, nudging John toward the driver's seat.

John sat down, feeling a bit cramped in the small car, and saw that the key was in the ignition. He started the car and turned to Bill. His voice was trembling a bit as he said, "I sure wish you were coming with us, Bill. I can't believe you're doing all this. You're probably saving our lives." Bill looked steadily at John as he responded, "For eight more weeks."

Propelled by the intensity in Bill's words, John hurriedly shook hands through the open window, drove out of the Blake's parking lot, and headed onto I-40 west-bound. It was good to have a short-term objective. Maybe by the time they reached San Diego, two days from now, the world would have woken up from its nightmare. In the meantime, it looked like he needed to start taking it a lot more seriously.

CHAPTER 33

Thursday, Feb 13 (Day -56)

Patrick had been back in Anchor Beach for two nights and already he felt restless. Maybe he should have accepted Leslie's invitation to stay longer—she had seemed sincere enough, and John had talked about a collaboration to decode the Titan message—but after many years of estrangement, it had seemed best to leave while they were still feeling friendly.

So Patrick was back in his cabin by the sea, trying to decide whether it was his new home. It still amazed him that he had developed new relationships with Hank and Emily and with his brother in the few short weeks since leaving Montreal. Which reminded him—one day soon he would have to return to his old apartment and get some closure on his life there. He should at least collect a few mementos and his computer. As for his clothes, now that he had lost 50 pounds and was continuing to shed more, maybe he would just donate them all to the Sally Ann.

There was no doubt about it: he felt restless. He could only enjoy taking so many walks along the same stretch of beach. And a grown man could only feel good about so many free suppers at his surrogate parents' down the road. One particular thought kept coming into his mind—like a bad conscience—that this was his last chance to finally do something with his life. So why was he languishing in a little cabin by the sea, like someone unable to face life?

More worrisome was what was happening with John and his family. He had tried to call them last night, but the line had remained busy for the entire time he was at Hank and Emily's for supper. He was tormented by the sense that something was supposed to happen in Hawaii tomorrow and that he should be there. But what would be the point? No one had contacted him to say that anything had been arranged. On his own he would be unable to do anything there, and if something was going to happen he certainly hadn't been invited.

He hadn't spoken to his brother since Tuesday evening, at which point John had known nothing about the administration's plans. Then last night there had been that horrifying news conference in which the President had hidden so much more than he had divulged. Why hadn't John answered the phone last night? Patrick had stayed at Hank and Emily's until well after midnight (10:00 p.m. Albuquerque time) in order to keep calling the only number he had for him. Maybe their home phone had just been off the hook, but somehow it nagged at him.

Sunlight fell on the blanket covering Patrick's legs. He was reclining on the porch swing, spending more time staring out into space than reading the book on his lap. He had cracked open one of the windows on this unusually warm February morning so that he could hear the ocean. Waves crashed onto the beach below. Closer by, icicles dripped off the porch roof.

Then he noticed another sound. Not so different from the rumbling approach of a wave, but with a high-pitched thread that kept getting louder.

Suddenly a red Trans Am skidded to a stop in the wet snow bank in front of his cabin. When no one seemed to be about to get out of the car, Patrick slipped on his boots and went out to see who it was.

The tinted window opened a few inches and he heard Ted Sullo's voice telling him to lean closer so they could talk privately. Wondering which concerned Ted more—the sea gulls or the neighbors a mile on either side—Patrick bent over to catch Ted's whisper. "This cabin is bugged. So listen, don't talk. You have five minutes to get out of here."

Well that solved the restlessness he had been feeling. A sense of urgency exploded inside his body and he was back out in the car with two packed bags in less than five minutes. The instant he slammed the car door, Patrick realized that he had not closed the porch window or turned down the thermostat. Well he would tell Hank when they swung by the store to say good-bye.

Ted nixed that plan, turned left onto the beach road and headed south toward Portland.

After about five miles, he suddenly swerved off the road and skidded about 50 yards down a snowy driveway until the Trans Am was hidden behind a boarded up A-frame. A moment later, a black car sped past, its tires throwing up a cloud of spray on the wet pavement. Not your regular tourists beating the summer crowds. Patrick and Ted glanced at one another, and Patrick suddenly knew that he had found the ally he had been searching for.

Ted waited a few minutes, before pulling back onto the main road and resuming their leisurely drive into Portland. Patrick had no idea where they were headed. It felt good.

He let himself sink into the comfort of the high-powered automobile, while fields of ten-day-old snow with salt grass poking through slipped past on either side. Already signs of the sea were falling away and the rhythm of a long journey on the asphalt river began to assert itself. It felt like an important moment. A second leg on his journey out of the dead-end life he had fled in Montreal.

Ted's first words were not so philosophical. "I discovered this morning that you and John have been targeted for elimination. My own boss has gone off the deep end. Those goons who passed us back there—they have orders to kill you. Probably your body would have washed up on the beach in the next day or two. And assassins visited your brother's house last night, but I think they got out in time."

Patrick swung around. "Last night? Why did you wait until now to warn me?"

Ted kept his eyes on the road as he negotiated a sharp turn. "If I'd warned you by phone, where would you have gone? My call would have just made them come sooner for you. So I gambled. I acquired this car, which cannot be traced, then drove non-stop for eight hours to get here."

When Ted didn't continue, Patrick asked, "Tell me again. Who wants to kill John and me?"

Ted's voice took on a harder tone. "His name is George Ball. He's a son of a bitch who controls things from the shadows. Some kind of defense contractor with more access to power than anyone should have in our so-called democracy."

Did Ted shiver? "I noticed that my boss is afraid of George, and I started wondering what the hell they talked about when they were alone. I bugged my boss's briefcase and you wouldn't believe the stuff I've picked up. My boss and George are thick as thieves. Thick as murderers, more like it."

Patrick forced himself to remain silent, allowing Ted time to pick his own pace. "My boss is using FBI operatives to kill North Americans. All George has to do is mention someone to him, then within a few days they're dead. A fatal car accident was reported on the news a few nights ago. Some well-known New Zealand psychic traveling in Canada, Mary Seer, who predicted both the comet and the Titanians a year ago, was in a single-car, fatal accident. Well guess whose name happened to come up in a conversation between George and Director Todd a few days ago?"

When Ted didn't continue, Patrick volunteered an answer. "Did George happen to mention how Ms. Seer was a pain in his butt?"

Ted nodded. "And now George is complaining about two more pains in his butt. Someone who works for me, or who I thought worked for me, picked up some calls John made to the TV networks last night. I was sitting in the control room with this other agent when the calls came through. The other guy immediately slipped out of the room, supposedly for a cup of coffee, and I sat there like someone on death row. If I reported the calls, it would be a death sentence for John. If I didn't report them, I would become the next casualty. Fortunately this other guy spared me the dilemma. And guess what? Within an hour, Todd's briefcase picked up a conversation with George. I have the recording with me."

They pulled into a gas station on the outskirts of Portland. Patrick wanted to call Hank and Emily, but Ted wouldn't let him. He said it would give too much information when the call was picked up, which it definitely would be.

Back on the road, Ted took a CD out of a jacket pocket and inserted it in the player.

Listening in shock, Patrick could scarcely breath. How could human beings discuss such horrors? He heard this abomination, George, sentence his brother, John, to death. Almost as an afterthought—maybe that was why Patrick had had an extra 12 hours—George added, "And put that fruitcake brother out of his misery, too."

Then George's voice became conspiratorial, as if he was now entering an even darker area than that of murdering two inconvenient civilians. "That Eagle Scout Pres is telling everyone how we've just launched a friendly welcome balloon. We're just going to check things out and ask the comet where it's going and if it doesn't mind we'd like to nudge it out of the way a bit." A cackling laugh, like the squeals of an asthmatic pig, followed.

Then Ted's boss could be heard. "What's wrong with that? In a month, the President will decide to either destroy the missile en route or target a particular surface on the comet." This last observation was greeted by laughter that sounded, even more, like some kind of animal, screeching in passion or in pain.

Then followed a voice from hell. George laid out his plan to assemble whaling boats in Hawaii by Friday—tomorrow—concluding in a conversational tone, "A few more thousand drowned dolphins and harpooned whales won't bother anyone too much. Just make sure I don't see any pictures on the evening news."

When the CD finished, they were 50 miles south of Portland. Ted removed the CD and gave it to Patrick to store in the glove compartment. "Put it in the 'Blood on the Tracks' case". Then neither of them spoke for the next 60 miles.

Patrick had never tried to initiate communication with the humpback of his dreams. He wasn't sure he knew how. Perhaps when he dozed off later that night, the whale would know that the killing grounds around Hawaii must be shunned, and would warn his kin. The horror would be there in Patrick's mind, awake or asleep, for his friend to read, like a telegram announcing the holocaust.

Frankie could tell them, but Patrick had no idea where Frankie was. And he knew Ted wouldn't let him use a phone to try and find out.

Ted's voice broke in on his thoughts. "There will be a hit out on me now, too. They'll know it was me who warned John. By now they must have found the equipment in my office. I left it running, still tracking on the briefcase."

So Ted really had come as fast as he could. He hadn't even taken the time to take his incriminating equipment off-line. Patrick felt a surge of gratitude. Ted had put his own life in jeopardy to warn them.

"Did that maniac, George, imply that the missile will never be turned off?" Patrick asked. "And why is he so concerned about dolphins? I can't get a handle on why someone who wants to show off his tracking system would give a damn about ocean mammals. It doesn't compute."

Ted asked if Patrick could drive and listen at the same time.

They pulled into a Taco Bell and used the washroom. Then they brought some take-out back to the Trans Am and Patrick slid behind the wheel. Tight fit. After giving himself more legroom, he ate a tostada and forced himself to leave his bean burrito with green sauce for later.

Patrick shifted into first, hesitated, and then turned to Ted. "I'm looking forward to driving this car, but where the hell are we going?" Ted stuffed a wrapper into the garbage bag, unwrapped a second taco, took a bite, and said, "I don't know." A few moments later he added, "I'm more clear on what we're running away from. Let's head towards Albuquerque. If we share the driving we can be there in two days. Then perhaps we can find out what happened to John and his family.

Patrick pulled back onto the highway. As they were approaching Boston, he saw a sign letting them bypass to Albany. He kept his eye on the road, enjoying the way the Trans Am handled, as Ted ate three soft tacos and then took one of the coffees. After he'd given Ted the chance to take a few sips, Patrick broke the silence. "What's George's issue about turning the bomb off? Surely, there's some ON/OFF switch activated by ground control."

"It's hard to get a straight answer," Ted responded. "I haven't been invited to the meetings where those kinds of things are discussed. But, like you say, it doesn't seem that it should be such a big deal to just switch it from ready to stand-by mode. It shouldn't be a problem. But when George says the bomb won't be turned off, it scares the shit out of me."

Patrick asked if the President was receiving geophysical studies confirming the danger of hitting the comet too hard.

"Judging from George's condemnation of 'fairies and do-gooders at the White House', I think the President has mixed feelings about his decision to launch a missile. He has drawn an incredible amount of criticism for his unilateral decision to launch an H-bomb at a moon-sized object that does not belong to the USA. On the other hand, now that images of a disturbing black-head in the Sun's umbra are starting to appear on the evening news, the President feels relieved that a missile is already on its way."

When Ted didn't elaborate, Patrick asked him about the even more appalling section of the recording they had just heard, "Why the hell does George want to kill whales and dolphins?"

Ted sighed and said, "How do you explain pre-meditated murder in any form?" Then he added, "I know what you mean, though. Why would an armaments kingpin give a shit about Flipper and Shamu? Especially now that his favorite toy is about to put him in the history books. You're right—it doesn't compute."

They drove a few more miles in silence. Patrick slowed down and adjusted the sun visor to block the late afternoon sun. When Ted hadn't said anything for ten minutes, Patrick glanced over and saw that he was asleep. That was just fine with Patrick. It felt good to be going somewhere. There might not be anything they could do in Albuquerque, but at least it was a destination.

By 5:30 p.m. it was already dark. Patrick drove non-stop for eight hours while Ted slept, his snores mingling with the road noises as the Trans Am ate up the miles. They reached the outskirts of Cleveland around 1:00 a.m., and stopped for something to eat at an all-night dinner. After filling the tank, Ted took over behind the wheel and headed south on Interstate 71.

After a few miles, Patrick reclined the passenger seat back as far as it would go and let the rhythm of the road seep into his body. He quickly fell into a dream where he was wandering in a desert and people dressed in business suits were running around with computer printouts. Their polished shoes were coated with red dust, their lips dry and cracked from the arid heat. No one seemed to notice the curved edge of a black shadow creeping across the parched desert floor behind them.

When Patrick opened his eyes again, the western horizon was tinged with pink from the morning sun. In the mirror, red clouds were sailing in a pale blue dawn.

He grunted. "Coffee."

Ted pulled off on a business loop and they found a small cafe with several pick-ups out front.

The eggs were cooked in bacon grease and someone's mother had made the strawberry jam. They both nodded every time the waitress offered to refill their coffee cups. About the fifth time this happened, she said, "You boys better be careful you don't float away. Speaking of floating away, did you catch this morning's news about the President?"

Patrick felt the bacon grease coagulating in his stomach. Ted swung around, as alert as a jackrabbit caught between sagebrush covers, and asked, "What news was that?"

The waitress laid her coffee pot down at a nearby booth and leaned her substantial haunches into the nearest table. "The President was admitted into Bethesda Naval Hospital. Said it was for a routine check-up. They showed him walking through the front entrance with his wife. Between you and me, he was leaning so heavy on her, she was about to have a hernia herself. And he looked as grey as last month's warmed-over beans."

The waitress swung her head towards the serving ledge where an order of pancakes was waiting to be picked up. The song playing on the portable radio had just been interrupted by a news bulletin. She bellowed, "Turn that up!"

The President was still at Bethesda, but reported to be feeling fit. Outside the White House, a nuclear protest was being held with an emphasis on not bombing other worlds. There was a short segment about a peace ceremony in northern India, which had attracted a million people.

Then there was a recap of the President's Wednesday evening announcement of the comet sighting. Since then—due to strong solar flares and calibration difficulties experienced by the Galileo probe—no new trajectory data was available.

Then Astronomer John Murphy was introduced.

Patrick and Ted sat like twin ice sculptures. The interviewer stressed Dr. Murphy's impeccable credentials, as if he was about to need them. Then they heard John talking about the mother of all comets, claiming that it was much more than the President had acknowledged: a world-destroying missile, on a collision course with Earth. Even to Patrick, his voice sounded hysterical, strident, panicky.

The interviewer asked Dr. Murphy how he knew so much about this comet, since no one else was claiming to have a definite track on its trajectory. Which telescope had he used for his observations? Dr. Murphy seemed to hesitate and then blurted out that the U.S. Government had a completely decisive calibration of the comet's course, but were suppressing this information. They were refusing to tell people about the danger this comet posed to every living being on the planet. And he expressed contempt for the Administration's claim that the Galileo probe was having problems with its equipment.

The interviewer interrupted to repeat his earlier question: How did Professor Murphy know all this? A moment of silence was followed by the professor's even more frantic voice, describing how a message had come from Saturn's moon, Titan, weeks ago. He had no opportunity to continue. Whatever else he may have said had been edited out.

The waitress muttered something about nut-cases coming out of the woodwork and went to pour coffee at another table.

There followed some comments from the White House press secretary. In a prepared statement, he said that the comet might pass close to Earth but that it was irresponsible to talk about a collision. He added that the comet was several months away, and that no one should panic. Then he added something not quite comprehensible about baseball. The gist seemed to be that if a fly ball did come towards you, then you either caught it or batted it over the fence.

Patrick could scarcely believe it when the waitress shouted out at the radio, "Straight on, mister. Smack the sucker over the bleachers."

Then she pulled out her pad and took an order for breakfast at a table where a family had just sat down, as if this news bulletin had been about the day's box scores. Patrick refrained from shouting back that catching a 200-mile-diameter comet could be bad for the health.

They paid the bill, walked out to the car and Patrick took over behind the wheel. After filling up, they continued west on Interstate 70. They passed a sign that put St. Louis 187 miles ahead.

Neither spoke, but Ted seemed agitated. He started flipping through the radio stations, but could only find the usual music, ads, and ranting talk shows. Some callers were talking about the comet, but it was as if they were all really talking about their private obsessions. Every half hour the same news bulletin was repeated. On an NPR affiliate station, there was an interview with the Coast Guard in Hawaii. Apparently there had been a huge jump in the number of whales spotted off Kauai during the past week. Patrick felt ill.

Suddenly Ted shouted. "Exit here!"

Tires squealed under them as the Trans Am swerved onto the exit ramp. They stopped at a Texaco station and Ted jumped out of the car. Before closing the door, he leaned down and said, "I won't be long. I'm going to check my phone messages at home."

Patrick sat in the car for a few moments, wondering why Agent Sullo had suddenly decided it was time for them both to commit suicide.

He got out of the car and met Ted as he was coming out of the office with a handful of quarters. "Don't you have a cell phone?" and when Ted sprinted to the pay phone, Patrick added, "And isn't calling home going to tell them where we are, however you make the call?"

Ted started dropping quarters into the pay phone at the side of the building, as if he hadn't heard Patrick. Only after he finished punching digits into the keypad, did he turn, with the receiver wedged between his shoulder and ear, and acknowledge Patrick's question. "You're right. It's almost insane. But how the hell else can we find out what's happening? Maybe Jane called."

Ted punched in some more numbers, presumably a security code for his answering service, then he stared straight ahead for about five minutes.

Ted slammed the receiver down and pronounced, "We're heading back to Washington," and ran over to the Trans Am.

Ted drummed his fingers on the roof of the car for a few moments. Glancing at his watch, he said, "It's 6:00 a.m. That's 7:00 a.m. in Washington and we have a meeting with the President at 10:00 a.m. That leaves three hours to make more than 1,000 miles. It doesn't work."

Patrick managed to speak. "Excuse me? We have a meeting with the President?"

Ted backed up a few frames. "There was a message from Jane. She didn't know about us being on the run. She asked me out to lunch after our 10:00 a.m. meeting with the President on Friday. That's today. Then she just happened to mention how glad she was that both Murphy brothers had also been invited."

This is what Patrick had been dreaming of ever since waking up in the Portland hospital two weeks ago. And now that a meeting with the President had been arranged, they were all running for their lives. How had John managed to get that interview? Was he still on the run? Or had the President's invitation been his ticket to freedom?

Suddenly Patrick had an idea. "We have an invitation from the President. Can't we hop a jet somewhere?"

Ted swung around. "That's it!" We need to turn ourselves in at a military base somewhere. Not the police. Not anywhere that might have received an arrest-on-sight order across their fax. Some military base where we can walk in and say: 'Take us to your leader. We have a 10:00 a.m. meeting with your Commander-in-Chief. Do you happen to have a jet parked out back?'"

Ted looked like his On-switch had just been flipped. He opened the driver side door, swung in behind the wheel and barked, "Get in, Patrick!" They squealed back onto West-bound I-70.

"Now you're paying your way. I know a Lieutenant Colonel at Scott Air Force Base. I think it's in Belleville, somewhere near here. Maybe we can still make it, if I really lay down the rubber. See if you can find it on the map."

Patrick felt himself sinking more deeply into the upholstery as Ted laid the pedal to the floor. The Trans Am was soon flying through the morning at close to 100 mph.

Patrick found Belleville, southeast of St Louis. It looked as if they could make it with luck. But not at this speed.

After giving Ted the route, Patrick remarked, "I don't think the police are our friends right now. Getting stopped would not only slow us down. It could be fatal."

Ted brought it down to 80. Awhile later they hit rush hour traffic and it began to feel like a hopeless cause after all. But once out of the St. Louis environs, they made better time again.

They pulled up to the Scott AFB gatehouse at 7:15 am. In response to the MP's polite greeting, Ted announced that Captain Ted Sullo was here to see Lieutenant Colonel David Lee."

The MP picked up the phone and spoke with someone. A few minutes later he hung up and came out to the Trans Am. "I'm afraid that the Lieutenant Colonel is on assignment, sir. It won't be possible for you to see him right now. It would be better if you called back this afternoon and made an appointment."

Ted shot back. "I know that didn't come from Dave. He wouldn't talk like that. Whoever you talked to needs to be told that this is an issue of national security. We have an appointment to see the President and we need transportation to Andrews Air Force Base."

The MP's reserve became palpable. He went back to the guardhouse but didn't even look at the phone. He returned with a form on a clipboard. "You can sign up for standby. If you're lucky, you might catch a flight to Andrews in the next week or two. Of course, you will need to be cleared for Air Force travel."

Ted didn't look at the clipboard. "Listen, Airman, one way or another we're driving on base. I'd sure prefer to have an invitation."

As the guard reached for his weapon, Ted put the gas to the floor. Patrick's heart sank. Captain Sullo had lost it. This couldn't possibly be the way to get to Washington on time. But when Ted told him to put the Dylan CD in his pocket, he opened the glove box and grabbed the wine-colored case.

Ted didn't try to evade the security cars. He came to a stop and left his hands on the steering wheel.

They were a little rougher on Ted but Patrick also had the wind knocked out of him as he was pushed against the side of the car and hand-cuffed.

They were escorted inside a nearby building and waited inside a locked office with an armed guard posted outside. It was 7:30 a.m. when an officer came to the window and looked in. As soon as he saw Ted, he shook his head and raised his eyes heavenward.

The officer waived the guard aside, walked into the room and immediately started haranguing Ted. "I don't know what you're up to, Sullo, but I think you've finally succumbed. This is not the enemy lines. You've just broken through the gate of a United States Air Force Headquarters. We have a four star general here. You're in deep doo-doo. I was in the middle of a preparedness review with the base commander. Headquarters command was there. I must be insane to come out here to talk with you. I'm keeping a Brigadier General and a Four Star waiting."

Ted blurted out, "Dave. You need to trust me on this one. The President is in extreme danger. My friend here has documentation in his pocket. He and his brother, John Murphy, are supposed to meet with the President at ten hundred hours today. Your Four Star can check."

Lieutenant Colonel Lee grimaced. "Ted, what are you on, man? I need to get back to inspection. I'll get them to serve you a breakfast and be back in two hours."

Then he nodded to the guard who immediately unlocked and opened the door. Lee walked quickly out as Ted shouted at his back. "At least call the White House about Patrick Murphy."

Lieutenant Colonel Lee took one more glance through the bulletproof window and wagged his head while looking skyward. Then his face disappeared. It was immediately replaced with that of the guard. This young man's eyes seemed only to see a room that needed to have two men in it for the duration of his watch.

CHAPTER 34

John prolonged his soothing shower in the San Diego motel room they had checked into that afternoon. His shoulders were sore from hours clenching the Datsun wheel and the hot water felt wonderful, washing away some of his exhaustion and discouragement.

He and Leslie had driven straight through to Los Angeles —after withdrawing all the money they could with their plastic before leaving Albuquerque—and had made it to L.A. by 5:30 AM that morning. Even at that hour, there was bumper-to-bumper traffic.

John still cringed at the memory of his strikeout with the media. All the TV networks had been closed to him. It wasn't just that 5:30 a.m. was not the ideal time to call. It was as if the people who answered on the news desks were expecting him and had been instructed to steer clear. No one even wanted to take a copy of his diskette with its excerpt of the Titan transmission.

So he had given public radio a shot and had found someone who was interested. They drove to the NPR-affiliated station and John had spilled his guts. Thirty minutes later—driving south towards San Diego—their worst fears about the interview were confirmed when they heard what made it through into the news summary—the ravings of a hysterical lunatic. When they finally checked into the Best Western motel three miles down the road from Sea World, John felt as demoralized as he had ever felt in his life.

Now he pulled his head away from the stream of water—someone was banging on the bathroom door. It was Eric and he was shouting something that sounded like, "Whose shoe should I pee in?" John forced himself to turn off the revitalizing stream of warm water, threw a bath towel around his waist and opened the door. Eric squeezed past and, with adolescent modesty, closed and locked the door the instant John stepped out.

John dried himself off and had just zipped up his gabardine slacks when the lock clicked and the door opened. It was Leslie, carrying Frankie and Chinese take-out in one hand, and a beat-up booster seat in the other. Marveling that his wife must have talked a Chinese restaurant into giving her a toddler seat, John lifted Frankie up while Leslie laid out the food. As soon as Eric came out of the bathroom they dug in.

Leslie mumbled something—her mouth full of Kung Pao chicken—got up and retrieved a folded sheet of sky blue paper from her fanny pack. By the time she returned to the table, she had swallowed enough to say, "I found this in a Laundromat next to the Chinese restaurant."

She handed the flyer to John and he read it out loud. It announced a presentation at 7:00 p.m. that evening at a local church. The talk was titled, "Earth, Moon, and a Visitor," and the speaker, Hal Nagen, was described as a western Yogi trained in Eastern Tibet.

The flyer included a phrase which caught John's attention: Sometimes the only escape is to let your enemy in and lead him into a different future.

Then John recognized the name. Patrick had described Hal as probably the only person who might actually know what was happening to the planet. Hadn't Patrick also said something about several pairs of brothers having been chosen? Yes. Hal was trying to find his brother, who was some kind of faulty link. And Hal was afraid the whole chain might break as a result.

John turned to Leslie and said, "We have to go to this."

Eric immediately reacted. "You promised that we could watch cable TV, tonight."

It was true. But John badly needed to go to this talk. In a half-hearted effort at reconciliation, John turned to Leslie and said, "I know we need to bring Frankie with us, but do you think Eric could stay here, if he promises to keep the door locked until we come back?"

John's suggestion was beneath consideration. Leslie turned to Eric and said, "You can have your night-with-cable at the very first opportunity. Just not tonight."

"Mom. My favorite TV shows are on Thursday nights. Why do I have to listen to some flake talk about astrology?" Frankie joined in, "Coming to Moon. Coming to Moon."

With an air of helplessness, Eric turned to Frankie. "Star Trek, Frankie. Star Trek. Going to stars." Frankie repeated himself, and Eric seemed to recognize that he was badly outnumbered.

* * *

They entered the church, paid the suggested donation, and found three aisle seats about 20 rows back. Frankie sat on John's lap so he could see the front where the speaker would sit. They were a few minutes early and John let his mind drift into the subdued whispering around him. Meanwhile Eric—in a kind of stage whisper, obviously intended for his parents' ears—started making sarcastic remarks about the setting: the burning candle at the front of the church was such a nice touch, an eternal flame of truth—live from San Diego! Both John and Leslie told him to cool it.

At the front of the church, there was a single empty chair and a low table on which stood—as well as the illuminated candle that had caught Eric's attention—a Buddha statue and an enameled bowl with a padded stick beside it.

The group that was assembling to hear the talk, "Earth, Moon and a Visitor" seemed quiet—probably relieved that no major riots had been announced, the President was out of the hospital, and the only photographs of the comet yet to appear were of a tiny black dot at the edge of the Sun's umbra.

At 7:05 p.m. a muscular, blond man, seemingly in his mid-forties, entered the church nave from a side door where there must have been an office. After he had walked a few steps towards the center of the platform, he stopped and scanned the room. His gaze was deliberate, unhurried; yet it would have been hard to say if he had found any sign of what he was looking for in the faces that looked back at him from the audience. His eyes seemed to linger on Frankie.

He continued walking across the platform to the armless, cushioned chair and sat down cross-legged on it. Then he didn't say anything as he continued to survey the room.

John found himself savoring the stillness that this man, Hal Nagen, seemed to be instilling into the atmosphere of the room. He was already glad they had come. One needs an incentive to just sit still and listen to the silence sometimes. This thought came into his mind at the very moment that the blond man spoke.

"I know why I am here. Do you know why you are here? Why have I been traveling around this continent for the past three months, and before that for six months in Asia, the Middle East and Europe—talking to people about a comet and about a race of beings who live on a moon which orbits Saturn?

Eric whispered, "This guy could get a job in elementary school. They always start by telling you how great they are." Both John and Leslie glared at him, and Eric slouched down lower in the pew.

"I expect some of you will have difficulty believing that I have been giving talks about this for the past year. Yet there is nothing I will say this evening which is substantially different from what I said in Sri Lanka eight months ago, in Athens five months ago, and in Little Rock, Arkansas five weeks ago.

"This evening is a test case for me. I need to discover, now that everyone is hearing related things on TV, whether anyone in North America can still hear what I have to say."

For a fraction of a second, John felt certain that the speaker's body became brighter. A giggle from Frankie, at that precise moment, corroborated his feeling. Meanwhile Hal, who still had not introduced himself, continued to sit silently, emanating an uncanny intensity. Then he was talking again. "Why are you here? Ask yourselves this question now, and don't stop asking it for the remainder of your lives. At the very least, don't forget it this evening. If at any point I sense that more than half of the people in this room have stopped asking themselves why they are here, then I will leave without a word of explanation."

Eric whispered. "I'm ready. Should we go?"

The blond man seemed to glance at Eric before continuing. "Perhaps some of you would like help in keeping this question in your minds. Maybe you don't have a lot of experience keeping your unbroken focus on something for two solid hours. Let me help you. Sit up straight. If you find yourself leaning against the back of the bench, or your legs stretching out in front of you, an alarm should go off inside your head. Watch your breath. Let yourself taste what you ate for supper from the traces of Kung Pao chicken in your mouth. Listen to what I say only if you want to, but don't let any of this —the breath, the residues in your teeth, or the words you hear spoken this evening—don't permit any of it to rob you of your unwavering connection with the only question that has any value. Why am I here?"

No one laughed as Eric sat up straight, looked around the room and whispered, "This is my grade 3 teacher, Mrs. Skilbomber. We finally have proof of reincarnation."

"I know why I am here. But no one can tell you why you're here. Not your therapist, not your confessor, not your Grade 3 teacher."

Eric went rigid.

"Don't pay attention to anything that doesn't help you answer this question. Let it keep hitting against your dullness, your fear, and your desire for the evening to end so that you can go out and get an ice cream, go and catch your favorite TV show.

"I may tell you things about the Titanians that you don't know. This is a pretty mixed group here right now. Some of you have had visions about them. Some of you are here because you're afraid your world is about to fall apart. A few of you are here because you've heard of me personally. None of that matters. What matters is that you use the next eight weeks to really understand, perhaps for the first time, the value of your human life. I wonder how many of you have the slightest inkling of how incredibly precious it is to be born a human being or a cetacean.

"Some of you think, since life on this planet may get annihilated a few weeks from now, you should wait and see what happens. If it doesn't get destroyed then you'll have lots of time to really get into this question of the meaning of life. But if it is going to get destroyed, then why bother investing any real effort in a dead-end species, and in a form of consciousness that is about to become obsolete? You may not have said that out loud, but look into your own mind. Look right now. Can you track down that kind of thought and corner it in its miserable, dark little cave? Can you see that you don't know whether anything is really worthwhile doing now?

"Ask yourself another question. Do you think highly enough of yourself and your world to feel some healthy, bottomless grief that it all now hangs by a gossamer thread?"

John glanced over at Eric. He was actually sitting up straight.

"Imagine that your mother or your child is going to die in eight weeks. A roomful of doctors has assembled to give you the news with an appropriately solemn air, before they all rush out to answer telephone messages, play golf, and file Medicare claims. They leave you in the empty waiting room to absorb the devastating news. Now you have to go and see your dear mother or child with the knowledge that in about eight weeks you will never be able to hug them or talk with them again. Would you feel like you do now, now that the doctors have pronounced that everything you know and love may be about to die?"

Then he didn't say anything for almost five minutes. The candle kept burning. Everyone kept breathing. A powerful quality of stillness settled over the room. Some outside traffic noises could be heard, but inside there was an astonishing absence of virtually all the sounds of restlessness with which people usually greet silence. No one scratched himself; no one shifted the position of a leg, coughed, or whispered something to their neighbor. It was as if everyone had remembered a solemn pledge made in a distant past, before his life had succumbed to distraction.

A memory of rushing six-year-old Eric to the ER with a fractured collarbone came back to John, as vividly as the day it had happened. Then Hal was talking again.

"How can we learn to value all of life as much as we value our own child? There's something strangely comforting in the thought that everyone may die together and that the cause is so cosmic that no one could possibly reproach us personally for it. No one, not Saint Peter, not God himself, can possibly accuse you of not having worked hard enough to save your children, your friends, yourself. And none of us will have to suffer any grief. None of us are going to have to wander around for years, maimed in our souls at the loss of the person we most deeply loved, the person without whom life can not ever again seem warm and friendly.

"That sounds pretty good doesn't it? No blame, no grief, no bitter prayers on behalf of loved ones gone long ago, by survivors still wailing in their endless nights. Sounds like the way to go, doesn't it? In fact it sounds so good that many of us who have never before been able to imagine the inescapable reality of our own personal death, are now able to glimpse it.

"Don't forget to ask yourself the question. What is the question? Do you remember?"

"Why here? Why here?" Frankie followed his refrain with laughter. A woman sitting by herself three pews ahead, turned around and stared at Frankie, her lips trembling and her eyes welling.

Hal said something in a guttural, foreign language, then continued in English. "Let yourself acknowledge that deep down you believe it's OK if we all go out in some cosmic event that's beyond our control. Then ask yourself again: Why am I here?"

Silence permeated everywhere, mist floating off the sea into a pristine forest.

"We may feel that we can't answer this question. Or we may produce some answer and then decide that means we don't have to ask the question any more. But don't let either of these illusions stop you from inquiring further. Can you contact something inside you that is interested in this question? Are you capable of being surprised at how easy you find it to consign everything to oblivion? Can you contact anything inside yourself that would be willing to make some kind of effort, maybe even learn to be a different kind of person, if that is what it takes to save Earth? Can you contact something inside yourself that would be willing to do this, even knowing that you personally won't live to see the benefits?

"Let me give you a hint. You can't contact this place unless you are able to feel gratitude for who you are right now. If you can allow yourself to feel grateful for what is already blossoming in you, then you will want to share it. You will want to put your gifts completely into the service of all of life, so that this life can continue to realize its destiny. If you can feel this deeply enough, then you won't ever experience another moment of boredom for the rest of your life. You will be permeated by a clear understanding of what is most truly worthwhile for you. You will feel like an eagle borne aloft on the winds of time. You won't ever again feel like a pigeon begging for a handout on some dirty street corner.

"Why would you? Why would you waste your time worrying about what the payoff is for you personally, or whether you're being given proper credit for your contributions, when every cell in your body has entered into the sacred work of saving Earth?

"Please understand this. If you don't remember anything else after tonight but to go on asking yourself, 'why am I here?' then that's enough. That's a lot. But if you have room to remember one other thing, then remember this. You personally have an opportunity in the next fifty-six days to bring a wonderful being into the universe. The planet Earth. If Earth survives this encounter with the Visitor, then it is destined to flourish as never before. It will become a world in which all beings care about what happens to one another.

"Our Earth can become a conscious participant in the cosmos. The Titanians have come in the sacred hope that they can help bring this new being into life. They are much older than us and can show us the great world that lies beyond our own little one. But first we have to want to be born into this new world.

"Make no mistake about it. There are examples right here in this solar system where the midwife was not allowed into the house. This will probably not mean much to you, since it doesn't have any counterpart in what you have been taught, but the planet Venus is the corpse of such a mother."

Despite his effort to stay focused, John stopped hearing very much of what Hal was saying. Was it safe for them to be here, at a talk about Titan and whales, with Bill's Datsun parked on the street nearby? The FBI could be tailing Hal. But leaving now, in the middle of Hal's talk could alert some FBI agent dozing in the back pew, who wouldn't notice them leaving in a crowd.

Suddenly there was a soft wailing sound that filled the church. As it continued, rising and falling with a deep resonance, he recognized that the sound was coming from the bowl on the table. As he watched, the blond man lay the padded stick back down on the tablecloth.

The undulating vibrations seemed to ride on the silence and become a mirror for its depth, gradually dying down, until only silence remained.

The talk continued. "What matters is how we greet our destiny. Let me give you an example of what I mean.

"Suppose you find yourself in quicksand. You struggle, squirm, thrash around, exhaust yourself—but you keep sinking.

"There's only one useful thing to do in this situation. You have to accept your own death. After you have done that, then you can ask yourself if you have left anything important undone in your life. If it occurs to you that there is something you really should try to get done, before you sink down into the suffocating muck, then you can go from there.

"Your situation may not be completely hopeless. Perhaps your feet will come to rest on solid ground. Perhaps it's the head of someone who was there last week and panicked." A burst of laughter greeted this last remark. Hal let it die down naturally, and then continued. "Another possibility is that someone will walk by and ask if you need a helping hand.

"But what if you just keep sinking? What if your prayers sink with you? That might be a good time to remember the question. What was the question?"

Several voices spoke out loud. "Why am I here?"

The blond man allowed silence to close over again. "Let me give you a method that has worked for me. You look for the nearest place that looks like solid ground, then roll there. First take a deep breath—it may be your last. Then you have to let your whole head sink down into the muck. There's no other way to get your legs up near the surface, so that you can roll toward the solid ground. If you have too far to go, then you will die. But if you are meant to have the chance to work on that unfinished business, then you will make it. You might even lose consciousness, but wake up with your mouth out of the muck just enough that you are able to breath. That was what happened to me."

Suddenly he pitched his voice differently. As if someone had just rushed into the living room and announced that the house was on fire. "The intelligent beings of Venus didn't notice the helping hand that the Titanians offered them. They let the comet destroy them. They were either sleeping or screaming when it hit."

Hal's voice returned to its earlier modulation, as he continued. "In many traditional cultures there is a rite of passage required to claim the rights and responsibilities of a full fledged member. Our Moon is about to be called upon to demonstrate that she can claim these rights.

"In many martial arts, it is necessary to let the opponent penetrate into our space. Then we move the space so that the force which has entered it will be harmlessly deflected. Our first impulse may be to strike out before our opponent has a chance to hit us. But then, if we miss, we will be worse off. It is better to let our attacker close, so that he will throw all this energy and balance into the empty space we suddenly offer him.

"The Moon must deflect the fist of this comet. Otherwise Earth will be destroyed."

This material was apparently harder for the audience to absorb. There were more indications of restlessness. John stole a glance at Leslie and was surprised to see how completely unbroken her concentration remained. He felt abashed at the contrast with his own weakened attention.

"I am going to ask that the four of you remain here for awhile longer tonight. You know who you are. My lecture is almost finished. Most of you have reached the point where you can no longer be very open to anything else I could say. So I will do us all a favor and let you leave while you still have the possibility of remembering what you have heard. Perhaps something will take root in the days ahead. I hope so.

"Let me finish up by asking each of you to send loving thoughts to our Moon. She is resting now, but soon she must face the dragon all alone. She will be alone in the vastness of space when the dragon comes upon her. So please remember her in your prayers and in your dreams. Please consider the possibility that this is why you are here tonight.

"What is the question?"

Seemingly relieved at the chance to take a more active role, a chorus of voices responded. "Why am I here?"

He held his palms together, bent low toward the audience for a few moments, then rose quickly and disappeared into the side door from which he had appeared two hours previously.

John looked at Leslie. He felt a pang of anxiety as he saw her continue to stare at the door through which Hal had just disappeared. John felt himself questioning whether he could be one of the four people this man had chosen. He sat there, while the church gradually emptied, feeling drained, empty, as if ashamed of something he could not quite bring to mind.

He stole a glance at Eric. Neither of them made their usual clown face. John looked away quickly in unexpected embarrassment.

When Frankie slipped down off John's lap and began the long trip up the aisle toward the front of the church, John stood up and followed. A moment later, he felt Leslie's arm looping around his waist and he felt a surge of gratitude.

They all stepped onto the raised platform and headed toward the side door. Frankie reached up toward the doorknob but it was too high. John found himself opening it instead of knocking.

As the door swung wide, the blond man stood up and faced them. Then suddenly the yogi's face was trembling and he was on his knees, his forehead and forearms pressing into the carpet, as Frankie laughed and tottered happily forward to greet him.

CHAPTER 35

Friday, Feb 14 (Day -55)

Hal had succeeded in talking John out of all his excuses for not visiting Sea World—such as concern for the attention they would draw if Frankie and the dolphins started interacting. Hal had also shared some incredible things. About how the Titanians had chosen pairs of brothers to try to communicate with. He claimed that John and Patrick were one such pair. Hal himself, together with his brother, was another. When Hal spoke of his brother, George Ball, and how he had tried to kill him when Hal had finally tracked him down, you got the feeling that there was not a lot of hope for the world.

Now it was Friday, the day the Titan Ocean was due to swing back into view of Earth, and John wondered if the world's radio telescopes were waiting. He had made a lot of phone calls, written a lot of letters, and not everyone had treated him like a madman. They left the Pinnaped show early, unable to feel entertained by contrived gestures performed in exchange for food. As they made their way out of the amphitheater, Eric provided a running commentary on what the animals were really saying. "Clean your ears, Mildred. I didn't say piss on me, I said Listerine. Use Listerine."

John could feel his heart pounding as they followed the signs for the dolphin exhibit. They walked past the food concessions and spectator arenas, where shows were offered at posted times, until they reached the building where bottlenose dolphins could be observed through plate glass viewing windows.

As soon as they entered, Frankie started kicking and wouldn't stop until John put him down on the floor. Frankie ran up to one of the viewing windows and a dolphin immediately approached, placing its snout directly against the glass. Seeing that Frankie's fingers could only reach the window ledge, John knelt down and lifted his son up onto his knee. Frankie immediately pressed his forehead against the glass and the dolphin shifted so that its melon was on the other side, directly opposite.

In a few moments, all the other dolphins in the pool approached. John could hear a couple behind them agreeing that in all the years they'd been coming to Sea World they had never seen the dolphins behave like that, hovering flank to flank ten feet below the surface, all staring at the human visitors.

John started to feel frightened. It wasn't so much the dolphins' overt behavior that affected him—although that was unnerving—as what was happening inside his mind. Something was beginning to deeply infiltrate his image of himself and the world.

With a shock of recognition, he realized that the dolphins were trying to talk to him. His mind felt crowded and invaded and he heard his own silent voice crying out, "Stop! One of you at a time."

To John's amazement, the dolphins immediately understood. They started swimming around, exchanged intelligent looks, then all rose together to the surface, presumably to breathe. After a few minutes, one dolphin returned to the window and pressed its melon against the glass in front of John. He understood that he was being invited to touch the glass with his own forehead, so he leaned forward until his cheek was on Frankie's hair. Then something very unusual happened. He became aware of being in the presence of a great community of minds. Hundreds of thousands of beings were avidly waiting to learn if John could accomplish something that they had been unable to accomplish.

They weren't interested in anything on the level of, "Greetings from my species." They wanted to corroborate with

John in an attempt to communicate with the missile that had fallen silent for JPL scientists. Thousands of dolphins, together with their cousins the whales, had congregated at several locations in the world's oceans in order to transmit a message to this missile.

The cetaceans would utilize the Titanian's capacity to send a stream of electrons across millions of miles of space, aiming this stream of electrons towards the missile. The environment being probed in this way would somehow be able to feed back information about what was found, as if the stream of electrons was itself a living, swimming entity.

John was wondering if the Titanians had reestablished contact with Earth, when the walls surrounding the pool and the tiled floor beneath him disappeared. Eyes and ears had sprouted all over his body. He was swimming in vast space and could directly experience everything that appeared in that space. He was overwhelmed by the intelligence and sentience of the world. The oceans were full of beings whose calm, intelligent minds had all congregated together for a very serious purpose.

Astounding images of the missile filled his mind. Glints of starlight reflected off the missile's conical nose. Minuscule vibrations from small impacts with cosmic dust could be perceived in the shimmering reflections. In other images, it was possible to directly apprehend the relative motions and positions of the comet and the missile.

John knew that, even with the aid of computers, it was far beyond the reach of human precision to correlate electrons, returning after a journey of many millions of miles, with the corresponding electrons that had left Earth a minute or so earlier. Dolphins, however, lived in this kind of milieu. The process by which sonar echoes are processed and interpreted requires an incredibly accurate recognition of just this sort of returning signal.

There were also images of the interior of the missile, real-time snapshots of a complex machine which was by now far too distant from Earth for any human-made instruments to record anything other than a radio signal sent from it. Yet John was at that very moment seeing images of the bomb's interior with its intricate control mechanisms. His early training in robotics helped him to make sense of what he saw.

He intuitively understood that the beings who were producing these images had not figured out how everything worked. The parts that resembled an animal's body—shell, structural elements, circuits, insulation, transmitters, and sensors—had all been organized well. The images had the clarity of anatomical drawings in which the systems for the skeleton, muscles, arteries, veins and neurological pathways all stand out distinctly. But the dolphins were obviously having difficulty visualizing how something capable of making such an exciting journey and communicating back to Earth about it would be logically organized around a mission to destroy the first thing it approached larger than a basketball.

John suddenly realized that the dolphins had been looking at this missile for weeks. If they could have figured it out on their own it would have already been destroyed. In a way it seemed surprising to him that they hadn't figured it out on their own. After all, what was so different between a switch designed to detonate a bomb and the anatomical/neurological features in the dolphins' own bodies that allowed for coordination of breath and digestion and the incredibly sophisticated processes of sonar communication?

It was surprisingly easy to see where the dolphins had made their mistake. They had failed to draw a link between the main processor, which communicated with JPL, and the detonation processor, which was connected with the bomb. The way they had drawn it, there was no physical channel through which mission control could affect the detonation, in any way.

John suspected this channel probably ran through an area of the missile's interior which was shielded from the electron flow by intervening material.

Not knowing what else to do, John willed his mind to draw on one of the images, as if he were using a felt marker on an overhead. He simply drew in a communication cable to join the two processors.

There was a strangely lifeless quality to his effort, as if in making this modification he had cut himself off from the immense energy and intelligence streaming out of the world's oceans. But he could sense the cetaceans collaborating with him. They incorporated his superimposition into the drawing. They let it remain in the image, its intended meaning clear.

Time passed. John knew that they were waiting out the interval it took for electrons to reach the missile, interact with the area in question, and return to Earth. They waited until the image changed. His overlay of the missing pathway vanished and something like the original drawing reappeared —as brilliant, alive and intense as any reality he had ever experienced.

The message was devastatingly clear. There was no such connection. The hardware simply wasn't there. The detonation processor was connected to a barrage of sensors—such as infrared cameras—and it was connected to the bomb. But it was completely unrelated to any command that could be sent by the Deep Space Tracking Center at JPL. Ever.

Suddenly all the images disappeared. No further discussion needed. John frantically tried to initiate new lines of inquiry. Could they utilize the electron stream to affect the path of the missile directly, or sweep up interplanetary dust into sufficient concentrations that passage through it could activate the heat-sensitive trigger in the cone of the bomb housing?

The dolphins must have been over that kind of territory countless times. They didn't need humans to brainstorm with them. They had contacted humans because humans had made this abomination, and because there might have been a possibility that humans would be able to turn it off. Well, the humans couldn't turn it off.

John felt like someone whose own behavior has helped kill someone's dear relative. Now he was being led politely to the door by the grieving family. They wanted to be alone.

Sea World came back into consciousness. Frankie was still on John's knee. Leslie and Eric were also leaning against the window. His wife looked like she had just woken up to a sudden crack of thunder—disoriented, groggy and afraid. Then Leslie screamed.

Frankie was having a fit. Leslie snatched him from John and together they looked at their youngest son. His limbs were thrashing and pink saliva was oozing from the corners of his mouth.

Eric's horrified voice added to the dreadful experience. "Look at the dolphins. They're trying to kill themselves."

John took a quick glance through the viewing screen and saw that the dolphins were dashing themselves against the walls of their enclosure and colliding with one another, as if acid was eating them alive.

John felt himself being grabbed roughly by men wearing dark blue uniforms.

Then Sea World disappeared again. John was in open ocean. There was blood all around. A ring of boats was tightening around a pod of whales. The boats had shining cylinders with dark mouths from which vicious, sharp things launched.

Then John was sitting in an office. There was no sign of his family. Handcuffs prevented him from moving his arms. He tasted blood in his mouth. There were two men in police uniforms sitting across the room.

One of the officers stood up, knocked on the window into the corridor and shouted, "He's awake again."

The other looked contemptuously at John and sneered. "Now I know why the warrant said, 'arrest on sight. Take alive if possible'. You're some kind of devil, aren't you, man? You killed at least two of those dolphins. Don't try any of your mind games on me. I'll be real happy to tell them it wasn't possible to take you alive."

Welcome to hell.

CHAPTER 36

Patrick watched Ted pace back and forth in their Scott Air Force Base hole-in-the-wall. A security guard stood at ease in the corridor outside, staring straight ahead. Breakfast trays lay untouched on the desk.

The wall clock indicated 8:00 am. Ted's old Air Force buddy had been gone for 30 minutes and now there was only an hour left until their 10:00 am (Washington time) meeting with the President. It no longer seemed possible that they could make it.

Suddenly the room vanished. In its place was a scene of horror. Whales were being slaughtered all around him. He struggled to regain control of his mind—telling himself that this had to be a projection of his own fear of being killed, fed by what he had heard George say on the CD. But the images wouldn't go away.

He seemed to be seeing everything with eyes that were sometimes in the air, sometimes just below the water. Suddenly a harpoon gun discharged and the sea turned red. His head was full of a terrible screaming, at a pitch that was too high for his ears to hear. Then just as suddenly as it had vanished, the room came back into focus.

Patrick could hear a commotion in the hall. He saw the airman on the other side of the door window come to attention. "Yes, sir! Immediately, sir!"

Was it Patrick's imagination, or had this guard not seemed quite so impressed previously by Lieutenant Colonel David Lee?

The door flung open, and three officers entered the room. Patrick couldn't prevent himself from rising quickly to his feet, as if the principal had just walked into his grade-school classroom.

One of the men had four stars on his jacket.

Lee spoke. "General, Sir. Brigadier, Sir. These are the two men who drove through the gate this morning. Ted Sullo and Patrick Murphy. They claim they have an appointment with the President this morning at ten hundred hours."

The four-star general pinioned Patrick with his gaze. "Why the hell would the President want to see you, Murphy?"

Patrick felt his heart beating rapidly. He had never been too good with authority figures, but he managed to answer, "I believe it's because I know things about the comet, sir."

Four-star shot back. "What do you know about this comet? And how do you know it?"

Here's where they'd get locked up in the loony bin. "It's 200 miles in diameter, it's due to impact Earth 55 days from now, and it will shatter into a squadron of lethal, flying mountains if that bomb is detonated. I know this because I've been in contact with a whale who saved my life 40 years ago. This whale tells me things which I would have no normal way of knowing. I believe that the President has asked to see me because of this."

Lee turned to the General. "I'm sorry to waste your time with this, Sir."

The General raised his hand, his gaze remaining unwaveringly on Patrick, and Lee immediately fell silent. After a moment, the General announced that he was going back to his office. He nodded through the window and the door was quickly opened.

When the Brigadier and Lieutenant Colonel started to follow him out into the corridor, he told them to stay where they were.

The four men remained awkwardly in the small room for what seemed like a long time.

Then the phone rang. Patrick glanced at the wall clock. It registered 8:07.

The ranking officer picked it up. "Yes, Sir. Right away, Sir. Your own jet, Sir? Yes, I understand. We'll be there immediately."

Ted grinned. He held up his hands to indicate the handcuffs. But the Brigadier appeared not to notice the gesture.

The Brigadier turned to Lieutenant Colonel Lee. "Both these men have warrants out for their arrest. Very serious National Security violation charges. However, they are to be flown immediately to Andrews Air Force Base in the Commander's personal jet. The President's Chief of Staff has affirmed that there is a meeting scheduled for ten hundred hours, Atlantic Time, to which Sullo and both Murphy brothers have been invited."

The Brigadier General grimaced. "Air Force has drawn security detail on this one. We are to escort these two gentlemen all the way to the White House. We are to release them to the President's own Security personnel, who will have a disposition signed by the Commander-in-Chief. We have our orders."

Lieutenant Colonel Lee whistled. At a glance from the Brigadier General, the door opened and all four men quickly moved into the corridor.

They were driven at high speed to Headquarters Command. Lieutenant Colonel Lee had become more communicative. He explained to Ted and Patrick that he was a squadron commander, the Brigadier General was Base Commander, and the four-star general was Headquarters commander. He shook his head in disbelief as he told them that they were now on their way to the four-star's private Lear jet, on which they were all going to fly to Andrews. He made it clear that not everyone who gate crashed at Scott was offered this experience.

Patrick tried to rub his nose with his right hand, and was caught up short by the handcuffs. Suddenly he remembered his horrible vision. He interrupted in a loud voice, "The whales around Hawaii are in danger and the President needs to know."

Lieutenant Colonel Lee looked at Patrick and said, "I heard about that on the radio when I stopped by my office. I thought that kind of shit was over. The Greenpeace guy they had on the 7:30 a.m. news said more than 20 whales were killed this morning."

Then he looked more narrowly at Patrick. "I didn't see a radio where you were waiting. How did you find out about it?"

Patrick forced down the bile that was rising in his throat. "You need to get us to the President. I felt it happen. This is exactly why the President wants to meet me."

Lee didn't seem too impressed.

The car came to a sudden stop beside a Lear jet, whose engines were already fired up. Patrick was pulled out of the car into the noise and wind, propelled up the stairway, then pushed and seat-belted into a chair. Within 10 seconds they were rolling down the runway. Within two minutes they were airborne.

CHAPTER 37

John felt numb. No one answered his questions about his family. They treated him like someone outside the realm in which common decency operates. Matters had improved marginally when San Diego Naval Security had taken over. At least now he wasn't being guarded by some guy who thought he was Damian, child of Satan.

But still, no one was talking to him. He sat handcuffed in a small windowless room, somewhere in a Naval yard.

So much for telling the world about the comet and about the amazing communication from alien beings. He would be lucky to ever see Leslie and his kids again. His abortive attempt to tell people had been an utter failure. He had come across as a complete flake on the radio. And now he was under arrest for some undisclosed crime, apparently so heinous that people were afraid of being in the same room with him.

For the first time in a decade, John felt a wave of nostalgia for his Canadian childhood. He wished he were there now. Living some low-profile life as a professor at McGill University in Montreal.

The door opened and a guard informed him that he was being moved to a different location.

He spent the next three hours moving to this different location. First he was taken by helicopter to a small airfield. Then he was flown by jet clear across the continent. During the flight, he was given a dry sandwich and a cup of coffee, both of which he had to lift awkwardly with both hands because of the handcuffs. If he weren't so frightened, he could have laughed at the image of himself as too dangerous to eat a sandwich normally.

They landed—he assumed at Andrews Air Force Base. No one would affirm or deny anything, let alone give him the slightest idea about what was going on.

They drove into town. He couldn't believe it when their limo was waved onto the White House grounds.

Still in shackles, John was led to a room in the basement. There the Navy guard relinquished him to another security group. The Navy people spent a surprising amount of time scrutinizing the documents which the new security force handed over.

A door was opened and John was led into a room where a meeting appeared to be already in session. The room looked larger than it actually was because of a wall-length mirror at one end. It flashed into John's mind that this could all be a psychological experiment, with a tank full of Titanians watching in an adjacent room.

With a shock, he recognized his brother and Agent Sullo. Patrick raised his wrists and flashed his handcuffs in John's direction. John felt a sudden burst of relief.

A clock on the wall indicated that it was 2:45 p.m., Washington time.

John couldn't believe who was chairing this meeting. It was the President's Chief of Staff, Phil Black. To his left sat some kind of high-ranking Air Force officer, with four stars on his jacket.

Phil Black was talking. "Now that Dr. John Murphy has arrived, we can get down to the nitty-gritty. Thank you for coming on such short notice, Professor."

A few people chuckled. But the atmosphere of suspicion and hostility which he had felt since waking up in a Sea World office was still very much in evidence. He felt it most strongly from a man who sat immediately to the right of Phil Black. This man seemed to glower at John with undisguised hatred.

Phil Black sat at one end of the long table—the end which faced the mirror. At his right sat the glowering man, then a lean-faced man with a thin mustache, who appeared very nervous, and further down the table sat Sullo and Patrick. Immediately on Phil Black's left was Four-Star, followed by a few empty chairs. A security guard pulled one of these out for John.

Tough-looking men stood on the perimeter of the room, staring straight ahead with an air of alertness. Some were clustered behind Patrick and Sullo, others moved in behind John. And John was surprised to see that there were two men, who seemed to be poised on the balls of their feet, immediately behind the man whose eyes flashed with loathing in John's direction.

Phil Black now addressed the man with the thin mustache. "Director Richard Todd. Please fill us in on what's happening here. Tell us why there are warrants out—under your signature—for the arrest of Patrick Murphy, John Murphy and Ted Sullo."

The room was silent. Director Todd looked like a caged rat. When he spoke, John could hear a tremor in his voice, "I don't think I need to explain to you, Phil, that there are some very strange things about these two brothers. I was calling them in for questioning. I have ample documentation that John Murphy contacted the media with the declared intention of going public with national security-sensitive material."

Phil Black interrupted. "Why arrest the other two? And what about the wording, 'Alive if possible'? That sounds like strong language to use when bringing in three men for questioning, especially when none of them have a prior record of wrongdoing. Wouldn't you agree, Director Todd?"

Director Todd dabbed his forehead with a handkerchief, although the basement room was on the chilly side. John couldn't help noticing that the man seated between Director Todd and Phil Black seemed increasingly agitated. Whereas Director Todd seemed nervous, the other man seemed on the verge of catatonic fury.

The director stammered several times during his response. "In retrospect, I would reconsider my actions, Sir. I may have been a bit carried away with the madness of the current situation. But now that we know the comet is heading straight toward Earth, it looked as if these Murphy brothers could be very dangerous. How did they know about it three weeks ago? I may have been excessive in my response, Sir, but I was trying to address a major security problem."

The four-star general spoke. "Why Agent Sullo? Isn't he one of your own men? Why did you issue an arrest order for him? And why the hell, if you want to know what the Murphy's connection is with the Titan message, would you risk having some paranoid cop shoot them?"

Director Todd mumbled something about the extraordinary times which they were all living through. But Four-Star wasn't listening. He turned to Ted Sullo. "Agent, why did you insist that we invite this man, George Ball? What the hell does a contractor in the defense industry have to do with all this?"

Mr. George Ball leaned towards Phil Black. His whisper seemed designed to carry around the table. "I have to agree, Phil. This is not the right context to discuss how the Murphy brothers' violated Umbrella Project security. I don't see why I need to be here."

Phil Black glanced at George Ball briefly, then immediately gave his attention back to Four-Star.

Four-Star kept his unwavering gaze on Ted, as if no one else existed in the room.

Ted returned Four-Star's gaze with silent intensity. Then he turned to Patrick. "Give him the CD."

Patrick started fumbling in the breast pocket of his jacket. After a few moments, it became apparent that he was having trouble retrieving the cassette with handcuffs on, and a security officer stepped away from the wall and pulled it out. John recognized the cassette jacket as 'Blood on the Tracks' by Bob Dylan. The officer handed it to the general, who inserted it into a CD Player which lay on the desk in front of him.

Then the General looked at Ted. "Fill us in on where this comes from."

John listened in amazement as Ted outlined how he had bugged his Director's briefcase because he sensed that the FBI's relationship with this particular man, George Ball, appeared to be irregular. "It just didn't make sense that the Director of the FBI would cringe at a look from a Defense contractor. I wanted to know why."

John's view of Agent Ted Sullo did a complete somersault as he listened to why Ted had warned him to get out of Albuquerque fast, and how he had then driven to Maine to snatch Patrick, moments before the arrival of Director Todd's assassins. As Ted spoke, Director Todd turned deathly pale.

Finally Ted concluded. "I copied one of the most incriminating conversations onto this Dylan CD. It starts a little ways in on cut 2."

The general pushed the PLAY button and skipped to track 2.

They listened to a little bit of Dylan and then suddenly there was a man talking. It was George Ball. The faces around the room became increasingly grim as they listened to obscenities about the 'pussy-whipped President' and his wife. Then came a harangue about the spineless degeneration of modern life, in which particular emphasis was placed on the deplorable assent of women into positions of power and influence. There was particular mention of the President's wife and a woman named Jane. George's greatest hatred was reserved for people who claimed to know things clairvoyantly —and the rising influence of such people in the world.

Then the two men got down to business. Business consisted of cold-bloodedly reviewing a checklist of who had been killed and who needed to be killed. In this particular conversation there were three targets enumerated: John, Patrick and some cetaceans who were rumored to be congregating around Hawaii.

What struck John as most appalling in this conversation was that the two men seemed to accept as given that there really were alien beings who were talking to the cetaceans, and that he and Patrick really did talk to a whale. George seemed to accept this more readily than John himself ever had, and it was in the context of this intra-species communication that enemies were being identified who needed to be eliminated.

Why bother? In the presence of such extraordinary things, how could anyone be concerned about defending themselves and their prejudices? And then John noticed something profoundly weird: George hated clairvoyants; but how did he himself know all this stuff about the Titanians and the whales?

The recording moved on to a ghastly plan to slaughter any aquatic mammals that showed up around Hawaii. That appalled John at a deeper level than anything else. It almost made sense that someone might want to kill Patrick and himself. But to kill more whales and dolphins, out of some kind of military/industrial paranoia? This lay outside any psychological model comprehensible to John.

Suddenly Dylan music was playing again. The general leaned forward and pressed the STOP button.

John realized that nothing on this CD adequately explained why Director Richard Todd was carrying out this vile agenda. At one point in the recorded conversation, George had observed how important it was to the President to count on the loyalty of his intelligence agencies. There had followed a remark that clearly carried some powerful innuendo for Director Todd: "Be sure to say hello to Carlos when you see him. And tell him from me that he's not paying you enough." It was only after this remark, John now recalled, that the Director had agreed that the Murphy brothers were indeed a very serious problem.

Phil Black appeared to have been shocked into silence by what he had heard. It crossed John's mind that the White House in general, and the President in particular, may have had a few questionable links of their own with this man, George.

John shifted his gaze to Four-Star. In spite of himself, he found himself hoping that the general would take over the meeting. It was time for someone decisive, and untainted, to take charge.

John followed Four-Star's gaze to the two men whose conversation had been bugged. Their respective demeanor could not have been more dissimilar. The FBI Director looked like he was going to cry, faint, or shit his pants. George looked like he would love to personally pluck the eyes out of everyone present.

Then the Director started blathering. "One mistake. I made one mistake. Only George knew about it. Before I knew it, I was in too deep to turn back. I started signing things that I didn't even look at beforehand."

The first thing John noticed was that the security detail was suddenly in motion. Then he noticed that George was standing. His hands gripped Director Todd's head like it was a football he was about to toss.

Too fast to really see, he spun around and one of the security guards slumped across the table.

Director Todd's head was now lying flat against one of his shoulders.

A security guard managed to land a decisive blow and within seconds they had George in handcuffs, his elbows cinched behind his back and his ankles knotted tightly.

John couldn't believe it when George started talking. The man was like a wolverine, leaping against the wire mesh of its cage.

"Baaaa. Baaaa. Baaaa. The sky is falling, the sky is falling. Let's send up a bomb. No, wait, we better turn it off. We mustn't upset the clairvoyants and the giant eels."

George's expression had shifted into a kind of leering joviality, as if he had slipped over into some psychotic realm which he had previously managed to keep hidden. He started shaking his head and tut-tut-tutting to someone no one else could see. "Mr. President, Sir! Did you think I'd let you just shut down our missile? Did you really think that? I'm afraid that's not going to happen, Sir! Cause Georgie Boy is going to make a hero out of you. And then don't you be forgetting your old friends—you hear!"

It had become increasingly obvious that George was addressing someone who wasn't physically present in the room. Meanwhile his voice had become more slurred, perhaps from the blow on the back of his neck.

John turned toward the large mirror at the end of the room. Could the President actually be watching all this? Would George know about a room equipped with a one way-mirror at the White House? Or was he talking to some hallucination, incarcerated within a mind that had now completely succumbed to madness?

Four-Star's voice sounded surprisingly gentle. "Take him away. He won't be telling us anything useful for a while. If ever. And please remove the corpse."

Everyone got up and cleared a path while they took George out of the room. There was no struggle from the man who had just killed with such lightening speed. John found himself on his feet, well clear of the door, even though George seemed to be effectively bound.

As George was being carried through the door he suddenly turned towards John and smiled. "Give my best to your family. What's your youngest son's name? Frankie, isn't it?" Then George disappeared into the corridor and the door closed behind him.

John felt cold.

A few minutes later, the security detail returned and three of them removed Director Todd's body—one at the shoulders, one at the feet, and one cradling the head like it was a newborn infant.

After the room had been cleared, everyone returned to their seats.

Four-Star spoke with the kind of quiet authority that everyone in the room must have been craving. "If it was my decision to make, I'd take the cuffs off these three men. They're not criminals, they're heroes. And I personally would have no trouble working with Agent Sullo as interim FBI Director. Would you care to respond to that, Sir?"

John noticed that the general, like George earlier, was definitely talking to the mirror. Following his question, Four-Star sat silently.

After several moments, the door opened. There was a gasp and suddenly everyone was on his feet.

The President looked pale, almost ashen. He gestured for them to sit back down, but everyone remained standing until he had taken the seat at the head of the table, which Phil Black relinquished.

The President nodded to Four-Star. "Thank you, Peter. Please plan on remaining in Washington for a few days. I need you."

He turned to Ted. "Director Sullo, I'd appreciate your presence at the 5:00 p.m. staff meeting in my office. I'll let Peter and Phil fill you in on the agenda."

Then he looked at Patrick and John. "Which one of you should I talk to about harnessing the Moon?"

John bowed in Patrick's direction. "My brother can take you farther along that path, Sir."

The President turned to Patrick. "We don't have a whole lot of time left. This is the way I see it. We need to harness all possible resources and that means I need to get back on TV and tell people what's really happening. We need to talk to anyone who can tell us how to move the comet."

With a visible shudder, he added, "It looks like we have a problem with the missile that's already on its way. JPL can't get it to respond to commands. I'm afraid the project chief for that mission was George Ball."

As if the subject was too painful to explore further, he turned to his Chief of Staff. "Phil, set up an Address to the Nation for 8:00 tonight. An hour should be enough."

Phil Black looked surprised, seemed about to say something, then rose from his chair and started making phone calls from a corner of the room.

The President turned his full attention to Patrick. "Whom do we contact, Patrick?" Then with a wan semblance of his trademark grin he added, "I want you to know that I'm not prejudiced against whales and dolphins, but if I can have a few humans around at all times, I'd feel more comfortable."

There were chuckles around the table, but Patrick didn't join in. "About Hawaii, Sir."

The President waved his hand. "There won't be any more killing. I give you my word on it. I've ordered a full mobilization out of the Hanauma Bay Naval Base on Oahu. Any boat found with whaling gear will be impounded and stripped immediately. And anyone on board such a craft is looking at jail time. The same with any illegal nets. Hawaii will be clean within 24 hours."

Then Patrick and John told the President what they knew. They told him about George's brother Hal and how Hal had said that the Titanians needed George to be a channel. The President sneered when George's name was mentioned, and John felt relieved that the head of the free world shared his own sentiments on this piece of human garbage.

For some reason his brother wouldn't leave it alone. Patrick insisted that George remained a critical factor, and that he needed to be kept safe from his security guards.

The President shrugged, glanced at one of the security men standing at the edge of the room and said, "Make sure our prisoner stays healthy." Then he returned his attention to Patrick and John. After a little more persuasion—mainly from

Patrick—the President agreed to set up a conference call with Hal Nagen the next day.

At 4:45 p.m., Phil Black had to remind the President about a meeting at 5:00. By then a plan had been made to meet in Hawaii two days from then.

On his way out, the President suddenly turned and asked John if there was anything he wanted. John answered without thinking. "I'd like to listen to your address this evening with my family in Albuquerque."

Before the President could respond, Four-Star clapped John on the shoulder. "My jet is parked out at Andrews, and my boss says I have to hang around for the next few days. You might as well use it."

John didn't refuse.

He and Patrick promised that they would see each other in Hawaii in a few days. Then John let himself be hurried through corridors and into a limousine. He was amazed at how quickly he was in the air. Then he was talking with Leslie on the phone. His relief at hearing her voice, safe and sound at home, was immediately dashed. Her voice sounded so flat that he could scarcely recognize her.

John felt the shadow of some unspeakable predator settling over his heart, as Leslie sobbed, unable to speak. An image of George smilingly inquiring after the health of his family came back now, bearing its full weight of horror.

John leaned his forehead against the seat in front of him. Except for the hand pressing the cellular phone hard against his ear, his body felt like it had no bones in it. Leslie's words echoed in a space where the last light was already extinguishing. "Oh, John, they've kidnapped Frankie. Our baby is gone."

CHAPTER 38

Patrick listened to the Address to the Nation from inside the White House. In addition to giving a sobering, but still downplayed, description of the threat posed to Earth, the President announced the formation of a task force to study the feasibility of harnessing the Moon's gravity against the comet.

After the talk, Ted remarked that the President had not said anything about the bomb that no one could turn off, nor had he shared that the purpose of his planned trip to Hawaii was to collaborate with whales and dolphins.

Patrick looked squarely at Ted and asked, "Would you have mentioned those things?"

Ted thought for a few moments before responding, "Maybe not. I was impressed with how much he did say. Now we'll have to see if civilized life as we know it breaks down."

They watched TV for a while. It was hard to turn it off. Every single channel was delivering on their promised non-stop coverage of the comet and reactions to the President's Address. In addition to live commentary, the networks seemed to have an incredible amount of material, continuously fed by packs of roving reporters.

One news item came from a bar in Paris. After a lot of chattering in French, a patron was found who described, in English, the new rage sweeping Montmartre cafes. He himself seemed to have already imbibed several of these smoky drinks which he referred to as 'the comet'. An ounce of brandy—the nucleus around which the drink was built—was surrounded by a milky aura of Pernod, while a dash of dry ice created a cometary train affect. Judging from the condition of many of the patrons, this combination packed a comet-sized wallop.

Patrick was deeply struck by a news report on the World Peace Ceremony in northern India. Millions of people had overrun a small rural area in the mountains—ten times more than in any prior year. A group of Americans told the interviewer that this gathering was in contact with the world's whales and dolphins.

Patrick felt stunned. Millions of people had gathered together in the mountains to communicate with whales. Why wasn't he there? He felt like a fool. Here he had been clutching onto his own experience as if it was unique. But he was not some isolated freak. It was time for him to join the dance.

The phone rang. Ted picked it up quickly. "Yes, he's right here."

Patrick put the phone to his ear and said, "Hello."

At first no one responded. After a moment, someone announced that his caller was on the line. Then he heard John's voice.

Patrick felt the blood draining from his face.

Frankie was gone. It had happened in the Albuquerque Airport parking structure. Two men had thrown Leslie and Eric to the ground and snatched Frankie. By the time Leslie had regained her feet, it was just in time to watch helplessly as a white van squealed down the exit ramp. No one else saw the incident. Later the van—which had been stolen in Memphis three weeks before—was found abandoned on the West Mesa. Nearby there were signs that a small plane had landed and taken off.

Patrick was surprised at the conviction that filled his voice. "We'll find Frankie. I know we will. We need to get in touch with Hal Nagen."

Leslie was suddenly talking on the extension. "Oh, Patrick. What can we do? Who took Frankie?"

Patrick felt Leslie's terror and it fed the clarity he was feeling as he responded. "I'm so sorry, Leslie. But I know you will get Frankie back. I know who took him, and there will be a way to bargain with that person."

John's voice broke in. "Who took Frankie?"

Patrick responded immediately. "George. Who else? That's why he mentioned Frankie by name at the White House"

John's voice was full of fury. "What the hell does he want with a two-year old boy? And what does Hal Nagen have to do with any of this?"

Patrick spoke quietly. "This afternoon, when we were all sitting in that room with the general, I started getting this strange feeling about George. I had a weird intuition about him. George needs Frankie, and that's why Frankie will be safe."

John interrupted viciously. "What the hell do you mean?"

Patrick wished that Leslie would say something. When she remained silent, he forced himself to respond. "I think both George and Frankie have a direct link to the Titanians. But in George's case it has made him psychotic."

A moment later a slam sounded across the phone line.

Leslie's trembling voice came on the line. "John can't handle any of this. He blames himself for what has happened to Frankie. That was him slamming the front door. I'd better go find him. Thanks for trying, Patrick. I'll talk with you later, OK?"

The phone went dead before he could say good-bye and he slowly laid the headset back in its cradle.

Ted wanted to know everything Leslie and John had said. Then he wanted to know everything about Patrick's hunch.

Patrick tried to explain. "The Titanians are feeding George all his technological breakthroughs, and George has developed a craving for it. But psychologically, he can't handle it."

Ted wanted to know where Patrick got this from, and Patrick said he had probably got most of it from Frankie himself, the week before in Albuquerque. Then Patrick stopped in mid-sentence. "Ted, I need to talk with George. Can you set up an interrogation?"

Ted grimaced. "That guy scares the jeebies out of me. Let someone else interrogate him."

Patrick didn't miss a beat. "I'll interrogate him. I just need you to arrange it, and I need you to be present. You can keep your distance or get close. Your choice."

Ted made no response. Then he got up and walked over to the phone.

George was locked in a basement room with two muscular Secret Service men outside the door. They were both on their feet before Patrick and Ted reached the room.

The service men called Ted, "Sir," and did everything he asked without question. Word of his promotion must have got around.

Then Patrick and Ted were alone in the room with George. The prisoner's ankles and wrists were shackled, but he sat ramrod straight in a hard chair and looked directly at Patrick.

Patrick pulled a chair away from the wall and positioned it so that he was facing George, about 10 feet away. He forced himself to sit up straight and return George's gaze.

He wanted George to make the first move.

After five minutes it became clear that he could never beat George at a waiting game and Patrick broke the silence. "What do you want in exchange for the boy?"

George leered. "Respect. I don't get no respect."

Even in sarcasm things are revealed. "How would you like this respect to be expressed?"

George raised his shackled arms, and shook his head.

Patrick didn't let himself get sidetracked. "Are you saying that you'll tell us where the boy is, in exchange for your own freedom?"

No response. George was no longer smiling.

This time Patrick remained silent. After awhile, George responded with a sneer. "You gonna set me free, Dolphie Boy? Does the fruitcake think he's the President's special pal now? If you bring me the President, maybe I'll talk to him. You aren't a messenger for the janitor of this rat hole."

Patrick was surprised at how calm he felt. "You're mistaken about one thing, George. Unless Hal comes, I am your only link. I'm the uncle of the boy you've kidnapped. And I know who you are. There isn't anyone else available to you here who is connected to both you and Frankie as strongly as I am. You may not like it, but no one else is going to be able to tell the President about you."

The sneer had slipped off George's face, and he looked at Patrick with a new wariness. Patrick continued. "Do you know what you are? I think it's possible that you don't really know."

Patrick fell silent, this time determined to wait it out. George seemed to be trying hard to keep up an air of disdain, but it was dissolving. "I guess you'd better tell me, Dolphie Boy. What am I?"

Patrick let him hang for a bit. Then he started to pull in the line. It wasn't that he exactly knew. It was that he seemed to be picking things up as he sat in the same room with this man and tried pushing various buttons. "You and Frankie have both been chosen. I think it's possible that you two are unique—the only two. But I have no way of really knowing that. You both get some kind of direct transmission. I don't know why the whales choose either of you."

Patrick watched as all the loathing flowed back into George's face, and he knew that he had taken a false step. Before George could say anything, Patrick blurted out, "I don't mean the whales. I mean the Titanians."

George's eyes became narrow and seemed to burrow into Patrick like lasers cutting through steel. Patrick kept going. "It is just you and Frankie, isn't it? It's just you two who have a direct contact with the Titanians. You two alone in the human world."

Then Patrick thought he was going to die. He felt himself falling off the chair onto the hard linoleum floor. He heard Ted's voice calling out to the guards.

No one had laid a hand on him, but his head felt like an egg being fought over in a pit of vipers.

CHAPTER 39

Sunday, Feb 16 (day -53)

John, Leslie, and Eric landed at Wheeler Air Force Base on Oahu early Sunday afternoon. With Frankie missing and his whereabouts unknown, John was oblivious to the stunning ocean views on the coastal road, the lavish buffet at the manor where they were given a luxurious suite, and when he introduced Leslie to Helen, the First Lady, that evening, it was a rote, social act.

Eric, on the other hand, didn't hesitate when Helen offered to escort him to the buffet tables which were laden with food. Nor did he object when she told him he was welcome to take his heaping plate into the adjacent game room.

Looking up from his self-absorption, John was surprised to see Leslie and the First Lady outside, walking toward the beach with their arms linked, and with two husky men following at a discrete distance.

"Alfred and Jimmy won't let anything happen to them." The President's voice startled John. "I can't tell you how hard my own wife is taking this. We lost a son years ago and now it's like it's all happening again for her."

The President escorted John to a secluded corner of the large room and introduced him to Jane Grinyer and Henry Sloan of NASA and to Phil Black, his chief of staff.

John scarcely heard the ensuing discussion about the next day's meeting at the Oceanographic Center, but then suddenly his attention was yanked back.

"John, I've already told the others a bit about Hal Nagen," the President was saying. "He's going to outline the parameters for tomorrow's meeting with the cetaceans."

At the mention of Hal's name John's stomach clenched into a knot. If it wasn't for that charismatic asshole Frankie would still be with them.

As soon as the President excused himself, Henry took the opportunity to hold forth on what seemed to be a favorite subject. "The scientific community has not followed up on John Lilly's dolphin studies, which took place just down the road from here. Our model for measuring intelligence always assumes the centrality of object manipulation, but couldn't echo-location lead to a graphic-based language?"

The room fell silent as the President entered with Hal Nagen at his side. Hal walked quietly at the President's side, with his hands folded in front of him, and each time they stopped at one of the tables, Hal bowed. Such gestures in someone who probably attended grade school in Scandinavia struck John as worse than ridiculous.

John noticed Leslie and the First Lady entering through the patio door and he tried to catch Leslie's attention. However Helen guided her over to her husband and Hal. Eric was standing on the edge of the room, as if called by an inner voice, his hands folded just like Hal's. Great. His wife and oldest son were all ready to start genuflecting to the man who was responsible for Frankie's disappearance.

Then the President and Hal reached John's table, with Leslie and the first lady in attendance. John tried to resist the impulse to stand up, but then found himself standing, telling himself that it was only for the President and his wife.

Hal looked directly at Leslie as he spoke. "You will be reunited with Frankie later today. In the meantime, please know that he is completely safe. George cannot survive without Frankie and that's as good a protection as any of us can ask for right now."

Then Hal stepped next to Eric, who had now joined his parents, and whispered something. John could have sworn he heard the words. "Pay close attention, Eric. Never forget that you will be the voice for a silenced world."

The President cleared his throat and announced to the room at large that he had asked Hal to say a few words about the "Hawaii Team".

Somehow Hal had convinced the President that he belonged in the corridors of power. And he and Patrick had paved the way for that to happen.

Hal walked over to an armless, padded ottoman. He sat down cross-legged, the same way he had in San Diego, with his back to the buffet table. Eric's face was shining with excitement, his eyes following Hal's every move, as Hal started to speak in the silent room. "The bomb will strike the comet thirty days from now. It is not possible to turn it off, and the comet will be broken. Some of the fragments will hit Earth 53 days from now."

John was surprised that the NASA people, Henry and Jane, didn't interrupt at this point. The room remained quiet as Hal left a few moments for this to sink in. Then he continued. "There are several reasons why Hawaii has been chosen as our command post. One is that it offers an ideal place for humans and cetaceans to work together. Another is that Hawaii will not survive. Wherever the fragments strike on Earth, Hawaii will be destroyed as a result. The only question is whether fire or water will get here first. I am of course referring to the volcanic eruptions and the Tsunamis which will be unleashed by the impacts."

The attentive silence accorded Hal's words served to increase John's agitation. And when he saw that both Leslie and Eric continued to give Hal their complete respect and attention, it was all he could do to remain in his seat.

Suddenly Hal was speaking in a strong, clear voice that rang throughout the large room. "No one who remains here at the Command Center will be alive two months from now."

The President cleared his throat and Hal quickly added, "There will be administrative oversight from Washington. But the fire fighters, here on the front-line, will be stranded in the burning forest, with no way out.."

John saw that the President, apparently satisfied with Hal's clarification, nodded.

Hal continued, "In the next seven weeks, we will find ourselves being drawn into intense relationships with beings whose families our species has murdered."

Hal let that sink in. "We'll be collaborating with intelligent beings whom our kind have slaughtered by the millions, merely because it was the easiest way to catch tuna. At least when we slaughtered millions of buffalo and left their carcasses rotting on the prairies, we took their skins. At least when we slaughtered hundreds of thousands of whales we used their oil for our lamps and their spermaceti for our perfumes.

"Soon there will be a reckoning. It will be like the New Testament Parable of the Talents."

In spite of his simmering anger, John was drawn into an attempt to apply this parable to the present situation. In Christ's parable, two sons are given equal allowances by their father, he recalled. One saved it and one invested it. The father's response? He gave more to the one who had increased his wealth. John had never liked that parable, because it was so often used to justify the rich getting richer off the backs of the poor.

"The New Testament wasn't written for Blacks," Hal continued. "Neither those who walk upon the land nor those who swim in the sea. But Christ's Parable of the Talents is now coming to pass. The dolphins and whales have developed what they were given and so will be given more. But we humans have blighted the land and fouled the seas over which we were given dominion. Volcanic activity, and direct strikes at the poles will cause the icecaps to melt. The oceans will rise and cover a greater portion of Earth's surface. The creatures of the sea will thus literally inherit more of Earth, and the creatures of the land will retreat to small isolated islands."

Hal paused and looked at each person in the room before he continued. "It would be pretty easy to just doze off now, wouldn't it—to continue living exactly as we have been? Like a prisoner receiving a death sentence, our first thought may not be to help the beings we will leave behind.

"Isn't it strange that we know so little about our past?" he continued. "We rely on written documents which take us back only a few thousand years. We examine rocks and bones and magnetic orientations for earlier times, but each generation we lose the living memory of living beings. For instance, humans have no memory that Venus was struck by a moon-sized object 9,000 years ago.

"But the dolphins and whales remember the cries of billions of beings whose futures were all obliterated in the space of a few seconds. This knowledge is a fundamental item of literacy for the millions of cetaceans living in our oceans. They remember the last Ice Age on our world. They have an oral culture that preserves these memories.

"Humans often have the impression that dolphins are like playful kids, but the dolphins' appreciation for what has led up to the present moment is far more mature than our own.

"They know more than humans about the kinds of behaviors that cause pain to all concerned—patterns such as the mass extermination of fellow creatures, and the oblivious harvesting of resources without a thought to what went into their creation. As a species they have already evolved to a point where they don't each individually have to experience, through their own private pain, what their ancestors learned to avoid in the past. They teach their children enough that each new generation doesn't need to experience such horrors all over for themselves."

John suddenly interrupted. "If humans are such scum, why do the Titanians bother with us at all?"

John thought that Eric winced. And that Leslie sat more stiffly.

Hal nodded at John. "I've asked myself that same question many times. Humans are more highly evolved in some ways, and it appears that the Titanians feel some sympathy of us. Perhaps they appreciate how our capacity for manipulation has got us into a lot of trouble."

Henry took advantage of the break John had caused to speculate, "No wonder that when a race of beings more evolved than either humans or cetaceans contacted our planet, they found the cetaceans better company, and developed a friendship only with them."

Hal nodded. "There are a number of reasons for that. The cetaceans physically resemble the Titanians more than we do, and both species use direct, personal communication in contexts where humans rely on technological artifacts.

"When the Titanians first spoke, the cetaceans immediately knew who they were. They were deeply moved that older and wiser beings were befriending the inhabitants of Earth. They responded like children, starved for the attention of adults who care enough to teach them. In contrast, humans responded like adolescents who just want to do whatever they feel like doing."

Hal then asked if anyone else wanted to say something. The first to speak was the First Lady, Helen. "What about those of us who have been affected by a new vision? Can we be part of this communication between Titan and Earth, or have the Titanians concluded that we're basically a broken species?"

Hal nodded. "No one knows at this point. We don't even know whether any humans will survive.

"However, I have two speculations that touch on your question. One is that the Titanians will be much more likely to communicate directly with human beings, if in the next few weeks they become aware that we are capable of acting unselfishly. My second speculation is that even if humans can only harvest new knowledge through the cetaceans, that may not be a bad thing. For humans to learn to communicate with another terrestrial species in ways that respect our complimentary talents would be as revolutionary a step in the process of human evolution as anything that could come from extraterrestrial contact. Until that happens, we don't really have much to offer the Titanians or the cetaceans. I expect you have felt that directly, Helen. It was probably the most exciting experience of your life, but did you feel that you were able to offer anything in return?"

Helen shook her head.

Hal smiled at her. "When the cetaceans and the Titanians talk there is a real sharing. The cetaceans give something back in the sheer aliveness of their interest. Humans feel strong emotions when they see the extraordinary beauty of the Titanian constructs, but very few humans respond with an inner determination to move into the heart of that beauty. Some humans make a step in that direction, but for a whale who has swum for miles under the ice, not knowing if she will reach the next blowhole, all along the way experiencing the extraordinary beauty of the blue light raining down throughout her world, much more than emotion is evoked by the Titan images. That whale can swim in the Titan image with her whole being. And in that swimming, she tells the story of life on Earth on behalf of her species. She gives the Titanians a book that they can read, a book full of new knowledge. Humans can't do that. For one thing we don't understand where we have come from, and even if we did, we have never learned to be so open that we could share that understanding with another species."

Henry spoke up. "Will we have a chance to talk with the cetaceans?"

Hal smiled. "I have good news for you, Henry. To talk with a dolphin requires exactly what you possess. You need to feel their presence and you need to appreciate them. Tomorrow you'll get your chance to try."

The astrophysicist's face broke into a boyish grin.

Then the President spoke. "Hal, we're going to need a working plan of action that means something to the people who launch missiles. At what point are we going to work that out?"

Hal responded immediately. "We can't actually launch anything until the comet has been shattered. Only then will we know whether our planet has any chance of survival, and if so which fragments are the most critical to intercept with laser cannons and nuclear payloads. The greatest likelihood is that there will remain a massive core, in the order of two hundred kilometers, continuing on its path towards Earth. By the time we know this it will be too late to significantly deflect it's inertial vector. The Titanians continue to believe that Earth's only chance centers on harnessing the Moon's gravity on this large fragment, and the cetaceans are in charge of that effort. What humans need to do in the next week is to get all the world's missiles and bombs ready to launch and to develop a unified command center for their deployment. We will need to implement George's new technology on all these missiles. Nothing else has a chance to succeed under such challenging conditions."

The President's expression made it clear that he couldn't give his approval for such a plan. But before he could say anything, Hal added, "Let me suggest, Sir, that we take things one step at a time here. We can explore options, without committing ourselves to any one course of action. I would also like to say that once the comet has shattered, I believe no one will see any option to using BallMaker control systems. But by then, performance test results will be in, and you will be able to make an informed decision on their basis."

The President nodded, and Hal returned his attention to his audience.

John suddenly couldn't prevent himself from interrupting. "What about Frankie? When I first met you, you treated him like he was central to all of this. Now he's gone and you haven't even mentioned him."

Hal looked at the President. "Sir, do you have a timeline for the arrival of Frankie and the others"

The President responded. "I've asked to be notified the instant they contact us. Still no word yet."

John stood up, shaking, “What! You know where Frankie is.”

Hal addressed Leslie. "You and your family will see Frankie later tonight. But let me fill you in on some background about your youngest son. For all of his life, Frankie has been in communication with a dolphin. Frankie's presence is crucial tomorrow, because that dolphin will be there. This dolphin has spent the past week swimming across the Pacific in order to meet with us. Of all the humans who will be present, it is only Frankie who has ever spoken with him. Frankie is the only one who can reassure him that the humans gathered together here are not the same kind of humans as those who have slaughtered millions of his brothers and sisters."

John felt another wave of anger overwhelm him. "You're talking about our missing two-year-old. Leslie and I haven’t known if we would ever see him alive again. And now you're making plans to put him to work as soon as he shows up? What could Frankie possibly do that you couldn't do yourself?"

Hal considered John for a moment before responding. "I believe Patrick has already told you something about this. The

Titanians communicate with humans exclusively through whales and dolphins, with two exceptions. Those two exceptions are Frankie and George."

The image of George killing a man in an adjacent chair, as if he were swatting a fly, came back to John, along with the knowledge that George was responsible for Frankie's kidnapping. He was about to start shouting when, feeling Leslie's hand on his shoulder, he fell back helplessly into his chair, his rage suddenly turning to anguish. In a strangled voice, John said, "You have no idea what it's like to be the father of a two-year-old boy. If Frankie dies, I'm the one who took him to Sea World, at your suggestion. Don't you feel responsible for anything? Isn't this madman, George, your brother?"

Hal didn't take his eyes off John as he spoke. "I know more about regret and remorse than I pray you will ever have to experience, John. I am responsible for the death of my father, and for the psychological disintegration of my brother, George. And now I must helplessly watch as my unspeakable karma ripens before my eyes. Millions of beings will die because of what I did, when I was ten years old. If any harm comes to Frankie, the hounds of hell will rip me to pieces. Nothing you or anyone else might say could stop them."

John felt a deep chill gripping his spine. He somehow knew that Hal was speaking the literal truth.

"Frankie and George had to connect." Hal continued. "Now that they have done so, there is finally some hope for Earth again. Now the Titanians can at last communicate to us about missile launches. This communication needs to be directly between Titanians and humans. The Titanians cannot use cetaceans as intermediaries for this. The technology of mass extermination is too utterly foreign to the whales and dolphins."

Just then a Secret Service man came to the edge of the room and nodded to the President, who immediately excused himself. The room remained completely silent in his absence, as if expecting bad news, but John's anguish felt somehow more bearable now that he knew Hal shared it.

The President returned a few minutes later, looking pale. He looked at Leslie as he spoke. "Frankie is on Air Force One.

They are due to touch down in 30 minutes. I'm afraid that George is also on the plane."

The President added in a soft voice. "My limo is waiting for you out front. If you leave right now, you can be on the runway when they touch down."

Leslie grabbed John's forearm and pulled him out of his seat. Out front there was a stretch limo with the engine running and its rear door open. The President stood close by, as John, Leslie and Eric climbed in. Then the door closed and they were speeding down the long driveway to the coastal highway.

With Leslie's head heavy against his shoulder, John knew that the guillotine blade was still poised over them. Why else was George on Air Force One? But for now, his whole being flooded with relief and joy. His son, Frankie was alive!

CHAPTER 40

Patrick was sitting on Air Force One, Frankie lying on the seat opposite with his eyes closed. He could see the top of George's forehead over the seat cushion twenty yards ahead. A sizeable detail of service agents, including Ted Sullo, were stationed in between. Patrick knew it was not necessary, but remembering how easily George had snapped a guard's neck he was glad they were on the plane. Patrick wanted his own neck to stay intact awhile longer. And it would be a shame to miss any of this.

Without knowing the details, it was clear that even in handcuffs, George continued to exert some kind of power. Perhaps a missile could target the White House or Air Force One at a word from him.

Patrick wasn't really worried. Perhaps because Frankie was not worried. As if in confirmation of this thought, Frankie opened his eyes, looked straight at his uncle and said, "Teach George swim."

When Patrick looked back uncomprehendingly, Frankie elaborated. "George not swim. Water scary."

With a flash of insight, Patrick understood. George was scared shitless of the Titanian mind—its shifting motility, its lack of any recognizable rubric to catch the quicksilver movement of thought. George had become addicted to the power that the Titanians gave him—to affect the material world in which he lived—but the alien mind that made this possible terrified him.

George was like a sailor afflicted by nightmares about sea-monsters. While he culled the fruits of Titanian insight, he lived in horror of falling in and drowning. Frankie had singled out the crucial issue, and Patrick now understood what had to happen.

When Patrick glanced toward the other end of the plane he saw George looking at him, with an expression something between agoraphobia and rage. Then the captain announced their final descent, and George sat down again.

One thing was certain: wherever this radical new technology had originated, George was the only one who could implement it on the massive scale now called for. Whether George's phenomenal accomplishments came entirely from the Titanians, or whether the Titanians had picked George because of some unique ability, Patrick didn't know. In either case, the Administration had no real choice: George was vital to the comet defense project because the Titanians were not talking to anyone else about missiles and bombs.

Patrick shuddered as images came back from the basement interrogation of George at the White House. Without warning, Patrick's mind had been invaded by masses of writhing serpents. He had been defenseless against the unspeakable horror of George's experience. Then the snakes had transformed into a mesh of interacting segments, like the scales of a fish, across which it was possible to change direction by moving from scale to scale. The Titanians seemed to open up an alternate way of moving in space—perhaps even in time. They showed George how to intercept a flying rock by getting the position and timing just right. And George passionately craved the power this intelligence gave him. Maybe the Titanians really had picked their man carefully—given that they wanted to explode bombs. But something seemed to have gone wrong.

Patrick was yanked back to the present, as Air Force One bounced lightly, its engines screaming. Wheeler Air force Base appeared in the window. They taxied to a stop, the cabin door opened, and a stairway was secured to the aircraft.

George left first, still in handcuffs, surrounded by four security men, Ted a step behind. Patrick left the plane next, his young nephew in his arms, and was immediately greeted by the pleasant sea breezes of a warm February evening on Oahu. Fifty yards away, he saw Leslie and John stepping out of a stretch limo and start to run in their direction.

Frankie squirmed loose and ran headlong into Leslie's arms. She scooped him up as John put his arms around them both. Eric stood back until Frankie held out his hand. Then Eric took a step forward and leaned into the pyramid. Patrick inhaled deeply as he looked at this brother's family. It must be nice.

After a moment, he glanced across the tarmac and saw George getting into the back of a dark limo—one of two identical cars parked at the edge of the runway.

Frankie called out, "Bye George."

George glanced in their direction with a dull look that seemed beyond appeal. He was still staring as the tinted glass of the limo door closed over him.

"What in hell does that killer have to do with us?" John asked harshly.

Ted Sullo remained at a discreet distance, but his manner made it clear that all the Murphy's were to follow him. They walked across the tarmac together and Ted opened the passenger door in the other limo. After the others had entered he climbed in and the caravan immediately pulled out.

After a 25-minute drive, the two limos came to a stop under the portico of the Oceanographic Institute. Hal was waiting for them. He stood aside as George, accompanied by security, entered the building and then the Murphy's followed, John carrying Frankie.

They convened in a room full of networked computers. Most of the equipment was already turned on. It didn't mean much to Patrick but George immediately exclaimed, "No. No. You have it all wrong."

George sat down in front of a console and started typing on the keyboard. The handcuffs made it difficult.

Patrick grabbed a chair near the door and watched in amazement as the images started to dance gracefully on the screen.

After a moment, Hal told the security detail to remove George's handcuffs, and one of the uniformed men inserted a small key into the locks, and removed them. George didn't acknowledge his new freedom. He just typed more quickly, seemingly unaware that on all sides people were watching him.

As Hal began to talk, he gave the impression of being unconcerned whether or not George cared to listen. "At least Frankie and Eric have a father—unlike the rest of us. In fact you might say that Frankie has two fathers."

George was now looking over the monitor, out a window that overlooked the sea, his hands motionless.

Patrick kept his eyes on George as Hal continued talking. "I'm talking about Patrick and John, and I'm also talking about George and myself. The loss of our fathers has been the defining event for all four of us."

Watching George's face, which had begun to grow ominous, Patrick suddenly remembered how he had killed a man, while a dozen people stood by like statues.

Hal seemed not to notice. "Another interesting question. Why have Frankie, his father and his uncle all been contacted by cetaceans? Does it have something to do with an unusual family gene? How much have the Titanians had to do with choosing these three people from a single family? And how do George and I fit in? Why again have two alienated brothers been chosen in both these cases?"

George whirled around on his chair and screamed. "Liar! You fucking liar! Get out of my head. I'll kill you if you don't get out of my head. I don't have a brother, and I don't need one. You read my mind, and then you think you can manipulate me. You find some tiny thing, then you weave complete bullshit out of it. Get the fuck out of my mind, you god-damned asshole!"

Hal continued as if there had been no interruption. "I was ten years old when I ran away from home. I didn't just run around the block. I hid aboard a steamer one Sunday afternoon, when my family was out for a stroll on the Stockholm docks. It was meant to be a kind of prank. I watched my parents calling out my name on the wharf below and I just let the joke go a little too far. Suddenly the metal plates were vibrating under my feet and I watched in horror as the roof of a wharf-side storage shed started moving away from me."

Hal stopped talking for a while.

Patrick couldn't take his eyes off George. He looked as if he might have an epileptic fit at any moment.

Hal looked directly at George as he continued, but George stared straight ahead, his eyes glazed. "The rest doesn't concern anyone but you and me, George. For now, let me just say that Dad was contacted by the captain and a few days later he booked passage on another steamer. After he arrived in New York he was killed in a freak automobile accident on his way to the foster home where I was being held. Our father left behind a pregnant wife, who died in childbirth, and you and I were brought up in two different orphanages, on two different continents. I didn't even know about you until a few weeks ago."

George had turned to look at Hal and now didn't take his eyes away. Hal held George's gaze as he continued to speak. "One other interesting event happened during my boat trip to America. I felt so guilty that I jumped overboard in the middle of the Atlantic Ocean. It was the middle of the night and no one on the skeleton crew noticed."

Hal stood up so quickly that even George flinched. His voice suddenly had a vibrant, penetrating quality that made it impossible not to listen. "We can't imagine what the Titanians have given up to help us. For thousands of years, they will go on living in cold darkness, maimed in their innermost being, because they sent part of themselves to Earth. And now comet strikes will obliterate our planet's ability to send them home."

Patrick stopped breathing. Although he had seen how the Titanians could adopt perspectives outside their ocean-dwelling bodies, and had glimpsed how there was a symbiotic connection between the two distinct elements of their embodiment, nothing had ever suggested that some of them had sent that symbiotic part of themselves to Earth.

Hal continued. "They've given up more than their eyes and ears. Losing a child is closer."

Hal seemed to lose his self-assurance as he continued. "I was the direct cause of our father's death. I am to blame that you grew up without love. And I take complete responsibility on my own soul, for all of time, for any harm you have ever done."

Then, without giving George any chance to respond, Hal turned to Frankie. "I can help provide some stability, but it must be you, Frankie, who lead us all into new waters."

Patrick quickly pulled his chair closer to the others. Then he couldn't stop himself from asking, "How did you get back on board ship?"

Hal kept his eyes on Frankie, as he responded. "A school of dolphins carried me, while a fin whale crossed in front of the ship's bow. Eventually the crew saw me and pulled me aboard. They had no idea where I had come from."

Frankie's face was so still and peaceful. His eyes were closed. Patrick was looking at Frankie when the room disappeared. There was the rushing sound of water. Light, carried by billowing mists, pervaded every corner of Patrick's consciousness. And it wasn't just his own consciousness. A congregation was assembling. Like individual instruments warming up, Patrick recognized familiar voices in the cathedral: everyone in the room, the old dolphin, the dolphin who had saved him at Anchor Beach, and the humpback who had saved him as a child.

With a sharp pang, he recognized Hank and Emily. How could he have let weeks go by without calling them? This wonderful couple that had saved his life. He vowed to call them that very day.

Some of the beings had been there all along, conducting their own vigil. Some had just that moment been startled awake in their beds. Thousands of humans arrived, new voices coming into focus with each passing moment. And virtually every whale and dolphin on Earth was there. They had been waiting for this moment for a long time, and now it had come.

But there was something else present. The Titan children really were here on Earth. What strange creatures they seemed to be. It was as if they had no will of their own, but could only serve others. On Titan they served giant ocean worms with no organs of perception in their own bodies, allowing them to experience the cosmos.

Patrick felt weak as understanding seeped in. The Titanians had sent away their soul mates and now these vehicles for greater life were stranded here on Earth. The question was, was life on Earth worthy of such sacrifice?

Terrible recognition brought deep insight. Even all the humans congregating together around the planet in prayer and hope, fell far short of the marriage of spirit that had been sacrificed on Titan to make this possible. It was the whales and dolphins who had created the basis for this sacrifice. And the main task of earning it now rested in Earth's oceans, on the congregation of beings who lived there.

How terrible this must be for George. He was the center of attention for millions of beings. And he was beyond any helping hand, smothered in a writhing pit of snakes. Patrick had glimpsed this before, but now it enveloped his own consciousness. He found himself screaming in horror, unable to separate himself from the terror.

Then he heard Hal's voice. "Look at what's really there! It's millions of beings just like us."

Suddenly, for Patrick, the snakes became the bodies of dolphins—heart-rendingly graceful, full of joyous embodiment.

But George couldn't let himself see. His mind closed down, clinging to justifications for the murders he had committed. How could a dolphin be beautiful, an emissary of healing, for the man who had ordered the slaughter of these creatures?

Patrick was plunged into the pit again. No, now it was an ice cave where creatures like moray eels writhed and coiled around one another for warmth. Similar creatures outside herded clouds of small serpents into the cave, apparently for food. The sea creatures outside the cave appeared alert, intelligent, and alive to their environment, poised on the edge of vast understanding.

Then Patrick was deeper than ever in a landscape dense with the thrashing, coiling bodies of serpents. He was sinking down in some living hell. Hal was saying something, but Patrick couldn't hear. Suddenly he remembered running in the woods as a child in the suburbs of Montreal, where he had grown up. He had stumbled on a tree root and pitched down an incline into a natural pit. It had been full of snakes.

He could hear Hal's voice but not his words. Snakes were coiling around his eyes. When he raised his hands to brush the snakes from his face, they just brought more snakes with them.

Patrick dimly understood that this hadn't ever happened to him. As a child, he had stumbled at the edge of a den of writhing snakes and run home terrified, but none had actually touched him.

Suddenly a monstrous serpent was coming straight for him. It grew larger and larger, its mouth opening. Then the serpent was Frankie and he was throwing his arms around Patrick. But Patrick wasn't Patrick anymore. He was George.

And he was wailing. Begging for another chance. A chance to redeem all the terrible acts he had committed out of fear and loss of contact with his own human being.

Suddenly, Patrick was in a beautiful ocean, inside a body that could glide though the water with a simple flexing of its spine. With a strong thrust, he broke through the surface into the air. For a few wonderful moments he could see all the way to the horizon, across miles of undulating ocean alive with wind-blown spray and flashing sunlight. Then slowly, cleanly, he dove down into the silent rapture of the sea. Deeper, deeper, until the world grew dim and an inner breath reached every cell, penetrating every old memory and hurt like a mild breeze in early spring.

Without Patrick being aware of the shift, the teaching started. The Titanians told them about the Earth, the Moon and the life that held them together. George was with them now. Like a young child invited to sit on his father's knee, he clambered up into the light. Patrick realized that they had all climbed out of the snake pit together, whatever that had meant for each of them. And it was Frankie who had climbed in deepest, so deep that he had been able to lead George out.

Patrick rubbed his eyes and then opened them. The room was full of people. Leslie and Eric were sitting next to John. Frankie was still on John's lap.

Hal leaned forward and said something to Eric in a barely audible voice. It sounded like, "You need to remember all this. You more than anyone need to remember it."

Patrick got up and moved his chair until it was almost touching John's. Eric was asking his Dad to explain what had happened.

John smiled. "Well, I can't claim to understand what's going on, Eric, but I think I finally understand how the Moon is connected to us and to the planet we live on."

What John actually said seemed hardly to matter. As Patrick watched both their faces, Eric seemed to be listening to his Dad with every pore of his being.

George, now looking more like a scientist contemplating a research problem than a meth addict looking for a fix, slipped quietly out of the room. Leslie was watching her husband and two sons. Then she turned and looked at Patrick. Only then—he was sure for the first time in many days—did Leslie's face relax into a beautiful smile.

CHAPTER 41

Monday, Feb 17 (Day -52)

John and his family drove to the Oceanographic Institute before sunrise, sharing a van with the President's wife, Helen. Henry, Jane, and Ted followed in another. Outside the long-neglected building, they were welcomed by Hal—who had spent the night at poolside.

Without delay Hal led John and Frankie to the innermost of several holding pools, where an old dolphin with scars on his head and body waited.

John could feel Patrick's presence, squatting behind him at the water's edge, as he and Frankie and Hal waded through the shallow end of the pool. When the water became too deep for Frankie, Hal picked him up.

Hal seemed nervous, and John remembered that this was the first face-to-face meeting between Frankie and the old dolphin. Would Frankie make the connection that this dolphin was his lifelong companion of the mind? Did the old dolphin really understand that Frankie was a human, the species responsible for the death of his family?

Now that Frankie was free from George's clutches, John felt reconciled to Hal. He had to admit that Hal had explained many things which John had never understood before. On a personal level, it was now much clearer what an extraordinary little person his son Frankie had always been.

This research center had been chosen because it allowed direct access between open ocean and several artificial pools.

Decades ago, in the process of dolphin research, these pools had been used as permanently gated holding tanks, under the assumption that too great an investment had been made in the captive dolphins to allow them to return to the sea.

Now there was no question of confining this old dolphin or any of his friends who dropped in to visit.

The pool sloped down gradually from a dry area, where the humans were gathered, to a depth of about six feet. At any time, the waiting dolphin was free to swim into a channel, through another pool, and back into the ocean—just as the humans were free to walk through a door back into their familiar world of restaurants and shopping malls.

John glanced at Frankie. Hal was holding him at arm's length, as they slowly waded towards the old dolphin. John felt relieved that he wouldn't be responsible for keeping Frankie's face out of the water. Especially now that very frightening images were coming into his mind.

The dolphin mother was helping her newborn baby to the surface for its first breath. There was no indication of any problem. The baby dolphin was alive and well and was participating in his first ascent towards the surface.

Then the abomination arrived. Suddenly she couldn't swim, and every flexion caused knife lines of pain to tighten around her body. Some of the other dolphins started screaming, as if they too were in pain. In the confusion that swept through the pod with the arrival of the drifting nylon horror, no one but the mother noticed her baby sinking into the darkness of the ocean depths.

By the time the others understood that she was not screaming for herself, and dove down to retrieve the newborn infant, it was too late. The baby dolphin could not be induced to breathe. He was dead.

The mother died soon after that. She didn't reach the surface on her own and when her friends lifted her face into the air she didn't breathe.

It was apparently then that a strange connection was formed between Frankie and the dead baby's father. In the same few moments that the baby dolphin had failed to reach the surface and take her first breath, Leslie had given birth to Frankie and Frankie had taken the first breath of his new life.

In those moments, the Titanians had created a link between Frankie and the bereaved father dolphin.

Why the Titanians had established this connection was not known. Had they chosen Frankie deliberately—because he was already special—or had some random connection between the attempted dolphin birth and Frankie's own birth been forged in some dimension inconceivable to either the human or cetacean mind?

In any case, the father who lost both his newborn and his life-mate formed a strong bond with Frankie in those moments. Ever since, he had treated Frankie as if he was a survivor of the family that had been taken from him, and their minds had remained linked.

John was yanked cruelly back to the present. Frankie, who had never before been in deep water, was swimming by himself in the deep end of the pool. As John watched, the old dolphin and Frankie both dove to the bottom of the pool.

Leslie screamed and struggled towards their son. John caught her and put his arm around her. "It's all right. They know what they're doing. The dolphin is teaching Frankie how to swim."

As John and Leslie watched, it became increasingly clear that they didn't have to worry. Frankie was completely at home in the water. He knew how to judge when it was necessary to head back to the surface, and how to relax so that no effort was required to keep his mouth above the surface.

Suddenly Frankie climbed onto the teacher's back and they made several tight circumambulations at the deep end of the pool. Frankie was laughing and shouting the whole time. Once, when he slipped into the water, the dolphin made an incredibly agile maneuver, ready to nudge him back to the surface if it were necessary. It wasn't. Frankie swam to the surface by himself and succeeded in climbing on to the dolphin's back again. John could feel Leslie slowly relax and lean more heavily against him.

John was not prepared for what happened next.

For some time they had been hearing the cries of other animals outside, and now the dolphin raced into the channel that led out of the enclosure—with Frankie on his back.

Leslie struggled through the water to the edge of the pool, climbed out and headed toward the door out of the building. John dove into the water and headed for the channel into which the dolphin and Frankie had just disappeared.

His heart was pounding, even though he and Frankie remained in almost constant communication with one another. More than was possible for Leslie, he felt reassured by this contact and recognized the immense trust that Frankie felt in the dolphin's protection. At the same time, John knew how useless he would be if anything dangerous were to happen in this environment.

When he reached the other pool, he was stunned by what he saw. There were about a dozen dolphins swimming in a graceful, counter-clockwise circle around the perimeter of the pool. The one carrying Frankie was swimming in a somewhat tighter circle and John realized that this was so that if Frankie were to fall off he wouldn't hit the hard edge of the concrete enclosure. Another dolphin was riding guard beside them. As John watched, Frankie started to slip and this outrigger nudged him back into the saddle, without either dolphin missing a stroke.

Suddenly one of the dolphins broke away from the circle and swam up to John. She did a slow turn, her flank rubbing against John's knees. John just kept treading in place in the deep water. Then he heard Frankie. You ride too.

Frankie better be right. The last thing he wanted to do was give offense. And grabbing a fellow creature without permission, especially in order to ride her, like humans have ridden horses for thousands of years, might definitely qualify as a major social gaffe.

After more encouragement from Frankie, John caught hold of the dolphin's fin and let himself be pulled around the pool. He felt a heady mix of embarrassment and delight.

Frankie's voice echoed in John's head once more. Like me.

John couldn't make himself do it, but then the dolphin dove down and a few seconds later came up directly beneath him. He had to grab onto her dorsal fin just to avoid capsizing. There could be no further doubt. He was being offered a bareback ride by this creature.

Once he had settled, the dolphins all started swimming through the open gate that separated this deep-water pool from the open ocean. The last two to leave were the ones carrying John and Frankie. John heard Leslie's voice calling out after them, but he couldn't have done anything, short of deliberately falling off, to affect what was happening. And the truth was that, even apart from the question of staying with Frankie, he wouldn't have missed this ride for the world.

Outside the gate it was like a surprise party, sprung the moment you open your front door. There were literally hundreds of dolphins of many different species. Further out, in the deeper water, there were humpbacks and other species of whales. It was soon clear that they were heading directly for a particular group of humpbacks who were waiting about a mile off the shore.

John’s dolphin tried to keep up with the others as the open sea raised a swell around them. But after John fell off twice, the pod moved ahead of them. Eventually John got the hang of it, alternately anticipating the drag of the water against his legs and thrilling at the sensation of being air born, floating above the expanse of undulating water all around. To John’s amazement, Frankie was standing up, astride his old friend, as if the two of them were one being, a glorious centaur of the sea.

When they reached the whales, John’s dolphin suddenly dove down and away and two other dolphins slipped into place on either side, supporting John under each arm. Then three more dolphins arrived from the Research Center. Hal and Patrick riding on two of them and the third towing an inflated rubber dingy.

Frankie climbed into the dingy. John, Patrick and Hal all floated, bobbing up and down, and supported by dolphins on either side.

Then it started.

The humpbacks started singing. John felt completely unprepared for the effect this had on him. The humpback song seemed to cause organs, or energy centers he didn't know he had, to throb and vibrate.

Then the dolphins joined in. John knew that his ears couldn't hear most of the register being used by the dolphins, but something was getting opened up inside him. It felt as if an organ of perception at the top of his head was opening up like a huge flower.

Then he heard Frankie's voice.

Daddy. Nice people? Want to know nice people.

John understood Frankie's question. Hal had alerted him to its possibility the night before. What John wasn't sure of was how the communication was supposed to take place. In particular, what would Frankie's role be? What could Frankie possibly make of John's perception that Helen, the President's wife, would give her life for the whales and dolphins, because she had not been able to find a way to give it for her own son? And what would it mean to Frankie that Jane desperately wanted to use nuclear weapons for a peaceful purpose, and thereby vindicate the years she had spent at the Pentagon, before she'd transferred to NASA? Or that the President saw this as his last chance to redeem himself for having given the order to launch a missile two months before?

But those issues paled before the question of what he could possibly say to these creatures about George. How could he explain to them that the man who had slaughtered hundreds of their brothers and sisters a few weeks ago was now a crucial ally?

Hal came to his rescue, talking in John's mind, as Frankie had a moment before. Leave George to me. When the time comes, I will have a lot to say about him. All you have to do is think about these other people. Every once in awhile, think of Frankie too. You don't need to feel limited by what you imagine Frankie is personally able to understand. It's more a question of keeping your heart open to him while you're talking. Frankie's mind will be a receiver for whatever you think. Frankie doesn't need to understand it all, but if he doesn't understand some of it then his mind will cease to be a good conductor. The beings who need to understand you are the whales and dolphins. It would be helpful if you think of yourself as addressing that humpback directly in front of you.

John looked at the humpback. It was hard to establish much eye contact, because the whale's eyes were spread so far apart on the sides of his head. The instant that thought arose in John's mind, the humpback turned to his right and John could look directly into his left eye.

He intended to tell the humpback about the others. But instead, he found himself apologizing for the way humans did things without concern for the beings who were affected. He found images of animal slaughter rising unbidden in his mind and for a moment he imagined that the humpback was considering attacking him. Hal uttered a few calming words, as one might rub the neck of a skittish horse.

Then John heard his brother's silent wailing. An immense feeling of loss swept through him. It came from Patrick, but it was as if it were also his own.

Hal was still nudging him forward, now very gently, into the task he had been assigned.

John forced himself to think of the people he had talked to the night before. It was hard. He wondered if the Titanians were around. Hal responded. No, it's just us terrestrials.

And then, without warning, John found himself opening up in a new way, swamped with feelings for the frailty of life. He remembered Helen's glistening eyes as she had talked about the son she and her husband had lost. He remembered the old dolphin's mate and child. And Danny—Hank and Emily's son, —Patrick's voice broke in.

John thought of the millions of animals and people that humans had killed within just a few decades. And suddenly he understood why Hal had said that they all needed to relinquish any hold they had on their own survival if they were to be of any use to Earth. He heard himself promising to stay in Hawaii when the comet hit, to stay here with the dolphins and the whales, even though it meant that they would all die.

Hal interjected that all of the animals assembled there had vowed to remain in congregation around Hawaii, and die together. Some of them were such strong swimmers that they might have a chance to escape to deep water in time, but they would be included in the roll call when life in the vicinity was annihilated.

More and more, John could feel the presence of the calloused old whale who floated in remarkable stillness, just 20 feet in front of him.

Then the memory came flooding back to him, the memory of how his father had died before he was born, when Patrick was three.

The old humpback before him was the whale who had saved his brother's life. Patrick had known it right away.

It was like his old dream. But this time he knew that he and Patrick were dreaming it together. This time it was like a memorial for their father. The old whale had risen in the chapel to give remembrance to the heroism of a human life, making it shine, telling the surviving children about their father whom the sea had taken. A burial at sea, forty years late in coming.

And John realized that no other living being had ever really spoken to him about his father.

He felt how the memory struck like a hammer against his brother's heart. Their father's vow, to never let go of the chain, had been what had saved Patrick. It had caused the whale to rise up, catching the sled and the two bodies on his broad head. It was what had prompted this huge, compassionate creature to lift them to the surface and slide the two bodies back onto the ice.

And now, in present time, with the whole Earth watching and the executioner coming steadily nearer, these two beings were following in his father's footsteps. Neither Patrick nor this whale were going to let go. They would hold on now for the sake of future beings. Not their own children—they were both alone in the world—but the children of strangers, who through no fault of their own were about to fall into a realm of bitter cold and darkness.

And then John realized that he and his own family would be denied this terrible certainty. Frankie could not be allowed to die. Too much depended on him. And John, as this exceptional boy's father, needed to build a refuge in a world that was about to be shattered.

But Patrick would die. In less than eight weeks. Patrick, his shining brother, wearing their father's mantle, would plunge fearlessly into the dark, treacherous waters until his last breath ran out.

CHAPTER 42

Wednesday, March 19 (Day -22)

After an absence of more than a month, John and his family touched down at Wheeler AFB. Out on the tarmac, John saw Patrick standing beside a limo and they waved. As soon as the door of the limo closed and they began the drive down the coast road, John started talking.

"This morning, before dawn, I trained my telescope on where I knew the comet would appear in the solar umbra. George's missile really did shatter the comet, didn't it?"

"Yesterday," Patrick confirmed.

"It's happening, isn't it?" John continued, remembering the swarm of little cometary tails visible for a few moments before the full glare of the dawning Sun had overwhelmed the image. He refrained from adding how that probably spelled the end of terrestrial life as they knew it.

Patrick simply nodded.

"What are Henry and Jane saying? What's the diagnosis from JPL? When will the armada of missiles launched last month engage the fragments?"

Before Patrick could respond to John's barrage of questions, Leslie spoke. "Why did Hal want Frankie back here?"

Patrick looked at Frankie for a moment before responding. "Actually according to Hal, it was the old dolphin who called Frankie back. But I know Hal is also concerned about George. George hasn't slept for several weeks. He's always in front of his computer, working on specs for missile deployment guidance systems, personally involved in every step. The President may be in charge of the aerospace/military complex, but George is in the cockpit."

Turning back to John, Patrick continued, "Hundreds of armed, space-faring missiles, similar to the one that shattered the original comet yesterday, are now on their way. They all required the accelerated production of missiles, bombs, guidance systems, rocket fuel, complex computer code, lasers, cameras—the entire inventory of items needed for observing, responding, controlling, and destroying. Henry and Jane can tell you more about all that."

Remembering the image he'd seen that morning in his telescope of a tight swarm of tiny comets escaping from the core—as if a rock had been removed from a nest of centipedes —each one already growing a tail of its own, John shuddered and said, "If all that armament still had a single giant rock to push around, Earth might have a chance. Now, I don't know."

No one responded to this remark and after another mile, Leslie turned to Patrick and said, "You look exhausted."

"I've been spending all my time with George. Hal is always doing things with the dolphins, so I get to watch George. And George never sleeps," Patrick said.

Why do you need to watch George?" John asked.

"I can't get it out of my mind that George might revert to the guy who blew up the original comet. On some deep level, like some modern-day Shiva, George might be addicted to the sheer act of destruction.".

John didn't need to be convinced of George's murderous side and hated the fact that Frankie had been called back to be close to this man. Following up that concern, he said, "When you're sitting with George for all those hours, are you linked with his mind?"

His brother seemed not to understand the question for a moment. Then Frankie, sitting on Leslie's lap, laughed. Suddenly, Patrick's expression transformed into a look of certainty.

"I've just seen something that I didn't understand before," Patrick said. "I've been watching George do his thing for the past several weeks, and sensing all these other minds looking in from time to time. I felt that I was the one who couldn't break contact, and that may have been true, but not because I was keeping George balanced and sane. All this time, Frankie has been doing that. Frankie needed me to be there, in close proximity, so that he could be in touch with George through my mind."

Patrick looked at Frankie and they both laughed.

John shuddered inwardly, as the limo pulled under the portico of the familiar manor. While Patrick continued on to the Oceanograpic Institute, John and his family were escorted to the same suite they'd occupied a month before.

Leslie and the kids elected to hang out in the comfortable suite but John, feeling displaced in time and space, grabbed a jacket and headed toward the beach. But walking through the lounge, he heard a familiar voice, "John, I heard you were back."

Henry, who was just the man who could answer his many questions, beckoned him over to a nearby table. They moved to a table next to an open window, through which the surf could be heard breaking down below, and without preamble, John launched forth.

"I saw the shattered comet this morning, I saw with my own eyes that there is now a school of little fragments spreading out from the giant core. It's obvious that George's bomb has greatly increased the number of objects heading our way. So now what do we do?"

Without waiting for an answer, John continued, "Are we going to keep bombing everything until we have a hundred thousand hunks of rock and ice aimed at Earth? Everyone is so impressed with the great reflexes of BallMaker Control Systems but what can it really do but smash things into finer pieces? And what exactly did you mean by your varnished pillow analogy at that White House meeting last month? I assume you meant that there is a harder surface somewhere on the original comet, against which a detonation could push without shattering the whole object. Now that the worst has happened, is that still an option?"

Henry seemed happy to respond. "The gigantic fragment is our main concern. Anything less than perfect accuracy—a nuclear detonation directly above the rocky shelf—will create the same horrific shattering which we are now desperately trying to mop up.

"There are two basic strategies being implemented on the fragments," Henry contined. "There are about fifty fragments that we know about, each more than a mile in diameter and each larger than the asteroid believed to have killed off the dinosaurs. Nuclear explosions will be used on them. And laser cannons will be used on the thousands of smaller fragments—some capable of destroying millions of people if they land in the middle of L.A. or Taiwan. BallMaker tracking is central to both these strategies."

Henry confirmed that this technology had never been approved by any President or Congress but now no one was complaining that BallMaker Electronics was able to put into space a laser cannon capable of pulverizing, in three seconds, rocks the size of a city bus, and re-sight on its next target with speeds comparable to hard-drive access times.

"But a major problem remains," Henry continued, his face grim. "BallMaker control systems, as presently configured, cannot be used directly on the gigantic fragment, which is still about two-hundred miles in diameter. The plan is for a missile to pass the huge comet core on its starboard side and detonate at the precise moment that the rocky shelf swings past. This means that the missile's automatic targeting mechanism has to shut down a few seconds before impact so that it can be redirected slightly off target. This is not a simple matter. Operating at incredible speeds, the system's fundamental imperative is to stay on track until impact destroys its target."

Henry seemed to view the Hawaii Team as a shoestring operation, completely inadequate to its task. The President was never there—for reasons of State. Hal spent almost all his time at the Oceanographic Center with the dolphins and whales. Henry, Ted and Jane were almost always somewhere else—Cape Canaveral, White Sands, JPL, Russian launch pads —supposedly in frequent computer contact with George about launch schedules and flight programming. But the few words that anyone ever heard coming out of George's mouth asserted that these proposed modifications to his system were not only untested but contrary to its fundamental design.

On a personal level, George had become mild, sometimes even tearful, but on another level he seemed as isolated and intractable as he had a month before.

John and Henry were still deep in conversation when Hal came in and walked up to their table. Henry took one look at Hal and immediately stood up, stuffed some pretzels in his pocket, and waited at Hal's side. Hal found a moment to thank John for coming back and promised that he would talk with him and his family later. He affirmed that it was the old dolphin who had wanted Frankie back: because George needed it, and also because he wanted to say good-bye to Frankie in person.

As they were talking, and as if called by a hidden voice, Eric appeared, with Leslie and Frankie a few steps behind. Hal immediately asked John if he could borrow Eric for the rest of the day.

"Can I, Dad?" John glanced at Leslie and they both nodded.

As soon as Hal, Henry and Eric had slipped out of the dining room, Leslie turned to John and said, "I thought Patrick looked exhausted, but Hal looks twenty years older than he did a month ago."

After lunch, John, Leslie and Frankie drove over to the Institute. While Frankie and the old dolphin played in the shallow pool, the adults sat in deck chairs. Leslie still kept a vigilant eye, reacting to every shout and splash, but John felt relaxed enough that he was able to give his attention to Hal as he filled them in.

" The Moon is awakening. Like an infant stirring in her mother's womb, she is becoming aware that she is not alone. The Moon, the Earth, and the envelope of life around Earth are beginning to relate to one another in new ways. Much more than humans, the whales and dolphins are deeply involved in this transformation."

John allowed these images, so alien to the perspective in which he had been trained, of how gravity affects matter, to wash over him. He listened, as a patient for whom Western medicine has come up empty-handed might listen, in hope of the healing interventions of a shamanic healer.

CHAPTER 43

Friday, March 28 (Day -13)

A week later, on Friday, March 28th, the President held a press conference. Patrick listened with interest, as one might listen to a news report about an accident to which one has been a witness. By now someone would have had to be living underground in a root cellar with no radio or TV not to know that there was a battalion of comet fragments flying through the inner solar system. Thousands of cometary trails were streaming away from the Sun like ugly tears in the blue fabric of the morning sky. Hundreds of whirling swastikas slashed the heavens, all terrifyingly visible to the naked eye for people everywhere.

For the first time, the President spoke openly about contact with Titanians, and the collaborative effort to move the comet core onto a path from which the Moon could draw it away from Earth. A detailed graphic was available which clearly illustrated the scenario.

He also tried to prepare people for the inevitable cometary debris that would hit Earth in less than two weeks. He spoke about the whales and dolphins, and called them "our brothers and sisters of the sea." Finally he announced that Earth's best hope lay in prayer. He actually said, “If we all pray for the wellbeing of the Moon, then our survival will be assured.”

After his prepared remarks, he fielded questions for another hour. The questions ranged from heart-felt thanks for his honesty to bitter hostility. The hostility targeted two opposite offenses. Either the President had waited far too long to tell the truth, or he was assumed to have finally broken under the strain and lost his mind.

Afterwards there was commentary from panels of experts in all the network studios, but this quickly gave way to news bulletins. Malls were being ransacked. Fires had broken out, interstates were filling up and bridges had become impassible.

One dramatic incident, filmed from a helicopter, showed motorists responding to a blocked lane on the Golden Gate Bridge. Like hundreds of ants carrying a beetle, they lifted the stalled car to the edge of the bridge and dumped it against the suicide barriers. Then they raced back to their own vehicles.

The commercial networks all seemed to downplay the importance of the President's revelations and preferred to air footage on the riots and panic in the streets. A few channels preferred to report the activities of people who were holding vigils, and reminded their viewers that there were beings on Earth responding with calmness and courage to the possible end of life.

Patrick turned off the TV, went out to the end of the dock where George, like a monk living in cyberspace, spent his days and nights, and once again felt reassured that there was absolutely no need for him to hang around. Patrick remembered how, within a few hours after Frankie's arrival the week before, George had become a different person. George had actually eaten supper in the main dining room that first evening and when Frankie had whispered something in his ear they had both laughed like kids playing a game. Now it finally sunk in. He didn't have to watch George anymore.

Now that Frankie had pulled George out again, the Murphy's would probably be leaving in a few days. There were only two weeks left before the comet fragments would reach Earth. Perhaps smash into Earth. It flashed into his mind that Hal had never once given the Earth a clean bill of health. Even after the incredible success in launching a fleet of defense missiles into space, Hal always spoke as if there was some terrible price to be paid.

Patrick hitched a ride to the manor and on his way to the corner of the building where John and his family were staying, he met John coming down the corridor. John called out,

"Patrick! I was just coming to look for you. Frankie says we should all go the Research Center for a swim. One last visit with the dolphins together."

The two brothers were standing close to one another in the corridor, when John continued in a gentle voice. "Hal says we need to get going tomorrow. The world is becoming too dangerous to count on safely flying three thousand miles later this week. A cabin in the Laurentians has been set up for us."

Patrick forced himself to try to visualize what was going to happen to John and his family. "Why the Laurentians?"

John responded. "They're an ancient range of mountains, far from any volcanic or tectonic sites. They're high enough and far enough inland that they won't get inundated by tidal waves from the Atlantic or the Great Lakes. They're basically worn down mountains that can ride like skateboards over any magma waves unleashed under the earth's crust. Hal has set up a cabin for us in the woods about 80 miles north of Montreal—somewhere near St. Jovite. It's stocked with enough provisions to last ten years."

Patrick nodded. He knew the general area well. Then, for the first time since he was ten, he put his arm around his brother and said, "Let's go for our swim."

As they walked down the corridor together, Patrick realized how important John had become to him. What a strange, sad life. They had been enemies for so long, friends for a month or two, and now all that was left was a swim in the ocean.

CHAPTER 44

Patrick stood on the runway. The plane had disappeared five minutes ago but only now was it fully dawning on him that he would never see John or Leslie or Eric or Frankie again. His world was already saying good-bye to him. From now on, more and more would be for the last time.

Finally he turned, nodded to the driver and said, "Take me to the Institute, please."

As he sat alone in the back of the limo and watched the seaside landscape rolling by, he wondered what the last two weeks of life would bring?

When Patrick arrived at the Oceanographic Institute, Hal and George were out on the wharf. SLIP communication cables and power chords ran along the edge of the weathered planks, feeding computer equipment which had been set up at the end of the jetty.

Dolphins surrounded the two men, and the dark shapes of whales could be glimpsed bobbing up and down farther out. Patrick wasn't given the chance to go out—Hal had left a message for him to go back to the manor and get some rest. And the message had added a final, enigmatic phrase, “Some friends from the dolphin world are there to see you.”

Dolphin friends? What in the world could that mean, Patrick wondered as he drove back along the familiar few miles of coastal road? He stepped out of the shuttle van at the manor and was about to walk down to the beach when a rap against a window drew his attention. Peering through the glare off the lounge windows, Patrick was suddenly transformed back to that day in January two and a half months ago, which felt more like a lifetime ago, when he had stepped out of his Honda hatchback outside a little general store in Anchor Beach, Maine. Recognizing their dear faces, he struggled to ward off tears as he stumbled toward the door.

Inside, after hugs and greetings, Patrick managed to get out, “How in the world?”

Hank, smiling, responded, “How many chances do you get to take a one-way trip to Hawaii?”

Emily cut in, “All those cold winters in Anchor Beach, I couldn’t count the times Hank and I would dream about spending the winter here.”

Hank, looking at Emily for a long moment, added, “But we were waiting for the sea to return our son.”

Neither Hank nor Emily spoke for a bit, then Emily, looking directly at Patrick, said, “A man who said his name was Ted arranged for us to fly directly here from Portland on a military jet. And when he told us you’d be here, we knew we had to come.”

Like two voices speaking for one soul, Hank finished her thought. “We’ll be joining Danny in a couple of weeks, according to what Ted told us. What better place to cross over than from this glorious Pacific Ocean. I bet Danny will want to know how big the waves are in Oahu.”

Patrick added, “I’ve heard a big one may be coming. A rogue wave to end all rogue waves.”

Somehow they all found this hilarious.

They spent the weekend taking lots of walks by the sea, and then the following Monday, together with Ted and Jane and a roomful of people, they watched a launch on which the fate of the smallest microbe on Earth would depend.

George, who was now working on the same agenda as everyone else, had put together a modified BallMaker control system to launch against the 200 mile-diameter fragment. That morning's rocket—appropriately a "Titan"—carried a hastily designed payload and a lot of prayers. It was leaving Earth so late that it was now their only hope of diverting the monster fragment. If it didn't work, then Earth would become another Venus.

The Titan rocket lifted into the sky beautifully. It accelerated upwards, enveloped in a flaming contrail. Mission Control at JPL announced a successful launch, and the Titan rocket separated from its payload. Then a nuclear warhead, mounted on a small secondary rocket and controlled by a modified BallMaker system, was on its way to a rendezvous with the core-remnant of the gigantic comet.

ETA: ten days from then, on Monday, April 7th, three days before the whole cometary mess would scream through Earth's orbit, and maybe into Earth herself. But first would come the waltz of the invading dump trucks, tumbling cathedrals, and careening high rises, any one of which could turn out the lights for generations to come.

* * *

Thursday afternoon, April 3rd, at 2:37 pm, Hawaii Time, the initial umbrella of missiles, launched two weeks earlier, would engage the squadron of comet fragments. A large screen had been set up in the lounge and an hour before the moment of truth (literally, it would be a moment or two) the room was packed. Patrick decided that he wanted to be closer to the action and—telling Hank and Emily that he would see them for supper—he headed over to the Oceanographic Institute.

Patrick's hope of being with Hal and George was quickly dashed. The two brothers stood alone at the end of the jetty, surrounded by the glistening black heads of dolphins. Now and then Hal glanced at the monitor next to them but George's back could have been sculpted out of stone as he stood facing the open ocean.

A grim-faced man stood with his arms crossed at the entrance to the jetty and shook his head when Patrick indicated his interest in walking out. Frankie was gone and Patrick was apparently no longer needed. Perhaps that meant that all the cards were already in play and now even George could no longer change a Jack into a King. So Patrick turned around and joined Ted, Jane, Henry, and a few others in front of a large screen poolside. They all waited in silence.

At 2:37 P.M. Hawaii Time, the most important sixty seconds in the history of planet Earth arrived. The two armadas swarmed through each other like flocks of rabid hummingbirds. Their speed relative to one another was about 50 miles per second and the entire engagement was over in less than one minute. The window of opportunity for each missile and its target came and went within a minuscule fraction of a second.

Then the screen went blank. With little idea of what he had just seen, Patrick turned to Henry and said, "Who turned off the camera?"

Without taking his eyes off the screen, Henry said, "There aren't any cameras out there. This is a simulation from JPL based on pictures coming in from the Hubble Telescope."

Henry said nothing more and so Patrick returned his attention back to the blank screen. The screen suddenly came back to life. From a wider focal angle, and at a slower speed, the engagement was replayed. Patrick could see the entire field of cometary debris, like a mother duck and her brood strolling through the yard of the inner solar system. Then an army of foxes was in the yard. Hundreds of ducklings were slaughtered but the mother was untouched along with five of her largest offspring.

Jane spoke. "Oh My God. Five got through?"

A voice spoke from behind them and all heads turned as one. It was George. "I've shattered the comet and there's no way to pick up all the pieces now."

Patrick, who felt connected to George after weeks of sitting beside him, addressed his ravaged face. "What happened just now? Did you get what you were hoping to get?"

George didn't answer, but Hal, standing at the edge of the pool where several dolphins had entered, did. "Most of it. Two pieces, each about the size of a large city block, were not visible to Hubble and were not targeted. Three other targeted pieces escaped because of malfunctions. So five large fragments are still coming our way. As well as the core, of course."

Ted, sitting beside Jane, spoke. "Why does George think we can't get those five fragments with the next barrage? Another wave of missiles is on its way, right? Isn't the result of this first engagement pretty impressive in its own right?"

Hal didn't answer right away, and watched George wander back outside toward the ocean. Then, looking at Ted, he said,

"Yes, those five fragments can and will be targeted by the second wave of missiles, a few hours from now. But George feels personally responsible for shattering the comet and the inevitable deaths that will be caused, whatever happens. And there is a more terrible possibility. George is one of two humans who are in direct contact with the Titanians. Perhaps he already knows what is going to happen."

No one had much to say after that and Patrick made his way back to the manor, walking most of the way along the beach.

The Moon didn't rise until after midnight. Patrick couldn't sleep so he walked down to the beach. He knew that the Moon wouldn't look any different. He just wanted to feel her presence in the Hawaii night sky.

Sitting on the sand, looking out over the ocean, Patrick watched the light from a quarter moon dancing on the face of the water. Far out, he could see the black shapes of whales and dolphins riding the swell. As he sat there, a feeling for both Moon and Earth came alive in him. The Earth felt so steady under him. How could anything ever hurt her?

Patrick must have dozed off for a while, lulled by the sound of the waves crashing rhythmically against the hard-packed sand. He awoke with a start as a hand pressed hard against his shoulder. It was Hank.

"Sorry, I stumbled in the sand just now," he said. "Emily asked me to look for you. They're saying that something important is about to happen."

As they walked back up to the manor, Patrick felt surprisingly peaceful. Whatever was about to happen million of miles away, somewhere out in the solar system, this kind old man and his wife cared enough to call him inside for the show.

Images of the cluster of comet fragments were on the screen when they entered the viewing room. Henry immediately turned to Patrick and said, "Have a look at these images. They're a composite of images from Hubble and VLA data. An interesting alignment should be coming up any moment."

As Henry was talking, a series of slides appeared on the screen. They were the best pictures Patrick had seen. You could actually see the landslide of cometary debris—thousands of dark rocks, many of them with bright tapers streaming out—seemingly suspended in their headlong dash to the finish line. The largest fragment dominated the picture like a rhino in a cloud of birds.

Patrick noticed that the focus was widening with each successive frame, until eventually only the single monstrous fragment remained visible—a small dark dot from which a long feathery tail streamed out. Henry told Patrick that the comet fragments were still 12 million miles out. Then he said to watch carefully.

The cometary train, streaming away from the small dot, filled the screen and blew off the right side of the frame. Then, suddenly, shockingly, the bright rim of the moon broke through the left border of the image. Earth's future was suddenly in the room, spelled out in a clear alphabet of meaningful symbols—as Hubble caught a fleeting visual alignment of Moon and comet.

It seemed to take forever. Patrick wished he'd visited the bathroom before sitting down, but now he didn't dare leave or take his eyes off the screen. This second wave of nuclear- and laser-armed missiles would be the last chance to take out the five massive fragments which the first barrage had missed. Other launches had been attempted in the previous weeks, but for various reasons none of them had succeeded. Nothing else was on its way and nothing else would be.

Optimism was running high. But everyone knew that anything that got through unscathed now would hit Earth in two days.

The technology behaved with incredible precision. Within a period of 20 seconds, all five fragments had been destroyed. Elation swept through the room. It now appeared that of all the large fragments only the core remained.

This mood of elation didn't last long. Incredibly, two fragments—previously cloaked by successfully targeted, larger fragments—now stepped forth into the sunlight. Despair and anger welled up in many of the people who had worked without sleep for days. How could a mere five fragments have been hiding two others? Why had they even bothered trying? Suddenly people could be heard talking about George in a way that had not been heard for weeks. He was to blame.

Others immediately tried to explore alternatives. But there was no nuclear armament in a position to do anything about these two surviving fragments. The truth stared everyone down. Two predators had made it across the barriers, and the pearl-blue planet would not escape their ravening jaws.

The only nuclear bomb still on its way toward the cometary debris had an even more important mission than destroying either of these two mid-sized fragments. That bomb carried the only hope that Earth would not become another Venus, on which not a blade of grass could grow for billions of years.

New missile-launches were planned to occur within the hour. But everyone knew that it was too late to intercept the fragments significantly beyond lunar orbit. Shattering at that range—a deadly fraction of their mass would strike Earth with 100% probability.

Then more bad news started coming in. Canaveral was knocked out when a Titan rocket exploded on a launch pad. A fuel leak at White Sands closed them down. And there were no more BallMaker control systems in Russia. No missile could be launched within the next 12 hours and by then it would be too late to affect anything.

A flurry of activity continued to rage around Patrick. The third squadron of missiles, all armed with swivel-mounted laser guns, performed flawlessly. In the space of a few minutes, they cleared away all lesser debris. Hundreds of bus-sized pieces were blown off course. Thousands of pieces—all larger than anything that had struck Earth in Patrick's lifetime—were vaporized.

It was a stunning accomplishment, one that might have, under other circumstances, saved hundreds of millions of human lives. But now no one even raised his voice in the somber viewing room.

They all now knew what Hal had somehow known all along. Earth was going to be hit by two large comet fragments. The early word coming in from JPL was that one of these fragments was about two miles in diameter and the other approximately one mile.

Within the hour, further corroborations of Hal's predictions came in. The larger of the two fragments—now upgraded to 2.6 miles in diameter—would land in the Pacific, a few thousand miles west of Hawaii. It didn't take a genius to know what would happen to all islands and costal areas around the globe a few hours after impact.

The smaller of the two fragments—now identified as being 1.3 miles in diameter—would strike Antarctica. The water thereby released from Earth's southern icecap would disperse across the globe, increasing the level of the world's oceans dramatically. Hal's version of the Parable of the Talents was coming true.

There was no time for the Hawaii Team to become philosophical about what this meant for the future of life on Earth. But the mood changed. Everyone became completely concentrated on what they were doing. And now there was only one thing worth doing. Unless they could shift the path of the comet's core by a few degrees—so that the Moon could sling it away from Earth, then in a few days there would not be a gnat left alive on Earth.

All capacity for excitement seemed to have drained from Patrick's mind. The fate of individual entities seemed to hardly matter anymore. Everything took on a transparent quality. It was not indifference or resignation that had fallen over him. He felt strangely alive and connected to everything.

When Ted said that he and Jane were going over to the Institute, probably for good, Patrick agreed to join them and they drove the few miles down the coastal road together.

They sat down with a group of people who were gathered around a large monitor at the entrance to the jetty where Hal and George were working.

Patrick looked out to the jetty. Hal sat beside George, and both were gazing out to sea. Hundreds of dolphins floated quietly on the surface, around and beneath the wharf where the two men sat cross-legged on cushions, surrounded by computer equipment.

Ten minutes passed, as everyone waited for the fate of Earth to be determined in a final coin toss.

A series of Hubble images succeeded in holding the massive fragment in focus. The fuzzy dark ball danced back and forth in the upper left corner of the image. Henry whispered to Patrick that they probably wouldn't see the missile because it was traveling too fast.

Suddenly the entire Hubble image flashed brightly. Then the screen went black.

Everyone sat still as stone statues. Patrick became aware of waves lapping against the pylons and the sound of George tapping on his keyboard. He heard Henry whisper, "At least we know the bomb went off."

For what seemed like a long time everyone sat in utter silence. Either their monitor had blown, or Hubble itself had been knocked out by the intensity of the flash.

Then, for the first time in weeks, he felt his mind being drawn into a realization that life on Earth was on the cusp of a new era. There was a quiet awareness of great loss, a deep leave-taking of all that had been known, and within that deep sadness there was a glimmer of hope, an element of something like gratitude, born of the recognition that life on Earth had risen to a terrible challenge.

Patrick closed his eyes. He no longer needed to wait for some image to reappear on the screen before him. He was able to see what George was seeing. The giant comet core was turning. It had not yet broken, as the Moon reached out and they tugged at one another. It was as if the lookout on watch on the Titanic had found the misplaced spyglass, and had glimpsed moonlight glistening off the iceberg ten minutes sooner. Now the passengers, crowding the deck, waited helplessly as the massive ship moved degree-by-agonizing-degree to port—not one of them knowing if there remained time to avoid collision.

To his surprise, Patrick realized that even George did not know what was going to happen. And with a rush of awareness, Patrick saw how George had risen from the ashes of his madness and that he had not wavered for an instant in the terrible role assigned him—once the Titanians had recognized and corrected some of their own mistakes. Like parents who only slowly understand what it means to guide a child, they had been unaware that George's mind had broken under the gravitational pull of their alien intelligence.

More and more Patrick felt as if he were suspended in time, or as if he were under water. Everything seemed clear, vivid and personal. He felt no need to cling to life. Instead he felt immense gratitude for all that had happened. He thought of Hank and Emily, of John and his family, of the contact he had been given with dolphins and whales. He thought of the thrilling knowledge that there was other life in their solar system. How could he begrudge his personal death, after these incredible wonders that had been given to him?

It wasn't as if he didn't care whether or not Earth would be destroyed. It was more that he no longer had to feel anxious about things that were clearly out of his control. Now that there were no more practical steps to take to try to save life, he could give himself over completely to appreciating it.

CHAPTER 45

Thursday, April 10 (Day 0)

Patrick left Hal, George and the others and made his way down to the beach. The Moon was three quarters full and high in the sky as dawn approached in Hawaii. At 5:32 am, Hawaii Time, the two fragments, already visible to the naked eye, disappeared behind the Moon. They both reappeared seconds later, noticeably on a slightly altered path. Patrick had been told that, traveling at 30 miles a second, they would reach Earth in about three hours.

With all life histories, the years that in the beginning seem endless eventually give way to an accelerating finitude. Years, months, days, and finally hours come starkly into focus, and finally it can no longer be denied. There is not much left of life. Suddenly, strangely, everything is for the last time and time itself is hurtling past. Or perhaps, at last, time is running straight into the heart.

While the comet was still far beyond Pluto, an observer could have watched for days without being sure in what direction it was heading. But now its shattered pieces were inside the Moon's orbit, flying towards Earth, and time itself was an arrow piercing its target.

Patrick felt an intensification of the pressure he was feeling inside his skull. Perhaps the approaching comet fragments were disturbing the magnetic field. Or perhaps it was the strain of concentration.

He could not prevent himself from being more and more drawn into a global concentration, and now the Moon felt as close as a frightened child, cradled in her mother's arms.

Wanting to be with the people who had become his friends, Patrick climbed up to the coastal road, hitched a ride, and made it back to the manor in time to catch the final News Broadcast of the era in which he had been born.

News that the first comet fragment, 1.3 miles in diameter, had sliced into the Antarctic ice fields came at 8:28 a.m. Within minutes, Patrick imagined that he felt a new static charge in the southerly breeze. An amazing calm fell over the islands—broken only by an ugly black scar rising slowly out of the ocean to the south.

Moments later, right on schedule, a 2.6 mile-wide ball of rock and ice plunged into one of the deepest parts of the Pacific Ocean, the 35,000-foot deep Marianna Trench just east of Guam. If this fragment had been gently laid in the Pacific trench, like a stone placed in a shallow bowl, it would have sunk harmlessly out of sight with about four miles of water above it.

Instead it arrived at a speed of 30 miles a second. It pierced the thin veil of Earth's atmosphere like a bullet flying through mist. The 6-mile depth of ocean water, which the leading edge of the asteroid traversed in about a second, offered little more insulation than a bowl of Jell-O would to an exploding land mine.

Patrick walked outside. The islands were still quiet. A breeze seemed to have picked up on the ocean, coming out of the West. It gradually became more difficult for the dolphins to float on the surface. The whales off shore seemed more and more to vanish beneath the increasing choppiness of the swell.

For the Hawaii Team and for Patrick, the last moment would not be the rendezvous between Earth and the comet core (slowed now by its change of trajectory). The massive core of this ancient comet would not cross Earth's orbit until later that morning, at 10:55 am. Long before then, the islands would be destroyed by the affects of the two asteroids that had already struck.

Patrick knew that he would never know if their efforts had been successful, but he kept his concentration on the Moon, feeling the presence of countless other beings joined in vigil. And he felt their deaths, one by one, as the devastation spread outward across the globe from the two impact centers.

A bizarre kind of hopefulness survived. It was as if, with the death of beings around the world, some kind of energy was released. Was it possible that even in death, their will to save Earth was surviving? Were the Titanians continuing to harness the psychic energy of every soul who yearned for Earth to remain alive?

A passage from Franz Kafka came into Patrick's mind—how the fate of Paradise was also changed, when Adam and Eve lost their chance to live there.

A heartfelt wish took form in his mind. Let Paradise survive, even as I leave it forever.

A rapidly spreading pillar of black smoke from the asteroid strike off Guam could now be seen to the west of Hawaii. Even from 3300 miles away, the immense column of ejecta was clearly visible. Then the islands started shaking.

Lines of rubber dinghies were waiting at the shoreline. Hank, Emily, Hal, Jane, Ted, George, and many others ran to the dinghies, which were then towed out by dolphins. They wore scuba gear, for when they would be cast beneath the waves. Perhaps it would buy them a little time.

They were about a mile off shore when the volcanoes started spewing black smoke, followed by upwelling streams of flaming lava. Patrick caught a final glimpse of the Moon before the sky disappeared under a pall of funereal emissions. Then hurricane winds in excess of 500 miles per hour arrived. They ripped out every tree and leveled every building on the islands. Patrick barely had time to start the oxygen flow and bite down on the mouth plug, when his dinghy was plucked from the crest of a twenty-foot wave and flung shoreward like a blown leaf. He dropped into the sea, his body slapping against the side of a wave.

Struggling against the sudden weight of a gigantic swell passing over him, he turned and looked upwards. Through the goggles, the sky was dark and far away.

Then suddenly he was being lifted to the surface. His heart froze as he felt the strong body pushing against him. For an instant, a fear of sharks grabbed at his mind. But just as quickly, something familiar in the way he was being held broke through, and his fear turned to joy. It was the dolphin who had saved his life two months ago.

Under conditions that would otherwise have killed a human, the dolphin allowed Patrick to witness the ferocity of a storm from hell. The wind ripped away the top of each cresting wave and flung it across the sky.

Then the dolphin would deftly pull Patrick down beneath the surface in time to escape the full fury of the wind.

There would follow a brief interlude of uncanny quiet. Submerged 10 feet under the cresting wave, the water above would slowly fall away until they broke through into the air again and were floating at the bottom of a gigantic, gleaming valley.

Approaching inexorably, towering 50 feet overhead, would be the next wave. The carnage wrecked by the wind, as it ripped the heads off the peaks on either side, seemed to be happening far above.

The dolphin remained close to Patrick, supporting him and pulling him down to safety whenever a breaking wave would otherwise have crushed him under tons of water.

It was the ride on the tiger's back of which every child dreams. That was what was so deeply moving, Patrick suddenly realized. For the first time in living memory, he was a child under the protection of a being he could trust.

Then her behavior changed. She seemed to want Patrick to stay close to the surface, even when this risked his life. It took a while before Patrick understood why.

At first it seemed that a dark mountain of storm cloud was coming in from the West. The air felt as dense as the water. There was a sense of being in a riptide, of being sucked towards the roiling wall of storm.

Then he understood. The word echoed in his mind, like the closing chord in a symphonic poem. Tsunami. The horizon rose up to the sky. The face of the sea lifted upwards until there was no more sky and darkness fell around them.

Perhaps time slowed down. Or perhaps his mind had no way to judge the distance of a two-mile high wall of water.

He had time to review his life. Most of all he felt a great gladness to have lived these last few weeks. In the darkness, he caught glimpses of the dolphin beside him. The face of the ocean was now as flat and wide as an Alpine meadow, with a wall of mountain towering above it to the west.

Patrick felt his body being lifted up and flung sideways. He had imagined that he might get to experience what it was like to be a sperm whale two miles below the surface. But he lost body consciousness almost immediately.

Then he saw his father's face. How could he have forgotten? Lying on his back, he felt those hands reaching into the crib, lifting him into the air. And both of them were laughing.

CHAPTER 46

It all felt so familiar to John. Snow melting off the eaves in the afternoons. Maple trees, with sap dripping from spigots into tapered silver buckets. The air, so unlike New Mexico's dry desert air, redolent with deep woods smells.

Their cabin looked like any ordinary cabin on the Laurentian Shield, 80 miles north of Montreal. But under the pine lapstreak siding, a skeleton of steel was embedded in a massive concrete underground living area, far larger than the visible cabin. A special computer gave them contact with control centers at JPL and Hawaii. Their food—which filled a sandalwood-lined vault under the cabin—was mostly dehydrated, with a few years' worth of canned delicacies thrown in.

The last few evenings, they had all sat in the darkened cabin, the light from a three-quarter moon visible outside on the snow. It would seem to John that Frankie was enveloped in a blue aura. John and Leslie never saw him sleep.

Thursday morning, before sun-up, John, Leslie, Eric and Frankie huddled around the computer display. They saw Hubble photos of the two fragments passing across the face of the Moon. Then they waited. For John, the unbearable pressure of waiting had the effect of driving him into a heightened sense of appreciation for ordinary life: the smell of coffee, birds singing in the pale dawn light. He went outside onto the front porch and sat down on the stoop with his cup of coffee. A delicate breeze wafted into his face, carrying the smells of melting snow and forest vegetation. But he couldn't sit there for long. His mind was too much on other places and other people. Patrick was living the last day of his life. And maybe that was true of every living being on the planet.

John returned to the cabin just in time to hear Frankie moan and hold his head in his hands. Minutes later, satellite photos of the first fragment strike at the South Pole came onto the screen.

It was strange to see images of devastation on a little monitor—while outside the warm April breezes soughed soothingly in the pine forest. John reacted by turning his mind to the beauty around him. Leslie spent a lot of time with Frankie on her knee, while Frankie himself didn't really seem to be present to his surroundings. As for Eric, he acted like he wanted to jump in a car and keep driving: he twice dropped his plate of toast on the floor, and repeatedly went outside, then came back seconds later.

By 12:30 p.m., Montreal time, the Guam strike had occurred. Hubble images of this strike showed a column of flame, then a mass of blackness rising up out of the ocean and spreading across the familiar marbled face of the blue and white planet. Close-ups showed a gigantic wall of water riding eastward across the Pacific.

By mid-afternoon, JPL and Hawaii were both off-line. For a little while Hubble images of the Moon continued to transmit —presumably via some other earth-based receiving station. Then the computer went blank and stayed that way.

All afternoon, they felt faint tremors under their feet. None of them had ever experienced an earthquake, so they weren't sure what to expect. John sensed that the movements in the Earth weren't like what was experienced in an earthquake zone. It was more like being on a large ocean liner where there is some vibration and a slow swaying. He visualized that they were experiencing shock waves from the fragment hits, but that the Laurentian Shield was riding the agitated magma like a heavy barge.

They all felt the moment Patrick died. It was as if the cabin had suddenly grown unbearably cold. There was a sudden shift in Frankie. He started crying and wouldn't stop until Leslie gave him a bottle of warm milk—his first in six months.

George must have died at the same time. John wondered if that would end Frankie's contact with the Titanians. With the death of the old dolphin, the humpback, Patrick, George, Hal—all that extraordinary connection might now be lost.

No. John could dimly sense that some powerful force was continuing, but he was just too drained to focus on anything.

He heard Eric announcing that he was going for a walk, and Leslie arguing with him. Then the cabin door slammed.

John looked at Frankie sleeping on the sofa, his almost empty bottle lying on the cushion beside him, and let his own head rest against the back of the easy chair. He would have time to be with his family later. There was so much to share that he hadn't shared, but now he just needed to rest for a moment. Exhaustion swept over him like high tide covering a shoal.

He awoke to the sound of Leslie screaming and Frankie crying. What was it? Frankie didn't seem to be hurt.

Outside the forest was thrashing. As he watched, a large maple branch snapped and flew past the window as if it were a twig. He remembered that this sturdy log cabin had heavy shutters outside, which could be bolted across the windows. Why hadn't he fastened them earlier?

He ran to the front door and tried to open it. It seemed to be locked shut. Putting his shoulder against it, he realized that the weight of the wind was pushing against him. Leslie was still shouting something when he forced himself outside. Then the door slammed shut between them.

John managed to close the shutters. For a few moments the wind slackened and he was able to open the front door. He had not cleared the threshold when the wind hit the house with such power that the closing door hurled him into the middle of the cabin. Struggling to his feet, John shouted at Leslie that they needed to go into the storm shelter under the cabin.

She just stood there, holding Frankie in her arms, shouting something back. He had to put his face right next to hers before he could hear what she was saying.

"Didn't you see him? The door must have slammed in his face. Can't you hear him knocking on it?"

John's mind refused to understand her. He made her spell it out. Leslie screamed, "Our son, Eric, is out there!"

The roar of wind and branches smashing against the cabin roof hurt his ears. John and Leslie pushed against the front door as hard as they could, but it didn't budge. Then John used a crowbar to wedge it open a few inches. But when a twig stabbed in through the tiny crack, making a deep gash in John's hand, the message was clear: anyone out on the porch would already have been swept away and dashed against the nearest tree trunk.

They heard the sound of shattering glass and turned to see the jagged end of a tree branch protruding through the kitchen window. The 1" plywood shutter held up around the puncture, but a heavy pot blew off the counter and a flurry of napkins flew around the cabin.

John knew that if a sizeable hole opened anywhere in the house, the whole building could be torn off its foundations.

It was Frankie who launched them into action. "Eric OK. Need go in ground now."

John found a large flashlight, opened the trap door, and led Leslie and Frankie beneath the house. With the heavy door bolted securely above them, the wailing of the storm seemed much farther away. But one of them was still out in this storm. And, despite Frankie's assurances, his parents felt they had just pulled his tombstone over their heads.

EPILOGUE: THE TIME NO ONE WANTED

When I was a child, the Moon moved around the Earth in a regular orbit that took about 29 days. On a clear night you could see its bright, friendly face watching over Earth.

All of that has changed. The comet pulled the Moon into an eccentric orbit which takes 122 days to complete. And the atmosphere is so contaminated that the Moon is only rarely visible—only when its full face coincides with its closest approach to Earth.

Even though I can't see the Moon, I have plotted its path by measuring the behavior of the tides. The tides vary a great deal. Neap tide is scarcely more than a foot, while rip tide is more than 200 feet in height. The psychological effect is also variable to an alarming degree. When the Moon is at its closest point, I am truly a lunatic. There have been occasions when I have been brought back to shore, almost dead, by dolphins who found me trying to swim across the ocean.

This document—perhaps I will indulge myself and call it a book—describes what happened during the months immediately before the collision of cometary fragments with Earth. It is based on a kind of journal that Hal gave me—thin as a Newsweek, shrink-wrapped, and slung in a gossamer harness which he told me to wear at all times under my shirt. Hal made me promise that I would always have it with me, even when I slept or washed. Along with pages that Hal himself recorded, there were writing materials: a box of #2 pencils, three thumb-sized pencil sharpeners, and some kind of paper, hundreds of sheets, very thin, which twenty years later still seem unaffected by the passage of time.

I had this backpack with me when I was separated from my family, the day the comet struck. I kept Hal's notes, but it was years before I could bear to look at them. When I did finally break the shrink-wrapping, I discovered a shorthand description of the lives of my family and a few other people—covering the months immediately before the destruction.

I have organized and amplified these notes, trying to be true to what I knew about the people involved. I sometimes imagine that I have muses in my head who fill in important details. Call it fiction, if you prefer.

At first I wasn't going to add anything myself (with the exception of some elucidation of an incident that occurred to me in a schoolyard), but I've changed my mind.

Let me emphasize that I didn't open this journal for sixteen years. It was four years ago that I began to work on it, overcoming great reluctance to do so. This has been partly out of necessity. No one is bringing me food, or gathering and chopping firewood for my hearth. I don't have electricity to keep a lamp burning—even if I did have the energy to sit up in the bitterly cold evenings to write. So I write just a few hours a week, if I am lucky.

My snail pace also stems from a gut revulsion to dealing with this material. I get very angry whenever I think about this time, and about all that was lost in the year that I turned 13.

And one may well wonder why on Earth I need to add my own final thoughts to such a dismal story. Considering that it will likely be read only by people who live in the same world that I now inhabit, if by anyone, of what possible value will it be for me to describe what it is like to live in this cold, dark reality? Who could I possibly imagine would read such a thing?

This is precisely the issue for me. Who will read this? More specifically, will it be read by my contemporaries in the present era, or will it be read by the contemporaries of my parents, in the era before the comet struck?

If you have read the document that precedes this epilogue, then you will have heard of the man named Hal. Hal died in Hawaii, in 2014, along with my uncle and almost everyone else mentioned by name in this document.

I was separated from my mother, father and brother a few days later, at the very moment that the comet fragments were devastating the planet. I have not seen them for 20 years. I have to assume that they are all dead.

Hal insisted, much against my wishes, that I needed to survive in order to record these events.

It seems surprising to me that, two decades later, not only do I remember what he said, but I find myself acting on his words, as ridiculous, even irrelevant, as they ordinarily seem to me.

Hal claimed that the Titanians know how to communicate with other times.

He said he had personally seen evidence of this capacity. He was certain that if the Titanians had something useful to transmit, recording the human experience of this catastrophe, then they could transmit it back to the time that preceded the great collisions. In other words, they could replace the warning which was sent to Earth at that time with something more effective. For instance, they could transmit something to the President that would catch his attention at a deeper level than the basic warning about a comet did.

I am not convinced.

Then why am I writing this document? After all, why does anyone alive now need to know about the events that led up to Earth's collision with a comet? The whales and dolphins will always teach each other about it, and if I can learn from them so can other humans. If there are any. Why describe our past mistakes? It is enough to learn how to live well, without dwelling on the insanity that ruled so much of human life in the early 21st century. That's what I think.

But Hal insisted that I needed to tell this story. During the last week my family was in Hawaii, he used to wake me up early in the morning, and we'd walk out on the beach for an hour. He kept drumming into me that my story would be crucial. Even if I couldn't understand why, he said I needed to tell it.

It's like he placed some alarm clock in me that started ringing a few years ago. Now I can't go back to sleep.

Hal told me on these walks that it was too late to avoid catastrophe. I could never understand how he was so sure, so early. But then he promised me that there was still a way to avoid the world in which this catastrophe had become inevitable. At some time in the future, the Titanians would try to communicate back to the humans who lived on Earth prior to the arrival of the comet. There was no question in his mind that they were able to do this. His only question was whether a document I wrote would be included in a transmission whose main purpose would have to be something more central to the intentions of the Titanians.

Anyway, I couldn't say no. I started writing this document four years ago and at least I am able to sleep a little better now.

* * *

I've just been told that I need to have my document ready by the next full moon. That's ten days from now. The idea seems to be that whatever I have written will be read directly from my mind and then sent to present-day Titan.

Who told me? I have no idea. When I was in mid-school something similar happened. I could sense what other people were thinking. I always had the feeling that other people, like my Uncle Patrick, did that regularly. Right now it doesn’t seem important to figure it out. For the past twenty years, the dolphins have talked with me, and maybe they’re the ones who are telling me what to do now. But it feels different. It feels like someone is giving me the final exam, after twenty years of study. I just know that the dolphins know way more than I do about what’s going on on Earth. And they’re waiting for me to get going.

So here I go. The teacher has set the timer. If something useful happens as a result, then I suppose that my present status as a 33 year old orphan will lose its antecedents in time, and some other Eric Murphy, perhaps still with family and friends, will come into being.

I'm ready.

So what is my part? First, it's to finish writing this epilogue. There are some things I want to say, just in case people, who were alive before the comet struck, ever see it. Then I have to do my best to learn this document by heart. Like the Tibetan monks used to do with their sacred texts. Maybe still do, for all I know, somewhere in the Himalaya if there are any mountain chains still standing on the planet.

When the Titanians look into my mind, I want them to be able to find a text that really expresses what those people were experiencing in 2014. There I said it: I'm getting ready for the Titanians to visit my mind. I don't have a photographic memory, but if I live with this material for the next ten days, perhaps they will be able to find something coherent. I think I have enough food to stay alive that long. Maybe, maybe not. But the dolphins share with me whatever they find in the waters around this tiny island.

First of all, I want to say that I don't enjoy living this way: I didn't choose to be a hermit.

I know I also need to remember to feel appreciation for my present life. My connection with the dolphins and whales is very important. I feel lucky to be able to communicate with other beings whose minds are so rich and whose experiences open up whole new realms to me.

I wouldn't be alive if it weren't for my friends the dolphins and the whales. I live on fish. I lost the boat I used to have and now I try to catch fish in a kind of pouch made out of vines. Very crude. Now and then I catch something. But I know that I wouldn't be alive if I didn't have friends to chase fish into the shore for me. Sometimes I can net ten or twenty in an hour and then I smoke them over my fire. It's quite a gift they give me. There aren't many fish in the sea these days. Although now that it's possible to see a faint shadow once more, I think life in the oceans is increasing. That's what my friends tell me anyway. They say that there is more plankton and that some of the baleen whales are slowly putting on weight again. The dolphins aren't breeding yet, but I have the feeling that they are feeling some optimism. In any case, they will have to breed in the next decade because not many of them will live longer than that.

Every time they send me fish I feel a kind of awe that they would share such meager pickings with me.

Let me say it again: I haven't seen another human being for twenty years. I think that there are other humans left on the planet. The cetaceans have told me there are. They have told me that Mom and Dad and Frankie are still alive. But they must be mistaken. I know I would feel Frankie's presence if he were still alive.

They say there are human settlements here and there. Sometimes I think I should risk everything to try to link up with one of these communities. But I've heard that some of them are rough. They might kill any new arrival, out of fear that one more mouth to feed would be too much for whatever meager foothold they have worked out for themselves. Some have become cannibals. In any case, I don't have a real boat anymore, capable of crossing a large expanse of water. And how could I navigate in this dim haze?

I was somewhere in the Laurentian's when the storm hit. I was very upset that day. I knew my uncle had died. I could feel everything through Frankie. I don't know how Frankie could stand all the dying. I couldn't. I went for a walk. I had probably walked 2 miles by the time the winds came. They weren't ordinary winds. I was on top of a rock looking down over the woods below when I saw a full-grown maple tree rip out of the side of a hill and fly through the air.

I'd seen a cave of sorts while clambering up to the top of this rock. Fortunately it was on the leeward side of the promontory from which I saw devastation being visited on the forest below.

I managed to get off the top in time. I was terrified of being plucked off the hill by the suction of the wind sweeping around it. My ears were stabbing with pain as I reached the cave and clawed my way inside. It offered meager protection, but it had a slight indentation on one side so that by compressing my body into the jagged wall of this crevice, I could escape direct exposure to the elements.

The wind got even worse. Trees repeatedly smashed against the mouth of my cave. Then suddenly the ground under me was flying violently upwards. The acceleration was so great that I passed out. When I awoke again there were fires. I passed out again, this time probably from lack of oxygen. Somehow I survived. I sat for days while an incredibly heavy rain fell outside my cave. To have stepped outside would have been like walking into the middle of Niagara Falls. The puddles in my cave were bitter but drinkable.

When I ventured outside again, I think about five days later, my body so stiff that I could scarcely crawl, it was with horror that I viewed my world. I was on a small island.

In the dim light I could see no other land. Not then. Not for the next 20 years. Maybe I was confused about the orientation of the cave I spent those five days in. Maybe in being flung upwards on a river of erupting magma, my little island was turned around. I thought I would only have to swim out a couple of miles to reach my family. But after two days of dog paddling on a floating log, there was still only sea. I had been so sure that I would get home that when I finally gave up I had no idea how to get back.

I would never have been able to return to my little cave if the dolphins hadn't carried me back. But they couldn't guide me to my family. They had heard of my family and me. But with the death of Dolphie, Frankie's friend, and the old humpback who saved Uncle Patrick, no one knew how to talk with them. Or how to find them. The dolphins told me that they were on a continent, near a fresh-water lake, separated from the coast by impassible terrain. They said that even if they took me to the coast, I would never be able to find my parents.

I returned to my island exhausted and discouraged. For years I lived like a zombie—my only daily company a crab, whom I called Rock, and a salamander I called Rose.

Then one day the dolphins showed up with a decrepit old rowboat. I was ecstatic. I set out like a new man, my heart daring to hope again.

A storm smashed my boat the second day out. Again the dolphins brought me back. That was four years ago. It was then I started writing this book. Suddenly I was ready.

With no boat—and no large trees on my little island to make one—I survive on rainwater and the fish that are herded into shore. I have gradually noticed that the more time I spend writing, the more likely I am to find a fish in my net. At least the dolphins think this is a sane thing for me to be doing.

So here I am addressing the memory of dead people, and fanning the delusion that some beings from another planet are going to deliver this letter for me. I guess 20 years without talking to another human takes its toll.

That's not all. My mental condition is even more precarious than that. Not only am I now working 20 hours a day, with very little sleep and even less food, to pursue this absurd project, but I feel more alive doing this than I can ever remember feeling. Quite frankly, there is a level at which I believe everything that Hal told me, and everything that the cetaceans now tell me. I do so with a kind of begrudging recognition that the state of my own sanity is probably beyond the point where I can accurately judge anything.

Besides, loneliness will drive a man to any kind of company, even into the company of the dead. And I do commune with the dead. Whenever I read the old documents about these people's lives, I see them again, and I actually feel that I am talking with them: Mom, Dad, Frankie, Uncle Patrick, Henry, Ted, Jane, even George—the whole shining roll call of all that I have loved and lost.

When it comes to Hal, he is like a voice inside me that tells me what to do. I think they used to have a name for that: psychosis.

These days he is telling me that I must not be sleeping when the Titanians come. That sure makes it easy for a guy to relax.

* * *

Ten days have come and gone, and the Titanians are looking into my mind right now. My chance to write anything more has passed.

It's the night of the full Moon. There are an incredible number of whales and dolphins off shore. A hundred times more than I've ever seen before. My cave looks out over the open ocean as it stretches away into the distance towards the east. The Moon has already come up and I can make out the dim outlines of thousands of beings riding on the black sea. And there is something I have not seen since I was a child. I can scarcely believe it. In the thick obscurity of the smoggy night sky—a rainbow!

For better or worse the Titanians have already picked up the entire document. I was surprised how quickly they got it out of my mind. I was even more surprised at how precise and detailed it seemed to me as they pulled it out. I really felt that they got every word that I have written down over the course of the past four years. It felt as if I was reliving those times—not only what I had written, but everything I have ever felt or known seemed to rise in me like a golden flock of birds.

One memory stands out strongly.

I was adding some seaweed to the fire—I think it was about three years ago—so I could continue writing a bit longer, when suddenly I heard a seagull's cry. I looked up towards the curtain of woven seaweed that hangs across the mouth of my cave, so stunned that I could not breathe. I had just finished writing about how my grandfather drowned under the ice. That seagull's piercing cry, the only birdcall I had heard in 16 years, uttered a promise of other lands. It reminded me of something I read in my childhood, but whatever book that may have been is now permanently checked out.

That single cry filled me with such longing and pain that I was not able to write for many, many months after that. And I have never found that other land.

My memories ran through me like a torrent, as the document was being drawn out of me. It may all have taken place between two breaths. Now, in the silence that follows, I can still feel their presence. They aren't going away. Gradually I understand that they want something else. They're now going much more slowly.

They seem to be probing me for something different from what I spent the past four years writing. I can feel that they will use part of what I wrote, but now (at this very moment) they want something more spontaneous. That was why I mentioned all those heads out in the water, looking up at this cave. The Titanians seemed to want that.

They want me to say something about them. But I don't know anything about them. The last time I had contact with the Titanians was 20 years ago, and back then I was always with my parents and Frankie. Now something different seems to be happening. It's as if they are telling me how they feel. About their own loneliness.

I never experienced that 20 years ago. Hal gave the impression that Frankie and George were the only humans who had direct contact. Now I'm getting that kind of feeling too. At least I think I am.

I may as well just barge ahead. I don't know what else to do. The Titanians seem to want me to just say what I feel right now with them talking to me inside my head.

So here goes. This is my understanding about the situation on Earth. For the cetaceans, and me it's miserable. More dolphins and whales survived than humans, but it's been very hard for them to keep alive. Many have starved to death, in addition to the millions who were killed at the time of the comet.

With that as a background, it may sound strange to say this, but for human life on this planet, a kind of renaissance has begun. A new influx of energy and understanding has arisen from contact with the Titanians. However, the estate of human life has been so profoundly reduced that it is extremely difficult for our species to benefit from new understanding right now.

The cetaceans are also experiencing a renaissance of sorts. Although they have been in touch with Titanians for thousands of centuries, their new communication with humans has radically deepened their relationship with Earth.

As for the Titanians, they preferred whales and dolphins from the very beginning. I say that without any bitterness whatsoever. It's the most natural thing in the world that the Titanians would choose dolphins and whales over humans. They are able to talk together and immediately understand one another. Part of that is due to similar experiences. Both have lived in the ocean for millions of years. Both have a system of communication in which intimate knowledge spans eons of time and connects the lives of countless individuals. The cetaceans know how to preserve the deepest insights and values that have arisen for their species as a whole. For humans there is science, which abstracts away from feeling; and religion, which imposes its values from outside.

Probably the main reason that the Titanians feel more at home with whales and dolphins is that they noticed when the Titanians first contacted Earth. It's as if a grandfather had two grandchildren, one of whom lights up whenever he visits, while the other has to be dragged out of his room. The grandfather is much more likely to enjoy spending time with the one who is delighted to see him, right? Well, humans are like the kid who would prefer not to be disturbed, while cetaceans, recognizing that there was a new voice speaking on Earth, gathered round like children bright-eyed at a campfire.

In certain traditions there is the promise that a new era will be ushered in with the arrival of a being who can lead humans out of suffering and confusion. One name for this being is the Messiah. Unfortunately, there is no guarantee that humans would recognize this being, or be willing to initiate drastic change in their ways of thinking and behaving, even if they did think such a special being had come. Humans have always assumed such a Messiah would be humanoid, so they would not even notice a non-human Messiah if one knocked on their front door.

Most humans probably have not been capable of either recognizing or welcoming a Messiah for many centuries. And we also did not know how to welcome a very intelligent, highly evolved species from our own solar system.

The whales and dolphins knew how to welcome them.

It's an interesting difference in our two species. There really isn't anything in human life comparable to this ability, shared by the entire cetacean order, to become aware of a new presence on Earth. For humans, there is always some frozen "sense of reality" that functions like the walls of a prison. We feel threatened if anything arises which challenges our view of reality. We would rather ignore a whole new realm of experience than be obliged to revise our comfortable explanations for the way things are.

Now I'm being pushed in another direction. The Titanians want me to say more about this present era. This wonderful, terrible, new time that is unfolding on Earth: where cetaceans play the largest role, but where there may still be a place for humans as well. In spite of tremendous losses, something significantly new is unfolding.

So why should an effort be made to go back to the past and change it?

Why did Hal tell me 20 years ago that this was why I had to survive? It hardly seems worth it. The world is about to emerge from a very difficult time, and a brand new future is dawning. A life form other than the human is in the ascendant. With the support of the Titanians and the eclipse of the human species as an overwhelmingly dangerous force on Earth, it really seems that the cetaceans can now blossom into the role of dominant species. With millions of years to evolve, what could such an intelligent and peaceful order of beings not bring to fruition? Surely this is a good time for humans to step aside and let a new future come into being.

However, even now as I ask these questions, it's clear that the Titanians wish Earth had been spared those two devastating cometary impacts. Why? I'm asking this for myself, as much as for anyone else who might ever see this.

The answer comes back crystal clear: for cetaceans, for humans, and for Titanians.

Why would the cetaceans be better off? They would be better off because they would be spared the terrible losses they have suffered—in individual deaths, in the extinctions of whole species, and most importantly in the fact that for the next ten years very much still hangs in the balance. It is still possible that many more species will vanish from this planet.

Why would humans be better off? Because we have lost almost everything. We've lost most of the knowledge base that guided human life. That is not all for the bad. It's good for all beings of Earth that we can no longer make the weapons that for half a century were capable of doing more damage than the comet fragments did. It's also good that we are no longer in a position to slaughter other species as we did, nor to despoil the environment shared by all living beings. Nonetheless, the Titanians would rather sponsor an Earth with human beings fully present on it. Why?

This has partly to do with humans themselves and partly to do with the Titanians.

Something shifted in human consciousness during the time of the comet. Otherwise the large fragment would have collided and no intelligent life would have survived on Earth—not humans, not cetaceans, not the Titanian children. It seems that humans in the end showed themselves able to be the friends of life, rather than its despoilers. At least some humans discovered what it means to give without hope of reward. Our species showed itself capable of growing up, of devoting its energy to interests greater than its own self-assertions. Without those final efforts—freely given without hope of personal advantage—not a single terrestrial being would have survived.

The Titanians haven't forgotten the belated heroism displayed by many human beings, and they are willing to act on our behalf if the opportunity arises to do so.

Why do the Titanians want a new time?

I remember Hal talking about this in Hawaii. But only now has the terrible depth of the Titanian sacrifice hit me full force.

The Titanians want a new time because they can't get home. If a space program had survived on Earth, they could have told us how to equip a ship to take them back to Titan. But they cannot do this by themselves. Titanian emissaries were able to reach Earth because their community developed a transmitter, harnessing the electromagnetic energy of Saturn, to make it possible. One day, some natural confluence of bodies might occur that would allow the Titanians to hitch a ride home, but the only possibility of which they are aware lies thousands of years into an indefinite future.

The Titanians resemble terrestrial butterflies in some ways. Except instead of a caterpillar turning into a creature with wings, they remain both the caterpillar and the butterfly. Part of them remains confined to a blind, groping life in the cold dark ocean of Titan, while another, symbiotic part soars aloft. Not only are they physically confined to the water (as Earth's cetaceans are confined), but their experience of this home realm is very limited. They can hardly see or hear or feel without that part of their embodiment which is free to fly in the atmosphere, also free to fly above the atmosphere (which is very deep on Titan), and even in the vast magnetosphere of Saturn. And to survive in the ocean, they rely on these free-flying eyes and ears.

It is these symbiotic parts of their embodiment which several Titanians sent to Earth, and which are now stranded here. So they have their own motivation for wanting a human-based space program back in the picture.

A vital part of these Titanian beings are here on Earth: the part that reaches out to embrace life. Without it they are like sentient beings who have been turned to stone. They know what it is to reach out but cannot do so; they know what it is like to thrill to beauty, but cannot even bring to mind a clear image of what they most love.

Humans can't really understand the nature of this loss: how these beings, marooned on Titan, can't see or hear or feel, how they can't enjoy experience of any kind.

The final anguish of their situation is that they are still in touch with one another, across hundreds of millions of miles, like two imprisoned loved-ones touching fingertips through barbed wire.

Animal life being what it is, it is this Titanian exile that allows me to hope that a new message might actually get delivered back into the time when I was still very young. I was thirteen when the comet reached Earth, but presumably a new influence would reach Earth earlier than that.

In my mind's eye I can wonder what might start changing in my life. I would like to be able to go back and watch, as an observer who also knows what I have experienced in the past 20 years.

Of course, if the Titanians actually do change the course of human—excuse me, terrestrial—history, then I won't ever know it. I'll just be a person with a certain unfolding life story, and this story will always seem like the only one I know, or ever knew.

Won't it?

Except I find myself wondering about that young boy, Eric, to whom my heart goes out. If he encountered a manuscript that purports to be about his life, written decades later, might he look off into a vaster kind of space and time? Might he for a moment look towards where I am sitting now and give a small wink?

CPSIA information can be obtained at www.ICGtesting.com
Printed in the USA
LVOW040323120712

289646LV00005B/1/P